The

BOTTOM DWELLERS

The

BOTTOM DWELLERS

BY

LEAH DEVLIN

ISBN-13: 978-1-942756-42-1(Paperback)
ISBN -978-1-942756-43-9 (e-book)

BISAC Subject Headings:
FIC008000 Fiction / General
FIC031010 Fiction/ Thrillers / Crime
        Editing: Chris Paige
        Cover Illustration by Christine Horner

Address all correspondence to:

Penmore Press LLC
920 N Javelina Pl
Tucson AZ 85748

The Bottom Dwellers

Book One of
The Woods Hole Thrillers
by Leah Devlin

to be followed by
Ægir's Curse
and
The Bends

Author's Note

Woods Hole is a real village on the southwest corner of Cape Cod. However, all characters in this novel are purely fictional. Their resemblance to persons alive or dead is coincidental.

Dedication

For Jenny

Chapter 1

Newport, Rhode Island

The woman shuddered... *writhed under a rain of glass and blood, amidst shrieks and screeching metal...* and awoke shaky and distraught, as she did every morning after that nightmare. Then it registered... this was not her bed. These sheets felt clean and smooth, whereas those on her boat were rumpled and sandy. Nor did this place smell of salt pond and scotch whiskey, but like floor wax and disinfectant. Where had she passed out this time? Twice in the last few weeks she'd awoken in strange places. Once on Stony Beach, her hair briny with salt water and clothes inside out—skinny-dipping obviously—and another time in someone's rowboat along the seawall at Eel Pond. Her hands slid with trepidation across the sheets. Hopefully this dawn she wouldn't have to fumble in the darkness to locate her clothes, then tiptoe out some back door. And there was always the issue of her car; inevitably she'd have to wander the side streets searching for it. Her hands crept further across the sheets. The bed was definitely not hers, as this was a single. She exhaled with relief; the bed was empty. This encouraging discovery prompted her to open her eyes, but a fluorescent ceiling light struck them like lightning. She ducked under the pillow. She'd glimpsed just enough to see that she'd landed in some hospital. So that was it. She'd finally gone insane. Someone had committed her.

The entrance of a nurse prompted her to peer from under the pillow.

"What day it is?" she asked.

"It's June 15," the nurse answered. She glanced at the patient's name on the board. "How are you feeling, Lindsey?"

"Like shit."

"I'm going to get you something to make you feel better."

"A beer?" Lindsey said hopefully.

"No."

"What state is this?"

The question didn't surprise the nurse. "Rhode Island," she said, departing.

Lindsey's eyes finally came into focus. The place was definitely a hospital, but how she got there was anyone's guess. She'd emerged from a blackout in another state once before, with a favorable outcome. Her destination had been Mardi Gras, but she'd inexplicably found herself in Big Kahuna's Bar in Fort Lauderdale during Beach Week. After the trip she'd proudly strutted down the hall of her dorm, holding aloft a first place trophy in the tequila shots contest, and a third place in the limbo contest.

Rhode Island... this was a small bit of good news, as it wasn't too far from home. She could make it back to work by tomorrow. When was the last time she'd been to work? Did she still have a job? How the hell had she wound up in Rhode Island?

The room swirled momentarily as she struggled into a seated position. The thin, white blanket slid to her lap. It wasn't dawn at all. The light through the window was the pale orange of late afternoon. In a hedge outside the window insects chirped, and cars droned along a distant highway. She'd worked in a hospital before, but for only a year; the whole ordeal had been a disaster. It had been her shortest stint of employment. Teamwork was not for her.

A few days ago—a week?—She'd informed Sara that she was taking a few vacation days to go a boat show in Newport. She *had* told Sara that, hadn't she?

It was June 15th and she couldn't remember the past few days of her life.

She kicked the blanket off her legs and looked at herself, aghast. The clothes were unfamiliar and frightfully garish. The miniskirt was made of some unidentifiable synthetic fabric resembling pink leather. The fashion designer who'd created her flimsy shirt must have done so on a dare. It was a leopard-printed, sleeveless job with a low swooping neckline designed to maximally expose cleavage. The black bra underneath was lacy and see-through, not her usual sports bra.

Her hands shook, but that was normal. So was the pounding headache; nothing that a few beers and extra strength aspirin couldn't handle. Her brain, she figured, resembled a minefield, memories sunk irretrievably into deep craters. No matter. As long as it could navigate her to the nearest package store, all would be fine.

She continued to survey the damage. Her legs and arms were very sunburned. Her wrists ached and were circled by red marks. The knuckles on her left hand were split open and bruised. A long scrape ran down her calf. Thankfully there were no tattoos. She peeked under the miniskirt to check what panties she might be wearing.

"Oh my god," she moaned aloud, collapsing back into the pillow.

She whipped her legs over the side of the bed, her feet bumping into a mobile bedside table. The table careened across the room and crashed into a chair. The nurse hurried in, carrying pills and a water bottle,

"You need to take this pill."

"What is it?"

"Valium. It'll take the edge off the withdrawal," the nurse nervously responded, bracing herself for the unknown and unpredictable.

"Whatever." She lifted the bottle and pill towards her lips, and swallowed. "What is this place?"

"The Narragansett Eastbay Clinic in Newport."

"A clinic for what?"

"This is a drug and alcohol rehab. You're in detox."

"What! I don't have a problem with drugs and booze. What time is it? I need to get home!"

The nurse consulted her watch. "4:45. Dinner's in a little while. Get something to eat. You'll feel better."

"I need a shower!"

The nurse pointed. "Everything you need's in there."

Lindsey dashed to the bathroom and tore off the strange clothes. Her reflection stared back from a full-length mirror. She turned around and gazed over her shoulder. The entire surface of her body, with the exception of her pubic area and rear end, were a deep red; evidently she'd been sunbathing topless somewhere.

She ripped the paper off a small bar of soap and stepped into the shower. She lathered soap and shampoo over her body and hair again and again under a trickle of lukewarm water, and then dried off. In the bathroom was a small kit of toiletries. She brushed her teeth and then struggled to move a limp black comb through her long, wet hair.

Circling the room, she searched for *her* clothes and *her* shoes, but found no belongings. Unless she was willing to remain in a small damp towel, there was no choice but to change back into the slut attire. The rumblings of an appetite arose. She had no recollection of where or when she'd last eaten. The towel draped over her head, she hurried from the room.

A cloud of blue cigarette smoke floated over a table in the designated smoking area where five ghostly men played cards. They eyed her scanty outfit, but she ignored them and headed with deliberation to the nurses' station.

"Did a bag of clothes come in with me?" she asked anxiously, leaning against the counter.

A wrinkled nurse behind a computer monitor said a bit tiredly, "I wasn't on duty when you came in."

Lindsey glanced over her shoulder to the table of men. "I have a big problem," she whispered emphatically.

The nurse waited with baited breath to hear of the "big problem."

She tugged at the leopard shirt. "I don't know whose clothes these are, but I need to get them off. These clothes are hideous. I look like a hooker who shops at Walmart!" She glanced over once again to make sure that the men were out of earshot. "And worst of all, I don't have any underwear. I can't be walking around these slimy men in this microscopic skirt and no panties!"

The muscles in the nurse's jaw tensed, suppressing a guffaw. She grinned broadly. "Okay, honey. We'll get you some." A metal canister of dinner trays rattled down the hallway, smelling of institutional food. "Go eat," she continued. "I'll see what came in with you."

The arrival of food spurred the men from the blue cloud to a dining table across the room. Lindsey's plan was to grab her food tray and go eat in the solitude of her room, but one of the men placed hers on the table amongst theirs. She dropped glumly into a chair; she seemed to be the only female inmate in the asylum. The men of different ages and castes chatted amicably with one another, having bonded during an afternoon of cards, as they waited to see whether their insurance would let them stay, or cast them and their addiction back onto the streets.

Within blurry seconds of the introductions, she'd forgotten all of their names. Stereotypes would have to do, since her short-term memory centers were mush. The jovial man wearing a yellow polyester shirt and plaid pants she named 19th Hole. He was an oafish good ole boy, quick with jokes that were decades old. No doubt he was a salesman. Next to 19th Hole sat Hayseed, a loquacious redneck who nervously picked at the scabs on his arms. On her right sat L.L. Bean, who looked abashedly down her blouse while whining that the nurses had taken his smartphone. At the head of the table sat a handsome Army Ranger. To her left, the window looked down to a parking lot where heat radiated off the black top and pollen floated languidly in a yellow haze.

She turned back to face inside. Directly across from her was a man who was not easily pigeonholed like the others. His shaggy blond hair and a scruffy beard reminded her vaguely of a Doonesbury character. Like Hayseed, the man's forearms were spider webs of scarred blood vessels. His Che

Guevara t-shirt reminded her of a sophomore Political Science course. How was it possible that she could remember undergraduate courses—not even in her major—but she could not recall the last few days of her life? The blond man studied her intently. There was a vague familiarity to him, and she wondered if they'd met somewhere before.

Throughout dinner her outfit received numerous compliments, and she was barraged with intrusive questions. "What's your name? Where are you from? What's your drug of choice?"

"Don't know, don't remember," she answered curtly.

Distracted by the ridiculous skirt riding up her thighs, she had little appetite for the vegetarian lasagna. The men were happy to grab the roll, pudding, and salad that she offered up. The blond man didn't eat or say much either, and finally limped away toward the smoking area. One leg of his jeans was cut to the knee. His lower leg was in a hard cast, his toes wrapped in gauze. 19th Hole followed her gaze. "He was in Afghanistan," 19th Hole said, nodding in the direction of Che.

She squirmed in her chair once again. The men's wishful stares and ceaseless questions had become intolerable. So was the unmistakable sensation between her legs. It was not the relaxed feeling after having had sex once or twice, but the twitchy burn from having ground it out over several hours. Was it a fun romp, orgy, threesome... rape? Perhaps it was best not to remember the whole ordeal. For the moment the amnesia was a blessing.

She looked desperately at the clock. The shakes in her hands were at their worst at this time of day. Were she back home, she'd be settling into her throne, her favorite barstool at the Kidd with a direct view to the giant TV screen. This was the time of the day she lived for... Happy Hour. She muttered some lame excuse to the men, jiggled her tray into the food rack, and walked the length of the ward. The corridor doors seemed escape-proof without the proper tools to deactivate the locks. And if she attempted a jailbreak through the fire door, an alarm would blare and she'd be easily captured. Trapped, she skulked back to her room. She wanted to hide under the covers, pull the pillow over her head, and sleep until morning, except that it was only six o'clock and still bright outside. To kill time, she lay under a blanket and looked for constellations in the rough surface of the ceiling panels. Her mind was sluggish and only Orion's Belt and Capricorn could be identified.

Che appeared in the doorway. "What are you looking at?" he asked, looking curiously at the ceiling. A halo of cigarette smoke circled his head as he exhaled.

"Constellations," she answered flatly, so as not to encourage further conversation.

He was unfazed by her unaccommodating tone. "You're right." He pointed upward. "There's Ursa Minor, Leo, and the Big Dipper."

She sat up quickly and searched for these star patterns, vexed that he'd spotted them before she had.

He dropped a gym bag onto the bed. "The nurse found your stuff. We're starting a game of poker if you want to join us." He wandered away.

She sprung from the bed. It was her blue overnight bag with Hopkins Lacrosse printed in white lettering. She shook its contents across the blanket. Thank god, her hoodie. Hospitals always cranked the air-conditioning to arctic extremes. An unfamiliar plastic packet was immediately torn open. Cotton underwear! Thank you, Wrinkled Nurse! One size fits all. It didn't matter that they were the style that she wore in second grade, or that two of her could fit into them, or that the waistband might stretch up over most of her rib cage. She shut the bedroom door, flung the miniskirt into a trashcan, and wriggled the baggy white underwear over her sunburnt legs and hips.

Only a few t-shirts and pairs of shorts had been packed for a short trip to the boat show. She opened her wallet. Another piece of good news... her credit cards were present. This meant that she wouldn't have to endure a tediously long phone queue listening to dentist office music, all to cancel a lost credit card. In the slot for cash was three hundred dollars; this caused a surge of panic. She was lucky if she carried a twenty at any given time. Where had she come upon three hundred dollars? What if in the blackout she had robbed someone! Or, was it payment for a favor?

The nurses had clearly searched her bag for drugs, weapons, and other contraband, because her cosmetic bag and cell phone had been confiscated. They could have the phone—the data plan was a complete rip-off anyway—but the cosmetic bag held absolute-must-haves: a bottle of extra-strength aspirin and her birth control pills. She continued the rummage through the pile. Her dive watch. Her car keys! Wonderful... she'd driven there! Her Jeep must be nearby!

She'd leave tomorrow morning—first thing—after settling the bill with the business office. She tore off the tacky shirt and heaved it across the room toward the rejected pink skirt. She stepped in front of the bathroom mirror and looked at herself appraisingly. Nice... the black see-through bra was a definite keeper. She pulled on her *own* shorts, t-shirt, and hoodie. Comfort and confidence were restored. Glorious release from the nuthouse imminent, and Valium now coursing through her bloodstream, she decided to enjoy herself. She strolled out of her room, prepared to show those bottom dwellers huddled in the blue cloud how to play poker.

A Forest in Tennessee

"Bess, wake up... c'mon, wake up. If we leave now, we might make Alabama by tonight."

Maggie emerged from under a blue tarp strung between the trees. The first rays of dawn sifted between the branches. Not even birds were awake at this hour. Behind a tree she slid down her shorts, squatted, and peed. She wiped herself with napkins stolen from a donut shop in Nashville, pulled up her shorts, and returned to the campsite. She ducked back under the tarp.

"We're almost out of napkins," she grumbled aloud. She knelt over her traveling companion—her only companion. "C'mon now, wake up!" She nudged Bess' shoulder. No response. She gnawed urgently on the cuticle of her thumb and eyed Bess' cosmetic bag that contained the syringes, powder, blackened spoon, and matches.

"Bestie?" She reached tentatively for her friend's cheek and instantly retracted her hand. She bit her nail again and bent fearfully forward. She rested her ear on Bess' breast. She gasped. All in her friend was silent.

Maggie crawled frantically toward her backpack, scrambling for her cigarettes. Terrified, she fled the shelter of the tarp, quickly thumbed the lighter, and inhaled deeply. She paced the woods some distance from the tarp to avoid the passage of Bess' wicked spirit to some netherworld. Her lungs heaved... this was the third dead body, and in less than a year!

Tears filled Maggie's eyes and the forest blurred around her. "What, what, what? Bess carried the drugs, the money, the maps... Bess made the decisions... she was older, smarter, prettier, stronger, meaner.... What, what, what to do? No, no way can I talk to the police!" she stuttered to herself as she kicked through the leaves. "They'd send me back to Minnesota for that horrible... don't fuckin' think about that! Contact Bess' family? Did she have any? Where was she even from? Louisiana? Yes, it was probably Louisiana. Bess always avoided that state. What to do? Bess loved camping in the woods. I'll bury her here," she finally decided. "In the woods... that she loved."

The sound of a living, human voice, if only her own, was slightly consoling, so Maggie continued chattering to herself. She returned to the campsite and tossed her cigarette butt into the fire pit. She grabbed one of the plastic plates that they had stolen from a family campground near the Dismal Swamp in Virginia. That had been a wonderful day. She and Bess had waited in the woods for the family to leave their campsite. They had walked casually down the trail—who would suspect two teenage girls—and unzipped the screen tent over the picnic table and made off with plastic plates, silverware, and other wonderful treasures. For two fabulous days they stuffed themselves with hot dogs, hamburgers, potato chips, and Cheerios. For two perfect days they didn't have to pull tricks for food.

Not far from the tarp Maggie found a place where the ground was soft and thick with ferns. Dazed and sniffling, she got on her hands and knees. With a plate for a shovel, she began to dig a hole.

The Bottom Dwellers

Woods Hole, two years earlier

"Amazing deal for a case of summer ales," Lindsey said to herself. Her foot jumped onto the brake of her Jeep and she veered off the road. "What a find... Dave's Marina." The bait and tackle shop had a number of great beer bargains, plus it served lunch. She ordered a sandwich at the deli counter and hurried off with the key to the ladies' room. After returning the bathroom key to the redheaded clerk named Sheila, Lindsey paid her bill and stepped outside.

Sandwich and cold beer in hand, she strolled along the dock, admiring the boats and shaking loose the stiffness in her legs and lower back from the drive up Route 95 N from Baltimore. The marina was lively for a midweek afternoon. In the stern of a Bayliner, a paunchy middle-aged couple reclined on chaise loungers and listened to Jimmy Buffet. Two rednecks in camouflage loaded rods and bait onto a bass boat; a retiree on a pontoon boat read the *Boston Globe*.

She dropped onto a bench next to a fish-cleaning table and thumbed through a real estate guide from a rack in the bait shop. Housing prices were ridiculous; Cape Cod had become a bedroom community for Boston. And a waterfront home on her salary... forget it. Now that she was on her own, only a small, temporary place was required, until she was sure that the new job was for her. It had been fifteen days since Duncan had walked out on her. Who gave a shit about the departed husband? That bastard had taken the dive boat and her scuba tanks. So she'd sold their remaining junk at a sidewalk sale, closed up their apartment in Baltimore, and accepted a job in Woods Hole, Massachusetts. Where she was now was none of his damn business.

The salt pond in front of her was enclosed by sea grass sprouting from acrid mudflats. Over the water's surface dragonflies flew dizzying patterns through the heat. Bug chirps and buzzes and gull caws mixed with low rattles of outboard engines. It was a soothing blend of sounds reminiscent of Uncle Charlie's boatyard on the Severn River in Annapolis. A narrow passage of olive-brown water cut a swath in a field of sea grass, and at the mouth of the passage beat the low surf of the Vineyard Sound.

Boats rocked gently in their slips. They were a middle-class assortment of boats: cruisers, a banana boat or two, small sailboats, and motorized skiffs. Two dilapidated houseboats floated at the far end of the pier. She tossed her sandwich wrapper and empty beer bottle into a trashcan and wandered down to have a look.

Both houseboats appeared to be vacated. The one on the end had seasons of dried leaves on the deck. A red and white FOR SALE sign was duct-taped to its transom. She hopped onto the deck and pressed her face against the back window. The boat had a traditional houseboat floor plan, a living area aft, a galley and helm. Steps disappeared to a head and cabin in the bow. A teak interior, mildewed carpeting, sun-faded cushions on the sofas. She sidestepped along the gunwale and examined the hull, cleats, and seams, then the railings for rust and other potentially costly problems. Structurally the boat appeared fine. She glanced at her watch, then upward at the sky. In the summers the boat would be in direct sunlight from late morning to late afternoon. She climbed halfway up the ladder and looked across the flybridge. That space would be ideal for sunbathing, reading, or working on a laptop. There were no breaches or cracks in the fiberglass. A creak of feet on the dock caused her to quickly climb down, as she was trespassing.

A weathered, unshaven man said, "It's for sale."

"I see that. How much?"

Dave named a price.

She was astonished. "No way... it's practically free. What's wrong with it?"

"Everything. It's a floating piece of junk. The owner is in Alabama with a sick wife and is anxious to unload it. The couple's very old. They're not coming back."

"Do the water pumps work? Does it have electricity? How about the fridge? Does it work?"

"Yup, but the engine's seized."

"I'm not going anywhere. I'll take it."

After signing some papers and writing a deposit check in Dave's office, she moved her Jeep to a parking space next to the houseboats. Dave offered her a wheelbarrow from his workshop, and after a few short thumping trips across the dock, her boxes and bags were unloaded onto the faded sofas. The houseboat had not been opened up in years, so the air was an oppressive ninety-plus degrees. She lifted the windows and wonderful blasts of salty wind pushed through the screens and lifted her spirits.

Dave pointed her down the highway toward a strip mall that had both a liquor store and grocery store. She returned later with the essentials: whiskey, food, and cleaning supplies. The first priority was swabbing the fridge so that the case of summer ale purchased from Sheila could be chilled. She changed into shorts and an old T-shirt and attached her iPod to her belt loop. Joni Mitchell sang "Coyote" and she decided that she was in love with the man in that song, but reminded herself that she was never thinking about men again. She guzzled down a beer, realizing that she had never, until this point, lived alone in her own place. She'd always answered to a man: her father, then to

Mark Willis, then to Duncan. Wildly exhilarated, she cracked opened another beer, swallowed a shot of Scotch whiskey toasting her good luck and liberation, and began to scour every inch of her tiny yet wonderful parcel of dockside real estate.

The following morning she woke damp and sticky, smelling of rubber gloves and lemon-scented cleanser. She had peeled off her clothes the night before, flopped onto the bed, and fallen into a comatose sleep on top of the sheets. A symphony of pond sounds woke her. Although the windows were wide open, without a fan, the cabin was smothering. She chugged down a beer to cool off and clear away the cobwebs, then went to the head to clean up. In an attempt to look respectable for her first day on the job, she twisted her hair into a loose bun and tossed on a blouse, khaki slacks, and sandals.

Lindsey stepped onto the dock and noticed Sheila, Dave's wife, stepping down the backstairs from an apartment over the bait shop, two small children, Brianna and Max, in tow. As the children climbed into a minivan, she asked Sheila how long a walk it was down the road to the marine lab. Sheila directed her to a path through the marsh and said that it was quicker and more scenic to walk the bike trail that wound along the shoreline. The lab was about a mile down the trail, Sheila explained.

Despite the early hour, the bike trail was a flurry of activity with dog walkers, joggers, and bicyclists streaming by. Lindsey walked at a brisk pace, thrilled to work in a lab again. She had wanted to work at this particular lab since attending a conference there as an undergraduate. It had been a big... *huge*... mistake to think that she had any of the requisite 'people skills' to work in a hospital, but Duncan had insisted because he wanted her to make "big money."

The bike trail ended in the village at the ferry launch to Martha's Vineyard. She stopped at a cyber café and bought a large coffee and pastries. At the bascule bridge she peered downward into the green water of Eel Pond to see a cluster of translucent ctenophores undulating in the slow current. Water Street, the narrow main street through Woods Hole, already bustled with scientists, tourists, and children from the science school parading through town with their nets and buckets in hand. A large gold sign advertising the Captain Kidd drew her attention. She squinted through the screen door, noticing a colorful pirate mural and a long wooden bar. The barstool at the end she claimed as hers from six until whenever.

She continued down the sidewalk, past the gray clapboard shops and window boxes with purple and yellow pansies. Across the street was the oceanographic institution whose submersibles had discovered life at the ocean's deep volcanic rifts and the ghost ship *Titanic*. A large sign in front of the marine lab read that this was the oldest marine laboratory in the U.S. and that more than fifty Nobel Laureates had worked there.

Her new place of employment was easy to find as it was in the largest building at the marine lab. After climbing three flights of stairs she located her new boss' office. Mort Somers seemed delighted to see her and wrung her hand again and again while coffee splashed across her blouse. They'd met once before when her honors thesis advisor, Anne Davids, had introduced them at a Neurosciences conference when she was still an undergraduate at Hopkins. Somers reminded her somewhat of Yoda, ancient and gregarious.

"Your lab is this way," he said, pointing down the hall. "Dr. Kauni will be your assistant. She just finished a post-doc in electrical engineering at Cornell."

A low hum grew louder as they approached the end of the corridor. A nameplate next to door read: Biomedical Imaging Technologies. Director: Lindsey Nolan, M.D., Ph.D. Chief Engineer: Sara Kauni, Ph.D.

The hum emanated from a blimp that hung in the airspace in the middle of the room. Lindsey moved directly under it, watching the two whirling propellers. "Very cool. Ferdinand Zeppelin's LZ-1. It's a perfect replica."

Sara Kauni was a black-haired woman in her twenties who at the moment held a remote control in her hands. She wore a sleeveless tie-dyed shirt, faded jeans, and flip flops. "Are you sure?" she asked teasingly.

"It's definitely the LZ-1," Lindsey stated.

Sara smirked. "You're right. I've been bored out of my mind waiting for you to come, so I've been building tiny drones."

"Impressive," Lindsey marveled, still watching the hovering blimp.

Somers chuckled. "I'll leave you two to your own devices. Sara will show you where everything is. I'll meet you both for lunch to discuss our research plans. How about one o'clock?"

"Sure," Lindsey answered distractedly, wanting only to investigate the aeronautical models lining the windowsills. Somers hobbled out the door.

Sara maneuvered the blimp through the air and lowered it onto her desk. The landing was not a delicate one and a rudder broke off.

Lindsey walked along the windowsills. All of Sara's models were precise replicas. "The Montgolfier Balloon,

U.S.S. Akron, Henri Giffard's Dirigible, the Wright Flier... whoa! That's Leonardo da Vinci's Aerial Screw, the prototype for the modern helicopter!" She couldn't resist holding it. The rotators were made of rice paper; the framework was of balsa wood. "Brilliant. This model flies, doesn't it?"

"Yes," Sara answered. "Da Vinci's design never would have flown, though. The four men supposed to power it would never have been able to create enough lift. I made a few modifications to it, let's call it poetic license, so it would fly."

Lindsey walked over to assess the damaged blimp. "I can show you how to buffer that landing so the rudder won't break."

"How?" Sara asked from under raised eyebrows, testing her new partner's knowledge of aerodynamics.

"Attach a tiny sensor to the nose cone. Program it to detect a distance of six inches off the tarmac. Then gradually reduce the rotation of the propellers, in transitions to make the descent softer. You could also change the angle of the elevator flaps to reduce the pitch." Lindsey smiled. "But you already know that, don't you?"

"Yes," Sara admitted agreeably.

Lindsey scanned Sara's desk and work area. Digital photographs of a small boy were tacked to Sara's cork board. Other photos were of atolls and coral reefs. A case of bottled water was under Sara's desk, along with a rolled-up yoga mat. Her screen saver showed changing images from an old TV show, *La Femme Nikita*.

Sara rifled through a drawer of electronic components. From her shoulders to wrists ran an intricate pattern of tribal tattoos. She noticed Lindsey's curious look.

"I'm from the Marquesas. Of all of the groups in Polynesia, the Marquesans have the most elaborate tattooing practices." She put two new batteries in the back of a remote and snapped the cover closed. "Watch this."

The rice paper fins began to spin and Leonardo's flying machine lifted into the air with a gentle whir.

"Bravo!" Lindsey clapped with delight. She dropped her backpack down on the empty desk across the lab.

She was home.

Chapter 2

Newport

A muted rustling across the room woke Lindsey sometime around dawn. Lifting her head from the pillow, she found the room gray and silent. Her hospital gown had twisted itself around her body, so she struggled to close it. Maybe the visitor was a night nurse closing the curtains? She squinted through the darkness; odd, the curtains were still open. She sat up, suddenly on alert. Someone had definitely been in the room. She could sense it. Had one of those creepy men ogled her while she'd slept? She hurried to the door, but it didn't have a lock. Spooked, she lay awake for some time, her ears straining to hear the slightest of sounds. She finally dropped off to sleep.

Swishes of rain and wind against the window woke her later that morning. Sitting up, it took her a moment to recall where she was. Neither the hospital gown nor the blanket had provided much warmth during the night. She remained in bed, trying to rally the courage to step onto the cold floor tiles. She finally padded briskly to the bathroom and showered, and then returned to her blue gym bag.

Her eyes widened with surprise. Her overnight bag had been zipped up the night before, she was sure of it, but it now gaped open like a hungry mouth. She burrowed quickly through the clothes for her wallet, and to her amazement, it was there. Her credit cards and cash were intact. But her sandals no longer sat side by side under the chair where she'd left them. One sandal had been kicked into the far corner of the room, while the other was under the bedside stand, presumably by the intruder of the night before. Or maybe one of the men had a foot fetish and had used her sandals to... so disgusting. The sandals would be thoroughly washed with the hand sanitizer in the bathroom. Her space had been violated, and she had been watched while she slept! Goosebumps rose across her skin. No matter, she thought to calm herself; by tonight, she'd back in her own houseboat on a quiet salt pond in Woods Hole, sipping *slowly* from a glass of scotch whiskey. A lesson had been learned the hard way, ending up in detox, having had sex with some forgotten man. From now on she would be moderate in all things... beer, scotch whiskey, and men.

A nurse poked her head in the door. "The doctor will be by shortly."

Lindsey nodded distractedly. Her thoughts were still wispy from the sedatives, so she was not particularly conversational. It was best not to concern the nurse with a failed attempt at petty thievery. Besides, it was probably commonplace for the staff to deal with addicts searching for drug money. It was best to say nothing, avoid all complications, discussions, or extra forms to fill out. If the paperwork went smoothly, and her car could be located, she'd be back at the lab and working with Sara by noontime.

She dressed and packed her bag. At the window she impatiently fondled the car keys in her pocket. From this view of the parking lot she could not locate the Jeep; after the doctor released her, she'd roam the parking lot until she found it.

The identity of the intruder or voyeur was easy to surmise. During last night's poker game, 19th Hole had mentioned his country club and a recent golf holiday with his wife to St. Andrews, Scotland. Che wore a Rolex and smoked Dunhills, and L. L. Bean had boasted about his prestigious law firm of Blah, Blah, Blah and Associates. Ranger did not play cards with them, but quietly read AA pamphlets by himself. It was doubtful that any of them rifled her bag. That left Hayseed. He'd mentioned that he was a plumber and had invited her repeatedly to his apartment in Taunton. "I can cook. In my spare time, I fix stereos and TVs. I can give you stereo speakers for free."

"I only listen to an iPod and don't have a stereo system on my houseboat," she had said.

"Your loss," he shrugged, "I have a really decent pair of speakers. I'd just need to clear a rat's nest out of the back of one of them."

Though not a smoker, it was pacifying to smoke with the men while the spoils of victory, a pile of cigarettes and coins grew in front of her. She'd shown them no mercy in a game that they had just taught her called Texas Hold'em.

"Shit, I've never seen such beginner's luck," L. L. Bean had said irritability.

"It's staggering intelligence," she had rejoined.

"I agree with Ted," 19th Hole had remarked. "You have amazing beginner's luck."

It was no use arguing with a bunch of dimwits. How could they possibly know *who she was*?

The Valium did little to quell Hayseed's heroin withdrawal, so he had dropped out of the card game and bounced from sofa to sofa in his red high top sneakers until the night nurse bolted from the nurses' station and ordered him down. She was a big, beefy girl twice his size, so he'd slunk obediently off the furniture. The sofa hopping had agitated Che; the cards shook uncontrollably in his hand. Her impulse was to reach across the table and steady his hand, but she reminded herself that all contact with men, of any kind, was over. Instead she'd preoccupied herself by calculating the probability that her full house would beat out the hand of 19th Hole. L. L. Bean had nothing; he pushed his glasses up the bridge of his inflamed nose every time he was bluffing. Che folded. L. L. Bean angrily tossed his cards onto the table. "Let's play a different game."

"Name it," she'd said. "I'll beat you at any card game."

Che had smiled tacitly at her, as if they shared a secret.

L. L. Bean looked furtively toward the nurse's station. "Strip poker," he announced quietly, staring at her breasts. "And the winner gets to choose what comes off the loser."

The Army Ranger looked up from his pamphlet and watched cautiously from across the room. The beefy nurse had keen hearing, because she stomped from the nurses' station, grabbed the deck of cards, and ordered all of the card players to their rooms.

The rest of the night had been uneventful, until some creeper lurked around her room while she slept! The door squeaked open; she started, dropping her car keys on the floor.

"You're jumpy," the doctor said.

"Because this place is full of perverts and lunatics."

The doctor introduced himself, but she didn't catch his name. The red monogrammed stitching of his name on his white lab coat was impossible to read in her impaired state.

"I have the results of your blood work," he said. "Your liver enzymes are quite elevated, indicative of alcoholic hepatitis."

The breakfast cart arrived in the hallway and she was eager to eat, settle her bill, and be on her way, but he continued to admonish her about the general debilitated state of her health: the liver damage, anemia, weight loss, malnutrition, thiamine deficiency. Irked by his patronizing tone, she asked him what medical school he'd attended. She'd never heard of the place... the Podunk College of Second-Rate-Medicine of West Virginia. He was only one step better than a chiropractor.

"Can I see those test results?" she asked.

He reluctantly handed her the folder.

"Hmm," she said, scanning the medicalese gibberish. She handed him back the folder.

He grimaced from behind his Clark Kent glasses, and then stated dourly, "If you had not gotten here when you did, you might have been dead by the end of the summer. Your liver function is impaired." But then he added, "The good news is that a bed is opening up in the rehab. Your insurance will cover the thirty-day stay. We can have you there by lunchtime."

"Thirty days! You're kidding me," she protested. "I have to get to work!"

"Discuss it with Dr. Waters, the director of the rehab, and see what she says." He scanned her documents again. "Why's your name familiar to me?"

"Who knows," she replied dismissively. "It's an ordinary name."

He continued to stare at the name. "What do you do for a living?"

"You guess. Choice A: Harvard Law Professor. Choice B: Back-up singer for Lady Gaga. Choice C: Stripper." She added ironically, "Choice D: Fucking Genius."

He assessed her attire, a tight black t-shirt and faded shorts. He was clearly unimpressed. In fact, his expression was one of repugnance. "Stripper?"

"Correct!" She smacked him heartily on the shoulder. "Buy that man a beer!"

With that, he signed off on the paperwork that authorized sending her to Purgatory for a thirty-day sentence.

A Marine Laboratory in Woods Hole

Dr. Sara Kauni gazed out a window of the Nolan-Kauni bioengineering lab toward Eel Pond. She sipped her coffee and checked the time on her cell phone again. It would be another day her boss did not show up for work. Lindsey must be too drunk to leave her houseboat. In the past, even when loaded, she'd had the courtesy to call in sick, albeit with some ludicrous excuse. But today there was no call, and Sara's stomach knotted. Troubling images emerged: Lindsey's Jeep over a guardrail, Lindsey having picked up the wrong man in the wrong bar, Lindsey fallen from her boat and adrift or, worst case, drowned at sea.

Sara drained the last of her coffee and sent a text. "lin im really pissed. txt or call me. i hope ur alive. i need to know that ur ok."

The Bottom Dwellers

At the coffee machine, she poured herself a third cup, fully aware that it would only exacerbate her foul mood. She wanted to wallow in her anger this morning. It was time to find a new job—and really follow through with it. She walked to her computer, clicked open her personnel folder, and reviewed her résumé. She scrolled straight to the References section and deleted Lindsey's name, replacing it with the contact information for Dr. Derick Briggs, a microbiologist and friend from graduate school at Cornell.

But where to apply? Sadly, she'd have to leave Cape Cod. In a short period of time she had found many close friends within the Cape's gay community. Woods Hole was a safe village with undiscovered beaches and clean sea air in which to raise her five-year old son, Zephyr. Having grown up on a remote island in the Marquesas, she preferred quiet, natural environments to cities. The marine lab was the best of both worlds, state-of-the-art laboratory facilities located in a beautiful seaside town. She checked her smartphone again; there was still no word from Lindsey. Alcohol had taken a steep toll. Because of it, Sara's own career had come to a screeching halt. And she, unlike Lindsey, who was committed to nothing and no one, had another mouth to feed. There was no choice but to move on.

It was fortunate there were so many engineering departments around the Boston area. Perhaps she would not have to move far. Between graduate school and her post-doctoral fellowship, she and Zephyr had made far too many moves. The plan had been for Woods Hole to be their last stop, but that was clearly not to be. She knew the engineering professors, Ken Housener at Harvard, and Inga Davis at Tufts Medical School. Maybe they were looking for an electrical engineer to work in their labs? What about Karen

Battersby at Boston Technological Institute? Karen was a Johns Hopkins-trained engineer like Lindsey. Though Lindsey did not know Karen personally, she'd once remarked that "Karen Battersby's research was very solid, though not particularly novel."

Sara paused in composing her queries to Housener, Davis, and Battersby. Was she willing to settle for "very solid" when her boss—in the rare instances she was sober—was one of the most creative inventors in the U.S.? During the two years of their collaboration at the marine lab, their list of publications and electrode designs was nothing short of astonishing. Additionally, Lindsey didn't give a damn about first authorship on their manuscripts, unlike so many academics and lab chiefs who demanded credit for and ownership of all ideas emanating from the lab, even when they'd actually contributed nothing. She and Lindsey simply alternated first authorship on their papers, despite the fact that the original idea for the project invariably sprouted from Lindsey's fertile imagination.

And there was something percolating in Lindsey's brain, behind the red eyes and amidst the vaporous thoughts, some magnificent... *something* was germinating; the pieces, like living cells, arranging and re-arranging themselves into a functioning organism. Sara could sense it. During her few lucid moments, Lindsey would scrawl equations across a yellow legal pad, or draw some device with a computer-aided design program. Yes, something stunning was forming in that over-sexed, whiskey-sodden brain.

She checked her phone again. It was past ten and still no word from Lindsey. This morning her partner was too drunk to even find the speed dial on her phone—or find her phone. Sara swallowed another slug of coffee. Her heart now pounded. In a muddle of sadness and anger, she finished composing the job inquiry to the three engineering professors, attached her updated résumé to the email, and hit SEND.

A Forest in Tennessee

Maggie dropped in exhaustion against a tree. The horrible task was done. The dirt on her knees and hands was too ingrained to brush off. Sometime later that day, she'd need to find a bathroom with running water, or maybe a stream, to wash away the grime and refill the water bottles. Her head pounded from fatigue, dehydration, and hunger. It had been a sweaty, dirty task to drag Bess through the underbrush.

The worst part of all was tossing dirt on Bess' cold, naked body and long, strawberry blonde hair. But Maggie had had to remove her clothes. Her own shorts were almost threadbare. Bess had newer stuff. Bess was better at everything, including shoplifting. Her own sneakers had holes in them. Maybe by summer's end she'd grow enough to fit into Bess' cool Nikes.

Maggie had broken down the campsite by herself for the first time. The tarp was rolled up and ready to go, and lay next to her in the leaves. But where to go? Now she'd have to think on her own. It had been so much easier when Bess told her what to do.

That jumpy, itching, irritating feeling returned, so Maggie fumbled with the shoelace around her forearm. Tennessee and Alabama were so fuckin' hot in June! She rhythmically pumped her brown hand. Why had Bess wanted to go Alabama in June? To find that old boyfriend, who was a dick and cheated them in that last deal! She urgently flicked the syringe with her middle finger. This forest was a fuckin' swamp, with steam and ticks and mosquitos. Maybe she should head north? It would be cooler there. Think about it later! She squeezed her fist again and a large vein popped near her wrist. She'd use this one this time. Her heart beat in anticipation. This was her reward for a morning of hard work... to obliterate the sorrow... the loneliness. The prick of the needle sent a euphoric shudder through her body, and a warm, peaceful wave coursed through her blood. Her head dropped back against the tree trunk. For a moment she was transported to that wonderful, fantastical world inside her head... In a World... of warm food, beds with clean sheets, and gentle people.

Chapter 3

Rehab

"Plumbers make a lot of money," Hayseed explained, leaning across the counter of the nurses' station. "I'll be able to pay my bill. I promise, I will! Please let me work out a payment plan..."

Plumber, right, Lindsey thought. Hayseed was a thief, plain and simple. He probably trolled suburban neighborhoods during the day, pilfering TVs, stereo systems, and computers. He had ransacked her bag searching for her wallet, and then flung her sandals across the room. The faster she could be rid of him, the better. "He's welcome to my bed," she said enthusiastically to the nurse. "If there aren't enough beds, he can have mine! If you sign my release papers, I'll drive straight to an AA meeting this very minute."

"I'm not going to a VA hospital," Che interrupted forcefully. "I've been in too many of them. I'm staying here."

"I'm serious. He..." Lindsey couldn't recall Hayseed's name so she pointed, "... can have my bed if beds are the issue."

The old battle-tested nurse was unmoved and stood with her hands resolutely on her hips. "Beds are not the issue. It doesn't work that way," she explained. "He doesn't have insurance…"

"Before you release me, I'll need my phone and cosmetic bag," Lindsey insisted. "It's the pink one."

"My wife is Samantha Harper," Che interrupted again. "She might be able to help the hospital… make a donation. I'm not going to a VA hospital."

"Someone must remember taking a pink cosmetic bag from my overnight bag," Lindsey broke in.

"Please let me go to rehab. I wanna heal!" Hayseed pleaded.

The nurse turned to Che. "What name did you say?"

"Samantha Harper."

"The Newport socialite?" the nurse asked, her curiosity piqued.

"That's the one," Che answered, smiling pleasantly.

"Wonderful," Lindsey cut in. "Now that's all settled, can I have my phone and cosmetic bag? I need my birth control pills. I need to find my car so I can get to my AA meeting."

"There was no pink bag, Ms. Nolan," the nurse said. "Get yourself ready. You can discuss this with Dr. Waters in the rehab. Only she can sign your release papers at this point."

Moments later Lindsey, Che, Ranger, L. L. Bean, and 19th Hole were buzzed through the security doors of the rehab. The only consolation was that the thief with a shoe fetish was left behind in detox. Her blue Hopkins gym bag slung over her shoulder—sans the pink cosmetic bag—she approached the first rehab counselor she could find.

"Can you direct me to Dr. Waters' office? I need to talk to her immediately."

The counselor was a kind-faced Latino. "It's her day off. But she'll be in tomorrow."

"Tomorrow? You're kidding me! Who else can sign my paperwork... Ramon?" Lindsey peered at the counselor's name tag.

"No one, chica," Ramon said unflappably. "It'll have to wait until tomorrow. Let me show you to your room. It's on the female side of the ward, across from the Fishbowl."

"Fishbowl?"

"The smoking lounge," he said, pointing.

"I've been reduced to a fish in a bowl," she muttered, dragging behind him. "I'm living my worst nightmare."

She inspected her assigned room, furnished with two single beds and a small bathroom with a toilet and sink. An old woman snored in the bed next to the window. Covering the desk were photographs, presumably the old woman's grandchildren. The curtains were partially closed and the sky beyond was swollen with angry, fleet clouds. Rivulets of rain ran down the pane.

"There's been big mistake," she whispered urgently to Ramon. "My room in detox was a single. I live alone. I'm used to being alone. I need to be switched to a single!"

"There are no singles. Everyone has a roommate," he whispered back. He departed with a smile.

She dropped her gym bag onto the free bed next to the closet. There was no reason to unpack, since she wasn't staying. Besides, opening the dresser drawers would wake the ancient woman.

She quickly cased the ward that was shaped like a rectangle. No computers anywhere. How could she get anything done without access to a computer? In the rectangle's center was the glassed-in lounge, the Fishbowl, where Bob Marley, Gay Guy, Soccer Mom, Captain Ahab, and Harley Davidson were playing Monopoly. The sofas and chair sagged. The coffee tables were carved with obscenities and singed by tobacco embers. The magazine rack contained *Reader's Digest* and *People* magazines from 2014. She opened the refrigerator next to a coffee counter and winced. The leftovers were from the same year.

There had to be some way to get discharged other than Dr. Waters' signature. Waiting for one signature was ridiculous. The disease-infested refrigerator gave her a brilliant idea. The plan was to make herself so obnoxious that the staff would expel her by afternoon's end. Dr. Waters would never even know that she'd been there.

"This fridge should be sealed off with yellow caution tape," Lindsey said in a loud voice.

The Monopoly players turned.

"I mean it. Everyone should stay far, far away from this Frigidaire," she warned, pointing at the appliance. "The bacteria on the leftovers have mutated into lethal, man-eating pathogens. If they ooze out, they might envelope the room and suffocate us all!"

A staff member—not the pleasant Ramon—paused in the doorway. This was encouraging. "It's also possible that the bacteria might release some toxin, causing us all to drop dead on the spot. Then the bacteria will devour us all by the process of phagocytosis! We might be the subject of a reality TV show called *The Bacteria That Ate the Rehab*."

Gay Guy burst out in laughter. "If they make it into a movie, I hope I'll be played by Orlando Bloom!"

A few men from the Nautilus machines down the hall congregated next to Joe, the grim-faced counselor, watching from the doorway.

"When the CDC or NIH are called in to clean up the mess, they'll have the impossible task of trying to distinguish the bacterial cells from us inmates," she expounded, "because all of us will have been reduced to blob-like, unthinking prokaryotic organisms, left with only the capacity for eating and sex."

Joe had heard enough. He pointed his thick finger at her face. "You! Out of the Fishbowl for the rest of the day!"

Exit Strategy One having failed, she decided to implement Exit Strategy Two: checking windows and doors for a possible escape route. Unfortunately the rehab was on the third floor of the hospital and the branches from the nearby maples were too far from the windows, so jumping was not a viable option. Besides, she was not remotely athletic and it was still drizzling; so if, by some miracle, she did reach the branches, they would be too slippery to cling to, so she would break every bone in her body, which for a brief moment she considered an option. At least it would mean a transfer to the ICU.

Exit Strategy Three was to locate a box of tools. If she could get her hands on a Phillips head screwdriver, she could disable the alarm, disengage the lock, and then slip away to freedom. But no tools could be found, and with every casual stroll toward the security doors to study the locking mechanism, Big Nurse appeared out of nowhere, blockading the door with her giant, gelatinous body, thus thwarting all attempts at a jailbreak.

"Go do something useful, darling. Like read the Big Book," the nurse said repeatedly.

Whatever the hell a Big Book was.

That evening, after a dinner of unidentifiable food that she ravenously devoured, she settled herself in the dining room to play five-card stud. Again, relying on her system of calculating probabilities, she won nearly every hand. A treasure trove of cigarettes and lighters grew on the table in front of her until Drug Dealer sprung to his feet and flung his cards at her chest.

"Cheatin bitch!"

L. L. Bean and Insurance Fraud departed in a huff along with Drug Dealer, while Che sat, smiling. Big Nurse had heard the commotion and waddled into the room. "Lindsey, darling, you're banned from all card games for the next thirty days."

"Thirty days... right." She sulked off to her bedroom, carrying her winnings in the pouch of her hoodie. By the time she slipped into bed that night, amidst the tidal snores of Grandma, she'd agitated every fish in the bowl. But they had not sent her home.

Boston

Dr. Karen Battersby bent back the lid of Tuna Sensation as two identical black cats, a sister and brother, rubbed affectionately against her leg. She scraped the food into bowls and placed them on the kitchen floor. Pussy Willow and Puss-n-Boots hurried to the bowls.

"No, Boots," Karen said with a sigh. "The pink bowl is Willow's." She moved him to the blue one. "You stay away from her food. You're putting on too much weight."

She slid a frozen dinner into a microwave and poured herself a glass of milk from the refrigerator. She sat down at her kitchen table and reread the email on her laptop. Received hours before, the email was still confounding. Sara Kauni leaving the Nolan-Kauni lab at the marine lab... you gotta be kidding me! Lindsey Nolan and Sara Kauni were the most productive team of bioengineers in the country. Now

The Bottom Dwellers

Sara Kauni was seeking another job? Had Lindsey fired her? Was Lindsey replacing her with someone better—but who was better technically than Sara Kauni?

The email was unnerving in many ways. Her life was all about disastrous timing. In the 13.8 billion years of the universe's existence, her birth had to coincide with that of Lindsey Nolan's! Not only did they coexist temporally, but out of the three trillion planets in this galaxy, they resided on the exact same planet, attended the same university, Johns Hopkins in Baltimore, and studied in the same exact engineering department. Lindsey the Wonderful was two years ahead in the program, which meant suffering through endless ceremonies where she'd received the departmental engineering awards. And then Lindsey married the most gorgeous guy on campus, that All-American in lacrosse, Duncan McLeod. To add insult to injury, she develops an electrode to detect aneurysms that BioCorp buys for a zillion dollars! After that, no one in the department paid any attention to her own electron oscillator. The Battersby oscillator was a far more sophisticated invention than the Nolan-BioCorp electrode, but who ever heard of it?

A throbbing headache coming on, Karen reached for Pussy Willow to soothe her. She'd worked through her "obsessive Lindsey issues," as her therapist, Dr. Samuels, called them, years before. She was sure of it. The days of obsessively Googling Lindsey were in the past. Nor did she check PubMed or Medline anymore to see if Lindsey's publication rate exceeded her own. Besides, they conducted research in completely unrelated fields now. They didn't compete for the same pool of grant money, or for the same top grad students. It was sheer coincidence that she and Lindsey now lived in the same state. BTI had made her the best job offer, she had tried to explain to Dr. Samuels. That was the *only* reason she moved to Massachusetts! It had nothing to do with the fact that Lindsey lived there! She was so much better now; even Dr. Samuels agreed. *She was so much better now.* Lindsey hadn't crossed her mind for some time.

But then came Sara Kauni's email!

What was that all about? Had that sly Lindsey put Sara up to it? What was she up to? The microwave beeped. Dinner was ready, but Karen was too distressed to eat. Instead, she opened Google to check on her nemesis's activities.

Chapter 4

Rehab

Lindsey lingered around the reading room the next morning, pulling random books off the shelf. Single words were recognizable, but it took her many passes before she could decipher a sentence's meaning. Comprehending entire paragraphs... forget it. In despair, she leaned her forehead against the windowpane. She was brain damaged. With slop for a brain, her career was over.

She still, miraculously, had the ability to count. Three packs of cigarettes had been won off the men in the poker game. And she could do multiplication. Three times twenty was sixty. She had sixty cigarettes. Smoking was a ritual that was both relaxing and time-consuming, so she pulled one from her pocket. As a simple mental exercise, she'd count how many cigarettes she'd smoke today until Dr. Waters released her. This was cigarette number four. Equally miraculous was the fact that her eyes had come into focus enough to see the hands on her dive watch. Were she in Woods Hole, she'd just be arriving at work. Sara would assume that she was taking an extra vacation day. Somehow she'd have to contact Sara, but there were only two antiquated pieces of technology—pay phones—down the hall, which were always occupied by some jittery body slumped against the cinderblock wall.

The rattle of metal food carts announced the arrival of breakfast, so she stubbed out her cigarette and headed to the dining room. The patients—they were *not* inmates, Big Nurse had kindly informed her—settled themselves at three parallel tables in a dining room and opened plastic bags to get at their plastic silverware to eat what she suspected were plastic scrambled eggs. The golfer, Curtis, and Ethan in the Che Guevara t-shirt sat with the CEO and the Goth. Curtis waved for her to join them, but she shook her head and remained alone in the corner. There was no point in making mindless small talk with a bunch of strangers. Remembering actual names was an unnecessary task. Why bother? In a few hours she'd be gone. Lobsterman, Bling, NRA, Dead Head, and Poodle Trainer chatted about an old episode of *Breaking Bad*. Her roommate, Grandma, appeared to be friends with Captain Ahab, Gay Guy, and Bob Marley. Barbie Doll and Soccer Mom quickly zeroed in on Mitch, the Army Ranger, and sat themselves on either side of him. The dining room quickly filled. There were about thirty patients in total.

Posters on the dining room walls had slogans and quotes by some guy named Bill W. and there was a list of twelve nonsensical steps. Ethan left his conversation with the others and moved his tray next to hers, interrupting her self-imposed ostracism. He clearly had some level of intelligence for he spoke at some length about the failure of the international committee to act fast enough to contain the Ebola virus in Nigeria, while she struggled to remember on which continent Nigeria was located. Ted, the preppie lawyer from detox, was still resentful after her victory at five-card stud and glared at her. Drug Dealer ignored her completely, as he was hitting on the beautiful teenager, Jailbait. Ethan had little appetite, ate only a few bites of breakfast, then excused himself to smoke in the Fishbowl. Insurance Fraud quickly appropriated Ethan's vacated seat. He leaned oppressively close and bounced his knee against hers.

"How's our lovely gambler this morning?" he said quietly, his breath hot in her ear.

"Fine," she replied, fidgeting.

His finger stroked the red mark circling her wrist, and he smiled suggestively. "Let's you and I play some games later." He stood and left without waiting for her response.

Having lost her appetite, she headed for the Fishbowl. She had a cigarette with Ethan and was playing Solitaire with a sticky, incomplete deck of cards when a middle-aged woman strutted in.

"Let's talk in my office," the woman said imperiously.

"Glub, glub," she answered.

The woman laughed outright. "I heard that you were a pain in the ass."

Lindsey followed reluctantly and glanced at the woman's nameplate as she entered the office. Katherine Waters, Ph.D. Clinical Psychologist. Waters eyed her cautiously from behind her desk. Lindsey eyed her back. Waters was about fifteen years her senior. Her brown hair was streaked with gray. Her face was hard and attractive. She was slightly overweight. Most unnerving were Waters' seen-it-all eyes that cut through her like blue glass.

"I'm Kate. I'll be your counselor for the next month. Please sit down." She gestured to a chair.

Kate was a monosyllabic, easy-to-remember name. "I definitely won't be staying that long," Lindsey replied, obstinately standing. "In fact, I want you to sign my release papers immed—"

"Yeah, we'll get to that," Kate broke in, staring into her laptop. "Let me get some background information on you. You weren't too forthcoming with it the ER. Your name's Lindsey Nolan, correct?"

"My name's inconsequential because I'm not staying."

Kate glanced up from the screen. "That's an interesting spelling of your name. L N D S Y."

"What?" Lindsey asked, flustered.

Kate added flatly, "When you signed yourself in, you forgot the vowels."

"That's not funny!"

"No, it's not funny. It's not funny at all."

How could she not remember how to spell her own fucking name! She had mastered that task when she was three years old. She could read by four. She suddenly craved a cigarette—number six—and reached into her shorts for the pack. The psychologist left her desk and opened the window. A rush of humidity moved through the screen. Lindsey's thumb flicked frantically over the lighter, without success. Kate took it from her hand and lit the cigarette for her.

"Do you remember *anything* from the ER?" Kate asked.

Lindsey remained silent as Kate's infuriating blue eyes cut through her once again.

"Your tremors will continue for a while. Today you'll stop getting Valium. Eventually the tremors will stop, but it takes time. Everything about this process takes time. You must be patient." Kate lit herself a cigarette, Camel non-filters, and inhaled deeply. "Your address is listed as Massachusetts. Why are you in Rhode Island?"

"I was at a boat show. I think."

"You think? You don't know?"

Best not to respond, Lindsey decided.

"And what do you do back in Massachusetts?"

"I work."

"What do you do for work?"

Lindsey was silent.

"Let's try this again. What do you do for work?"

"I work in a lab," Lindsey answered evasively.

"Doing what?"

"I care for animals, clean tanks, wash glassware, stuff like that."

"So you're a lab technician?"

"Yup. Something like that." An overflowing ashtray sat between them on the windowsill. "Do we want to empty this thing?" Lindsey asked, hoping to change the subject.

"No. A lab tech must have some education. Where did you go to school?"

"Why is this relevant to anything?"

"I was just wondering. What's the big deal?"

Whatever. What random school to pull out of the blue? "Penn State." Right, like she'd ever attend a public state university.

"I've forgotten... what's that mascot of theirs?"

Lindsey stalled. Shit... what was it? Something blue and white. "The Hoyas."

Kate glanced doubtfully at the patient. "Do you abuse any other chemicals besides alcohol?"

"I don't do drugs. I just drink too much sometimes."

"How much is sometimes?"

"Fuck! I don't know!"

"We don't use profanity in the rehab. We treat each other with respect and civility. Is sometimes every day?"

"Possibly."

"Possibly or definitely?"

"Possibly definitely," Lindsey quipped with a sarcastic smile.

"You definitely drink every day," Kate stated, shaking her head.

"Yes, definitely."

Kate scowled. "How much?"

"It varies. Less on weekdays, more on weekends."

"And excessive amounts at boat shows," Kate added.

Now Lindsey scowled.

"How old were you when you began drinking?" Kate continued.

"I'm not sure. Maybe fourteen?"

"So you've been drinking about half of your life. Where does your family live?"

"I don't have one."

"Everyone comes from somewhere."

"My husband lives in Virginia."

"Do you have children?"

"No, thankfully."

"Does he know you're here?"

"No. He spends summers in Edinburgh."

"What does he do?"

"He's a professor."

"You live apart. Why?"

"We can't stand each other."

"So why don't you divorce?"

"We enjoy torturing each other."

"How often do you see each other?"

"He visits me every few months."

"How do get along then?"

"He wants to screw the whole time and I want to be in the lab. He stays too long. I get drunk. He gets mad. We fight. He leaves. And the cycle repeats itself the next time."

"Do your fights always revolve around your drinking?"

Lindsey remained silent again.

"Maybe you didn't hear me. Let me rephrase my question: If you did not drink, would you two have anything to fight about?"

Lindsey snuffed out her cigarette in the pyramid of smelly filters, and scanned the cars in the parking lot below. "There's my car!" she announced happily. If she could find a way through the security doors, she'd be home free and at work in one hour, maybe less if she sped.

"Which one?"

"The green Jeep in the corner."

"That's the most alcoholic car I've ever seen."

The canvas roof was held together by duct tape and wire, and the fender tilted from when she'd backed into the dumpster at the marina. "It's a bit beaten up," Lindsey conceded. "But the engine runs perfectly. I tune it myself."

"Who was the man who brought you here?" Kate asked.

Lindsey's head spun around. "What man?"

"What man!" Kate said incredulously. "The man you were screaming at and fighting with outside the ER."

Cambridge

The best bench near the Wood Sailing Pavilion on Memorial Drive was unoccupied, so Karen Battersby scurried toward it. The water of the Charles River was quiet except for a few scullers and kayakers; to her right, a stream of rush hour traffic lurched and honked its way across the Harvard Bridge into Cambridge. This morning required a Grande coffee from Starbucks; she'd had little sleep. Yesterday's email from Sara Kauni was still disconcerting. There were a number of possible reasons why Sara had sent that email. 1) Lindsey had fired Sara. 2) Sara wanted to live in the city. 3) Sara and Lindsey had a proprietary dispute over an invention. But reason number 4 seemed most plausible... Lindsey's fecund imagination was drying up. So Sara was being sent by Lindsey to infiltrate her BTI lab for purposes of spying on her—and stealing her latest inventions. Yes, that was surely the reason.

"So that's the game Lindsey wants to play. Challenge accepted!"

Karen tossed the remaining bits of her cranberry muffin to the pigeons, then pulled a tablet from her brief case. Her response would be polite, professional, and very brief. She would request a meeting in person to carefully observe Sara's body language for any signs of subterfuge and treachery. She typed her reply.

Dear Dr. Kauni,

I was pleased to receive your job inquiry yesterday and was very impressed by the interesting projects that you've been involved with over the past few years. I'll be on the Cape next week visiting an elderly aunt if you'd like to meet somewhere then.

Regards, Karen Battersby, Ph.D.

SEND

Chapter 5

Rehab

Kate Waters agreed to sign the dismissal forms *after* Lindsey attended a few AA meetings and group counseling meetings on the ward. Besides, it was nearly the weekend, the psychologist had pointed out. "Let your mind clear for a few more days, over the weekend. Then maybe you'll be ready to go back to work next week."

Maybe the rehab was a safe place to wait it out for a few days, Lindsey decided. What if the creep that she'd fought with was waiting for her in the parking lot? Had she met him at the boat show? Was it the same jerk that she'd had sex with? The guy who bashed up her knuckles, scraped her calf, put her in that obscenely short pink miniskirt... with no panties! The same asshole who'd bound her wrists! The red marks might as well be flashing neon, they were so obvious. Now every man on the ward was hovering around her.

This was all a colossal mistake.

She glanced around the room, at the circle of human flotsam on folding metal chairs, sitting in a smog of cigarette smoke, at her first AA meeting. What man, what fight? If only she could focus on the words of British Airways... In her cheery lilt, the flight attendant described her bottom. She'd been nipping from bottles of Smirnoff Blue all the way across the Atlantic, taken a fancy to a brawny Air Marshal and begged to see his sidearm, thereby breaching airplane security somewhere over Iceland.

"She wanted to play with his gun," Lindsey blurted out loud, laughing.

Kate stared aghast and sprung from her chair. "Sharing at AA meetings is supposed to be cathartic and instructive, not subject matter for callous comedy! Out, Lindsey!"

"The story's full of ironic humor. How can everyone not see that?" she said in rebuttal.

"I said out!"

"I'm cast out of the outcasts," she muttered to herself, slumping out of the meeting room.

She found her bedroom congested with bodies. Grandma's daughter and son-in-law were packing the old woman's bags, as she had just completely the thirty-day program.

Grandma had been an excellent roommate, as she had slept all the time. It was a smart strategy to pass the thirty days. At the moment the old woman was circling the room in dazed circles as the daughter closed the suitcase. Before bed the night before, the old woman had said that she was from a farm in western Rhode Island. Her daughter had initiated an intervention. The daughter's logic was somewhat questionable, Lindsey thought, as one might be set in ones ways by the age of eighty-six. The daughter had hid the keys to the minivan to prohibit her mother's trips to the liquor store. Having run out of wine coolers one afternoon, the irked old woman instead drove the John Deere down the interstate to the liquor store. Thirty days in rehab was a stiff sentence, Lindsey agreed, especially as there were no driving violations en route. The family was taking an extended vacation and needed a safe place to deposit the old woman for a few weeks, she guessed.

"Okay, Mom. It's time to go," said the daughter with the golden tan.

"You be a good girl," Grandma said, patting Lindsey on the cheek.

"I will. Good luck with everything."

"Just for one day, sweetheart. You can do it, just for one day," Grandma said, hobbling toward the door in her worn bedroom slippers.

Lindsey nodded. The encouragement was touching and gave her a glimmer of hope after a morning of bad news and the public admonishment in the AA meeting.

"Mom, what have you done with your shoes?" the daughter asked with a sigh of exasperation.

Lindsey peered nervously into the closet and then under the beds. The scuffed brown shoes were mysteriously missing.

"How was your evening?" Kate asked when Lindsey entered the office the next morning for their counseling appointment.

"Fabulous. I went dancing and bar-hopping in Newport with Rob Gronkowski. What kind of question is that? You know how my evening was. It sucked! I was stuck here, bored out of my mind, twiddling my thumbs, doing nothing."

Actually the previous evening had been spent surreptitiously studying the patients in the Fishbowl. Which weirdo stole Grandma's shoes? And why those shoes? They were old and ugly. Was it the same weirdo with some freakish shoe fetish who kicked her sandals across her room in detox? Curtis, Ethan, Mitch, and Ted had been in detox with her. Curtis and Ethan were unlikely, as both were pleasant and wealthy, and Mitch's sole interest was the Nautilus equipment and chin-up bar outside by the patio. The culprit had to be Ted, the surly lawyer who wanted to play strip poker. He would be avoided at all costs. Her sandals had been hidden away under her mattress throughout the night. And sleep, forget it. The doors had no locks. Who could sleep with some creep with a shoe or foot fetish lurking around?

"My evening was very interesting. I Googled your name and had a number of hits." Kate opened a folder and read the headlines of the printed articles. "Johns Hopkins—not Penn State—undergraduate," she said, "sells patent of non-invasive imaging electrode to BioCorp. Nolan Electrode now standard equipment in all U.S. hospitals. Here's my favorite." She chuckled. "Dr. Lindsey Nolan: On the Road to Stockholm?"

"I'm on the road to nowhere sitting in this asylum." Lindsey dropped her head on the desk.

"A future Nobel Laureate in our midst. This certainly explains the pomposity," Kate replied.

Lindsey quickly lifted her head. "Sara's going to be panicking by now. Thinking that I've been kidnapped by some terrorist group or rogue government, coerced into making neurotoxins or rockets to knock out entire armies. Perhaps the CIA and FBI have been called in to hunt for me."

Kate shook her head in disgust. "You live in fantasyland."

"I can't get on the goddamn phones! I need to send two emails. Please?" she pleaded. "One to Sara at work. One to my husband, Duncan. Just to let them know I'm alright."

"And if I allow it, you'll make an effort to cooperate and participate in a constructive manner at all AA meetings and group counseling sessions? No rude laughter when other patients are sharing their thoughts?"

"I promise."

"And keep an open mind about the lessons of AA and the Twelve Steps? And not bitch and moan for the next thirty days?"

"Thirty days? I've been here two. That would be twenty-eight."

"Good." Kate smiled triumphantly. "So you *are* staying the remaining twenty-eight."

"Wait! I didn't say that!"

"But you'll keep an open mind about it... and an open mind gets you on the computer."

"I'm very open-minded."

Kate rose and gestured Lindsey into the chair, but she hovered nearby.

"Stop watching me," Lindsey said.

"I don't want you touching any of my files. Just send your emails and get off my computer."

Lindsey's fingers moved across the keyboard. "Dearest Duncan... I'm lying across the bed at rehab in a black leather teddy. Silk straps around my—"

"Why did I agree to this?" Kate snatched up her pack of cigarettes, moved to the window, lit a cigarette, and blew streams of smoke through the screen.

Lindsey typed two quick messages to Sara and Duncan, hit the SEND button, and joined Kate at the window with cigarette number fourteen.

"Thank you," Lindsey said genuinely, a tone which Kate hadn't heard before. "That's a load off my mind."

Kate searched the patient's face for signs of insincerity, but there were none. "I spoke with a technician who saw you outside the ER. The man who dropped you off was wearing sunglasses, a t-shirt, and shorts. Does that bring back anything?"

Lindsey shook her head dismally.

"He said that the two of you were... physical. He was trying to hold you, restrain you. You were trying to escape him, screaming and cursing at him, shoving him away."

Woods Hole

Sara watched a wave rush up the beach and fill in the moat around Zephyr's sand castle, then the water percolated away into the sand, leaving the moat empty again. Stony Beach was her son's favorite place, so on most evenings in the summer, after his summer camp and her work, they had a picnic on the beach. Stretched next to her on the blanket was Zephyr's hero, Derick Briggs. Just at that moment Zephyr looked up from his sand castle to check on Derick's whereabouts. Derick responded with a growl and threw a clump of seaweed at him. The seaweed hit Zephyr's arm with a wet splat, and he grinned. Zephyr was fascinated with all things Derick. Derick wrestled grizzly bears. Derick's motorcycle could turn into a space cruiser. And Derick wore black leather clothes for his job as an intergalactic bounty hunter.

The next wave made off with the plastic shovel. Zephyr rose quickly and chased it into the shallows. Out in deeper water, teenage boys tossed a foam football, so he wandered out to watch.

"Not too deep, sweetheart," Sara called after him. She turned back to Derick. "I've done an idiotic thing. I sent out inquiries for a new job, got a response from Karen Battersby at BTI, and agreed to set up a meeting with her. Right after that, I got an email from Lindsey. Turns out she's in rehab. Finally! If she can get better, we can get back to work again. I don't want to leave Woods Hole."

"That's not idiotic," Derick said. "You did what anyone in your shoes would have done when a job becomes difficult."

"What do I do about the meeting with Karen? I'd hate to waste her time." She turned her view seaward. "Zephyr, that's far enough."

"What if Lindsey can't get sober?" he wondered. "Then you're stuck in the same boat."

"I know. The last few months—no, the entire year has been a disaster." She sat erect. "That's way too deep!"

"Maybe you could meet with Karen, just to see what she's like and see what her lab's doing. You don't have to commit to anything. But you don't want to burn any bridges either way, in case Lindsey can't get it together." He removed his Ducati Racing Team ball cap and sunglasses, and placed them on a cooler.

"You're right. Karen's going to be on the Cape anyway. I'll invite her here, give her a lab tour, and take her to lunch. I'll make it a nice time so that if nothing pans out, then her time hasn't been totally wasted."

"That sounds like a good plan." He stood. "Let's swim with Zephyr." He pulled Sara to her feet and they walked to the foamy edge of the water.

"The bottom's so rocky. I should have worn my beach shoes." Sara dipped her toe in. "Yikes! The water's too cold. I'll just wade."

"You should be used to the Cape water by now."

"But I'm not," she admitted. "I'll just go out to my knees."

"Alright."

Zephyr turned to watch Derick and his mother approach. Suddenly Derick grinned devilishly and swooped her up in his arms. "Don't you dare," she screamed. Laughing, he strode quickly into deeper water. "This water's freezing!" she gasped, writhing and kicking. Suddenly he threw her high into the air. Delighted, Zephyr clapped his tiny hands as she hit the frigid water.

Zephyr loved it when Derick made his mother shriek.

A Rest Stop in Delaware

"Fuckin' finally," Maggie groaned, climbing out of the ravine. For nearly two fuckin' hours the state trooper had parked in front of the entrance to the rest stop. For nearly two fuckin' hours that fat turd had drunk coffee and stuffed his face with donuts. And a terrifying snake had popped its head from the tall grass and stared her right in the eyes! She had frantically heaved stones at it, hoping to drive it away. Bess would have killed it and cooked it. Bess would eat almost anything.

"Snakes are protein," Bess had once said. "Protein makes your hair pretty and shiny."

The Bottom Dwellers

Bess was smart like that. She knew about protein, hair, and other shit. Bess had told her that she could learn about hair protein in beauty magazines, but when Maggie had approached the magazine rack at a rest stop in North Carolina, the old bitch behind the cash register had said, "I'm sorry, but if you're not going to buy anything, you'll have to leave." Mean old bitch.

After scaring off the snake, Maggie had passed the afternoon drawing in the dirt with a stick. Her third grade art teacher had told her that her drawings were good. She'd periodically checked the time on Bess' watch, waiting for the police cruiser to pull onto the interstate. She was pleased with herself; not only could she draw but she could tell time. These things, Bess had said, caused something called Self-esteem.

Maggie brushed the dirt her off clothes and climbed over the edge of the ravine. The sun was just setting over the trees across the highway. This rest stop wasn't too far from the ocean, and seagulls swooped over the parking lot, searching for scraps of food. She looked stealthily around. No one was nearby except an old man and his poodle in the dog walking area, and he seemed too senile to notice her. She approached the trashcan in the picnic area where a young couple had eaten with their tiny children earlier that afternoon. Tiny children often couldn't finish their Happy Meals. She pulled the fast food bag from the trashcan. Her stomach jolted as the marvelous smell hit her brain. She tore open the bag. A half-eaten bag of French fries and a half-eaten cheeseburger! Heaven! Cheeseburgers were protein. She joyfully stuffed the delicious food into her mouth and pushed her way through the door of the rest stop.

She washed up and filled her water bottles in the women's restroom. Before leaving the building, she snagged creamers, sugar packets, and condiments—travel snacks—and snuck them successfully into her bag without the manager noticing. The sun had set beyond the forest and night was falling over the parking lot. Night always filled her with dread. She trudged listlessly toward the trucks. Night meant work, work meant old men.

Typically Bess would do the talking for the both of them, but now she had to do the talking on her own. What was it that Bess used to say? She hadn't paid the least bit of attention, as she always distracted herself by watching the parking lot lights reflect off the colorful paint of the trucks. Some trucks even had artwork like flames and swirls. She walked the row of trucks, her heart thumping in a sickly fear. That last trucker in Maryland had smelled horrible and been too rough. She still ached a day later, but he'd given her fifty dollars, which she'd promptly spent on cigarettes and crack in Baltimore. Which truck to approach? Each one was equally terrifying. She found herself at the end of the parking lot, having passed all of them.

Through the darkness, she spotted a van at the far end of the lot. Rain was forecasted for the next few days. A van might provide a dry way north. It was worth a try, so she wandered toward it. Two white surfboards were on the roof. The air around it smelled of marijuana. Surfer stoners were fun. If they had weed, they might have other good shit. Her spirits lifted.

The surfer in the driver's seat studied her cautiously through the open window. His friend in the passenger seat craned his head around to watch her approach. She flashed them her most dazzling smile. What was it that Bess said... that always hooked them... what the fuck was it?

Maggie reached forward and slowly ran her finger down the length of the driver's pinky finger splayed on the side mirror. She suddenly remembered. Bess' normal snarling voice would become a purring southern drawl.

"What are two gorgeous men like you doing all by your lonesome?" Maggie asked sweetly.

Chapter 6

Rehab

Lindsey did not share at all at the AA meetings; there was nothing to tell. There was no violent pimp beating her up; nor had she been to prison, nor contracted HIV from a dirty needle, nor lost children, nor had to declare bankruptcy, nor been raped by a father, brother, or uncle, or any number of horrors that beset the other patients. Then why did she drink so much? It made no sense; she was blessed in so many ways. When asked to share, she no longer wise-cracked "I'm Lindsey and I really meant to take the Fall River exit." Instead she just muttered, "Pass."

It took a few counseling sessions, but Kate and she eventually seemed to settle into a routine with each other. They'd talk for twenty minutes every morning, slouched against the windowsill, blowing cigarette smoke through the screen. All of the counselors were recovering addicts and alcoholics. Kate's drug of choice was vodka. During a fight at a steakhouse with her then-husband, she'd decided to pin his hand to the table with a steak knife. He'd got full custody of their three children and moved them to Oregon. She was a hardhead, she explained, going through rehab twice before getting the program. The chip on her shoulder, Kate admitted bitterly, was the size of Mt. Everest. Kate was assigned the most difficult cases, a fact that puzzled Lindsey. *She* wasn't difficult.

Between their two faces and the window screen, smoke hung heavy in the humidity. It had just stopped raining and the air smelled of freshly mown grass. On the sidewalk below, a woman in a gray suit, perhaps a hospital administrator, dashed through the front entrance, closing an umbrella. A father hopped puddles in the parking lot, carrying a pink and silver balloon that read *It's a Girl!*

"What are you feeling today?" Kate asked.

"At the moment, only one thing. Frustration. The booze dissolved my cerebral cortex," Lindsey explained sadly. "I've lost all higher brain function and the ability for abstract thinking. I am barely able to understand the mindless articles in the fashion magazines. Forget about reading *War and Peace* in the reading room."

She remembered that she worked in a bioengineering lab on Cape Cod, had an ingenious partner named Sara Kauni, and a sweetheart of a boss named Mort Somers. She had a great job... why did she drink so much? State-of-the-art scientific equipment covered her lab benches. There was more grant money than she could ever spend. She was developing some electrode, but what type she could not remember. Why did she drink so much?

"If I can't think, I can't work. I'm meant to work in a lab. My brain is my only tool. I have no other skills to fall back on."

Kate asked apprehensively, "If you don't get your mind back, what will you do?"

"I'll kill myself," Lindsey said simply.

Woods Hole

In preparation for Karen Battersby's visit, Sara decided to use the morning to straighten up the lab. And she would take Derick's advice—keep her options open in regards to job prospects.

With Lindsey absent, she could listen to her music without headphones, as they had diametrically opposite tastes in music. Lindsey listened to smooth jazz, honky-tonk, and the blues, whereas Sara liked blaring rock and roll. She scanned her rack of CDs and picked out something old, Alice Cooper. To keep herself company, she turned on the motors of two of her favorite planes, Manfred von Richthofen's *Red Baron* and a Sikorsky S-38 flying boat. The planes circled the air space above as she got to work.

Humming to herself, she started with the lab benches and moved the pipettes and soldering equipment back onto the shelves. The chemicals were placed back in explosion-proof cabinets and in alphabetic order. She wiped dabs of solder and conduction grease from the bench tops with an industrial strength disinfectant. At Lindsey's rack of electronics containing oscilloscopes, amplifiers, and assorted self-made components, she removed the spare cables that hung like snakes and returned them to the cable holder.

A key to Lindsey's small workroom was tacked to a corkboard next to her computer. The workroom was really no more than a closet, but Lindsey had managed to squeeze in a table, chair, and a metal electronics rack. Sara turned the key with dread. This was the place where Lindsey in the past few weeks—on the days she made it to work—retreated to drink.

It was no surprise that the room was trashed. Electrical components were strewn haphazardly across the table. She halted and stared downward. Amidst the debris, some unidentifiable piece of equipment was emerging. Lindsey was building something, but Sara had no clue what it was. She felt her blood heat. They were to work on all projects together! Nothing was to be done independently! That was their agreement. All profits from their inventions were a fifty-fifty split.

Behind a laptop was an empty bottle of Icelandic vodka. In a box of clamps were an empty bottle of Lindsey's favorite, Glenlivet whiskey, and a pack of breath mints. At the bottom of the box was something else... she could not believe her eyes!

"That shit!" she cried aloud. Her blood hit its boiling point. She dashed out of the workroom to a cabinet where the trash bags and rubber gloves were stored. Fuming, she tugged on the gloves. Returning to the workroom, she heaved the bottles of vodka and scotch whiskey into the trash bag, along with the breath mints... and condoms and sex lube!

That shit had been bringing boyfriends from the Captain Kidd back to the lab in the late evenings! In their intoxicated, frenzied lust, they couldn't make it as far as her houseboat, or his place! Instead had they staggered the few steps down Water Street to screw in the lab? Lindsey had made their workplace a bordello. Sara recoiled, not wanting to touch a thing. She could imagine it all too well; she had witnessed heterosexual sex *ad nauseum* in the movies, and even had it a few times herself with her Japanese friend from the Math Club for the purposes of conceiving Zephyr. Lindsey and...

whoever... standing up in some half-dressed tangle against the worktable.

Sara grabbed the trash bag and ran down the back stairs of her lab building. At the dumpster outside, she flung the trash bag upward. As the bottles shattered in the dumpster, she decided to take the interview with Karen Battersby very seriously.

Chapter 7

Rehab

New emotions upwelled in Lindsey in unpredictable, unwelcome surges. Frustration was soon replaced by guilt and embarrassment. Her two days in the black hole continued to obsess her. As for the mystery man outside of the ER, she wondered if the sex had been forced or consensual. The red marks around her wrists had disappeared, but the thought of being restrained somewhere by some stranger still unnerved her.

"If it's any consolation, you tested negative for HIV and other sexually-transmitted diseases," Kate remarked.

"I want go down to my car to search for clues," Lindsey said.

"I'd rather you didn't," Kate responded quickly. "You said you'd give rehab a try, and I don't want to see you drive off with none of your issues resolved."

"Then you go." Lindsey sprang out of the chair, left the psychologist's office, jogged across the ward, and returned with a cluster of keys. She leaned across Kate's desk. "You go.

Please," she begged. "Anything to help me backtrack my drunken footsteps."

Later that morning Lindsey watched from a window as Kate walked with an empty cardboard box toward the Jeep. The counselor frowned in disgust at the bottles, cans, and other debris in the seats. After searching the car and sifting through assorted trash, she hefted the box across the pavement and disappeared through the front entrance. As Kate buzzed through the security doors, Lindsey grabbed for the box, but Kate shouldered her away, saying, "I have to check this stuff first."

"You're kidding me," Lindsey said. "Like I have coke hidden in the pages of my lab notebook or something."

"I've seen stranger hiding places," Kate replied. "Aren't you supposed to be at your group counseling session right now?"

Lindsey returned later that morning to find the contents from her car spread across a table in the reading room. Kate, her arms folded across her chest, studied the items, as if trying to solve a mystery.

"That's not my brand," Lindsey said, lifting a sandy tube of sunscreen. A yellow Post-it note in a cryptic, drunken scrawl had a name and address of a local hotel. "That might be my handwriting." There was a matchbook from the same place. "I have no idea where that hotel is."

"I do," Kate said. "It's not that far from my house. It's a dive, a no-tell-motel on the coastal road. In your car were a black string bikini and Corona Beer beach towel. There were also blue swimming trunks, black flip-flops, and a straw Panama hat."

"The bikini and Corona towel are mine, but the men's stuff... God only knows."

The Bottom Dwellers

A lab notebook and some electronics were present on the table. Her iPod! Better yet, her tool kit containing a Phillips head screwdriver!

Her chip processor and circuit analyzer had had their metal lids screwed off and their interiors searched. She said facetiously, "So you found the top secret microchips I was selling to the Chinese?"

Kate's response was an unimpressed scowl.

"Was there a pink cosmetic bag?" Lindsey asked.

"No. But this is interesting." Kate presented a white paper. It was a map to the Narragansett Eastbay Clinic that had been printed on Lindsey's home printer. Her email address, time and date stamp ran along the bottom of the paper. The page had been printed out on June 13 at 6:43 pm.

"You meant to come here, Egghead," Kate said, pleased. "You consciously sought out this place. There's hope for you yet."

Kate lifted the iPod off the table and scanned the playlists. "Nice. Big Bad Voodoo Daddy. Ella Fitzgerald. Diana Krall. 'Cry Me A River'... that's my favorite song!" She excitedly placed the headphones over her ears and disappeared into the world of music. Lindsey pondered the items on the table, her frustration growing. None of the clues led her any closer to identifying the elusive Boat Show Man.

Cambridge

Karen Battersby taped the latest Dilbert comic to her office door. Her graduate students, she knew, found Dilbert as hysterically funny as she did. She returned to her office and studied the list of gamers' conventions and Comic Cons tacked to her bulletin board, next to images of Wonder

Woman, Catwoman, Deanna Troi, and Dr. Beverly Crusher. A number of Comic Cons would be held in the New England area over the next few months. With a yellow highlighter, she underlined those that were within a day's driving distance from Boston. She returned to her desk. The computer reminded her of the recent correspondence with Sara Kauni.

In a few days she was to visit Sara at—of all places—Woods Hole! Karen had imagined that they might meet at a restaurant in Falmouth, but Sara had instead invited her to Woods Hole. This was a stunning invitation and one that she had to carefully analyze. Was Lindsey Nolan setting a trap for her—in Woods Hole, on her home turf? Caution, Karen, caution. Her email back to Sara said that Woods Hole might be an awkward place to discuss employment opportunities should they run into her current boss. Sara then replied that Lindsey Nolan was out of town for the month.

Karen's mind wandered. What exotic place might Lindsey and that hot Duncan McLeod be traveling to for an entire month? Was it a romantic getaway to Barcelona, the French Riviera, Bora Bora?

Sara's email also conveyed that she'd like to give Karen a tour of Woods Hole; it was a scenic little village with nice seafood restaurants. Sara's response seemed innocent enough. Or was it?

Karen stared at her *World of Warcraft* screensaver, her thoughts darkening. What if Lindsey wasn't really abroad, but was planning to infiltrate Karen's lab in Boston? Was Sara luring her to Woods Hole so Lindsey could slip into her BTI lab? It would be necessary to warn her trusted grad students to be vigilant of any unusual visitors or activities.

But how clever was she to mention an aunt on the Cape! It was essential to keep Sara—if she were in fact a spy—far away from Boston for as long as possible, until her exact motives and intentions could be accurately gauged. Sara's invitation to Woods Hole truly was baffling. Was Sara 'going rogue' and deviating from Lindsey's game plan… to spite her boss?

Might it be possible, Karen wondered, to get a quick peek at what Lindsey was up to in her Woods Hole lab? Two could play the Infiltration Game.

Chapter 8

Rehab

"I have two pieces of good news," Kate said to Lindsey the next morning. First, I've assigned Myra to be your Peer Mentor."

Lindsey breathed a sigh of relief. "Thank god. She's the only sane person in this nuthouse." Myra was two weeks further along in the thirty-day program. She was on leave from her airline job and had checked herself into the rehab. "She was sick and tired of being sick and tired," she had said earlier at an AA meeting.

"And second, no one ever uses the corner table in the reading room, so you're welcome to use it for your electronics projects," Kate offered. "But only during recreational time and *after* you've done your AA readings."

"You're trying to prevent me from stirring up the waters in the Fishbowl."

"Exactly. The complaints about lethal, man-eating bacteria in the refrigerator have become quite tiresome. Today I want you and Myra to discuss Step Four with each another, one-on-one, as you'll do later with your sponsor."

"Which step is four?"

"*Made a searching and fearless moral inventory of ourselves.*"

"I hate that one," Lindsey grumbled.

"You're both alcoholics. This will help you two to identify any defects of character that perpetuate your drinking behaviors."

"Since I have no defects of character, I'd like to waive this assignment. Besides, I am not particularly interested in confiding anything to anyone *one-on-one.*"

"I'd like to remind you that non-participation will only drag out the process," Kate pointed out.

"One-on-one sounds fine with me," Lindsey readily agreed.

Myra found Lindsey in the reading room later that day. The tall, wiry Brit glanced at the table, where a number of mechanical and electronic parts were scattered. "What are you doing?"

"I'm designing a doorknob that can be opened in response to one's touch," Lindsey said over her shoulder. "A keyless, handprint-sensing doorknob."

"No retinal scanner?" Myra asked, amused.

"No. Do you know how difficult it would be for a drunk to stand motionless and non-blinking in front of a retinal scanner? It was so embarrassing to ask my self-righteous, asshole of a neighbor for *my* spare set of keys to get into *my* own boat twice in the last few months. That will never happen again. Drunks will thank me for this doorknob. Plus, it will give them something to grab on to after a night on the town."

"The Drunkard's Doorknob can wait. It's time to discuss Step Four. It's a beautiful day. Let's talk outside."

Lindsey followed Myra down the stairs, passing Larry the Drug Dealer and Jailbait Kelly groping each other in the stairwell. The two women spotted some unoccupied lawn chairs in the back of the garden.

Myra wiggled her feet out of her laceless sneakers and stretched out her long, freckled legs. "You go first. Tell me about your family and when you first started to drink.

Lindsey started to sort through her childhood memories, slouching deep into the chair. Her long-term memory was surprisingly intact. "I had a banal suburban childhood. My mother, Miriam, was a control freak. Everything was appearance, a veneer of normalcy and order, everything perfect, everything false. Michael, my father, was never around, avoiding her at every turn. He was a successful defense attorney and good-old-boy in the service organizations, a.k.a. men's drinking clubs. For four generations the Nolan family was a well-known legal family in the city of Annapolis."

"Are your parents dead? You talk about them in the past tense."

"I don't know."

"How can you not know that?"

"I haven't spoken to them in years. We had a falling out."

"About what?"

"I don't remember."

"You're so full of shit. Go on."

"My house was an ugly clone of every other one in a development of executive homes, immaculate and unlivable. Being the neighborhood nerd, I preferred the library to the playground. When I learned how to ride a bike, I was off through neighborhoods only to return at night. My two sisters had the cloying charm and social skills that my mother prized, and I lacked.

"It infuriated Mommy Dearest that I, but not my sisters, passed into the gifted programs at the school. My mother had my sisters tested and re-tested to get them into the same programs, but they couldn't make the cut. She bullied the school officials for years, but they would not relent. My mother's resentment of me grew and I withdrew to other places, both literal and figurative.

"I retreated to the library, or my uncle's boathouse. Uncle Charlie was the best. He was my father's youngest brother. Charlie and his partner, Elliot, ran a boatyard on the Severn River where I learned to sail, set rigging, fix boat engines, and electronics. They spoiled me rotten, and took me to Orioles games at Camden Yards where I learned everything about baseball. My mother was a homophobe and bitched endlessly to my father, 'Because of him, you'll never be Attorney General'."

Myra grimaced sympathetically. "Sounds awful, all right."

Lindsey was silent for a moment, remembering the smells and sounds of the Severn River.

"The boathouse was a magical place, full of fun gadgets for me to play with. In the corner was an old refrigerator where Charlie kept snacks and drinks. One day he and Elliot were down the pier and I went to get a Popsicle. I noticed a case of beer. I don't know why, but I grabbed a can and stuffed it under my shirt. I ran behind the boathouse, down the pathway to the mudflats where I hid in the tall grass by the river's edge. I cracked it open. It was a Coors Light. The sensation was immediate. I was twelve years old and I was tasting heaven."

Lindsey's thoughts drifted from the mudflats to a creaky stairway that led to Megan's basement. "Megan was my best friend. Her father's workbench was covered with bottles of homemade wine. One day after school we crept down the basement. We shared a bottle and then goofed off around the woods behind her stables, trying to sober up before her parents returned home. For the rest of the summer I prodded her to make trips in to the basement for us. She was normal; she could stop after one cup. Even then, I couldn't. And that's how it started."

Myra's drinking history was significantly more exciting than her own, Lindsey found. The Brit had grown up on the Southampton waterfront and was raised by two brawling drunkards that ran a pub ineptly. Regulars at the pub were a one-legged surfer (shark attack, he claimed), a doddering Arctic explorer, and various bookies and chippies.

"I joined the airlines to get as far from England as possible. But the job involved a lot of waiting around hotels and bars. I've slept with security guards, pilots, and baggage handlers. Married or not. I didn't care. And I didn't care how that might impact the men's marriages, or families. Men and alcohol," Myra explained regretfully, "are like the chicken and the egg. One perpetuates the other."

"You should write a novel based on your life. It would be a bestseller."

"I just want to repress the whole thing. I hope that that worthless bit of sod called England is submerged when global warming melts the polar ice cap," Myra said, rolling her eyes. "Your turn."

"I'd be happy to concoct a more captivating story for your amusement, rather than a story of a nerd from Annapolis, Maryland. First I ran off with gypsies, then the circus..."

"Just tell the truth! What about your relationships with men?"

"I'm married. That says it all. My sex life is stultifyingly boring. There's nothing to tell." Lindsey fumbled with her pack of cigarettes. "My relations with men are normal."

"Nothing is normal about us, and you're so full of shit! You're never going to get better if you can't share. You'll drink the second you get out of here."

Lindsey nervously lit cigarette number... she'd lost count. An image emerged. Her English teacher, Mr. Willis, was behind a desk at the front of the classroom, proctoring her exam. Why was she there after school? Then it came to her. She'd missed a midterm to attend the Annual Ann Arundel County Junior High Engineering Competition. In her assigned seat, she silently wrote in a bluebook. The room was a bland canvas of beige, beige desks on beige floor tiles, bordered by beige bookshelves. She wanted out of the beige everything and for the day to be over. She looked briefly up at the clock... it was 4:50... then to Mr. Willis. He smiled wearily. Her mind was drawn back to the final essay question on *The Heart is a Lonely Hunter*.

She stretched and squirmed on the hard seat, vaguely aware of him walking to the back of the classroom to close the windows. She glanced sleepily at the clock again, her stomach rumbling for dinner. It was 4:53. She closed the bluebook with finality and sat reflecting on the last question.

"Are you finished?" he asked.

"I don't want to think about southern writers anymore today." She handed him the bluebook. "I'm completely brain dead. My hand has no more ATP left it in. My arm is completely limp." She shook out her wrist.

"No ATP?" he repeated, smiling at her scientific vocabulary.

"None in my brain either. We had to be on the bus this morning at 6:30 to get to the competition. That sucked. My robot wasn't running right, so I had to make some changes to it on the bus. I ran it up and down the bus aisle a few times, finally getting it to work. Mrs. Stanton was really pissed at me for not staying in my seat." She bent to put her pens in her backpack. "I'll probably have to serve a detention for that," she added glumly.

"She's not upset," he remarked cheerfully. "Your tinkering must have paid off. It's terrific that you won. Your parents will be really proud of you. The headmaster mentioned your victory at our faculty meeting today. He said that the Engineering Club at Episcopal Academy hadn't lost that competition in twelve years. But now the trophy's ours! The faculty's really proud of you."

"My dad will be happy, but my mother will never acknowledge it. She hasn't spoken to me for three days since I didn't take out the trash when she wanted me to. She's so fu... messed up. You met her at the parent-teacher conference. Didn't you think so? What horrible things did she say about me?"

"Nothing. We talked about her. She reminded twice me that she was the Provost at the university. She's... intense," he answered conservatively.

"Intense! That's an understatement. You're just being polite. You and I both know that she's an anal-retentive asshole and control-freak to the nth degree!" She slouched farther down in the chair. "Shit, she..."

Mr. Willis interrupted, "Lin, your language. Remember, we're working on your language."

She replied brashly, "Well, shit, anyway! I'm not going home to sit there at the dinner table and be completely ignored. I'm going to scrounge change from my locker and go to *Burger King* so I won't have to deal with her."

"Here, take this." He pulled out his wallet and handed her a five. He looked out the window into the late October evening. "It's getting dark. Do you want me to drive you?"

"That's alright. My bike has a light. I like to ride around the harbor to look at the boats, and then study at the library. I usually do that. Thanks for the money. I'll pay you back tomorrow."

"Sure. Whenever."

Mr. Willis moved behind her chair and glanced again at the closed door. He slowly placed his hands on her shoulders. She sat rigidly, her heart pounding. He moved her long blonde hair off her shoulders and then massaged her shoulders, and then neck. His were not the tentative, clammy hands of boys her age, but skilled and warm.

Eventually her eyelids dropped. "You're making me sleepy."

"Does it feel good?"

"Yes," she murmured.

"I can show you a lot of things that feel good," he whispered.

She turned toward him, her eyes at his belt buckle. She looked up at his yellow dress shirt, blue and gold tie, trimmed beard, glistening eyes and soft curly hair.

"Let's celebrate your victory. Let me make you dinner tonight at my place," he had suggested pleasantly. "I have some imported beer. Do you like beer?"

Myra stared at Lindsey in wordless disgust. "You're the one who should write the book," she finally said.

"Nabokov's already done that. Mark and I were lovers until I graduated from high school. We were very careful. I'd ride my bike down the alley and hide it in his garage and then enter through the back door of his duplex. I more or less lost interest in boys my age. Backseats and movie theaters became frustrating to me when I could roll around on a king-sized bed, and strut around Mark's house butt-naked, swilling expensive beers."

"No matter how many times I hear stories like this, whether in person or in literature, they still revolt me. You do realize that that was statutory rape, don't you? You said your relations with men were normal. That's not normal!"

"But it never felt wrong."

"Christ! How can you say that! It was. He was your classic pedophile. He groomed you to trust him," Myra cried, horrified.

"But he was a great English teacher. And he taught me so many great sexual..."

"Stop! Enough! I don't want to hear anymore!" Myra interrupted, still sickened. "Do you know what your greatest character defect is?"

"Lust?"

"No! Rationalization."

The two women silently finished their cigarettes.

"I guess we're done with this assignment. I'll let Kate know." Myra slid her feet into her sneakers, her face still twisted in annoyance. "Are you going back to the reading room?"

"Yes."

The Bottom Dwellers

Myra stood. "I'll come with you. Can I get two pieces of wire from your spool? I left my shoes in the Fishbowl. When I came back later, the laces were gone."

Boston

Karen was giddy with excitement about her trip to the Cape. For days she'd trolled the Internet, reading every possible fact about Woods Hole. The village was renowned within the science community for its oceanographic institute, fisheries and aquarium, and a marine laboratory. The marine lab was a hub of cutting-edge biological research in embryology, neurobiology, physiology, and molecular biology. A few labs, like the Nolan-Kauni lab, were involved in bioengineering and the development of electrode technologies.

She placed an ironing board in the center of her living room and aimed a remote at the TV. Her wild, impulsive splurge to purchase a gigantic smart TV still thrilled her. Now she could watch *Two and a Half Men* in high definition.

She walked into her bedroom and scanned the clothes in a large walk-in closet. Warm weather was forecasted for the Cape tomorrow, so she chose a sleeveless pink blouse. The blouse always looked great with her cat earrings, but it definitely needed pressing. She returned to the living room and set the heat on the iron for cotton. As she waited for it to warm up, she watched the TV and burst into hysterical laughter. Though she'd seen this episode twice already, it never lost its hilarity.

She composed a mental list of the things to take to the Cape: her smartphone, sunglasses, hat, and comfortable walking shoes. She'd told her PhD student, Fiona, to carefully watch the lab while she was gone, in the off-chance Lindsey Nolan did appear, so that was all taken care of.

Now, what to say about the alleged aunt that she was visiting, should Sara ask? The aunt will be named Edith. And she'll live in Barnstable and be a retired astrophysicist that studied thermonuclear fusion in red dwarfs. Maybe Edith will be an expert on Proxima Centauri and be widowed. Her deceased husband, Alfred would be... hmm... an actuary. Edith's hobby will be decoupage, and she will meticulously tend to bonsai plants, and have three cats. The cats will be named after wine regions in France: Burgundy, Bordeaux, and Alsace, since Edith is fluent in French. As a girl, Karen spent the summers stargazing with Aunt Edith. Karen hesitated. Hmm... maybe best not to make Edith too fascinating, in case Sara wants to Google her. Maybe better to make her a bank teller...

Chapter 9

Rehab

Anton encouraged Nancy to share, but she stubbornly shook her head. Wampanoag Joe, the night counselor running the AA meeting, offered further encouragement, but the timid teenager buried her face in Anton's shoulder. Joe turned to the group and asked for other volunteers.

Harley Davidson raised his hand. "My lawyer says that if I attend rehab, the judge might increase my visitation rights. I hope that fucking lawyer is right. That man is robbing me blind, and the courts are unfair about..."

"I'm one of those fucking lawyers," Ted interrupted testily. "What's unfair is that we can't use our cell phones! We're in the Middle Ages here. For the exorbitant amount of money we're paying, you'd think that they could set up a table with computers so we can talk to friends on Facebook."

"We don't interrupt others when they're sharing," Joe said gruffly. "Policy matters, like cell phone usage, should be brought up at Ward Council, not at AA meetings. Who else would like to share? Lindsey, you haven't shared yet."

"Pass." She knocked a cigarette from her pack. Ethan swiftly pulled out his engraved lighter. A brief flame danced near her lips. She inhaled. "Thank you," she whispered.

"Sure, love," Ethan whispered back.

Mitch raised his hand. "Ever since that ambush, I can't stop drinking. A woman and old man called for us to help them. We started up the trail when the Taliban open-fired. The bastards even shot the woman and old man... they shot their own people... they're not human... the binges started after that. Those bastards killed Jimmy!"

Nancy finally lifted her head from Anton's shoulder and tentatively raised her hand. The room fell silent. Her story emerged slowly, not in sentences, but in fragmented thoughts and nonsense words. What was decipherable from the odd monologue was that by the time she was fifteen, trips out to her father's auto detailing shop had become a nightly routine. She would see that her parents were absorbed in some TV show, and set off down the back stairs of the apartment, her sketchpad in hand. A spare key to the shop was hidden under a rusty barrel and she'd quietly remove the lock. Her father might be painting bold flames across the hood of a street rod, or delicately stenciling pink roses under the door handle of a minivan for a middle-aged woman, every few days the cars and paint jobs revolving. She had inherited her father's artistic talent, and her art teacher said that she'd have her pick of any art school in the country. With anticipation, she walked to the shelves and unscrewed the lid of her favorite solvent. Just a few whiffs, she told herself, and her sketches would be so magical, so colorful...

The solvents in the auto detailing shop severed the strings to reality so that Nancy never made it to an art college.

The Bottom Dwellers

Lindsey looked around the room. Anton, Melissa the Goth, and the sorority girl, Dana, were all college students. Anton had lost his basketball scholarship at U Mass due to cocaine abuse. The Amherst student, Melissa went wild doing her junior year abroad in Amsterdam, pot-smoking in the coffee houses, the drugs escalating to meth once she was back in the states. Dana was a garden-variety drunk who got sloppy drunk at the URI fraternities and woke up in assorted regretful situations.

During her senior year in high school Lindsey had applied to three universities, Cambridge, Stanford, and Johns Hopkins. She'd chosen Hopkins in Baltimore for its science and engineering programs, its medical school, and proximity to Orioles baseball at Camden Yards.

It had been a tense trip from Annapolis to Baltimore that August day, she recalled. Thankfully it was not that long a ride. Her mother was furious at her for something—again— and wordlessly released her in front of a red brick dorm on 34th Street. Lindsey had lugged her bags and laptop out of the trunk and onto the curb. The glistening new Lexus abruptly sped away in a cloud of exhaust fumes.

The old dormitory was stifling, window fans doing little to move the heavy air. The suite reeked of mildew and ammonia cleansers. She was the first of her roommates to arrive. The suite would be shared with Megan and two other girls, Joanne from Connecticut, and Kelsey from Texas. Megan was also interested in science and hoped to be a veterinarian who specialized in the care of horses. Megan was absolutely nuts about horses and owned a beautiful palomino. Lindsey had convinced her to go to Hopkins with her, instead of Penn, where Megan's parents wanted their daughter to go.

"The pre-vets and pre-meds will take all of the same science courses. We could study together and be roommates!" she'd suggested to Megan earlier that spring.

Lindsey's small bedroom was off the common living area. The white walls would be covered with posters of Orioles players and sailboats. Megan's walls would be decorated with photos of the wild ponies of Assateague and Chincoteague Islands, and glossy photos of that Red Sox rookie that Megan lusted after.

The plan was to unpack, then hookup her laptop to the university Internet, but a large boy appeared in her doorway. He introduced himself, and immediately gabbed about Blue Jays lacrosse.

"I'm a freshman and I'm starting," he bragged. "I grew up in northern Virginia, near a number of Civil War battlefields. I'll probably major in history. What's your major?"

"I'm double majoring in biochemistry and biomedical engineering," she said tonelessly, hoping that would scare him off. She just wanted to set up her laptop without distraction.

"You must be smart."

She rolled her eyes, wishing for a quick end to the mindless conversation.

"What do you like to do for fun?" he persisted.

Do not answer that, she told herself.

He waited expectantly.

"I love the Orioles," she finally answered.

"I love the Washington Nationals!"

She suppressed a groan. The Nats were the lamest team in the entire league. She wondered if Megan had gone online to check prices for season tickets to the Os' games, as she'd promised.

"Do you want to go out for pizza tonight?" he asked hopefully.

She looked up from her laptop and gave the boy the once, then twice over. He was handsome and muscular, and she fleetingly thought that it might be fun to tumble around with him just once. But he was a jock and clearly an ignoramus; therefore she was determined to have little to do with him. Her protracted affair with Mark Willis was over; she was finally free of grasping, needy men.

"Thanks, but I've made some other plans. In fact, I have to go pretty soon." She ushered him out the door.

"Another time…" he called undeterred, heading down the hall.

For dinner that night she had potato chips and soda from a vending machine, and then explored the library for an hour or two. The usual, antsy feeling set in later that evening; she headed toward her dorm on 34th Street. That clingy lacrosse player looked twenty-one. Maybe he wouldn't get carded. What was his name again? Dane? Davis? Duncan? Maybe he wanted to catch a buzz that night?

A Boardwalk in New Jersey

"Trust no one, ever, ever, Maggie, only me," Bess had once said. "Not a nice waitress, a smiling man who gives you free lines, or a dealer who adds in a free bag of smack… no one, ever, ever." How fuckin' paranoid Bess had been! Bess told her the meaning of paranoid and taught her how to spell it, even though it was a long word.

What amazingly awesome luck to have met the surfers, Tony and Jed, and hitch a ride north with them! In fact, they were far better traveling companions than Bess had ever been. And they weren't paranoid like Bess. Bess was endlessly crabby and snarly, except when cajoling men to get work. Bess' charming, seductive act never failed. But after that unspeakable winter in Minnesota, everything changed and Bess had unpredictable outbursts of rage and violence. Most of the time after that Bess was terrifying to be with. In Minnesota, Bess had lost her marbles, which means going crazy. That was a metaphor. Bess had told her all about metaphors.

In contrast, Tony and Jed were happy-go-lucky all of the time. They laughed and chattered about music, surfboards, waves, beaches, and weed. They were college students, so they sometimes discussed history (old stuff) and politics (old white guys). She asked them to talk about art, since she was interested in learning about that, but disappointingly, neither of them were art majors. Sometimes they showed her funny stuff on their smartphones. Once Jed showed her paintings from a place in Paris, France. The museum was spelled L O U V R E and rhymed with MOVE. He showed her a painting of a brown-haired, white woman that he called the Moaning Lisa. Then he erupted in crazy, stoned laughter. This made her crack up also, though she wasn't sure what was so funny about that smiling lady. When she grew up, she told him, her first purchase was going to be a smartphone so she could look at paintings all day.

A comfy sleeping place had been made between them in the van. Sleeping bags were almost as wonderful as beds with sheets. The surfers cooked wonderful food on their small grill called a hibachi. One night they ate hamburgers, another night hotdogs, and last night, they stopped for fish and chips. Three hot meals in three nights! Her belly felt satiated, a smart person's word for full.

The Bottom Dwellers

Tony and Jed wouldn't charge her for meals, gas, or tolls, they had said at that rest stop in Delaware, as long as she had sex with them each night, and scrounged up crack while they surfed. Deal!

The sex with Tony and Jed was tolerable. They were the best kind of fucks. Pounders, Bess called them... young guys who simply climb on, pound away, and come almost instantly. Thank you very much! $50 in less than 5 minutes! Old men... ugh... take an eternity and like all the weird stuff. Bess called them Slugs since they take a sluggishly long time and their bodies are mushy, fat, and slippery. Bess had hysterical... which means really funny... names for all types of johns and their fetishes.

But Maggie didn't want to think about work at the moment; she was in too good a mood. She was on a beach holiday, strolling a boardwalk on a summer afternoon. She stopped at a concession that sold cotton candy, corn dogs, pretzels, and popcorn in all flavors: cheese, caramel, crab seasoning, and extra butter. She searched her pocket for change. Yes! There was enough for a funnel cake!

The other great thing, besides the funnel cake smothered with powdered sugar, was that Tony and Jed said that she could go to Maine with them. Her original plan was to go as far as Providence—the capital of Rhode Island—and then head east to Cape Cod. But these two stoners were simply too much fun. Besides, she had nowhere else to go and nothing else to do. What the hell was so interesting about Cape Cod anyway? Why not go to Maine? It's capital was Augusta.

Summer holidays are the best! She wove amongst the sunburnt tourists and peered into the shops selling t-shirts, floral dresses, flip flops, straw hats, and sunscreen. In the distance, she spotted Tony and Jed floating amidst the other surfers beyond the breakers.

No fuckin' way would she ever swim in an ocean with man-eating sharks, giant squid, and poisonous jellyfish! The guys couldn't even convince her to walk on the beach with them. The boardwalk was the place for her, out of harm's way. Besides, she had been entrusted with a very important job, to hold the van keys and their cell phones while they surfed. They were afraid that the keys and phones would be stolen if left on the beach for the day. She wouldn't let the guys down, she'd promised; she would guard them with her life.

She found an unoccupied bench and finished her funnel cake. Jed said that she could play games on his phone apps while she waited, but she found the games impossible to understand. Instead, she lit a cigarette and opened the Map app. For some time, she studied a map of the US that showed all of the state capitals. If she had a cell phone, she'd never have to carry around paper maps. Bess' paper map, stolen from that gas station in Arkansas, was crumbling to bits from overuse.

"There's no smoking on the boardwalk," a stern voice said.

She looked up, startled. It was a policeman on a bicycle.

"Can't you read?" he continued. "The signs are all over the place."

"I can read," she mumbled defensively. She quickly ground the cigarette into a plank, checked her pockets for the keys and phones, and hurried away. She squinted into the afternoon haze, over the wooden railing, colorful umbrellas, sand, and towels, out beyond the breakers. Jed and Tony were still on the water. It was time to hold up her end of the deal. Crack for them and smack for her. She wandered off the boardwalk and walked until she found a backstreet with massage parlors, seedy bars, adult movies, and nail salons. In front of an abandoned video store, an old burnout sat on a step and plucked at the strings of an old guitar. His eyes and nose were runny and red, his crooning mournful and toneless. He stopped playing when she approached, and gazed slyly at her. Druggies spoke in code and she knew it all. White house was a type of smack, but she wasn't particular. Any type would do. Any type would get rid of that crawly, jumpy feeling sensation that arose when that cop frightened her.

"I'm lookin' for the white house," she said quietly.

She was far too young to be an undercover cop, the talentless musician must have decided. "34th Street. Number 22 in the back."

Woods Hole

Karen Battersby smothered a gasp of surprise. Why hadn't she Googled images of Sara Kauni so she'd know what to expect? The woman greeting her in the lobby of the laboratory building was without a doubt the most striking person that she'd seen in real life. Sara had the rare beauty of movie stars and super models. She was a tall, graceful Polynesian. Her large eyes sparkled like black onyx and were fringed with long, thick lashes. Her teeth were the white of new snow. Her smile and manner were easy and relaxed. If hired, Sara would completely unnerve the male post-docs in her lab. And she wore no wedding ring. This might be a real problem... all things to consider when assessing the variables of the interview. The lab's productivity could not be slowed in any way, or her large Department of Defense grant would not be renewed.

Sara was an affable tour guide, Karen decided. It had been smart to wear comfortable shoes, as they walked for nearly two hours, first to the Visitor's Center, where they climbed into a life-size replica of the deep submersible, *Alvin*, and then watched an engrossing film on tube worms at the hydrothermal vents in the Pacific Ocean trenches. Then they crossed Water Street to the oceanographic institute where they were guided by one of Sara's oceanographer friends to the back docks to see an array of remotely operated vehicles, ROVs, used to study the ocean depths. Engineering masterpieces were found at every exhilarating turn!

After the tour they stopped for lunch at a restaurant. Karen had been watching Sara carefully throughout the tour. There was no indication of deceptiveness or cunning at all. The conversation over a lunch of crab bisque and salad was informative and interesting; Sara was simply impressing a potential employer. As a warm sea breeze moved through the open windows of the restaurant, they conversed about new developments in the field of robotics, and Karen mentioned the possible hip replacement surgery of her beloved Aunt Edith, whom she'd been visiting in Barnstable.

After lunch, they started down Water Street toward the marine lab. Sara suggested that they talk back in her lab.

Inside the Nolan-Kauni lab! Karen couldn't believe her ears! Or imagine what the lab would be like! Sara had definitely gone rogue and broken ranks with Lindsey Nolan!

They entered the lab building, passed a golden statue of Confucius where scientists placed coins in homage to good experiments, and climbed the steps to the third floor. The door to the lab was already open and two grad students were weighing out chemicals at an analytical balance.

The Nolan-Kauni lab was surprisingly similar to her own, except that a long row of windows, lined with plane models, overlooked Eel Pond, rather than a bustling street in Cambridge. The bench tops were glistening and free of debris, and the equipment was neatly placed on large metal shelves. Karen expected that Lindsey Nolan was a stern taskmaster, demanding that the lab be meticulous at all times. A row of electronics racks lined one wall of the lab, like in her own. An electroplating area, chemical preparation area, Faraday cages... it was all very familiar.

The two partners' desks were on opposite sides of the lab from each other. It was easy to determine which was Lindsey's workspace, as the wall next to her desk had pennants from the Baltimore Orioles and Johns Hopkins University, a map of the Chesapeake Bay, and a sailboat calendar. Sara's desk was surrounded by photos of coral atolls, numerous photos of a small black-haired boy, and the same boy on the back of a motorcycle with a roguish biker. The burly man was no doubt Sara's boyfriend.

Sara's demeanor changed when she entered the lab; suddenly it was all business. She asked the graduate students if they might use the analytical balance in the lab across the hall. The request was understood; she wanted privacy to meet with her visitor. After they left, Sara handed Karen a copy of her résumé and said that she wanted to discuss her qualifications for a job. She crossed the lab and wheeled Lindsey's chair next to hers. It dawned on Karen at that moment: she was in Lindsey's lab, about to occupy Lindsey's chair, all for the purpose of hiring away Lindsey's chief engineer. This day was too wonderful!

The more Sara spoke, the more convinced Karen was of Sara's abilities and that she would be a perfect fit in her lab. Sara had grown up in the Marquesas and become interested in engineering through her father, a seaplane pilot. She'd spent her youth hanging around the hangar with the pilots and mechanics. Originally she had wanted to study aerospace engineering and work for Boeing or NASA, but at Stanford, her undergraduate institution, she became interested in electrical engineering. During graduate school at Cornell, her thesis advisor was a bioengineer who developed electrodes for recording biological signals, which was how Sara ended up at the marine lab, working for the senior scientist, Mort Somers. Shortly after hiring Sara, Somers had also hired Lindsey Nolan to supervise a number of bioimaging projects.

Karen scanned the long list of publications on the résumé, all of which she'd already read. Kauni and Nolan had an impressive level of productivity, and Woods Hole was a beautiful setting in which to work. "If I may be so bold, Sara, why do you want to leave your employment here? It's such a lovely location," she asked, again carefully scanning Sara's face any signs of treachery.

Sara's answer was quick and candid. "There are a number of reasons, but two in particular, one personal and one professional. I'm thinking that my son might be exposed to more cultural activities in Boston. Secondly, I'm wondering if it's time to do something new, other than bioimaging and electrode development. Our productivity here has slowed recently. I'm thinking that I can be more useful somewhere else."

"Why has the productivity slowed?" Karen asked with concern. This was the first red flag of the interview.

"Dr. Nolan is dealing with personal issues, and our projects are not her priority right now. Frankly, I'm getting a bit frustrated waiting around. I feel I could be doing more."

"I see," Karen replied with relief. The lag in productivity was all due to Lindsey's problems, and had nothing to do with Sara's level of motivation.

A student bolted into the lab. "Dr. Kauni, we need your help! The heat coil's getting way too hot. I think it's about to melt, or catch fire!"

Sara rose quickly. "Karen, will you excuse me for a few minutes?"

"Of course." She reached into her purse for her smartphone. "I'll check my email."

Sara and the student rapidly departed.

Karen rose and breathed in deeply. She was in the lab of her nemesis. And Lindsey Nolan was losing her edge! What personal issue occupied Lindsey's attention? Had her Adonis husband left her for another woman? She wandered by Lindsey's bulletin board, but saw no photographs of Duncan McLeod. Nor were there any photos of children, only an ad for the Newport Jazz Festival and a boat show. Did Lindsey have a sick cat, or parent? What could it possibly be? Karen scanned the lab again.

What was that room in the corner? Why had Sara not shown her that particular room? Was it intentional, or had she merely forgotten? The door was slightly ajar. Karen tiptoed quietly across the room and peered inside.

The room was no more than a closet with a small worktable, chair, and electronics shelf. Like the other areas around the lab, it was immaculate and orderly.

What was that!

It was a mystifying device interfacing with two laptop computers and two smartphones. Never, ever had she seen anything like it! She hyperventilated with excitement. With quivering hands, she lifted the metal lid. The instrument contained numerous tiny chambers with tubes running between them. In discrete places the chambers were separated by rubber membranes and ion diffusers. Minute cooling and heating units were placed throughout, as well as atomizers, particle accelerants, thermocouplers, and microprocessors. She snapped a number of pictures of it, from all angles, with her phone. Sara would be back any minute. Karen scurried back to Lindsey's chair and struggled to slow her breathing. *What was it?* She logged onto to her personal email account to distract herself from the baffling device. *What, what, what?*

She struggled to focus on the emails. *What was that thing?* There were the usual pesky BTI-related emails from her department chair, colleagues, and grad students, but unfortunately there were no emails about The Dungeon to distract her from Lindsey Nolan's perplexing device!

Chapter 10

Rehab

"What's up with up? You've been bitchy for days," Kate asked, looking up from her laptop.

"PMS, I guess," Lindsey griped, slumping against the windowsill.

Kate lit a cigarette and joined her patient at the window. "Ever since Mitch shared about his DWI, you've hardly said a word. The whole time he was talking, you were staring into space as if you weren't there. You weren't listening to a thing he said."

"I was too listening! So Mitch nearly backed into two pedestrians while coming out of a nightclub. They jumped out of the way. They were barely scratched. Every inmate in this loony bin has had a DWI. It goes with the territory. Affairs, broken families, bankruptcies, arrests, and DWIs... BFD."

"These are huge BFDs to the victims." Kate eyed Lindsey suspiciously. "Have you had a DWI?"

"You saw my car. I knocked the bumper off my Jeep when I backed into the dumpster at the marina. Another time I scraped a fire hydrant, but I didn't knock it over, so no water squirted out; and one night, when I was really lit up, a boyfriend and I took the Jeep four-wheeling and got stuck in a sand dune by Provincetown. But we made the best of it. We had amazing sex until dawn, when the police and tow truck arrived."

Kate shook her head reproachfully. "I swear to God, you're an adolescent. Why can't you share at meetings?"

Lindsey hunched down and kept her mouth shut.

"What?" Kate asked suspiciously. "What are you not telling me?"

"Nothing!"

It was no use trying to work on the doorknob after the conversation with Kate. Instead Lindsey retreated to her room and dropped despondently onto her bed. Ethan and Melissa the Goth poked their heads into her room, but she pretended to be asleep.

What had happened that May was nobody's fucking business but hers! That DWI would not be shared at an AA meeting; it was not for public consumption. She forced her thoughts to other places, but the fragmented images of the accident returned like an insidious cancer....

The morning after the accident she fled to the lab of her honors thesis advisor, Anne Davids. The prying questions of the girls in the dormitory had become unbearable, and her roommates' furious parents had been a whole other order of stress. On a Sunday morning there would be no one around Professor Davids' lab. It was the perfect place to hide until she could think rationally, think calmly. A beer would settle her nerves, but fucking beer was what got her into this fucking mess in the first place! She sobbed into her arm at the desk where she kept her lab notebook and calculator. All was lost! When the university administrators found out about the accident, they'd pull her scholarship. She'd never be a physician that created cool biomedical devices! Without an education, the dreary decades of her tediously long life would be spent moving shopping carts around a parking lot.

The doorknob turned and her head jerked up. "What are you doing here?" she gasped.

Professor Davids halted. "It's my lab. That's what I'm doing here," she answered indignantly. "And I forgot some tests to grade. What, may I ask, are *you* doing here?'

Lindsey's red and swollen face twisted in despair. "I cracked up my mother's car coming out of Camden Yards last night! Her brand new Lexus! It's completely totaled."

"The Lexus is irrelevant," the old professor said. "Was anyone hurt? Are you alright?"

Lindsey had held up her hand that was in a cast. "I broke my arm. I spent the night in the ER. My mom came to the hospital. She was ballistic. She told me never to contact her, my father, or my sisters again. I'm the embarrassment of the whole Nolan family, she said."

"She was speaking in the heat of the moment. She'll cool down over time."

"You don't know her. She means it! I'll never see my family again. I'm an orphan now!"

The brilliant mathematician, Miriam Nolan, was not unknown to Professor Davids, as they worked at neighboring universities. Professor Nolan had a reputation for vindictiveness and mean-spiritedness, and those were her good qualities.

"Were you drinking at the game?" Davids asked.

"Yes."

"There are a lot of places where you can get help for this problem," the old woman said gravely.

"What problem?"

"What problem! You know what problem!" Davids cried.

To escape the professor's glare, Lindsey dragged herself over to the sink and pulled a paper towel from a dispenser. She pushed the abrading brown paper into her eyes. "Now I can't go home this summer. I'm going to have to stay here and find a place to live and work. The locksmith's shop is hiring."

Professor Davids dropped her leather satchel on a lab bench and paused while Lindsey honked into the paper towel. "I'm making this offer against my better judgment," she said, "but I can pay you out of my grant if you want to work as my summer lab technician."

"That would be awesome," Lindsey said weakly. "I'll do any and all of the experiments you want me to. And then more. I will not disappoint you."

"You already have, Ms. Nolan," the professor said caustically. "If you can't drink safely, I don't want you drinking at all. When you are in my lab, you are alert and in one piece. If I smell a drop of alcohol on you, we're through for good. Do you understand me?"

She nodded. "Yes. Absolutely."

Conducting experiments that summer helped bury the memory of that goddamn baseball game at Camden Yards. She'd tried calling, emailing, instant messaging Megan to apologize, but she'd been blocked. Megan's family allowed her no further contact with them. Miriam Nolan was quick to use this as an excuse to sever the umbilicus completely. Lindsey sent an occasional "Hey, what's up?" to her sisters, Colleen and Molly, but her emails bounced back unread. She logged on many times a day for months, waiting to hear from her father, but messages were not forthcoming. Never did she return to her hometown of Annapolis, Maryland.

To pay bills, she worked part-time jobs: at a lock store, and fixing lawn mowers and snow blowers at a gardening center. As promised, she did not drink at all that summer. By summer's end, she had completed two manuscripts that characterized the protein subunits composing a novel invertebrate neurotoxin. She was eighteen and first author on both of them. Upon their publication, the rising freshman was suddenly pressed under the cover slip of the scientific community, her career scrutinized under the highest resolution.

Boston

Karen turned on her new Alienware computer with the extra wide screen. She turned in her chair and looked out the window. Her condo had a spectacular view of Boston Harbor. Night was falling across the city, and a number of boats were illuminated on the water. As soon as she had been hired on the tenure track at BTI and became a permanent resident of Boston, she'd indulged herself and bought a waterfront condo. It was way beyond what she could afford, but the interest rates were low and the housing market depressed, so she'd got a wonderful deal on it. Besides, once she earned tenure as a professor of engineering, she was guaranteed a job for life.

Pussy Willow meowed at the door. Karen hated to do it, but she'd shut the cats out of her home office. No way could the twins jump up on her lap, or worse, step on the keyboard, while she was talking to members of her *World of Warcraft* Guild, the noble Guild of Centurion. She rose from her chair.

"Shoo, Pussy Willow, there's plenty of play equipment for you in the living room. You'll be fine without me for an hour or two," she said through the door crack. Next to the new leather sofa set and wide screen TV were two cat gyms; that should amuse the cats for a while. She checked her watch. It was ten minutes until the Guild met. She returned to her computer and clicked open the .jpgs she had sent to herself from her smartphone. Though the small device in the workroom had been snapped from all angles, she couldn't figure out what Lindsey Nolan was constructing. If she could only get her hands on the software from the interfacing laptops, it might be possible to determine what it was. She checked the time again. Five minutes until the online meeting of the Guild.

Tonight the Guild would be entering the most treacherous of places, the Dungeon of Zortan. She needed to prepare her avatar for the evening's adventure. For eight years, Diana, the Roman goddess of the hunt and the moon, had been her avatar. The goddess could talk to animals, which was why she'd chosen this avatar. Diana98 had the form of a pretty, slender woman, but with cat ears and a tail. She was not an elf, or a warrior, but one of the healers for the Guild. The battle in the dungeon that night might be bloody; she and the other healers would be busy. In the Guild's last encounter, in the Labyrinth of Minos, half of the warriors had been killed, including the Guild leader, Conqueror.

Diana98 had gained respect within the Guild over the past years because she'd never been killed in battle, and she'd donated considerable wealth to the Guild's armory.

The Bottom Dwellers

Karen placed the headphones firmly on her head and aligned the speaker over her mouth. Her Cherry Coke was placed within reach should she become overheated during the adventure. She logged on and joined the other avatars assembling at the entrance to the dungeon. Scarwing132 scurried around the border of the group, encouraging the warriors and elves to position themselves in proper formation. Diana98 stood next to Conqueror, as she considered herself the stalwart right hand of the Guild.

Diana98 was dressed this night in a diaphanous white gown. From her belt hung ampules of assorted potions. She carried a magic staff and a broad sword, just in case she was drawn into the action. Karen wondered if Conqueror was as attractive in real-life as his avatar. He vaguely resembled Conan the Barbarian, except that he wore a horned Viking helmet. His words through her headset were a melodic southern drawl. One night he had missed a battle to go to a Tampa Bay Buccaneers game, so she guessed that Conqueror was a resident of Florida.

Conqueror reviewed the columns of avatars and finally spoke. "I think we're ready to go, but we're still missing Odin18 and Charlemagne12."

"I'm here," said Charlemagne12, just logging on. Charlemagne12 was from somewhere in the mid-west, she could tell. He had an accent similar to hers. She was a native of Kansas. Charlemagne12 was ruthless in battle and one of the most skilled warriors in the Guild.

"Excellent," Conqueror replied. "Position yourself near the front of column two.

"Perfect," Charlemagne12 said agreeably.

"Does anyone know if Odin18's coming tonight?" Conqueror asked, sounding annoyed. Odin18 was a fearsome warrior also.

"He told me he'd be here," Diana98 answered.

"Alright. We'll wait one more minute," Conqueror sighed.

"Without Odin18, I calculate that we have only a 21.33% chance of surviving Zortan," stated Pythagoras3.14 with trepidation. Karen knew that Pythagoras3.14 was a graduate student in mathematics at Oxford University; they were friends on Facebook.

"If we stick to our plan, and stay in formation, we stand a chance," said AttylaHun88. "The battle in Minos was a fiasco because we didn't stay in formation!" AttylaHun88 always had a frantic, excitable tone to his voice.

"And because Troll303 was stoned again and led a group of us into the poisonous pit where we all perished," Manson72 added tersely. "That really sucked. I'm glad Troll303's not here tonight, or we'd all be doomed."

Odin18's voice crackled through Karen's earphones. "So sorry, I'm late," he apologized, panting. "There was too much traffic on the Beltway." Odin was a lobbyist for the cigarette industry.

"Glad you're here. Take the number one position in column one," Conqueror commanded. "Healers, move to the rear. Do you have the potions ready?"

"Yes!" Diana98 said with enthusiasm. She moved her avatar to the end of column one and positioned it next to Silk69 and BluntEdgeXP.

"Are we ready, Centurions?" Conqueror asked, pride filling his voice.

A resounding "Yes!" roared through her headset.

"Then let's kill these bastards! Centurions advance!"

The Bottom Dwellers

The two columns moved forward and descended down the slippery stone steps... into the black mouth of the dungeon.

Stamford, Connecticut

Maggie crept silently down the basement steps, praying that the pounding of her heart would not alert everyone in the tenement. Her destination was hell on earth, a dark, filthy dungeon. She proceeded carefully so as not to nudge the trash bags, full of clattering bottles, that filled the stairwell. Don't step on any of the cats, she reminded herself. Cats could yowl! She pushed the screen door open very slowly. So far, so good. It hardly creaked. If that old dog barked and Sneek appeared, she'd simply tell him that she had come back for another purchase. That was the plan.

She tiptoed inside, into the black mouth of the basement. The room was hot, humid, and smelled like a dump. After all, that's what it was. The cement floor was covered with rotting trash, empty food containers, and bottles. The worst part was the dog shit. The fuckers did not even walk that starving dog in the corner! The dog looked at her with glassy, defeated eyes, but had lost the will to raise its head. When she'd visited this place earlier that day it had been daylight; she turned on Bess' flashlight and wound carefully between the garbage and shit on the floor. Something stirred in the darkness off to the right. She stifled a gasp and quickly shut off the light.

"That you, Sneek?" It was a woman's faint voice.

"Just me..." Maggie stalled. "Sista."

"Sista?"

"Sneek's friend."

"Sneek know you're down here? He don't like anyone down here but me."

"I'm bringin him Beat. He told me to hurry."

"Give me some light."

Maggie flicked on the flashlight. The lifeless voice came from was a woman, all skin, bones, with hollow, dull eyes. Her bed was newspaper spread across a cement floor.

"Lost my light."

"Here." Maggie pulled a lighter from her pocket. She bent toward the woman, overwhelmed by the smell of body odor and urine. "Keep it."

"Thanks, lil sista." The woman lit a crack pipe and her skull-like face briefly glowed orange through the stench and gloom. "Hit?"

"Later. After I deliver this to Sneek."

Maggie navigated the maze of debris until she reached her destination. An extension cord snaked through a broken window, Sneek stealing power from some apartment above. Only a small light bulb lit up Sneek's stash. Across an old table lay a gun, analytical balances, cookers, propane grills and tanks, solvents, silverware, blades, bowls, and plastic bags. Her eyes fixed on a huge pile of white powder, most of it not bagged yet. Sneek's cooking shop was guarded by a crack-addicted skeleton and a near-dead dog! She had not been able to believe her eyes when she'd followed him into the basement that afternoon and he weighed out some tiny bags for her. The unbelievable volume of shit Bess would have called the Mother Lode, her term for a lot of anything. Maggie wiped the sweat from her eyes. She craved a cigarette, but there was work, very fast work, to do.

She was on a secret mission for Jed and Tony. After she told them of the Mother Lode in Sneek's basement, the van had prowled the neighborhood identifying alleyways and roads, her route of escape.

"You have to perform the top secret mission for us, Maggie, as two white guys are too conspicuous in this neighborhood," Jed had said.

"What's conspicuous?" she had asked.

"Easy to spot," Jed had explained.

She had nodded, as all of Jed's definitions were easy to understand... comprehensible.

"No one will pay attention to a skinny black girl around here," Tony had emphasized. "We'll sell coke all the way to Maine. And eat turf and surf every night."

"What's that?" she had asked.

"Steak and seafood. You'll be a millionaire, Maggie!"

Like guarding their keys and cell phone, she would not let the guys down. She glanced once more into the darkness, but there was no word or movement from the woman floating in some netherworld. She took a spoon from the table and began shoveling the white power, filling one ziplock sandwich bag after another, until her pockets bulged. She gently nudged open the back door. All she had to do was quietly climb the hurricane fence, creep down the assorted alleyways and... Mission Accomplished!

"Visualize your route, Maggie," Jed had said, as they scouted neighborhood. "Visualize means imagine it in your mind's eye," he had added preemptively.

She snuck up the back steps. The yard was a shit-hole of dirt and more garbage, a wrecked motorcycle, trashcans, a ruined child's playhouse, and shattered bottles. Men's laughter was heard from a window above. She tiptoed across the yard.

Grrr...

Her head swiveled instantly, and she dashed for the hurricane fence. A giant Doberman sprung from the plastic playhouse, its teeth barred. She leapt onto the fence and clawed frantically at the wire mesh. Furious curses rang from the window above. A bottle was hurled at her and shattered just above her shoulder; glass splintered against her cheek. The dog jumped upward. Its vicious yellow fangs clamped onto her ankle. Pain shot up her leg. The dog dragged her downward. She clung desperately onto the mesh. She glanced brief over her shoulder, into its demonic red eyes. She wildly shook her foot. The dog's teeth locked onto her sneaker, ripping it from her foot. She scrambled upward, the dog snapping the air below her. She finally reached the top, slung her legs over the jagged wires, and fell into the alley below. The dog threw itself savagely against the fence just inches from her. She struggled to her feet and headed down the alley. Bullets bounced off the dumpsters next to her head as she dashed into the darkness! Was she supposed to go to the left or right? Left! Left!... she was sure that Jed said go left! She veered off down another alley, then another, her heart heaving against her lungs. For minutes she was lost in a dizzying labyrinth of brick walls, dumpsters, and trashcans. She finally emerged at a small industrial park and limped quickly down the railroad tracks. Her shoeless foot was ripped from broken glass and stones, her ankle torn from the dog's jaws. Oh my god, thank god... she finally spotted it... the van waiting near the onramp. Jed must have seen her coming, as he slid open the side door and pulled her inside. Tony floored the van onto the highway. She collapsed, still shuddering, into the sleep bags. She reached for a cigarette. She was home free and she was a millionaire.

Chapter 11

Rehab

Anton stretched his wounded leg across the table in a conference room. Moments earlier, he had hurtled across the basketball court after tripping on another player's foot, to land hard. As he'd hobbled into the ward, a stream of blood had run from his knee and soaked his sock.

The hacker, Connor, shouted through the conference room door, "Anton, you're a dick!"

Anton went taut, ready to spring off the table, but Ethan placed a firm, restraining hand on his shoulder. "At least I have one! Yours is invisible!" Anton yelled back.

"Now that bitch will be sure to change the hours back to eight o'clock!" Connor ranted.

In Ward Council there had been a unanimous vote to get the evening patio hours extended. To avoid the tiresome pleas of the past three mornings, Kate had finally relented, extending outdoor recreational hours from eight to ten pm.

Ethan turned to Connor. "I'll talk to Kate tomorrow. This was an accident. It could have happened to anyone. You included."

"Beat it, Connor," Mitch said. "The doctors are trying to stop the bleeding." Mitch led Connor from the room.

Lindsey cleaned and applied pressure to the wound while Ethan wiped blood off the table with paper towels. He unlaced Anton's large sneaker and then placed it on the windowsill next to an arrangement of dried flowers. The blood-soaked sock he dropped into a trash bag.

After a considerable wait, a nurse practitioner from the ER arrived. According to her, an overloaded banana boat had had a gas leak and exploded off of Jamestown Island, so the staff in the ER was overwhelmed with burns and other severe injuries. A cut knee of a drug addict in rehab was not high on their priority list.

The appearance of a syringe on a tray clearly unnerved Ethan, so he averted his eyes, looking toward the window and dried flowers.

The nurse moved the syringe toward Anton's knee. "This is going to feel like a quick needle stick, nothing more."

"Is this going to leave a scar?" he asked worriedly.

"Maybe a little one," she answered honestly.

Mitch, Anton, Ethan and Lindsey were all in the same counseling group, so they were familiar with each other's respective drinking and drugging histories. Despite having been kicked off of his college basketball team for drug use, with the indefatigable optimism of youth, Anton was confident that he'd make the Celtics as a walk-on.

The nurse checked her watch and tapped Anton's knee. "Do you feel that?"

"Nothing."

She squeezed the flap of skin closed and blood oozed outward. She stitched up the gash and covered the wound with a gauze pad. Mitch entered with a pair of crutches and handed them to Lindsey. While Ethan distracted Anton with a conversation about basketball games that he'd seen at the Boston Garden, Lindsey adjusted the crutches. Anton was about six-six. Even set to their longest length, he'd be bent over.

"Lindsey, have you ever been to the Garden?" Ethan asked.

"Never, but I went to Fenway for the first time last summer with my neighbors, Rob and Danny." The memory saddened her. That was back when Rob would still ask her to join him and his son for excursions; before she became a hopeless drunk. Now he couldn't stand the sight of her, wouldn't let her anywhere near Danny, shunned her completely.

Nancy anxiously paced the hallway outside, obeying Mitch's order to stay out of the conference room until the nurse had finished. Finally the nurse peeled off the surgical gloves and dropped them into the trash bag that Ethan held open for her. "You're good to go." She eased Anton's leg off the table. "Try not to bend your knee tonight."

Lindsey handed Anton the crutches.

Mitch and the nurse assisted Anton from the room. "Hey sweetness, what'd you do tonight?" Anton asked Nancy.

"I made... you... an origami... bird."

"I'll put it on my nightstand and think of you," he said gently.

Anton was nineteen and had the sweetest heart on the ward. Lindsey hoped that one day she would see him wear Celtic green.

She and Ethan remained alone in the conference room. All was silent except for the low drone of the air-conditioning unit. They eyed their reflections in the windowpane. Their similarities were striking. They were the same physical type, emaciated blondes. His father was judge in Vermont; hers, an attorney in Maryland. They were both addicts early in life, she to alcohol in junior high, he dealing bags of pot and painkillers from a dorm room at his prep school. He'd entered a rehab while in college, but began using opiates when working in Africa as part of a mobile field hospital. Their respective medical schools, Hopkins and Georgetown were only fifty minutes away from one another in Baltimore and DC. He studied surgery, whereas she specialized in neurology and bioimaging technologies.

"We're a good team," he said.

She nodded.

Their murky reflections in the windowpane reminded her of how this disease had diminished them both. She couldn't look at herself any longer and started toward the windowsill. "Anton forgot his shoe."

"His room's next to mine. I'll take it to him," he offered.

"Okay." She squeezed Ethan's hand. "Goodnight."

He bent down and softly kissed her cheek. "Sweet dreams, love."

His words made her shudder. Sweet dreams had eluded her for ten years, one month, twenty-two days.

The next morning they waited for Kate Waters at the security door. Ethan had volunteered to tell Kate about Anton's knee, since almost everything about Lindsey irritated the psychologist. They had just left Anton in the Fishbowl, where Nancy was pushing on his sneaker and lacing it up for him.

"She's late," Ethan said, consulting his watch.

"She's never late," Lindsey replied curiously.

He held open a garbage bag for her while she dumped the contents of the trashcan into it. It was her turn to do the daily trash detail, so it was the first of many strolls around the ward, cleaning ashtrays, tossing abandoned soda cans into recycling bins, throwing away random wads of candy wrappers left on coffee tables, and emptying trash in the common areas.

The security door finally buzzed. She scurried down the hallway and appeared to be intently reading the activities board, even though all of the postings were from the day before.

Ethan sidestepped into Kate's pathway. "Good morning, Dr. Waters. You look lovely this morning."

She viewed him with suspicion and glanced down the hallway to Lindsey. "Good morning to you, Dr. Eldridge," she said skeptically. "What are you and Dr. Nolan up to?"

"Anton hurt his knee playing basketball last night, so Dr. Nolan and I stopped the bleeding while we waited for a nurse from the ER," he explained. "Their hands were full with a boating accident. We checked Anton's knee this morning. There's no infection; in fact, he's healing nicely."

"Then why is this a problem?" Kate asked.

"The basketball players are afraid that you'll cut the outdoor recreation hours back to eight o'clock."

Kate pondered his comment for a moment. "I see no need to cut back the hours. I thank you two for taking care of Anton."

Ethan studied Kate closely, noting her flushed cheeks and her hair hastily done. He smiled. "Truly, Kate, you do look lovely this morning."

She smiled back. "I feel lovely." She floated softly across the tile, her loafers' officious clack absent. She disappeared into her office and closed the door.

Ethan and Lindsey stared at each other, dumbfounded at the lightness of Kate's mood.

"Very suave, Ethan."

He grinned. "She had a good time last night."

"Or a good breakfast. I want what she had."

"You and me both, honey. Smoke?"

"Smoke."

They headed toward the Fishbowl. Though it was before breakfast, the room was already filled with cigarette smoke. She was now accustomed to the smell of smoke in her hair and clothes. On one sofa the golfer, Curtis, and Mitch shared parts of the sports page. Across the room, the soccer mom, Sharon, whined to the Barbie Doll, Trisha, about her dead-beat ex-husband not paying alimony and escaping with his girlfriend to some Caribbean island. In his plaid bathrobe and moccasins, Ted groaned a good morning, poured himself a black coffee, and shuffled back to his room. At the coffee counter, Lindsey brushed empty creamer containers, sugar packets, and stirrers into the trash bag.

Melissa bounced happily into the Fishbowl, her necklaces with pentacles and other Wiccan symbols swaying across her black t-shirt. Her lips were painted with black lipstick. She draped her arm over Lindsey's shoulder. "You're my new BFF!"

"Why?"

"Because of you, I can buy cigarettes for the rest of my stay."

"Explain."

"I'm running a raffle. I have one hundred percent participation from the ward."

"What are you talking about?"

"I'm running a raffle to guess the identity of Boat Show Man. I've collected over seventy-five dollars. When you regain your memory and disclose his identity, the winner who guesses correctly gets fifty dollars. Kate said that I could keep twenty-five for administrative fees."

"You're kidding, right?" Lindsey said, amused.

"Nope. Do you want to see the list of participants and their guesses?"

"Why not."

Melissa pulled a folded piece of notebook paper from a pocket of her black pants that dangled chains and straps. Lindsey scanned the list. Sharon had guessed Soccer Coach. Curtis, who had certainly noticed her sunburn in the detox, had guessed Lifeguard. Trisha had opted for Tennis Pro. Mitch had guessed Biker. Ted had gone for Bartender. Anton, with his one-track mind, had guessed a Boston Celtic. Nancy had guessed an Alien.

"Kate and Ramon entered also?" Lindsey said with surprise.

"Yes. So did the big nurse, Lorena. I told you that we had total participation," Melissa stated proudly. "You need to regain your memory soon so I can have my payout. This was the easiest money I ever made. Maybe I should change my major from English Literature to Marketing?"

"Definitely don't do that. Your poems are excellent."

Lindsey continued to read the list. Kate had guessed Scientist, and Ramon had written down Yachtsman. She handled the paper back to the college student. Melissa tucked it back in her pocket and said with a smirk, "Ethan was indulging in wishful thinking. He put down Surgeon."

"It was wishful thinking," he admitted.

"Can I enter?" Lindsey asked.

"I don't know," Melissa answered doubtfully. "What if you subliminally know who it is? Maybe we can put it to a vote at Ward Council. But I'll tentatively pencil you in. You owe me two bucks. What's your guess?"

Lindsey pondered this for a moment. "I don't know... my brain's still mush. Maybe the catcher for the Baltimore Orioles?"

"Now *that's* wishful thinking," Ethan said.

Melissa looked curiously at the white cotton fabric poking from Lindsey's pocket. "What's that?"

Lindsey quickly pushed the fabric into her pocket. "Nothing."

"It's definitely something. What is it?" the Goth persisted.

"It's the underwear that the nurse in detox gave me."

"You didn't bring underwear with you? What were you thinking about?" Trisha said with a mean-spirited laugh.

"I don't know. Maybe I did and lost them?" Lindsey floundered aloud. "I don't know what I was thinking. And I only packed two days of clothes."

"Maybe you did pack them, but now they're hanging on Boat Show Man's rearview mirror, next to his fuzzy dice," Ethan suggested.

There was a sudden hush, followed by an eruption of laughter. A red wave of embarrassment moved across Lindsey's cheeks.

"Ethan, you're so not funny!" She shoved him playfully in the chest. He grabbed her hands and locked his fingers between hers.

"So you carry them around in your pocket all day, like someone's going to steal those ugly things!" Trisha remarked again.

"No. I just found them on the shower room floor. Some jerk took the cord where we hang our hand-wash and tossed everything all over the floor. My underwear was covered with dust bunnies," Lindsey said, glancing uneasily at everyone's shoes.

A beach in southern Rhode Island

Love rhymed with dove and Louvre rhymed with move. She was in love, not louvre, Maggie giggled to her herself. Jed had told her that he liked her cornrows and their colorful beads, that her eyes were beautiful, and that her tits were not too small. They would grow when she grew up, he said. Jed used Jack Daniels to clean the blood from the dog bite, and where she cut her leg on the top of the fence. "Jack will kill any infection, Maggie. Jack is a cure-all." Jed gave her Self-esteem. Once when they were having sex, he asked her what she liked. No one had ever asked her that before.

And Jed had kissed her, and she'd kissed back. On the mouth! Would Bess be pissed! "Never, ever kiss them, Maggie, or look in their eyes. They don't exist. They aren't real," Bess had said to her a million times.

And these college guys were improving her vocabulary. Bess would be pleased. "A good vocabulary is important, Maggie," Bess had said. "We need to learn lots of long words. High price call girls, who make $1000 a night, need to talk like smart people to attract rich men. One day, Bestie, we'll share a penthouse apartment in Manhattan, with a hot tub and a view of something, and fuck movie stars and senators."

Maggie had remained silent during that discussion; she wasn't at all sure that she wanted to be a call girl when she grew up. On the other hand, if she was rich, she could walk around art galleries in New York City all day looking at paintings until she had to go to work at night.

"We're here," Tony said from the driver's seat. "Hot showers and lobster tail."

She looked out the van window. It was late afternoon, so many spaces were available in the parking lot at the public beach. The bathhouse was up a wooden walkway in the dunes.

"Here, Wonder Woman," Jed said, handing her a small hotel-sized shampoo and soap from his backpack.

The nickname the guys gave her after she lifted the Mother Lode was the best! "Show me her picture again," she said.

Jed tapped on the screen of his smartphone and an image of Wonder Woman appeared.

Tony slid open the side door of the van and rummaged through his backpack for his towel and shaving kit.

"I'm so hungry," Jed said. "Tonight I'm having stuffies."

"Lobster tail for me," Tony responded. "How about you, Maggie?"

"What was that thing you ordered for me last night? I want that again."

"Maryland crab cakes."

She studied the dark black lines and bright red, white and blue colors creating the Wonder Woman comic book character. "Like you'd ever see me in a gay skirt like that. Shit, I'd die first," she giggled. "She's probably wearing cotton panties."

"No way. Wonder Woman's definitely a thong girl," Tony said, grinning. "C'mon, poky pokes. Put that phone down. Let's shower. I wanna eat."

In her bare feet, she stepped gingerly up the wood walkway. All she needed was to get a splinter in her foot; her throbbing ankle and sliced toe were bad enough. The guys headed off to the men's side of the bathhouse, while she entered the women's side. In two hours time, she would be feeling nothing but Euphoria... which means really great feelings. Shower = hygiene. Crab cakes = satiation. Crack = anesthesia. She was getting so fuckin' smart hanging around with these college guys!

She peeled off her clothes, wondering how she might get herself to college. Maybe she'd have to do elementary, junior high and high school first. Shit... college was out of the question. She hadn't even finished fourth grade. She showered and dried herself up quickly, as all that talk of seafood made her stomach growl. At dinner she'd order a chocolate milk shake for her drink, and a banana split *and* cheese cake for dessert since she was rich.

She limped quickly down the wooden walkway. She halted. She put her hand over her eyes and scanned the parking lot. Maybe they'd moved the van? She walked the length of the parking lot, shifting her weight onto her good foot, but no van was to be seen. Maybe Tony had gone to pick up beer? He'd left her and Jed on the boardwalk once before while he ran to the beer store. She hobbled quickly up the walkway to the crest of a dune and gazed across the sand. There was no Jed on the beach. Her panic suddenly swelled. She hurried back to the space where the van had been parked, as if by hoping it might appear miraculously before her eyes. She needed a cigarette; she needed a hit. Suddenly she spotted it.

"Fuckers!" she cried aloud.

On the curb where the van had been parked was her rolled-up tarp. Gone was her backpack, clothes, money, drugs, cigarettes... all of her worldly possessions... gone! Those dickheads didn't even leave her shoes... Bess' cool Nikes!

Chapter 12

Rehab

Lindsey's fingers hung off the mesh of a hurricane fence surrounding the garden and she looked longingly down the bluff to the Sakonnet River and Rhode Island Sound. The meandering boats reminded her of her houseboat on the salt pond in Woods Hole and better times with Duncan. In college they'd scrimped and saved for scuba diving lessons and then bought a used motorboat that had sat for years in a parking lot of a local gas station in Baltimore. Over a couple of weekends she'd rebuilt the engine in the alleyway of their apartment building, while Duncan seemed to enjoy photographing her, sweaty and smudged with motor oil. The boat should be called *Beagle* (after Darwin's HMS *Beagle*), she had suggested, but he'd insisted on the name *Styx*. In a compromise, they had finally agreed on *Bluejay*, the Hopkins mascot.

The last time she'd seen *Bluejay* was on a broiling Maryland afternoon, attached to the towing hitch behind his truck. The afternoon he left her. The departure of the boat was more depressing than the departure of her husband.

Now it just sat neglected under some tarp, collecting seasons of leaves on his father's farm near the Blue Ridge Mountains.

Marriage had been fun for a while, and then suddenly the tectonics had shifted, knocking everything out of alignment. The rumbles of seismic activity had first appeared somewhere off the coast of New Jersey, in the vicinity of a sunken German U-boat that Duncan wanted to dive to. She had poured the remainder of a beer down her throat, while he had climbed out of the boat cabin and zipped up his wetsuit. He had not put a regulator on her yellow tank, so she stepped forward to do it herself. He yanked the regulator from her hands and placed it back in a dive locker. He solemnly leaned against the gunwale and pulled on his fins.

"Lin, you can't dive safely when you're impaired."

Impaired. She hated that word.

"Why not just say it, Duncan? Drunk. Fucked-up."

Anything but Impaired.

She had watched him tighten his weight belt and adjust the clasps on his buoyancy compensator. He spit into his dive mask to minimize fogging, then pushed the mask firmly against his face to form a tight seal. Regulator in his mouth, he fell backward over the side with a splash and disappeared into a burst of green bubbles. She wriggled out of her wetsuit and furiously heaved the flailing black rubber into the cabin. She grabbed a beer from a cooler of ice and walked to the instrument panel in the helm to check the depth sounder. With the amount of air that he had in his tanks, at a depth of fifty-eight feet, she guessed that he would be down for about thirty minutes. She consulted her dive watch. While he dove, a short experiment would be conducted, using herself as the test subject.

The Bottom Dwellers

Hypothesis: The test subject can drink six beers in thirty minutes.

Experimental Protocol: Pour one beer down throat of the test subject within a five-minute test interval.

Results: Six beers were consumed in thirty minutes by the test subject, thus confirming the original hypothesis.

Conclusion: The test subject would show him Impaired.

She leaned against the fence and pulled Duncan's postcard from her pocket and re-read it. The image was of Stirling Bridge. He taught a summer abroad course on the history of Scotland through his small college in Virginia. Frankly the postcards had become a bit monotonous; they lacked the substance, passion, and romance that she was craving. Instead, they were a cheerful travelogue from a mediocre travel writer describing his tour of Inverness, Loch Ness, the Battlefield at Bannockburn, and Hadrian's Wall. She had never been to Scotland; she had pleaded with him to take her. No doubt the rationale was to keep the wife away from the pubs and highland whiskey.

She crossed the lawn. Shirtless men darted around the basketball court, shouting, and cursing. Insurance Fraud (Vince) had weaseled himself onto a blanket and was enthusiastically rubbing sunscreen onto Jailbait Kelly and Dana the Sorority Girl. Under a picnic table umbrella on the patio, Kate, Lorena, and Ramon drank perspiring cans of soda while putting together next month's work schedule. At another table, Anton was letting Nancy win at checkers. Xbox (Stan) was in a lawn chair, his obese body jiggling as his thumbs pressed the controls of his GameBoy. Sharon and Trisha gawked at Mitch working out at a chin-up bar.

Basking on a blanket in the center of the lawn were Ethan and Gay Guy (Marcus). She could now remember the names of over half of the patients on the ward as her brain's association areas now allowed her to link stereotypes to actual names. This was encouraging; her brain was healing in fit and starts. She squeezed onto the blanket between the two men.

"The pickings at this rehab are sadly slim," Marcus said, watching the action on the baseball court.

Ethan glanced up from a dog-eared copy of *Jurassic Park* from the reading room.

"Will you rub sunscreen onto my back, Lin?" Marcus asked.

"Sure," she said, reaching for the tube.

She squirted a gob of white cream into her palm and rubbed slow circles around his skin. Marcus had already invited himself to visit her houseboat and to join her for meetings on the Cape. She had asked Ethan if he was going to visit her also. "Newport's not that far from Woods Hole," she had reminded him. He had said "Of course," but his tone was politely noncommittal. Once he healed, she figured, he would be off on his next assignment abroad. Ethan had incurable wanderlust.

"You have the best hands," Marcus said with a dramatic moan as she rubbed cream in to his lower back.

"Don't make erotic sounds like that," she replied in frustration. "I've blown it with my husband. When he finds out how I got here, with some strange man, that'll be it."

"Why should you care? You two don't even live together anymore," Ethan remarked irritably.

"I don't know, but somehow I still do," she answered.

After rubbing Marcus with sunscreen, she flipped onto her back and rolled her shirt up to brown her belly. She searched the clouds for familiar objects. "That one looks like a pancreas."

From behind his sunglasses, Ethan's eyes lingered across her belly. He also flipped onto his back. His pale torso was crosshatched with pink slices, small entry wounds where metal shards of a car bomb had sprayed him in Afghanistan. "You're right," he observed. "How about that one?" He pointed to the right. "There's a spleen and the thin bent one looks like the corpus callosum."

"Yes," she agreed.

"I'm not listening to you two," Marcus exclaimed in dismay. "Only sickos see body parts in the clouds." He grabbed for her iPod and pulled on the headphones. "Love it! Judy Garland at the Palladium in London!"

Ethan strained forward and removed a blade of grass stuck to the gauze on his toes. But she stared at his other foot. "What's with that?" she asked nervously. His sneaker was being held closed by a pipe cleaner that he'd gotten from his roommate, Priest.

"Wait, don't tell me," she said, her heart pounding. "Someone took the laces from your shoe."

Cambridge

In front of Karen Battersby was an auditorium of high school girls. When she was their age, she reminisced fondly, she had been the president of her high school Engineering Club and Math Club, taking math courses at the local college, as she'd already finished all of the high school math courses available to her. To earn tenure, she had to excel in three areas: Research, Teaching and Service. This was her favorite service activity, a summer recruiting event for girls interested in science and engineering. She was among five female panelists who were to give a brief summary of their career, followed by a Q & A session. Alongside her were a biotechnologist, a veterinarian, a pediatrician, and a marine biologist. She'd spoken first, so it was time to relax and listen to the other women. The marine biologist spoke about her research on changes in shark migration patterns due to global warming. Though Karen found the research topic fascinating, her mind was still in the Dungeon of Zortan.

They'd entered the dark chamber, and immediately large cracks had appeared in the stony floor, revealing molten lava, making it treacherous for the Guild to navigate. Only seconds into their journey, BladeSlinger and JewelMaster sustained serious burns. Then came the attack... giant hornets. Toxic spray from their glowing red eyes caused Guild members to freeze in place, rendering them easy prey for a horrible death by the stingers.

Diana98's senses were on their highest alert that night. "I think I saw a gargoyle move in the corner of the screen," she had said fearfully into her headset.

"You're imagining things, Diana," Malcontent61 had replied.

Conqueror had whacked a wing off an attacking hornet, causing it to career into a pillar and explode. "Just be ready for anything, Warriors," he had cautioned.

"They're crawling down the walls!" Charlemagne12 had shouted.

"Watch your flank! Here they come!" Conqueror yelled.

An army of gargoyles and their ferocious black dogs leapt off the dripping walls and swarmed the warriors...

"Karen, Karen?" The biotechnologist whispered and nudged her. "There's an engineering question."

Karen's face went red with embarrassment. "Oh, I'm sorry. What was the question?"

A girl in the front row stood and asked, "As a freshman, should I be taking physics with or without calculus if I'm planning on being a nuclear engineer?"

"You should definitely be taking physics with calculus," Karen answered confidently. "In that major, as an entering freshman, whatever university you go to, you'll probably be taking some combination of Engineering Design, Calculus I, Mechanics, Engineering Ethics, and some general electives."

"Thank you," the girl replied as she sat down.

The next question was on drug development, so it went to the biotechnologist. Karen's thoughts skipped back to the Guild.

After the exhilarating journey into the dungeon that night, she'd remained in the Guild Hall chat room for another hour. She was thanked twice by Conqueror for being restored to life by her magic potions, and praised by Charlemagne 12 for alerting the Centurions to the gargoyle and dog attack. "Many warriors were spared by your heads up play, Diana."

Pussy Willow and Puss-n-Boots had meowed loudly at the office door until she finally opened it. The cats had affectionately rubbed against her legs.

The wonderful adventure in the Dungeon had left her thirsty and drenched with sweat; she'd swigged down the rest of her warm Cherry Coke, then pumped her fist into the air. "Hail, Guild of Centurion!" She'd strutted to her new marble bathroom to take a cold shower.

Chapter 13

Rehab

"Today we talk about your favorite subject. Sex," Kate said, opening up the Nolan folder in her laptop. "Sit down please."

"Believe me, it's not," Lindsey stated. Sex was her fourth favorite subject behind science, alcohol, and the Baltimore Orioles, but this was not the time for elaborate explanations. She wanted to get through the sex chat as quickly as possible, since Marcus was waiting for her on the patio. In the outside world he was a dance instructor. He was teaching her to dance! "If I was marooned on a desert island with box of scientific instruments and the Patriots offense, including Tom Brady, I'd opt for tinkering with the gadgets."

Kate was unmoved.

"I live alone and prefer it that way. Besides, I'm celibate. There's nothing to talk about," Lindsey added.

"You're a twenty-nine-year-old science celebrity. The celibacy part is highly doubtful. Sit down, please."

Lindsey remained standing. "Marcus is teaching me to samba. I finally have tone in my legs and butt. When I get out of here, I'm going to be a man magnet."

"You just said that you have nothing to do with men."

"You're right. I don't."

"That's good. Because when you get out of here, you're going to avoid any romantic entanglements for at least six months."

"Yeah. No problem," she replied unconvincingly. She consulted her watch. "Are we done?"

"Sit, Lindsey. The tango can wait." Kate sighed in frustration. "How long have you been married?"

"Samba, not tango! The samba is from Brazil. The tango is from Argentina. They're not the same thing!"

"I don't care about South American dances at the moment. Sit, goddamn it! Answer my question!"

Lindsey dropped into a chair. "Who knows? I've repressed the whole ordeal," she said dismally.

"Answer me," Kate said in exasperation.

She slouched deeper into the chair. "Almost ten years."

"You were married very young."

"I was a college sophomore and too stupid and too drunk to know better."

"You mentioned sex after four-wheeling with a boyfriend. Do you have sex with individuals other than your husband often?"

"Why is this relevant to my drinking?"

"Because adultery is a character defect that you'll need to work on as you work through the Twelve Steps."

"Duncan and I live apart. For all intents and purposes, I'm single. I'm still married according to the law, but in no other way. Marriage laws are merely artificial societal constraints to enslave women to—"

"I'm not interested in your personal philosophy on marriage," Kate interrupted. "Are these sustained relationships or one-night-stands?"

"Quick quickies work for me," she answered flippantly. "I hate small talk in general, but particularly with men."

Kate shook her head. "Are you sober or drunk during these encounters?"

"I'm never sober. Isn't that why I'm here?"

"Does your husband know about your extracurricular activities?"

"Yes."

"How?"

"He asks, and I have this defect of character called 'telling the truth'."

"How did this start?"

Lindsey lit a cigarette and pondered the psychologist's question. "I was faithful to him all throughout college, but then..."

After college graduation Duncan toyed with idea of going into law enforcement like his father and brothers, all cops in northern Virginia, but his father insisted that his youngest son continue his education. "Go to graduate school like Lindsey," his father, George McLeod, had urged. So with a vague interest in Scottish-American history, Duncan applied to a number of graduate programs in history, all of which turned him down in the first round. During the year he had to wait before he could reapply, he took a web design course and worked in a game store with Benny, a buddy from the lacrosse team. They spent huge amounts of time together, all day at the store, and most evenings transfixed by Benny's computer or slumped in front of EPSN. She encouraged the friendship, for it released her to focus on medical school and her ongoing experiments with Anne Davids.

Duncan badgered her to buy a house near Benny and his wife, Charlene, in the suburbs outside of Baltimore. "We could use the money from your BioCorp electrode," he insisted.

"We should stay at the apartment in the city, at least until I'm finished with med school. I need to be close to the hospital and Anne's lab," she countered. "We're in the thick of so many research projects right now."

The fact of the matter was that Anne Davids' company was preferable to all others. Over the years, an unspoken pattern had emerged between the professor and her M.D./Ph.D. candidate. Every Friday afternoon the two women, master and apprentice, met in the lab to plan experiments for the following week, and then Lindsey joined Anne and her husband, Julius, at the Davids' house for dinner. Everyone had their unspoken, yet specific chore. Julius cooked. Lindsey set and cleared. Anne washed, and Julius dried the dishes, as the couple's row home was possibly the last in the city not to have a dishwasher.

Anne and Julius were both Hopkins professors, so invariably their conversation revolved around academic and university matters. Lindsey was excluded from the couple's nightly dish-drying ritual in the kitchen, and to ensure that she stayed in the dining room, Anne placed a plate of cookies, a pen and lab notebook in front of her graduate student. By the radiator, the dachshund dozed on a dog bed as Lindsey reviewed the week's results. Anne was slowing down a bit, and in the past months Lindsey had noticed small errors in the woman's computations, which she silently fixed.

One evening, while jotting some ideas onto a legal pad, she was distracted by a conversation coming from the kitchen. Julius, an English professor, was telling Anne of a faculty member in his department who was revoked of tenure. She had listened curiously, as it was possible that she might work at a university someday, so the tenure process was of interest.

"Only a complete idiot could be stripped of tenure," Anne broke in unsympathetically. "Either the man was having sex with his students, or he plagiarized another's work."

"He used university funds to pay for visits to porn sites so his wife wouldn't find out. Unbelievable, really. In one month alone, he ran up over three hundred dollars at a site called naughtywives.com," Julius said.

"Naughtywives.com," Anne had remarked, with a bitter laugh. "You can find anything on the Internet."

"Quite sad, really," Julius had added thoughtfully. "He taught a wonderful class on the American expatriates in Paris."

The faucet in the kitchen squeaked off, and the old couple shuffled around the kitchen for a few more minutes, Anne worrying aloud that the Doberman next door might jump the fence and attack her tiny dog.

Julius wandered into the dining room and patted Lindsey's shoulder. "I'm heading up early. My hip's bad in the damp weather."

She turned in her chair and squeezed his long, knobby fingers. "The manicotti tonight was your best ever."

He had smiled paternally. "You say that every week, sweetheart."

The Bottom Dwellers

Anne and Julius kissed at the base of the stairs. "I won't be up until I finish my mystery," Anne informed her husband.

"The butler did it," Julius replied humorously.

Anne briefly considered his words. "There's no butler in the story."

Julius had chuckled and labored up the stairs. Taking the hint that Anne wanted to finish her P. D. James novel, Lindsey pulled her coat off the coat rack and promised to meet Anne in the lab the next day. They had many projects planned and were producing two or three manuscripts a year. The Nolan-Davids neurotoxin papers had become the most cited in their field.

A fog off the Chesapeake had enveloped the city, obscuring the row homes across the street. The wooden planks of Anne's front porch were slick, so Lindsey stepped cautiously down the steps, grasping tightly onto the railing. She positioned her backpack on her shoulders and walked gingerly down the wet brick walkway. In the summer the walkway would be bordered by a burst of colors, annuals that Julius and Anne delighted in changing from year to year, but on that night the flowerbeds were naked strips of frozen mud.

Two columns of streetlights disappeared over a ridge in the street. It was trash night in Anne's neighborhood, so green recycling bins and trashcans lined the curbs. The old brick row homes were adorned with a variety of blinking Christmas decorations, icicle lights, inflatable snowmen, Santas, and polar bears. The mist was chilling, so she pulled a ski hat out of her coat pocket and tugged it over her head. A singular thought nagged her, poised teasingly between subconscious and conscious. She rewound the evening's conversations, hoping to nudge it free. The animated conversation from the old couple's kitchen contrasted starkly with the lugubrious silence of her own apartment where she and Duncan moved in tortuous pathways through the confined space. For the moment she longed to be old and forty years married, enjoying a comfortable friendship which had replaced an edgy sexual ache.

Her increasingly frequent fantasies featuring confident, skilled men were symptomatic of a dreary sex life with a neurotic, simpering husband. Recently she could only orgasm when she imagined that Duncan was not Duncan. And Duncan spent absurd amounts of time propped up against the headboard, clicking maniacally into his laptop so that he seemed a cyborg with a computer affixed to his crotch where genitals had once been. Some nights when she'd exit the bathroom, the lid of his laptop quickly closed, and he'd smile and aim a clicker at an extravagant new HD-TV.

Where had he gotten the money for a plasma TV with surround-sound speakers, the new mag wheels and a paint job for the truck when he was making little more than minimum wage at the game store? When she'd checked her bank accounts, she was relieved to find the BioCorp funds were intact, and so she decided to ask no questions about how he spent his paycheck.

His purchase of a new high-end digital camera caused her further dread. He was most aroused, he explained, by taking photos of his beautiful wife. Early in the marriage, admittedly, the attention was quite flattering and she was a willing participant in the photo shoots, for they were always followed by sex that was at least adequate. Then Duncan insisted on props in the photos, which quickly filled their small closets and soon overflowed to boxes in his truck. Sometimes she might be dressed as a firefighter in a fire helmet, raincoat (gaping open, of course) and galoshes. Or scuba diver with mask, snorkel and net (nothing else). Or construction worker with hard-hat, tool-belt and hammer. And predictably, there was the usual array of feminine attire: teddies, fishnet stockings, spiked heels, and dominatrix wear.

"I might be famous one day, Duncan, no face shots," she'd insist while posed motionless in some ridiculous stance.

"Never, Lin, trust me," he'd answer calmly.

Still, she warily inspected all of the photos to insure that her face was always hidden behind some hat, scarf, or outlandish feather. He complied. The photo shoots became their only foreplay and she became bored. Her suggestions of other erotic games that they might play together were invariably answered with his pathetic whimper, "Please, Lin... this is what really gets me off."

"Okay Duncan," she'd sigh in disappointed resignation. It was best to get the whole ordeal over with and get back to the lab as quick as possible.

The Davids' house was one block from the campus and she paused on a damp corner to watch some fraternity brothers huddled around a keg on the front porch of a frat house. An ice-cold beer would taste good right now, she thought. Bruce Springsteen sang "Santa Claus is coming to town..." from a stereo speaker propped in the frat's window. Across the street, the lights of the library reflected across the glistening grass.

Julius's words still nagged her and she was saddened by a talented teacher's career cut short by an addiction to pornography. In the library she found an isolated computer and logged on. She set up an alias account on yahoo.com. The library was nearly empty since finals had just ended; still she glanced surreptitiously over her shoulders and typed naughtywife.com into the search engine; she was sure, though she could not recall where, that she had heard of that site before.

The homepage was red and green and seasonal. A cartoon Mrs. Santa had her finger across her lips and a word bubble read "Shh." A cartoon Santa promised a gift, holiday photos of lovely nubile wives. Twenty dollars charged to a credit card would access the site. She searched for her wallet in the bottom of her backpack and extracted her credit card. She entered the numbers and expiration date into the appropriate boxes and clicked SUBMIT.

The heading read Santa's Little Elves. The images downloaded quickly on the library's fast Internet connection. The first elf, a voluptuous platinum blonde clad only in a Santa hat and a string of Christmas lights was explicitly posed with a life-sized inflatable reindeer. These photos were not funny or erotic in the least, just profoundly disturbing.

She scrolled down to the next series of photos. Blood ejected from her heart and slammed against her temples. She hyperventilated uncontrollably. Her heart felt like it was fibrillating. The second elf had been shot in profile. Also in a Santa's hat, the model was a slender woman, her face turned into the shadows. Draping her body was garland of popcorn as she was decorating a Christmas tree. Down her back, long blonde hair fell to her waist. Her breasts, belly and legs were tinted by the colorful lights of the Christmas tree. The second elf was unmistakably familiar. It was her.

The Bottom Dwellers

She glanced frantically around her. A librarian moved through some distant stacks. Finding no tissues in her backpack, she bowed her face into the cubicle and cried silently into the sleeve of her coat. That, she had thought, had been a wonderful evening. She, for a first, had cooked an edible meal that they'd eaten while listening to Christmas CDs. Then they cuddled on the bed, watching The Grinch. They pulled themselves apart long enough to decorate a Christmas tree that they'd bought from the fire station on the corner. He had handed her, already high and giggly, another potent eggnog, and reached for his camera.

She willed the tears to stop and struggled to slow her breathing. A headache throbbed behind her eyes. She scrolled upward to the images of the pervert posed with the reindeer. The platinum blonde was then recognizable. It was Charlene, Benny's wife. She suddenly remembered. At Benny's barbecue last summer, Benny, Charlene, and Duncan had lingered around the propane grill for some time. Their laughter about some website ceased suddenly when she'd joined them on the deck.

So the laugh was on her.

She logged off and hastily left the library, wondering which of the many props cluttering her tiny apartment—so many to choose from—she'd use to murder her entrepreneurial husband. Yet Duncan was twice her size and she hated violence of any kind. She smiled grimly to herself. It would take all of six words to terrorize Duncan and cause his frantic fingers to shut the website down in nanoseconds. *I'm going to tell your father.*

Her shaky hand pulled back the cuff of her coat to check her watch. She and Duncan had talked about seeing a movie later that night, but her plans had just changed. Down the street a yellow neon light with an image of the Parthenon glowed through the fog. She'd been to that bar a few times before with another med student who'd introduced her to a scotch whiskey called Glenlivet. She stepped out of the chilly night and into the Acropolis Lounge.

A group of office workers were celebrating loudly at one end of the bar, so she slipped into a barstool at the opposite end. "Rocking Around the Christmas Tree..." was sounding through the speakers while Ravens-Colts highlights played on the TV screen. A handsome Greek bartender slid her a drink and she slid some bills back at him. The office workers moved onto a dance floor, the men having tugged off their ties, which the women wore like headbands. They flailed and spun spastically, thoroughly enjoying themselves, which caused her to smile. The bartender smiled also. He glanced down at her empty glass. "Another?"

She glanced at her watch. Duncan would be worrying by now. "Why not?"

Watching the dancers, the bartender said with his exotic accent, "Tomorrow they will regret much." He slid her another scotch and again she slid some bills back toward him.

The meanness in her blood was dissipating, the scotch nestling warmly in her veins. It no longer mattered that thousands of lonely men, and maybe some women, had viewed pixels of her naked body, or that her husband was profiting from it.

"I hope they regret nothing," she said cavalierly. She held up her glass to the bartender. "To no regrets."

"No regrets," he agreed, holding up a plastic cup of Coke.

Two old men in flannel coats, possibly truckers or dock-workers, signaled to the bartender that they needed refills, so he wandered down the bar to pull beers from the tap. He then disappeared into the kitchen and returned with clean mugs, which he hung from a wooden rack overhead. Her attention was diverted to the TV screen by news of a possible trade of an Orioles pitcher for a shortstop and right fielder from the Braves.

She felt suddenly as if she was being watched and looked down the bar, but the truckers and tipsy office workers were focused on their comrades. The Greek's back was to her, but she found his shiny black eyes reflected in the mirror behind the bottles. Her eyes locked onto his reflection and he held hers unflinchingly. She was determined not to look away first and would not waver. Finally he turned with a wide, pleased grin.

She had already noticed the way his jet-black hair curled over his white collar, his gleaming white teeth and trim waist. She glanced at her cell phone; there were three emphatic texts from Duncan. Gloating, she shut off her phone for the rest of the night.

"Your drinks are on the house," the bartender mentioned.

"Nice," she replied quietly.

She unwound a wool scarf from around her neck as if removing a deep-biting yoke and slid her coat off her shoulders. With hollow legs and a hollow heart, she settled into the barstool.

Lindsey and Kate finished their cigarettes at the same time and stubbed them into an ashtray on Kate's desk.

"You and Duncan definitely have issues," Kate conceded. "Is there violence in your relationship with him? For your protection, we have to know this."

Lindsey shook her head. "No violence, but anger and resentment fuels our sex. Duncan resents me for making him earn an honest living and prohibiting photos. I resent him for exploiting me. Our sex lacks creativity, fun, and variation."

"You're bored and so you cheat."

"Precisely."

"And you rationalize your infidelities with the alcohol."

"Exactly."

"How often do you see Duncan?"

"Less and less. Thankfully."

"Why's that?"

"Since my neighbor and his son moved onto the boat next to mine, Duncan visits infrequently. He says that the boy, Danny, is too loud. It bothers him that Danny climbs around my boat all the time. He hates it when Danny jumps on my futon and shoots his dart gun at my wind chimes."

Kate studied the patient's face. "And what about the father?"

Lindsey shifted slightly in the chair. "I don't know. What about him?"

"I'm asking the questions. Is the father your age?"

"I guess."

"Attractive to you?"

"I've never paid much attention," she answered with an indifferent shrug.

"Have you slept with this man?" Kate asked abruptly.

"He can't stand me. And I think he's an asshole."

Kate's glare, like blue lasers, passed through her once again. "What are you not telling me?"

"Nothing!"

The Bottom Dwellers

Woods Hole, two years earlier

Lindsey's head jerked up from her journal article as an unfamiliar car pulled into the space next to her Jeep. What! This was her part of the parking lot! No one ever parked down by the two old houseboats, as she was the only one who lived there on a permanent basis. All activity centered at the opposite end of the marina, around the boat ramp, gas pumps, and the bait store. This was her side of the marina, and no one else's!

The intruder's car was a piece of junk, an old 1990's compact car. A man stepped out and opened the back door. A tiny boy in a bathing suit and sandals seemed relieved to be released from the constraints of his seat belt and bounded toward the dock. Her dock!

"Hey, pal, get back here," the man called. He zipped the boy into an orange life vest and followed the skipping child across her dock.

Shit! They were heading to the houseboat directly next to hers! She'd assumed that that dilapidated old houseboat, the *Green Monster*, had been permanently abandoned. Who in their right mind would name a boat the *Green Monster*? *Camden Yards* possibly, but the *Green Monster*... ridiculous!

The man and boy disappeared into the boat. A bit later the man stepped onto the deck. Looking up at her flybridge, he spoke to her in a nearly indecipherable Boston accent. She guessed that he said, "Do you have any socket wrenches?"

Her first impulse was to say, "No," so he'd leave her alone. But if she said, "Yes," a shot of rum would be her reward for retrieving the tools. "Yes." She rose off her towel and climbed down the ladder. In her galley, she took a long guzzle of rum, then grabbed the tool set.

"Here." She and the man leaned across the green column of water between their two boats as she passed the tools. His outstretched forearm was tattooed with the Red Sox team logo.

"Thanks." He turned away without further comment, while she climbed back up to the flybridge.

She pulled another beer from a cooler of ice. Except for the intruders, life was perfect... a full bottle of Pusser's rum... a new case of beer in the refrigerator... a sunny day to sunbathe... a nice buzz had settled in.

She'd become somewhat of a busybody, watching the bustle of the marina from behind her sunglasses, so she decided to turn her attention to the man. He contemplated the wrenches for a moment and finally chose the size that he was looking for. There was a wily, street-smart way about him that was off-putting. His tanned and rugged face led her to guess that he was a landscaper, carpenter, or construction worker. His nose had been broken and had not been correctly reset. Maybe he was a boxer? He retreated inside, and soon irksome banging came from his galley. His son, who was about kindergarten age, played with the plastic action figures of the Mighty Thor and Ironman up on their flybridge. He looked eagerly at her a number of times, but she ignored him by burying her face in her engineering journal.

"What are you reading about?" the boy finally asked.

"Calcium electrodes," she answered tonelessly.

He nodded as if to say "Of course." "What's your name?"

"Lindsey," she said grudgingly.

"I like your pirate flags."

She glanced at the fluttering flags of Jack Rackham, "Long Ben" Avery and "Black Bart" Roberts. If she didn't comment, maybe he'd stop pestering her.

"I never heard your name before," he said.

She sighed and finished her beer. The man's radio broadcast of a Sox-Marliners game was annoyingly loud. Either she could walk into the village and read in the marine lab library, or endure the noisy interruptions for a while longer. She cracked open another can. "It's a weird name, I guess."

"Now you're supposed to ask me my name," he said. "That's the polite thing to do."

"Is it?" she said with another exasperated sigh. "So what's your name?"

"Danny."

"Like Danny in the lion's den," she replied.

"Is that a story? How does it go?" he asked with sudden interest.

"I don't remember," she replied. "I think it's a Bible story. I don't go to church. I just remember the title."

Despite his apparent disappointment, he persisted. "I like your other flags. I know what most of them mean," he added proudly.

"Okay, smarty pants, what do they mean?"

He giggled at the funny name. "That's the flag of Massachusetts. That one's for the Baltimore Orioles. I don't know that one," he confessed, referring to the one with the red, black and yellow patterns.

"It's the state flag of Maryland."

"No!" The shout came from the galley. The father cried through the screen, "Dan, Garcia missed an easy pop fly to left field! That's his third error this week!"

"Garcia's a nitwit. They should trade him," Danny remarked, climbing down the ladder. "I'm so hot in this life vest."

The man stepped out of the cabin, took Danny by the hand, and walked him along the gunwale to the bow. He swiftly grabbed the boy by the waist and flung him outward toward the pond. The writhing, airborne boy squealed while she gasped in horror. Splash! Danny disappeared for a moment under the water, then popped into the air, laughing and shouting, "Do it again, do it again!"

The man grinned maniacally up at her and she grimaced back. Danny dog-paddled to the dive ladder on the transom, and the man heaved his delighted son into the pond again and again until they were both exhausted.

"Daddy, I'm hungry," Danny said, panting.

The man strapped small black sandals onto his son's feet, told him what to buy at the bait store, and warned him to be careful crossing the parking lot. He watched his son skip into the store. Moments later Danny returned with three orange Creamsicles. The man locked the door to his houseboat, and placed an ice cream bar and the tool set on the gunwale of her boat.

"Thanks," he said to her.

She chugged down the rest of her beer and looked down from her flybridge. "You're welcome. By the way," she stated with authority, "the best team in the American League East has always been the Orioles. The Yankees and Sox are entirely over-rated."

The man's eyes widened and he briefly moved his lips to speak. Best to refrain in front of his son. Instead, he took his son's hand and walked silently down the dock.

The Bottom Dwellers

Good riddance! She dropped onto her Corona beer towel to bask in the sun, her quiet, secluded kingdom restored to her once again.

A week or two later, as she was pushing her bike down the dock on her way home from work, she noticed some activity on HER SIDE OF THE DOCK. Dave and the man with the tacky Sox tattoo were talking by the *Green Monster*. Danny was by her boat, slashing the air in front of her plastic owl with his pirate saber. The man started hauling boxes from his car, using Dave's wheelbarrow. She had a very bad feeling, no, a terrible feeling about this. He was hauling boxes toward the *Green Monster*!

"I was down-sized," he grumbled in passing.

They were moving in? "How can you not see that the *Green Monster* is an irreparable hunk of junk?" she wanted to say. "With the next rainstorm the boat will sink, your boy will drown! You must leave immediately!" She made a hasty beeline to her liquor cabinet; an extra-large glass of Glenlivet was required to numb herself in the face of this horrible, horrible development.

Over the next few weeks, she watched her two neighbors with silent consternation. To Danny, the move to the marina was an enthralling seafaring adventure. With a black pirate hat and plastic hook over his fist, he investigated every inch of the place... including her boat, countless times. He was thrilled with her coconut head pirates and asked to see them almost daily. Thankfully the father never asked to come onto her boat. Danny quickly befriended Dave and Sheila's children, Brianna and Max. The father, Robert, was quite sociable as well, and chatted frequently with Dave and Sheila. Worse, other boaters now wandered down to her end of the marina to talk to him. Gone were her days of wonderful solitude.

Worse still, Robert had made no attempt to find other living accommodations; they were still there when the fall came. Every morning Danny climbed with Brianna and Max into the school bus in front of the bait store, while Robert seemed content to wander the marina all day, his faded Red Sox baseball cap tilted back on his head. Rarely did he change out of gaudy surfer swim trunks. It was a formal occasion for him to slide a t-shirt over his head. Every so often he worked in the bait store when Sheila ran out for errands; other times he helped Dave haul equipment or perform small maintenance and trash details around the facility. But most of the time he tapped away at the laptop in his galley while listening to music CDs.

Initially he treated her with polite disdain since her jibe about the superiority of Orioles. In New England, to put the Sox and Yankees in the same sentence was sacrilege. But eventually her insult was forgiven and she and he became somewhat conversational across the few yards of water that separated their two boats. He wrote a sports blog and was piecing together sports writing jobs to make ends meet, he explained.

In the afternoons, after the school bus stopped in front of the marina, Robert and Danny had the same ritual. In front of a green dumpster, the heel of Robert's sneaker carved a home plate in the dust. He instructed Danny on where to position his feet, how to grip the bat, how high to place his elbows, where to center his weight. Danny was pitched a series of tennis balls. He had a natural swing and was lean and athletic like the father, who gracefully pulled every catch from the air. From her flybridge, she listened carefully to Robert weave the fantasy.

"It's the bottom of the ninth, with two outs. Betts and Rodrigo are on first and third. The Sox are three runs down. A home run will take it to extra innings."

Danny held himself ready, his body taut like a spring, his heart dancing in his chest. The father released the tennis ball, a perfect arc over the plate. Danny's swing made contact. The ball soared through the air, dropping on the shoulder of the road.

"Home-run!" called Robert.

Danny sprinted around the parking lot, stomping on imaginary bases; then there was a joyous high-five at home plate.

Their boat's interior was illuminated at night. It was tacky with Red Sox memorabilia, trinkets, pennants, and posters. Bobble-headed Red Sox players were turned jestingly out the window toward her boat. She turned her coconut pirate heads to jeer back. After dinner, Robert helped his son with homework. When Danny was asleep on the foldout sofa in the salon, Robert sat in a lawn chair on the bow and gazed out to the marsh, the ember of his cigar moving like a firefly in the darkness.

Over the time the presence of the father and son became tolerable. After a while their sounds and activities simply melded into other rhythms of the pond. As she pushed her bike along the dock each morning, Robert stood on his stern with his cup of coffee.

"Shame that the Os have more unforced errors than any team in the entire league." Yes, she was painfully aware of the three dropped catches in right field the previous evening! And on another morning, "Could the Birds have a more pathetic bull pen?" True, the trade of the two pitchers from the Reds was boneheaded at best, but it was smart not to respond. On still another morning, "The Os are now eight games behind my beloved Sox... no way they'll make the playoffs now," he said with a goading grin. No, post-season was too depressing to think about! He was clearly following the Os' statistics very closely. Do not take the bait, she told herself... at least until your homework is done. At the lab, before she could start to work, she'd scour the Internet for any weak link in the Red Sox line-up, but sadly there was none. The Sox were having a fairy tale season.

Chapter 14

Rehab

A collision of fists and irate curses awoke the patients that morning. Flesh thudded against cinderblock. Everyone bolted into the corridor to find Marcus and Stan (Xbox) punching each other.

"You took my shoelaces, faggot!" cried Stan.

Marcus answered with a fist into the belly overhanging Stan's belt. "You took mine, you fat turd!"

Ramon and Mitch separated the flailing men. Blood streamed from Stan's nose. Marcus leaned over panting, his hands on his knees. Composing himself, he straightened, tucked his shirt into his pants, and patted down his hair.

The electronic buzz of the security doors startled everyone. The click of loafers approached down the waxed tiles. Briefcase and lunch bag in hand, Kate Waters cautiously eyed the tense, silent bystanders.

"What the hell is going on here?" she demanded.

"There was a fight between Stan and Marcus," Ramon answered timidly.

"That queer stole my shoelaces!" Stan screamed, pointing at Marcus. "And I think he broke my nose!"

"You go clean yourself up," Kate barked to Stan. "I want you and Marcus in my office pronto!"

Lindsey could barely eat breakfast that morning, and it was not because of the fight, or because Melissa sat across from her with facial piercings that looked painful and grotesque. Withdrawal symptoms were at their worst in the mornings. The pacifying Valium had long ago left her system, and for the last few days she'd been waking with some combination of shakes, sweats, and nausea. During breakfast, Kate switched the men's roommates. Stan moved in with the priest, while Ethan moved in with Marcus. While the patients were in a Twelve Step meeting, Kate, Ramon and Lorena searched all of the rooms but found no shoelaces. The day's pattern had been altered and Kate hated any deviation from The Schedule. This meant that she'd be an insufferable bitch for the rest of the day. The fight also delayed Lindsey's counseling session that day.

"Grandma's shoes were stolen, and Myra's and Ethan's shoelaces, and the cord in the women's shower room," she explained.

"Why didn't you tell me this sooner?" railed Kate.

"Because anytime I tell you anything about happenings in the Fishbowl, you scream at me to stop gossiping and focus on getting sober!"

"Thefts are different!"

"I've been panicky for days that there's a strangler on the ward. Any morning we might wake to find someone strangled! I've been barely able to sleep because of this creep. Every morning I feel tired and queasy from not sleeping."

For the moment Kate backed off on the questions and went to the window with her cigarette. Lindsey remained slumped in a chair, unwillingly to be a genial smoking partner.

Turning, Kate asked, "And *you* have nothing to do with this?"

"I can't believe this! Why would I want shoelaces?"

"For that contraption you're building in the reading room?"

"Shoelaces are not requisite components of doorknobs."

"You said that if you couldn't think or work, you'd kill yourself."

"That was a figure of speech!"

Kate blew streams of smoke through the screen. "You're right," she conceded. "You don't fit the profile. You have too much *joie de vivre*."

"Profile?" Lindsey sprung from the chair. "So that's all I am, a fucking profile?"

"And you know the rule about the use of profane language!"

"Fuck, shit, prick, asshole!"

Kate pointed toward the door. "This session's over!"

"Fine with me, Nurse Ratched," Lindsey huffed, heading toward the Fishbowl.

Ethan sat in a wicker chair in the Fishbowl. She carefully stepped over his injured leg so as not to jar his foot. He had just replaced the gauze around his toes, as he did many times a day. She sat between his spread knees on the edge of the coffee table.

"ARGH!" she roared. "I hate that bitch. I called her Nurse Ratched. Now she'll keep me here forever."

"Probably," he replied, laughing

"Will you two shut the fuck up? I can't hear my TV program," said the Barbie Doll, Trisha.

He continued to grin. He was different from the rest of the patients. He was always quick to hold the door for her, pull out her chair in the dining room, or light her cigarette, despite his chronic pain. After the explosion in Afghanistan, the field surgeons had almost removed his foot. His foot and ankle had been reconstructed back at Mass General.

At the moment, his eyes glistened their brilliant sea green from his painkiller. His pupils were constricted to tiny black dots and a slight sweat shone on his forehead and nose, indicating that he'd received a pill recently; for a while he would be light and cheerful. Later he'd become testy and withdrawn.

Lindsey glanced surreptitiously around the Fishbowl, her heart pounding. The lobsterman, Hank, and the gun-nut, Billy, were at the coffee counter, talking about re-financing their mortgages. Trisha, Anton, Nancy, and Dana watched music videos. All were out of earshot.

"I'm really nervous about the laces," she whispered, leaning close to Ethan. "More than nervous... I'm completely spooked. What if there's a strangler on the ward? Most of us have police records for something or other. Someone amongst us could be a murderer. The drug dealers have certainly killed people."

He whispered calmly back, "There's no strangler. Someone's still using. Intravenous drug users use a shoelace to constrict their vessels."

She shook her head, unconvinced. "Yes, *a* shoelace. But nine laces are missing, Stan's, Marcus's, Myra's, Grandma's and yours. Plus the cord for hanging the hand wash. An IV drug user doesn't need so many laces. Plus, who's going to use in a rehab! That's lunacy. We're all here to get better."

He reached for her hand. "Believe me, Lin, some IV drug user is still shooting up. No one's going to harm you, or any of us. You know that night in detox, I recognized you immediately."

"You're changing the subject."

"Yes, I am, because I don't want to be thinking about laces. It gets me obsessing on shooting up."

"Sorry," she said genuinely. "How did you recognize me?"

"Years ago I saw an article in *Money* magazine on the Nolan Electrode. I later bought stock in BioCorp. I remembered your photograph because I was struck by how young the inventor was."

"So that's why you were watching me during the poker game."

He smiled. "Yes, and to see if you were cheating. I used your electrode many times in the field. It's an amazingly accurate device." He then added comically, "I was a bit surprised when they peeled the great inventor, limp like spaghetti noodles, off a gurney in a detox in Rhode Island, of all places."

She flicked her lighter nervously. "I don't need to be reminded of that."

He leaned in closer. "All of the guys agreed that you had an adorable derriere."

"What!"

He whispered humorously, "We were all instantly in love."

Red heat suffused her cheeks. She dropped her face into her hands.

His quiet laughter continued. "You don't think we wanted you to play poker with us because of your IQ, do you?"

She drew her head upward and shook cigarettes into her lap. She pelted him with them, as if showering him with tiny arrows.

Woods Hole

"I don't believe my eyes," Sara whispered, upon opening her apartment door. Derick Briggs was dressed in a dress shirt and tie, instead of his usual biker leathers. "Where have you been, handsome?"

"To dinner with my fiancée."

"Shh..." She pointed to Zephyr asleep on an Asian sleeping mat in the corner.

He stepped quietly around bicycles in the doorway and into a tiny room that served as living room, dining room, and kitchen. He whispered, "I took Isabel out for lobster, and she didn't like it. And she doesn't like my apartment here, or the village of Woods Hole, or New England, or anything. I was hoping that if she came and saw the place that she'd come back here with me next summer. I get so much work done here in the summers. Do you have any aspirin? My head's throbbing."

"No, I avoid products from pharmaceutical companies whenever possible. They're so bad for the liver. For headaches, I go organic. I have weed."

"Anything will do at this point."

She disappeared into her bedroom and returned shortly. "Let's go outside." They sat down in two lawn chairs on a small, cement porch.

"Where's Isabel now?"

"Back at my place. Probably texting my brother, Jared. She texted him three times during the meal. It's like I wasn't even there. I don't know. I'm getting a bad feeling about everything."

She lit the joint, took a drag, and passed it to him.

"Everything feels wrong," he added miserably. "I don't want to talk it anymore. What happened with your job interview?" He took a long drag from the joint, exhaled, and handed it back to Sara.

"I think it went well. Karen was pleasant enough. I think that I could work for her, but I'd want to see her lab first. I haven't heard from her yet, so I'm a little worried."

"She's probably away on vacation. What are you going to do if she offers you the job?"

"I don't know!" she confessed. "I really need to see Lindsey soon to see if she's recovering, and see if there's any chance in hell she can stay sober. Can you watch Zephyr one afternoon while I drive to Newport?"

"Sure. We'll have fun. There's this new skydiving school..."

"No!"

He grinned. She smiled at her own gullibility and passed him the joint.

"No, thanks. That's all I need. The headache's gone. It's medicinal marijuana."

Providence, Rhode Island

"Trust no one, ever, ever, Maggie, only me," Bess had once said. "Not a nice waitress, a smiling man who gives you free lines, or a dealer who adds in a free bag of smack... no one, ever, *ever*." Especially not surfer assholes! Maggie inhaled a blunt that passed her way. The weed was laced with something... something very strong. The chemical hit her brain with the force of a train. Her eyelids dropped and she pressed her head against the wall to keep it from floating off her shoulders.

"Why didn't I listen to Bess? Bess had wisdom; she was always right," she muttered to herself. True, Bess went insane in Minnesota and whacked in Janine's head with a shovel, and maybe killed Russ with rat poison—though that might have been Janine—but Bess always spoke the truth. Never again, she thought, never in this lifetime will I befriend or trust fuckin' anyone! Forever ever I'm a solitary being roaming this planet on my own. People are shadowy, treacherous creatures in Out World only to be used for the acquisition of vital necessities: cigarettes, drugs and food. Retreat and hide In World, where it's safe and peaceful.

A nudge caused her to open her burning eyes. She squinted through the red smoke. "Where the fuck am I? I'm so fuckin' tired of travelin' to fuckin' nowhere!" The glowing blunt reappeared through the smoke so she took another drag. That weed made everything so slow, so blurry. Shadowy... treacherous... crazy, crazy party going on in Out World... the ugly man's hand slid into her shorts... the skeleton man tightened a shoelace around her calf... two bags, beauty... just like you asked your daddy... two bags this time... a needle pricked at her ankle... a shudder of pleasure... a wave of warmth... naked creatures stumble and dance... clinking bottles, screams, deafening music... if she closed her eyes, she'd disappear... no longer collapsed in a filthy shit-hole... a crackhouse... in which town?... go In World... close your eyes... In World... to that place of clean beds and warm food...

Chapter 15

Rehab

Sultry music played from a CD player and Lindsey and Marcus danced a tango. Lawn chairs and picnic tables had been dragged to the perimeter of the patio to make room for their dips and spins. Orange lilies bordered the patio where crickets fiddled loudly amidst the rhythm of the basketball in the court. Already the two dancers were wet with sweat. In exchange for massages, Marcus had agreed to teach her to dance. She was full of herself; the rumba, samba, and tango had all been mastered.

The next Twelve Step meeting was in ten minutes, at 10:30. They were to discuss Step 5: *Admit to God, to ourselves, and to another human being, the exact nature of our wrongs.* Marcus started a conversation, while dancing. "I got arrested at Heathrow," he confessed "I was only carrying a gun for my security. I hate London skinheads." He'd depleted his savings made from bartending and dance instruction, following actors and rock stars between LA and London, and finally, broke and coked out, had to move back in with his mother in South Providence.

Marcus, Lindsey knew, had already found a sponsor and hooked up with some long sober men in Gay AA. He shared frequently and honestly at meetings. She still could not share. There was nothing to tell. Her story was a non-event. She'd only hurt herself and Duncan.

"When my Uncle Charlie died in a motorcycle wreck, our family didn't attend the funeral," she reminisced sadly. "For weeks I roamed local cemeteries looking for his grave stone. My mother would tell me nothing. I never found out what happened to Charlie's body. I couldn't find his partner, Elliot. He simply disappeared. I'm sure that bitch did something to run him out of town. The boat yard suspiciously went up for sale, and then quickly sold. The chip on my shoulder against my mother is as large as the Eurasian Plate."

"That's not your wrong, sweetheart," Marcus said kindly. "You can't help it if your mother's a shrew."

Kate strode out the door, crossed the patio, and switched off the music.

"Speaking of shrews..." Lindsey whispered to Marcus.

"Enough dancing. Lindsey, we need to talk," Kate said.

"What have I done now?" She stepped away from Marcus.

"Come with me," Kate ordered. Lindsey followed her across the lawn to the hurricane fence. The psychologist turned abruptly, her hands resting on her wide hips. "What did you and Mitch do last night?" she asked accusingly. She lit a cigarette and blew smoke from the side of her mouth. "The night nurse saw you two talking for a while."

"Yeah, so what? We talk every day."

"What were you two talking about last night?" Kate said, demanding a more thorough explanation.

"About the time I crashed my sailboat on a shoal on one of the Elizabeth Islands. I destroyed the hull and outboard motor. I was stranded out there for over a day. The worst part was that I ran out of beer. I probably would have died of dehydration on that remote island had I not built a fire that a Coast Guard patrol boat spotted. Fortunately, by the time they showed up I was sober so they didn't arrest me for a BWI, boating while intoxicated."

Kate groaned aloud. "It's a miracle you're still alive. Is that all you talked about?"

"No. Mitch told me that I would have been able to survive indefinitely by eating mussels, crabs, and certain types of plants and collecting rainwater in my boat. Then he talked about that ambush on that trail again. He dragged his friend, Jimmy, into a cave during the firefight and tried to save him. Ever since then, he's developed claustrophobia that he never had before the incident. That's why he's always outside. He hates close spaces."

"He never mentioned claustrophobia to me or Ramon," Kate replied skeptically.

"He's upset that he won't be able to perform his duties anymore. His father and brother were Rangers. It's all he knows. The thought of being in confined spaces like helicopters or planes terrifies him. He's hurting. He still wants to drink really badly." She paused. "Why are you asking me all of this? I didn't see him at breakfast. Is he ill?"

"He's gone!" Kate's eyes were smoldering. "We've searched everywhere."

"Gone?" she repeated doubtfully. "No one escapes this maximum security prison."

"This is not a prison! If he wanted to leave, I would have signed his discharge papers, but all of his belongings are still in his room."

"A Ranger could deactivate the security door. I'm sure they're trained in all kinds of evasive maneuvers."

"We checked the footage from the security camera there. He didn't leave from that exit or the fire door."

"How about the window by the tree? Maybe he jumped over to the branches?"

"We checked that too. That window was locked from the inside. And it's definitely too high to jump to the ground. He'd break a leg."

"The missing laces!" Lindsey exclaimed, realization dawning. "He lowered himself out a window, using the cord and shoelaces!"

Boston

"No more Cherry Cokes," Karen Battersby thought to herself, as she read the number of calories on the can. "Just water." She returned the soda to the refrigerator and walked through her condo to the bedroom. She stepped on the scale. Yes! Three pounds had vanished! The morning walks and removing carbs from her diet were really paying off. The last vice to go was the fattening soda. She walked into her office and entered the Guild chat room.

There was a personal email from Conqueror. She read it repeatedly.

"Dear Diana98,

The Bottom Dwellers

Great time in the dungeon the other night. You really came thru for the Centurions. I have a favor to ask. I'm driving a large cargo of lumber between Washington State and the east coast and won't have time to access my computer for over a week. I'm wondering if you'd be willing to guard the Guild armory during that time? Hackers have been such a problem recently. I hope I'm not burdening you with this request. If yes, I can send you the password. All you'd need to do is check every day to see that nothing is missing. I also have an Excel spreadsheet that lists the armory's inventory if you want that also. If you could let me know by tomorrow, that would be great. Please feel no obligation. If you're too busy and can't do it, I'll ask Odin18.

So, Conqueror is a trucker. She imagined him much like the pictures of Brawny on her paper towels, or Paul Bunyan in her childhood story books, muscular and handsome, and clothed in a soft flannel shirt and jeans. And he was a trucker that could write well. The only misspelled word was "thru." To which part of the east coast might he be traveling? To the Boston area?

She responded immediately.

Dear Conqueror,

I would be honored to serve the Centurions in this capacity. You can count on me to check the inventory diligently every day to insure that nothing is missing. By the way, the comic convention is being held in Boston this weekend. Any chance you'll be there?

Conqueror responded within the hour.

Thanks so much, Diana98! I'm attaching the armory's inventory and password. So sorry that I won't be able to make it to Boston. Way too much work. In fact, I've never been north of the Mason-Dixon line. But Malcontent61 lives in New Hampshire. She might be there. I hope we can meet in person someday soon!

"That would be wonderful, Conqueror!" Karen typed. No wait, remove the exclamation point; it sounds too eager. "That would be wonderful, Conqueror. The armory's in good hands. Have a safe trip across the US. Diana98."

Chapter 16

Rehab

For the weeks after Grandma's departure, Ellen was Lindsey's roommate. She was a single mother from the fishing community of Point Judith who hired a babysitter for her two kids, and then headed out to her favorite watering hole to play pool, do shots, and slip into a back room to smoke crack cocaine. Ellen and Lindsey lived for weekends, when, like two excitable teenagers, they would primp for the Friday Night Narcotics Anonymous (NA) meeting in the outpatient wing. NA meetings meant bikers! Though Lindsey had promised herself after the death of Uncle Charlie that she would never ride on a motorcycle, there was something so arousing about men in black leather chaps.

Ellen was tall and curvaceous and turned biker heads; Lindsey wasn't and didn't. She was anemic and sickly thin. Worse, her attire alternated between the two sets of shirts and shorts from her overnight bag, and the oversized pair of hospital underwear invariably poked over the waist of her shorts. Not sexy. But there was good news; the big nurse,

Lorena, had told her during a weigh-in that she had gained three pounds.

And she was getting some sleep. Since Mitch's escape, the shoelace thefts around the ward had stopped; it seemed certain that he had climbed from one of the windows. Her night terrors and insomnia caused by the imagined strangler lurking amidst them disappeared. She was eating well, except during breakfast when she was queasy from withdrawal. If she smothered the rubber fish with tartar sauce, it would remotely taste like fish. She applied the same tactic with A-1 sauce on the rubber steak, and a blanket of Heinz 57 made almost any unknown substance taste edible.

With the mystery money in her wallet, Ethan's heiress wife, Samantha, who, Ethan explained derisively, had nothing better to do than shop, bought Lindsey new clothes. During one of the visitation hours, she'd given Samantha some cash and a list of her sizes. Samantha returned a day later with the items on her list. Samantha chose tastefully elegant clothes that Lindsey never would have thought to buy herself. Best of the all were the new bikini panties. Black silk, no less. The Annette Funicello underwear from detox were stuffed joyously into a trash bin.

Family visitation hours were on Saturday and Sunday afternoons, and Lindsey felt vaguely like she had in college, when there were family events and hers never came. Miriam Nolan had been true to her word; all contact with her family had ended on the night of the accident, when she was eighteen. Still, she wondered what type of women her sisters had grown into. She'd been close with Colleen and Molly in different ways. What were their jobs? Did they have families of their own? Where did they live? She had adored her father. Why had he never tried to reach out to her after all these years? Clearly some intractable deal had been sealed with her mother. Did anyone of them ever wonder, even once, what had become of her?

Regardless, visitation hours were enjoyable, as the ward was filled with balloons, baked goods, and excited children climbing over their missing parent. Stretched tautly across the faces of the significant others were the wary smiles of unknown, uncertain futures, and unresolved, unforgiven pasts.

Samantha wore such a smile. Ethan muttered in curt monosyllables to her, some private system of communication understood only by the two of them. His only interest was in talking to his children; for the most part, his wife was ignored. His twin daughters, in their matching summer dresses, clambered over him, competing for his hugs and attention. The oldest child, Samantha's teenage son by a previous marriage, shuffled aimlessly around the Fishbowl, eyeing Kelly and Dana, and obviously wishing himself anywhere but here.

The hallways and Fishbowl were a smother of bodies, so Lindsey typically retreated with a book to her bedroom. She could read again, understand, and even retain the symbolic meaning of words on paper. Sentences, paragraphs, even entire chapters were beginning to make sense to her. *Step 2: Came to believe that a power great than ourselves could restore us to sanity*, had relevance in her life now, and she thanked whatever forces moved through the heavens (a Higher Power? Was there really such a thing?) for the partially restored synaptic connections in her brain.

One Saturday afternoon, Ellen's mother and children had just left and she was painting her fingernails in their bedroom when Marcus rushed in. Lindsey glanced up from her book.

"Lin, some gorgeous man is signing in to see you. If you are not interested in him, I want you to introduce us immediately," he insisted.

Her heart sank. It was probably some prying science reporter. Her career was over. She turned hesitantly toward the door. A large redhead darted into the room. She gasped, leapt from her bed and into his arms, and pressed her mouth against his. They fell back onto the bed in a tangled heap while Marcus left in wordless disappointment.

She pulled her mouth from the man's just long enough to say, "Ellen, this is Duncan."

Ellen picked up the nail polish and put on her slippers. "Really? I thought he was your brother."

Lindsey looked up curiously at her. "I don't have a brother."

Ellen shook her head and left for the Fishbowl.

For a while she and Duncan kissed and fondled on the bed. After, she lay in the crook of his arm, her hand nestled under his shirt, against the warm skin of his chest.

"I've never seen you look so clear and beautiful," he said.

"I've gained weight," she said proudly.

"I can tell."

"I'm getting my breasts and hips back," she continued to boast.

"I can definitely tell. How's the withdrawal?"

"It comes in waves. But it's nothing like what the heroin and coke addicts are suffering," she explained. "But I'm always sleepy and hungry, sometimes nauseous. Will you drive to the Cape and get the booze off my boat?"

"Of course, baby."

"How are things going at work?"

He paused. "I'm co-authoring another grant with that administrator in Edinburgh."

"How about your manuscripts?" she asked reluctantly.

"Going slow," he answered glumly.

Duncan was a terrible writer. How many drafts of his college and graduate school history papers did she edit, no, practically write for him? His dissertation on "The Trade Relations between Highland Scots and Indigenous Tribes of Upstate New York in the late 1700s," she probably knew verbatim. He was on the tenure-track; the pressure to publish was intense. And she was distracting him from his work. She was to blame.

Kate tapped on the door and stepped into the room without waiting for their response. Her expression was the all-too-familiar 'remember-the-no-sex-rule' glower, on display whenever Lindsey spoke with Ethan, Mitch, or Vince (Insurance Fraud). Overlooking Kate's admonishing glare, Lindsey rose and introduced her to Duncan. Kate and Duncan exchanged a few superficial words, as they were civilized humans; Lindsey, however, decided that she was not. There was a matter of some urgency. When was the last time she'd had a good poke? (The sex with Boat Show Man didn't count because she didn't remember it). The second Kate left, she pulled Duncan into the small bathroom. Speed was of the essence; she unzipped his fly and stroked him in her hand. Her other hand whipped down her shorts. He pressed her against the wall and she pulled his hips into hers. Imagining Duncan to be Mitch or Ethan, she came quickly, muffling her gasps into his Izod logo. He still pushed.

"Don't come in me," she whispered in a panic. "I lost my birth control pills somewhere."

"I want to knock you up," he panted.

"Don't!"

"Yes!"

"No!" She pushed him off just in time to feel his hot release down her thigh.

Giggling, they cleaned themselves up and inched open the bathroom door. Kate stood fuming. Her trembling finger pointed at Duncan. "You can go now! You're not welcome back here!"

Duncan sheepishly mumbled, "Sorry."

"Your wife will not get better if you do not help her obey certain rules!" Kate turned to Lindsey. "And you should be packing your bags!"

"No, please, Kate, please..." she pleaded quietly.

"You, out!" Kate pointed at Duncan. "You, in my office. Now!" She stormed off.

Duncan and Lindsey slunk down the hallway toward the security doors.

"I love you," he said.

"I love you," she reflexively parroted back.

"Fuck the rules," he stated brazenly. "I'm gonna kiss my wife."

They kissed long and hard under the security cameras. A nurse buzzed him through the doors. Lindsey moved to the dining room, waited, and then watched him cross the parking lot. His rental car was parked next to the Jeep. She'd help him with his papers, and help him to get tenure. Once she was sober, she'd somehow make things right with him.

Cambridge

The Bottom Dwellers

Karen and the BTI computer science professor, Agnes Holcomb, decided to change into their costumes for Comic Con in a ladies' room of the Computer Science Department. Karen glanced into the mirror. The white toga that was tight on her at last year's gamers' convention was loose and flowing. She placed her Diana98's cat ears over her head and arranged plastic flowers randomly through her hair to appear like a goddess of the forest. Though she rarely wore makeup, that morning she had applied pink glittery eyeliner to match her pink lipstick and pink cat ears and tail. She looked critically at herself and liked what she saw. What a shame that Conqueror would not see her today! She tucked her makeup into her backpack that held her smartphone, laptop, wallet, water bottle, and change of clothes. Meanwhile, Agnes struggled with bobby pins to fasten two large buns onto the sides of her head. When they were finally ready, Karen inched open the bathroom door and peered out. Fortunately, no one was in the hallway. It was a Saturday morning, so the building was largely abandoned.

"The coast is clear," Karen whispered.

They dashed out of the building and waved down a taxi. They had decided to share a cab to the convention center since she, as the avatar Diana98, and Agnes, as Princess Leia, might attract unwanted attention on the T. The sidewalk in front of the convention center was already packed with gamers in cosplay when they emerged from the cab. They paid their admission fee and excitedly scanned the program. So many activities to choose from! A careful strategy was devised to navigate the large auditorium and optimize their time. They headed to the *Star Wars* area first, hoping to catch the parade of Boba Fetts. En route they stopped at exhibitions with high-end gaming computers, new video games, and a table selling sci-fi movies from the 50s and 60s. A Roswell alien pouring through the old movies said, "There's a rumor that Patrick Stewart's going to make a surprise appearance around three o'clock near the *Star Trek Next Generation* display."

Agnes spun towards Karen. "I already have the autographs of Leonard Nimoy and William Shatner! How cool would it be to get Patrick Stewart's autograph also?"

"So cool!" Karen said. "At 2:45, we'll stop whatever we're doing and check it out."

The two women hurried on their way. At the *Star Wars* exhibition, they watched the Boba Fett parade and voted on the costume they thought most authentic. Karen took photos with her smartphone of Agnes posing with Chewbacca, Hans Solo, Darth Vader and assorted Storm Troopers against a backdrop of the Ewok planet of Endor. After listening to a panel of screenplay writers from the Lucasfilm production company, they made their way to a concession stand.

Karen, contemplating the limited menu items, decided that she would allow herself, on such a special occasion, to slip on her no-carb diet and have Cherry Coke and funnel cake. She'd get back on the wagon tomorrow. The concession stand was crowded and the line of aliens, avatars, spacemen, and super heroes inched forward. She felt a bump against her backpack, and then a tug at her waist. Startled, she turned quickly.

A small girl, dressed as an anime character, lifted Karen's cat tail. The girl looked up at a paunchy Batman. "Daddy, could you buy me a tail like this for the next Comic Con? I really want to look like this lady."

"Sure, sweetheart." Batman turned to Karen. "Could you tell me where you got your ears and tail?

"At the Party Time store," she answered helpfully.

"Thanks. You two look awesome," Batman said to Karen and Agnes.

"I much preferred Christian Bale's Batman over Michael Keaton's," Agnes said to the man. "Bale's portrayal of Batman was so pensive and doleful. One could truly empathize with his torment and loss over his slain parents..."

"And his chiroptophobia that led him to become Batman was completely believable. That dark, claustrophobic pit with all of the bats was terrifyingly realistic," Karen added.

"What are those words, Dad?" the girl asked.

"Chiroptophobia is the fear of bats. Claustrophobia is the fear of small places," the man answered.

The three teenagers in front of the women, Spiderman, the Green Lantern, and the Joker received their food, so it was finally their turn. The women ordered, and Karen treated for lunch since Agnes had paid for the cab. With their food trays, they found a small, unoccupied table. As they ate, they perused the program and planned their afternoon, all of their movements through the hall, focusing on the paramount hour of three o'clock when they might meet Captain Jean-Luc Picard.

There was a sudden commotion at the end of the convention center near the *Star Trek* exhibition, and people surged in that direction.

"Do you think he arrived early?" Agnes asked, swiveling in her seat.

"We can't risk missing him!" Karen cried.

The two women jumped to their feet and made a mad dash for the end of the convention hall where a giant inflatable *Starship Enterprise* hung from the rafters.

Chapter 17

Rehab

Either Ramon was going to be a NFL quarterback in his next incarnation, or he owned stock in the NFL Shop, Lindsey decided. Yesterday he'd worn a San Francisco 49ers Joe Montana football jersey, the day before that a Russell Wilson football jersey, and three days ago, the gold and green of #15 Bart Starr. She watched him gaze at his laptop. It was impossible to imagine that the soft-spoken, gentlemanly counselor was once a gun-wielding drug runner for a South American cartel before he did jail time and found Jesus.

She poked her head around Ramon's desk to see what he was watching. His offseason was spent watching NFL Replays. At the moment, the Patriots were beating the Broncos 35 to 17. Tom Brady was hot; Peyton Manning was not.

Ramon smiled warmly. "Turn-overs, chica, turn-overs always determine the game," he said in greeting. "Que pasa?"

"Will you check something out with me? Somebody's been putting some shit in the washing machine, other than laundry soap. The smell's unbearable. I brought this up at Ward Council today, and no one admitted to knowing anything. But everyone agreed that the laundry room stinks to high heaven."

"Of course," he responded agreeably. He rose and they walked the long corridor together.

"If the smell doesn't improve, I'll have to resort to doing all of my laundry by hand-washing it in the sink in my bathroom," she grumbled. "I don't mind buying Tide or something from the hospital store that all of us can use, if we all agree to use it and nothing else."

"Patience, chica," he replied soothingly. "Let's see what the problem is first."

"Patience is not my strong suit." She looked into his kind, thoughtful face. His eyes were large and brown, overhung by bushy eyebrows. He had soft, thinning hair and a perpetual smile that had a pacifying affect on her.

Stepping into the laundry room, he halted abruptly in front of the washers and dryers. "Aye! I see what you mean!" he declared, wincing.

She grimaced. "And the smell's gotten worse since yesterday. What soap or chemical can someone be using that smells so revolting? I've never smelled anything so bad."

"I hear you. Maybe something died under one of the machines" He bent his head behind the machines. "I don't see anything, but there's a lot of dust and lint that needs cleaning out." He dropped to his hands and knees on the cement floor, and sniffed under each machine. "Nada." He rose stiffly and flexed his back.

They remained baffled. The same idea must have occurred to them both, for they looked upward. They noticed it at once. A ceiling panel, near an air duct, had a green stain.

"Gross!" she blurted. "Do you think that sewage is leaking from the toilets upstairs? What's upstairs anyway?"

"The psych ward."

"I thought *this* was the psych ward."

He smiled half-heartedly. "Hold the chair for me. I'll take a look."

She held the metal chair so that it wouldn't collapse. He stepped up gingerly. In her face was the #5 of a blue and white football shirt, made for the brief time when Tim Tebow was a Patriot.

"Someone didn't screw this grate in very tightly. I'm glad this didn't fall on someone's head. Hold these," he said, handing her down the screws. He slid aside the grate and looked into the air duct. His body quickly convulsed and the grate clattered to the floor. "Dios mio!" He jumped off the chair, dashed over to a sink, and heaved up his lunch.

She sprang onto the chair and peered into the darkness. Her eyes flew open wide, and she slammed her hand over her nose and mouth. Her other hand batted away a swarm of flies. Fluids had drained from the entrapped body for days. The skin compressed against the metal ductwork was broken and graveled. In his panic to find a drink, the claustrophobe, Mitch, had crawled into an air duct to escape....

Chapter 18

Rehab

Living on a houseboat made Lindsey acutely aware of seasons and time of day by the subtle shifts in heat or chill, and the reflection and angle of light off the pond. Time was gauged by the pull of the tide and the rocking of the hull under her feet. Once spring arrived, the boat windows remained open, despite wind or rain, until late fall, making the air in the boat persistently wet and salty. When ice rimmed the pond, she would finally shut the windows and turn on space heaters, which warmed the small teak interior within minutes. On the salt pond the rhythms of nature and her brain waves moved in harmony like two superimposed sine waves, but in the rehab time didn't pass in the same way.

Time was measured off by a calendar on Kate's wall, for there were no natural cues by which to determine time's passage. The air-conditioning was always a few degrees too cold and the cinderblock walls impermeable to sunlight. Therefore she went outdoors whenever she was allowed, impatient like a dog wagging its tail for the doors to open. Mitch had sought the outdoors for different reasons.

Every evening, weather permitting, she sat on the same bench at the same picnic table under the same array of stars. She drank the same type of tea and smoked the same brand of cigarettes, wrapping herself in these small rituals in hopes of finding any margin of peace and stability, but nothing felt harmonious after finding him. Some nights she'd try to distract herself with the moths flying frenzied loops around a light over the patio door. Other nights she'd remove her sneakers and roll a pebble around the cement with her toe, imagining the slab to be the beach near the marina.

Invariably, her thoughts returned to Mitch. Of all of the patients on the ward, he'd seemed the one most likely to make it on the outside. He concentrated seriously on the lessons in the Big Book, worked the Twelve Steps with determination and honesty, and shared often at AA meetings. She did none of these things. Her world was unraveled.

Addiction disorders defied all logic. As Kate had told her repeatedly, this was a rehab, not Alcatraz. People admitted themselves voluntarily, to get help, not to suffer some punishment. Had Mitch waited until morning, Kate could have discharged him. He was not a prisoner serving out some undetermined sentence. Yet, in an irrational panic, a man who was terrified of small spaces, climbed into a black tunnel in an attempt to make it to another ward and slip silently into the night, presumably to find a drink. His journey had been a short one. His shoulders became wedged during his desperate crawl forward. Frantic scratch marks cut into the dust and metal of the ductwork. His heart fibrillated and coronary arteries burst. If he had cried for help, his pleas had gone unheard.

She'd witnessed dead bodies before in medical school, as a resident and as a physician, but never one five days putrefied. By then his body cells had ruptured, expelling fluids into the body cavities and pooling in low-lying tissues. Methane and hydrogen sulfide gases had inflated his intestines, his abdomen distended and round like a walrus. His face was bloated beyond recognition. Sulfhemoglobin, produced by the frenzied action of bacteria, had tinted the seeping fluids green. But the worst were the flies; even in the isolated ductwork, the flies had found him. His mottled skin was speckled with clusters of fly eggs, some had already hatched, burrowing maggots feeding under his skin.

To fend off an attack from the enraged insects, she had shoved the grate back into place. Though she'd only seen Mitch's corpse for a few seconds, the image was etched indelibly in her mind. She had leapt from the chair like Ramon. He had still been retching into the sink in the laundry room, so she'd run to the women's bathroom, splashed cold water on her face, and scrubbed her hands and face with soap again and again.

It had taken the forensic team from the coroner's office nearly an hour to extract his body from the ductwork. Mitch's pockets were empty, but tucked into one of his socks were two frayed laces. They were the brown ones from Grandma's scuffed-up shoes.

Lindsey looked skyward, whispering a silent prayer for Mitch, one of many she had already offered to the gods. Where had he hidden the other laces, and the cord from the women's shower room? They were not found on his person, or in his belongings. Why had he only taken Grandma's thin, feeble laces on his journey into the air duct? They never would have held his weight had they been used to lower himself out a window. And why stash the laces in his sock, and not a shirt pocket or sleeve? In an air duct it would have been impossible to reach down to a sock. How did he replace the grate and screw it in behind him? That, too, would have been impossible. He had to have had an accomplice; someone had given him a boost in to the air duct and screwed the grate hurriedly behind him. Maybe one of his buddies, the NRA member, Billy, or the lobsterman, Hank, had helped him to escape? Mitch was an honorable soldier with a drinking problem, not an IV drug user or strangler. So why steal shoelaces? It made no sense.

She repeated her prayer to the stars and let her mind drift. It was a clear night. Constellations, distant fiery worlds slowly presented themselves. What was out there? Gods? Higher Powers? Other life? Yes, there had to be other life out there. She was convinced of it. It was hubris to think that only on Earth had life forms evolved.

How incredible would it be to transport oneself out of the insanity of rehab—if just for a moment—to a distant star! Certainly moving the solid bulk of a human body through time and space would be problematic. It would be more feasible, like in *Star Trek*, to break the body into its atomic components for transport and reassemble them at their destination, say Mars. This would require a comprehensive knowledge of molecular energetics, the breaking and making, of all of the trillions of molecules that compose the body. Before the transportation of the molecules across the galaxy, first the organism should be replicated, copied in some way, in case something went awry during molecular transport through the time-space continuum.

The Bottom Dwellers

Sara's splendid aerial screw on the windowsill of the lab came to mind. Contemporaries of Leonardo da Vinci must have howled in incredulous laughter at the idea of human flight when they saw his designs. Now, five hundred years later, human flight was commonplace. Perhaps five hundred years in the future, human transport in its molecular components would be commonplace. But it all would start with replication. If one could produce an exact copy of an organism, one would understand everything about the bonds that held the organism together. Replication, she was certain, was the first step....

Boston

It was a clear starry night when Karen emerged from the convention center. Although Patrick Stewart had never appeared, she and Agnes had sprinted to the *Star Trek* exhibition just in time to hear speeches by the new Uhura, Mr. Spock, and Scotty about the upcoming *Star Trek* movie. This was followed by a movie trailer projected on an enormous screen that reached to the ceiling of the convention center. There they were approached by two fearsome Klingons, colleagues from the Physics Department, and all together they spent the rest of the afternoon wandering the displays.

At the *World of Warcraft* exhibition, Karen had bought herself a new T-shirt that she could not wait to wear; she pulled it over her toga on-the-spot. The Klingons were also in *World of Warcraft* Guilds and described their experiences in the Labyrinth of Parnak. She had listened with rapt fascination, as the Labyrinth was the next challenge for the Centurions. A few Centurions were milling around the

WarCraft, booths so they took photos together in assorted heroic poses. BladeSlinger told her that there was to be a strategy session to prepare for the Labyrinth that same night in the Guild Hall chat room.

"I'll be there!" she had told him. "Two Klingons just gave me invaluable information about Parnak, which will certainly decrease the number of Centurion casualties." She checked the time on her cell phone. "Where has the time gone?"

It was nearly closing time; vendors were closing down their booths. Karen had left her Centurions friends and caught up with Agnes and the Klingons. As they had strolled through the emptying convention center, they'd run into other acquaintances, Wonder Woman and Obi-Wan Kenobi, who were going back to Cambridge for drinks.

"I'm up for bar-hopping," said one of the Klingons.

"Let's drink at a place where we can dance," Agnes suggested. "How about you, Karen?"

Karen had mulled it over for a minute. There were a few bars in Cambridge were they could go dancing in cosplay without being thought of as odd, but she had done far too much dancing recently, as all of her sorority sisters seemed to be getting married. Plus, it was imperative to be involved in the Guild discussion that night.

Karen's mind was made up. "I'm going to pass. I'll see you all at work next week."

"Alright," Agnes had replied. "Be safe and go right home."

"I will," she answered. "Same time next year?"

"Same time next year," Agnes agreed.

The two women had hugged. Agnes's party had headed toward the *Star Wars* exhibition to pick up some Ewoks that would be joining them, while Karen had stepped into the humid summer night.

The Bottom Dwellers

Despite the lights of the city, the stars visible between the buildings were unusually bright. She momentarily imagined the airspace above the cabs, cars, and street lamps filled with space cruisers zipping by at dizzying speeds. "I was born centuries too early," she lamented. Her attention returned to street level. At the curb, a short queue had formed, people waiting for taxis. She moved to a place at the end of the line. Two parents, Batman and Poison Ivy, with their sons, Robin and the Riddler, got into the first cab. Some minutes passed before another taxi appeared, so she decided to review her photos from the convention. The resolution of the photos on her new 5G smartphone was amazing, and she immediately posted a few to Facebook. A couple dressed as Smurfs climbed into the next cab that appeared. Only she and two snickering teenagers, the Mighty Thor and Ironman, remained on the sidewalk.

Suddenly Thor turned. His hammer, Mjolnir, hovered threateningly over her head. He knocked the cat ears off her head and they tumbled onto the cement.

"Why'd you do that?" she asked, stunned.

"Your Cat Woman costume sucks," Thor sneered.

"I'm not the Cat Woman! I'm my avatar from the *World of Warcraft*," she said indignantly. She felt a sudden tug at her backpack and clinched her arms across her chest.

"Give me your backpack," Ironman ordered from behind.

"No way, you dolts! My office work is in there."

"Dolt?" Thor laughed. "What's a dolt?" he inquired to Ironman.

"Who knows," Ironman said dimly.

"There's nothing in my backpack that would interest you. It's just my office work."

"Let me have a look." Ironman tugged again. "You're pissing me off, Cat."

"No! Get lost!" She arms remained locked across her chest, while her knees jittered.

"Give me the pack, or you get hurt," Ironman warned.

Thor's Mjolnir remained menacingly over her head. "Ironman's serious," he whispered fiercely. "And I'll bash your skull in if you don't hand it over."

Her muscles quivered and she blinked sweat out of her eyes. Down the sidewalk were some pedestrians. If she screamed out loud, would they help her, or would they think them acting out some scene from a comic book? Would Thor have split her head open by the time they arrived?

"The backpack, bitch!" Thor ordered.

Her academic work, patents, manuscripts in progress, data, and professional correspondences were all on that mini travel laptop! Her wallet contained about fifty dollars in cash, her credit credits, and her driver's license! And her condo keys! Would these jerks really kill her just for a backpack? Then Ironman's hands grasped her throat, her knees gave way, and all went black.

Woods Hole, a year earlier

Lindsey wandered down the bike trail, deciding to grab dinner in the village, as the refrigerator on the houseboat was empty except for a case of Belgian beer. Memories of Duncan's last visit wove through her thoughts. Why was he so determined to talk about money all of a sudden? That's why they had separate bank accounts and each paid their own bills. They didn't even live together anymore, she had argued, so why did they have to discuss money?

The Bottom Dwellers

It had been her plan to spend the afternoon on the beach with an ice-cold six-pack, not sit with financial records spread across her galley table when it was eighty-five degrees out, with no clouds in the sky, and a lovely onshore breeze blowing across the pond.

Duncan had perused her bank statements, copied down account numbers, and explained, "In case something happens to one of us, it's important for us to have access to the other's accounts. I'm doing so much traveling now, baby. If my plane went down, I want *you* and *not* the State to inherit my funds. It's not a lot, but it's something."

"I really don't want to talk about this," she had whined.

"Financial and estate planning are part of being a responsible adult, Lin."

Through the window of the houseboat, she had noticed that the pond was a shimmering green. Children were tossing bread crumbs to mallards near the boat ramp. "Well, I guess I'm not one. I just want to swim."

"The accountant, Lin, did you ever see him about the BioCorp money?"

"Yes, finally," she had sighed with disinterest. She grabbed a bottle of sunscreen off a bookshelf.

"What did he do with it?" he'd inquired.

She had put her leg up on the edge of a chair and spread the lotion up her calf and thigh. "Most is invested." She added tiredly, "But some is still liquid."

"Why? It won't make money that way!"

"It's my rainy day fund. I want it available. In case I want to buy another sailboat since the *Naughty Nymph* got torn up on the shoals." She looked through the window; the identical heads of Rob and Danny, towels slung around their shoulders, bobbed through the marsh on their way to the beach. "Can we swim now? Your name's also on the goddamn accounts should I die of a cirrhotic liver tomorrow. Don't worry about it."

"That's not what I meant! Some day we're going to live together again, like a normal couple, like man and wife in the same house, have a big family, retire together." His tone had sweetened. "Honey, we need to plan for these things."

The next day they had fought like savages—about what she didn't remember—in furious whispers so as not to disturb her neighbors. As Duncan left, she told him to get lost for good, but he said he'd be back soon.

During her walk toward the village, she was uncomfortably aware that she hadn't been laid in a while. But, she smiled to herself, her favorite playmate was in town; he would expertly handle her needs, and exorcise that horrid husband from her thoughts. Just as soon as the Orioles game was over.

At the moment she had the perfect buzz. Brilliant purchase, that home breathalyzer! Using herself as a human guinea pig, she had found in a series of experiments the specific blood alcohol content (BAC) where her shakes were silenced, headaches suppressed, there was no slurring of her voice, and yet where she maintained optimal mental acuity. Her maximal performance zone was between a BAC of 0.04 and 0.06%. It became the BAC she strove for each morning before leaving for work and then re-set at lunchtime with a hip flask. That evening, just before heading into the village the device read that she had a BAC of 0.055%. Perfect!

The sidewalk in the village was jammed with residents, summer scientists, children, dogs, and tourists. She threaded her way through the bodies on the sidewalk and entered a convenience store where she bought mints and gum. Next to the store was her home away from home. Large letters spelling Captain Kidd boldly proclaimed the bar's endurance and centrality in the life of the small village. Two carved fish swam on either side of the gold sign while red and green running lights gleamed over the front door. In any weather, foul or fair, she could leave the lab and look down Water Street to these welcoming beacons. A compass rose embedded in the sidewalk at the entrance guided her in. She stepped on it and pushed through the screen door.

Rows of red Coast Guard life preservers, ship wheels, old photographs and shark jaws decorated the dark wood walls. A colorful mural of Blackbeard and his pirates spanned the longest wall behind the barrel tables and chairs. Legend had it that Blackbeard's treasure was buried somewhere on the Cape; she was certain that it was on a place like Devil's Foot or Ram Island in Great Harbor. When collecting shells out on these islands she kept a hopeful eye out for pirate artifacts. She was sure that spirits of these pirates haunted the Kidd, especially after she knocked back a few. The air was rich with smoke, the tipsy banter of students, jukebox music, and clinks of plates from the adjacent restaurant, but her ears strained to filter through the din to find the voices of the sports commentators from ESPN.

On the TV screen, pitchers relaxed their arms while the umpires chatted behind home plate. Her throne was available, an omen that it was going to be a very good night. A few regulars were already slumped into their seats nodded their greetings.

This was Game One of a three game series between the Orioles and the Evil Empire, the New York Yankees. A knuckle-ball pitcher, Scott Michaels, was starting for the Birds. He was pitted against Eric Jones of the Yankees, whose fastball was often clocked at one hundred and two miles an hour. Both teams were still tied for first place in the pennant race, so this series was critical.

"What's it going to be, Lin?" asked Chris, the bartender.

"Scotch, beer, scotch, beer until I fall off the barstool," she kidded.

He frowned, not amused. "I don't know how you make it home some nights."

"I don't go home. I stop at an AA meeting. Can't you see how well the meetings are working?"

He pushed her usual across the polished wood. "That's not funny," he answered seriously. "Are things bad in the lab?"

"A minor setback, but hey, fuck it. All I want to see is the Spankees get spanked. From the warm-up it looks like Jones might still have an inflamed rotator cuff." She quaffed down half her scotch and squinted at the screen.

"Who's he?"

"The Yankee pitcher. I think he's still hurt. They brought him back way too soon."

She felt her long hair being lifted, so she swiveled the barstool and into the enchanting grin of a beautiful man with long dreadlocks.

"How's my favorite artist?" she asked coyly.

"Great now," the man answered in his low Jamaican accent. He lowered his face and pressed his warm lips onto her shoulder.

"Frigging magnet," Chris muttered.

"Pheromones, baby, potent chick pheromones," she replied humorously.

"Whatever," Chris said, moving to the far end of the bar.

The Bottom Dwellers

She held up her hand to her friend, Rodney, their eyes watching the locked fingers, alternating thick mocha and slender white.

"What are your plans for the night?" he inquired.

"I'm watching the game. Then spending time with you. I've been waiting just for you."

He laughed. "You're such a lovely liar. Do you want to slip off for a little while now?"

"If I leave now, you know I won't be back this evening. I'm not missing a second of this game. Meet me in two hours?" She ran her finger slowly from his neck, down his chest, belly and slowly traced the metal grooves on his belt buckle. "I'll make it worth the wait."

"You always do. I have something for you."

"I know you do."

"Besides that. In my pocket."

Her eyes sparkled with interest. "Front or back?"

"Front."

"Of course. Left or right?"

"Left, but you can check both if you like."

She slipped a small rectangle of paper from his jeans, an unlimited pass to the film festival.

"Thank you." She pulled him down for a kiss. "Do I get to sit in the projection booth again this year?"

"I'm counting on it." Rodney glanced with boredom at the TV screen. "I'll be in and out of the bar tonight. I'll look for you later." He knocked a cigarette out of his pack, and then offered her one.

She accepted, but had no matches. "Light me up."

"I will later." He pulled a lighter from his jeans. Her face glowed orange as she leaned toward the flame.

The Orioles choked in the eighth inning, giving up three runs and losing 6 to 4. Rodney faithfully reappeared in the Kidd. They drove in a Mustang convertible to a crowded bar in Mashpee where they danced on a sticky dance floor. Later they stepped outside to cool off.

Across the street was a small ice cream shop with assorted picnic tables scattered around a grassy field. They walked into the blackness, out of the glare of the lights and neon of the bar. Another couple had already claimed a dark corner of grass; the woman was truly enjoying her partner, or was skilled at faking it. Her gasps and groans whipped Lindsey's passion into a tornado. She tugged Rodney toward a dark grove of pine trees and they fell onto a soft mat of pine needles.

After, the Mustang skidded to a stop in the parking lot of Dave's Marina. She slipped on her sandals and extracted herself from the low bucket seat. She smoothed down her leather skirt, but wouldn't attempt to fix her shirttails. One was tucked in, one was out... no big deal. She was going straight to the shower anyway, and then collapse into bed. There was a lot to do in the lab the next day, as some colleagues would be visiting from Yale to look at a new electrode that she and Sara had constructed.

She leaned over the driver's side door and pressed her mouth onto Rodney's for one last kiss.

"Same time next year?" he asked hopefully.

"Same time," she whispered softly.

The convertible roared off toward the highway. Rodney was an independent filmmaker who helped coordinate the film festival. For a few days each summer they had a perfect romance.

The Bottom Dwellers

It was a lovely cloudless night. Nocturnal insects sang in the marsh across the pond. The only lights on around the marina were from Dave's storefront and the string of plastic party lights that outlined the *Green Monster*. Rob was on his stern with that same older guy who often visited, the white-haired man that drove a silver Jaguar. The two men sat on lawn chairs, talking quietly and smoking cigars. She strolled down the dock, wondering what amusing comment Rob would make about the Orioles' humiliating defeat that evening.

"Good evening gentlemen," she said slowly, hoping that her voice didn't sound too slurred.

"Hi, Lin," Rob answered tonelessly.

Though she waited expectantly, the O's jibe was not forthcoming. In fact, his face appeared solemn. Both men stared at her for a second, causing her quick, self-conscientious glance down her front. To her relief her blouse was buttoned and her skirt was zipped and almost straight. Maybe there were pine needles in her hair? His eyes darted briefly toward her boat. Her steps on the planks faltered.

A large, seething body was hunched on her deck. A duffel bag was at his feet. Duncan rose from a shadow. She fumbled quickly for the keys in her purse, though she wanted to escape into the marsh grass to hide. Sleeping with mosquitoes and ticks would be preferable to this. She stepped bravely onto the aft deck, a telltale cloud of whiskey and sex wafting off her. He moved uncomfortably close.

"Here's my fragrant flower," he whispered furiously.

Where were her goddamn keys! Her hand clawed through her purse, its jingle faint amidst the debris. Finally she felt the metal ring.

"You've been hard to reach," he continued.

"I've been working hard," she replied without looking up. The quivering key finally found the lock.

His insane gaze seared through her silky blouse. "Working hard at what?"

Rob and the man with the Jaguar stared holes in their shoes while Duncan's hand manacled her wrist and pulled her through the door. She prepared herself to fulfill a certain marital obligation.

Boston

Mr. O'Leary, the maintenance man, jiggled his master key into the door lock while Karen sobbed. "...When I regained consciousness, Thor and Ironman were tearing down the sideway with my backpack. I screamed at them to stop and started after them. I stumbled and scraped my knees on the sidewalk..."

It was too painful to continue. By the time she had hobbled to the street corner, whimpering in pain, Thor and Ironman had vanished. Limping back to the front of the convention center, she had recovered her smartphone, slipper, and cat ears and called 911. She was collapsed in a shaking heap on the curb when a police officer lumbered by and took her report. She could barely tell the cop what the perpetrators looked like.

"Ironman's head was concealed by a silver helmet, and much of Thor's face was hidden by a thick blonde wig," she had explained, weeping. "They were two white teenage boys." That was as specific as she could get.

"This is the sixth backpack or computer theft report that I've had to fill out today at this gaming convention," the cop had griped.

He had hailed her a cab and sent her on her way.

Mr. O'Leary pushed open the door to Karen's condo, glancing curiously again at her Diana toga. "I'll change your lock tomorrow, but I'll have to bill you for it."

"Whatever, fine," she sniffled, closing the door quickly.

She dashed toward the bathroom, ripped down her underwear, and urinated with relief. She had nearly peed herself when Thor's hammer hovered menacingly over her.

At her full-length mirror, she stood aghast. Her Diana costume was in ruins! Her mother would need to sew her a new toga gown before the next Comic Con... where she would *not* take her backpack.

Puss-N-Boots anxiously followed her to the kitchen, as dinner was hours late. She opened two cans of Salmon Fiesta and scraped them into the blue and pink bowls.

"Boots," she asked, "where's Willow?"

She searched the living room and found Pussy Willow stretched listlessly on the sofa. She carried the cat back to the kitchen and placed her by the pink bowl. Pussy Willow sniffed the food in disinterest and slowly wandered away.

"That's how I feel, too, Willow," she admitted sadly. "Too horrible to eat. You're so sweet. You feel my pain. We're indeed empaths." She blew her nose into a tissue. "It's going to be a long night with a thousand things to do. Something strong is required." She opened the refrigerator and, instead of a Cherry Coke, she pulled out a Red Bull.

The first order of business was to cancel the credit card and order a new one. She talked to a pleasant woman in Delaware. In the few hours since the theft, the only fraudulent charges made were at a Subway sandwich shop; the credit card was then confiscated at a liquor store when the under-age teenagers attempted to buy beer. The boys had escaped from the store before they could be apprehended. She checked the time. If she hurried, she might be able to catch some of the conversation in the Guild chat room. The computer booted while she took a quick shower and bandaged up her sore knees.

The Centurions were still discussing the Labyrinth when she logged on.

"Two Klingons at Comic Con," she explained, "warned me about deadly spikes that shoot up from the floor, snakes that slither from large urns, and dead-end tunnels where fierce ogres lurk." Her nerves still sputtered; out-of-the-blue she blurted, "Two dolts at Comic Con stole my backpack! My whole life was in my laptop!"

"That shit happens all the time there. My nephew had his backpack taken at a convention in New Jersey last spring," JewelMaster mentioned matter-of-factly.

"You took your laptop to a Comic Con?" Manson72 asked, astounded. "The hall is full of cyber thieves. Diana, are you a complete fool?"

"I guess I am," she admitted.

"Can we stay on task?" Odin18 chimed in irritably. "It's getting late. Some of us have to work tomorrow."

Tears flowed down Karen's cheeks again, and she clicked her microphone onto mute. She had expected, at least, some words of kindness and sympathy. Instead her Guild members had responded with callousness and indifference.

She logged off, grabbed a box of tissues, and dropped onto her bed. Despite the extra caffeine in the energy drink, she was exhausted. There were so many things still to do... get a new driver's license... contact Sara Kauni... check the armory... all could wait until tomorrow... for now just sleep...

Chapter 19

Rehab

The thirty-day program was more than half over. In a step meeting that morning, Lindsey's group had revisited *Step One: We admitted we were powerless over alcohol— that our loves had become unmanageable.* That was the single step that she had mastered; there was no doubt at all that alcohol dominated every aspect of her life. Through the orderly schedule of the rehab, some manageability, if only psychological, was slowly being restored. How could this sense of manageability be transferred to her life back in Woods Hole? How many bridges were burned? How many amends would she need to make? And she still couldn't remember a goddamn thing! Her panicky internal monologue over her uncertain future was interrupted when Kelly dropped down next to her at a picnic table and lit a cigarette.

"What's up?" Lindsey asked.

"Nothing," Kelly moped.

Before Larry had checked out that morning, he had been involved in the farewell ritual, an exchange of hugs, kisses, good lucks, and phone numbers that probably would never be called. Kelly had milled around the fringe of Larry's well-wishers, as if he was nothing more than a casual acquaintance. But during their brief affair, their souls had touched.

"He was a good man, Lin, really good," Kelly confided with a tone of closure.

Larry's court date was the next day. He had entered the program on the advice of his lawyer, since stays in rehab often got the jail time reduced. He had sold crack to an undercover cop and was looking at a long sentence, especially since that had been a second arrest. His teenage son had sold drugs with him out of the back of his girlfriend's wig and nail salon. Last fall his son had been killed by a rival dealer. The boy had been sixteen, Kelly's age. The price of this disease was too high. Lindsey's inappropriate sarcasm and giddiness of early recovery had given way to an intractable sense of unfairness and melancholia.

Melissa poked her head out the door. "South Park's on."

Kelly's cigarette hissed into a soda can on the table and she popped off the bench. "Later, Lin."

Within minutes of Larry's departure that morning the men were circling the teenager like sharks. Kelly was simply too beautiful; that was her burden.

An hour after a nurse had changed the sheets on Larry's bed, Bart, a tattoo artist, was moved over from detox. That evening he joined Lindsey at the picnic table where they watched men dart around the basketball court like bugs under a lamp. The insurance scammer, Vince, and the lawyer, Ted, watched the game with them for a while, before they wandered off to the fence. The two men conversed there nightly, whispering conspiratorially in the shadows. Both were about forty and, regardless of disparate backgrounds, oddly inseparable. Perhaps they had money interests in common. Despite Vince's amusing jokes and slick come-ons, she made it a point to keep her distance from him, and since their poker game that first night in rehab, Ted had made it a point to keep his distance from her. He complained vehemently to the staff about not being able to access email, Twitter, or Facebook. Ted at #addictedtosocialmedia.

Fireflies flickered on and off, signaling for mates. "Bioluminescent animals are the coolest," she commented. "A lot of people confuse bioluminescence with fluorescence, but they're actually two different things. In bioluminescence, the light is produced by a chemical reaction using luciferin and the enzyme luciferase. But in fluorescence, a source of light knocks an electron to a higher energy state, and when it returns to its lower energy state, a photon of light is emitted. Have you ever given anyone a tattoo of fireflies in a night sky?"

"No," he replied.

"Maybe you could design one for me?" she said, though definitely not meaning it.

"I won't be doing tattoos for a while," he mumbled quietly. "Do you want to see the one on my back?"

"Sure."

He tugged his t-shirt over his head, the movement catching the attention of Trisha and Sharon playing backgammon at the next picnic table.

"I got this one for my wife. I met her in Japan."

He turned toward the light over the patio door. Across his back was a dream-like depiction of a Japanese seaside village. Purple fog enveloped the mountains in the background. Tiny houses lined the shoreline. Junks and small fishing boats floated in swirling, mystical water. An insane urge to swim overtook her; she hadn't swum for weeks.

"My business partner designed it for me," he said.

His comment struck a chord and she wondered why there'd be no word from Sara. Sara had to have received the email sent from Kate's laptop; Sara had to know she was in rehab, not off on some endless bender.

Her focus returned to the tattoo. "That's the most enchanting place I've ever seen. I want to live there. I've never been anywhere. I'd love to travel one day." She outlined the sails of the junks boats with her finger. After a moment, Bart pulled on his T-shirt and sat down again.

"My wife ran off with my partner and took my two-year old son," he said despairingly.

Children... a terrifying thought. She silently thanked her Higher Power that she had no children, had left no innocents floundering in her drunken wake. She scanned the garden of misfits, many of whom were parents... another terrifying prospect.

The relationships formed between these misfits... these addicts... were unnatural compared to the outside world— intensely personally, volatile, vocal, physical, and short-lived. The patients quickly learned each other's defects of character. "He's a liar... rapist... pedophile. She's a thief... sadist... manipulator." They became non-judgmental and desensitized to the collective sins, for each of them was guilty of something. Their common bond was that their actions were chemically-induced, by fluids, powders or fumes, and administered by syringe, pipe, bottle, pill, lines, or aerosol can. Chemical addictions often exacerbated other addictions:

to sex, food, work, gambling, smoking, shopping, violence and social media. Dream it, and they were addicted to it.

"My using drove her off!" Bart bent his face into his hands and wept.

A quick stab of pain was felt behind her eyes, but no tears would come. That much she knew. Not one goddamn tear had flowed from her eyes since that bloody accident, when everything broke. She wordlessly draped her arm over his shuddering shoulders; no words could console him. As tiny specks of light burst over the dark lawn, she wondered if her tears would ever become unblocked.

Boston

Puss-N-Boots' purring woke Karen in the middle of the night. She found him pressed against her belly, having nestled into the pink flannel of her nightgown. Her head still ached from yesterday's trauma, and her thoughts were still fizzy and surreal. She was in shock. Her driver's license listed her condo address, and the teenager robbers had her car and house keys, a thought that stirred panic in her once again. Though hers was a gated condo community with a guard at the front entrance, she listened in the darkness for any unusual movements. The only sounds she heard were the quiet murmur of cool air blowing through the vents in the ceiling and an occasional car passing in the street below.

She reached for her cell phone. It was 4:05 am. There was a voice mail from her mother reporting that Cousin Betsy in Idaho was getting married. She moaned aloud... another wedding. Her mother's voice asked that she go to a tailor in Boston to get her measurements taken so that a dress could be altered for her. "Wonderful news, Karen! You're to be in the wedding party!"

She cursed. Another onerous task, like getting a new driver's license, which would take her from work. Her closet was bursting with frilly bridesmaid dresses that each perky bride had cheerfully said, "You'll definitely be able to wear this to other functions." She was an engineering professor... to what function could she possibly wear a floor-length lime-colored gown with fuchsia ribbons streaming down the back?

Too wired to sleep, she rose to go to the bathroom. The red marks on her neck from Ironman's grasp were gone. Thankfully, no bruises had formed that would require explaining to curious colleagues or graduate students. She just wanted to put the whole dreadful event behind her. Puss-N-Boots followed her into the bathroom and rubbed against her while she brushed her teeth.

"No Boots, it's too early for breakfast. Where's your girlfriend?"

Likely Pussy Willow had found a quiet place to sleep, in the laundry basket, or perhaps behind her snow boots in the coat closet, away from Boots' pestering.

"Oh my god, Boots, in all of the chaos of last night, I forgot to check the armory," she said, scurrying to her office.

She sat down in her new ergonomic computer chair and logged into the Guild's website. Where in the U.S. was Conqueror right now? Was he on his return route from his lumber run to the Pacific Northwest? She typed in the secret password to open the armory. The Guild of Centurion had very generous members, so the armory had amassed enough weaponry for a small army. Every year she donated her entire tax return, the equivalent of several thousands of dollars, to supply the armory with broadswords, battleaxes, bows and arrows, armor, shields, magic staffs, and potions. She clicked on the keyboard to inspect the armory's vast inventory.

Something was wrong. Had she typed in a wrong password and opened the armory of another Guild? She exited the site, and retyped the password very slowly to insure that she hit each key correctly. She stared at the monitor for some time, sweat forming across her nose.

"It's just a software glitch," she said to calm herself. She refreshed the page a few times, and then shut down the entire computer. She allowed it to reboot. The armory site was opened again. The same terrifying image appeared on the monitor! She swiped the sleeve of her nighty across her forehead. *War of Warcraft* was an online game, played around the world 24-7. Surely there was a 24-hour help desk. She clicked into a search engine and found the link for the help desk.

"Yes," the site manager told her, "the armory was accessed earlier this morning at 12:48 am." Karen's heart bounced wildly in her chest. She opened the armory again.

Not even one arrow or single potion was left on the armory's stone floor! On her watch the armory of the Centurions had been looted!

Detox

Maggie shuddered in her sleep... *she writhed under a rain of glass and blood, amidst feminine shrieks, brain spattered against a kitchen door, a shovel clanked to a floor, two living dead shrouded in tarps and horse blankets trudged through a Minnesota blizzard.* She shuddered again and awoke like every morning after that nightmare, shaky and distraught. The instant before opening her eyes, it registered... this was not her tarp. She was sure of it. These were sheets... that felt clean and smooth... whereas her tarp was tattered and sandy. Nor did this room smell like a garbage-filled shithole, a muddy storm drain or humid woods, but instead of floor wax and disinfectant. Where had she passed out this time? Twice in the last few weeks she had woken in some unknown place, or was it three times? Maggie opened her eyes.

Chapter 20

Rehab

Ellen, like Grandma, snored. Lindsey glanced at the clock. It was 4:05 am. She slipped from under the covers and walked to the window. On most nights she could sleep through the snoring, but that goddamn, unnerving conversation with Kate kept her awake.

The counseling session had started on a positive note. When she'd entered the psychologist's office, Kate had said, "You're starting to look like a healthy woman. You have color in your cheeks and your eyes aren't bloodshot anymore."

"Amazing, the resiliency of the human body, after all the abuse we put it though," she had replied ironically.

"Very true. How do you feeling today?" Kate had asked, lighting a cigarette.

"The cravings for a drink have pretty much gone away." Lindsey had presented her splayed fingers. "But look at that. I still have bad DTs. And I feel anxious and inexplicably alone. I'm the ultimate loner. I hate people. Why am I feeling lonely?"

"Humans are social animals. You're reconnecting." A cellphone buzzed on the windowsill and Kate glanced at the screen. She sighed in disappointment. "I thought it might be Myra. She still hasn't shown up at her Aftercare meetings, returned to her job at the airlines, or responded to any of my phone calls or emails. It's not a good sign. But I did get a text from Marcus this morning. He's doing well and has found lots of meetings. He's walking the walk."

"Maybe that's why I feel so lonely. I'm missing Marcus. I've become addicted to the endorphin rush during the dance lessons."

"By the way, I ran into the nurse that you screamed at outside the ER. After you left, she went back outside to finish her cigarette. The man that brought you here got into a beat-up black Trans Am. Do you know anyone who drives a Trans Am?"

She had shaken her head, baffled.

"He got into the passenger's seat of the car. He and the driver spoke Spanish to one another," Kate added. "Do you know any Hispanic men?"

"Only Ramon, and Dr. Ramirez at the lab. But I barely know them." She had paused, worriedly. "I have no idea who these men were! I can't leave here! The outside world's too dangerous. I won't be able to cope. I've become an institutional creature, accustomed to eating shit for food and dealing with maniacs on a daily basis. Perhaps you need an on-site assistant—one who would never leave?"

"Believe me, I don't," the psychologist had answered firmly.

"My Jeep will stop at the closest package store to the clinic!"

"People stop at package stores, people make bad decisions; cars do not. You're anthropomorphizing."

"Perhaps I could stay on as a tutor to the patients that are students? I'm already helping Dana with her chemistry course. And I've been discussing literature with Melissa, our poetess-in-residence. I tried to convince her that Robert Frost's *The Road Not Taken* is an argument for non-conformity and therefore a Goth poem."

"And what did she say?"

"That every time I open my mouth, her bullshit meter goes off-scale."

Kate had smiled. "That's about right."

"And I've been assisting Kelly with her summer school course in biology. I helped her solve some genetics problems last night."

"Alcoholism and other addiction disorders have a genetic component," Kate had said. "I don't remember any family function where my father or uncles were not shit-faced and did not throw furniture or fists at each other."

"Don't I know it," she had agreed grimly. "That's how I developed such quick reflexes. From ducking objects my mother hurled at my father after evening cocktails. One big happy family."

Lindsey had smoked silently at Kate's windowsill, contemplating the disease. Alcoholism ran in the Nolan ancestry since before recorded history, she had figured. The mutant genes probably appeared thousand years ago in some Mesolithic relative who'd become too fond of their berry brew. So emerged the Irish Virus somewhere in County Antrim. In the recent temporal scheme of things, she was the result of two lethal bloodlines that never should have mixed almost three decades before in Annapolis, Maryland. At the moment of conception, the fusion of one defective spermatozoa with one defective ovum, somewhere in the ciliated tunnel of Miriam Nolan's fallopian tube, the defective daughter was programmed to be a walking time-bomb, with no prayer for a normal life.

"Are you sure you can't remember any boyfriends who own a Trans Am?" Kate had asked.

Lindsey turned and glanced at the digital clock. It was 4:08. Hours later, the question still plagued her. Boyfriends, plural. The implication was not lost of her. During the blackout, had she slept with *two* Boat Show men?

Boston

Karen paced her home office for some time, hyperventilating and weeping. The inventory and password were in her laptop; the vast weapons hoard from the Centurion armory was now the property of two teenage thugs! The Centurions could not, under any circumstances, find out about the theft! Especially Conqueror, who had entrusted her with this important task! If they found out, she'd be unwelcome on the journey through the Labyrinth, at the online Guild banquet next month, or future Comic Cons. Her virtual life was virtually over!

But what to do? She leaned against the windowsill. The sun was just beginning to rise over Boston Harbor. The value of the armory she guessed to be around twenty thousand dollars. Where to get this sum of money? Her cash reserve had been used for the down payment on the condo. No way could she borrow the money from her father. He was a retired shoe salesman in Wichita; her mother, a homemaker. Her parents were barely getting by on social security checks.

And her father complained endlessly that she spent too much time online, when, in his words, "she should be looking for a husband." Her older sister had just been laid off from her job at a pharmaceutical company, and her handsome brother, a wanna-be-actor, was waiting tables in Los Angeles. And worse, she would not have a new credit card for days. By then Conqueror would be back in Florida... yes, her life was definitely over.

Wait—there was that American Express card that she used when she travelled to Europe, since many places abroad didn't accept VISA. She rushed to her desk. Oh, thank god! The credit card was in an envelope with her passport. One small thing was finally going right.

She dropped into her computer chair and created a new password for the armory with the site manager. A spreadsheet of the armory's inventory was printed out on her printer. She entered the virtual marketplace with dread. Christ! The broadswords of Eryx totaled four hundred dollars! Her finger hesitated over the keyboard. BUY. The healing potions were fifty dollars each and the armory had had six of them! In growing despair, she pushed BUY again. What!... the rare Shields of Zeus were eighty dollars apiece! There was no choice... BUY. She moved systemically down the spreadsheet, checking off each purchased item. BUY, BUY, BUY...

After two hours the armory was restocked, just as before. The trashcan next to her computer table was filled with soggy tissues; her nose was red and chafed. The Centurions would never know of the tragic misfortune at the armory. Exhausted, she collapsed into bed. Though it would take her forever to pay off the massive credit card debt, plus 18% interest, she fell asleep certain in her knowledge that she remained a trusted and respected member of the Guild of Centurion.

Woods Hole

The 4th of July fell on a visitation day, so the rehab was packed with friends and family. Lindsey spent the afternoon by herself in the reading room, refining the design for the handprint-sensitive doorknob. Last year on the 4th she had stood with her colleagues on the front lawn of her laboratory building. She and Sara had chatted with their boss, Mort Somers, and his wife, Ella while Zephyr wrestled in the grass with some small boys. Mort had asked her if she had spoken recently to Anne Davids and inquired about Julius' hip replacement surgery. Anne had been Mort's first PhD student when he was a young faculty member at Princeton. As Anne's student, Lindsey was in essence Mort's academic granddaughter....

Across the street in Waterfront Park, Danny was balance-walking along the back of a park bench while Rob held his hand. She and Rob exchanged a brief nod of recognition with one another, and then he turned back to some conversation with his sister and brother-in-law. Sara's comment about the resistivity of a new electrode under design drew her attention away from Rob's red, white and blue Uncle Sam hat. As the parade approached, Sara hoisted Zephyr atop her shoulders.

The parade floated down Water Street amidst notes of patriotic music. Kids from the Children's School of Science marched with their collecting nets and banners; children from the marine lab's summer camp wore lobster hats; grad students in grass skirts danced the hula; DNA splicers, the

"Splice Girls" pranced in drag; the Embryology students in three different colored t-shirts sang "2, 4, 6, 8, everybody gastrulate!" then arranged themselves into the different germs layers of a gastrula. Enormous jellyfish made out of clear plastic tarps undulated down the road. Bikes, wagons, strollers and cars were transformed into huge crabs, fish, or lobsters. It was a parade of quirky science humor, Woods Hole-style....

Instead of parade music, voices from families in the Fishbowl drifted into the reading room. To mute the sound, Lindsey readjusted her headphones and turned up her music, the blues. Her doorknob prototype was coming along well, except for a lack of certain key components that would need constructing in a machine shop. It was quite simple in design, and she was surprised that no one had come up with it sooner. All that was needed was one's handprint to be scanned. The prints would be sent to a tiny memory in the doorknob. The doorknob would have the capacity to memorize, in this first model, the handprints of ten individuals. The electronic eye built into the knob would read the ridges composing the handprint, and then release the locking mechanism if they matched. Her former engineering professor at Hopkins, who helped negotiate the deal with BioCorp, might point her to a company interested in her doorknob design. Sara could work out some refinements so she had a hand in its development, since everything they created was a fifty-fifty split. Thinking about Sara, she began remembering again.

After the Woods Hole parade last year, she had gone to a post-doc's barbecue with Sara and Zephyr. A keg floating in a tub of ice on a hot summer afternoon had been a glorious sight. She could still drink safely and controlled then, strictly limiting herself to three cups over the course of the afternoon; by Christmas time, however, that ability was gone. She would not permit herself to go to holiday parties, so she stayed at home in a solitary stupor....

After the barbecue, she pedaled back to the marina to spot Danny, Brianna, and Max doing cannonballs off the dock. Rob, in cooking mitts, turned shish kabobs for his sister's family. As she pushed her bike down the dock, he invited her to join them, but she politely declined and went inside to check her email. She and Duncan always made it a point to spend holidays together, but that year they had missed Christmas, her birthday, and now the 4th of July. He had more business in Scotland. No emails from him, she poured herself a large scotch, took a shower, and then retreated into the dark hole of her cabin to doze.

Laughter and splashes woke her sometime later. She had another scotch and wandered outside into the warm air to see Danny balancing precariously on the bow railing.

"Lin, watch my new trick!" he called.

Danny leaned forward, tucked his body into a ball, and flipped into the water. As his grinning face broke through the surface, she clapped and yelled down to him. "The Olympic judges award you straight 10s."

He beamed and climbed onto the boat.

Rob strode along the gunwale. "That is nothing, peewee," he said teasingly to his son. His Uncle Sam hat dropped onto a cleat. He strutted to the bow and stood balancing backwards on the railing, his arms straight out in front of him.

"Don't do this," she warned nervously.

Rob hesitated for dramatic effect. Then he flung himself backward, coiled in a ball. He spun, arms and legs sprawled outward in formless disarray, but he hit the water precisely.

"The judges award you 3s," she called down to him as he came up for air.

"3s?" he answered, astonished.

Danny bounced on his toes at her decision. "Dan, he's not in your league," she added.

"I heard that," Rob shouted, swimming between their two boats. "That was at least a 9.9!" He climbed up the slimy ladder of the dock and stepped onto her boat. Pond water from his stars and stripes bathing suit dripped across her deck. It was not often that he came onto her boat, and his presence started a lively beat in her heart. Her hands on her hips, she stood her ground, cautious of his intent. Danny watched fascinated.

"No," she said firmly to whatever he had in mind.

"Yes," he replied, grinning like a lunatic. He bent quickly and lifted her over his shoulder.

She paddled his back with her palms, while her feet wildly kicked the air. "Don't you dare!"

"Bad judges get dunked." He carried her easily off her boat onto the dock.

Danny shouted excitedly, "Do it, Dad!"

"Dan, how could you!" she cried.

Rob bent forward, whooping something reminiscent of a Rebel Yell. Their bodies separated in the air and they plunged into the pond. For a moment she let herself hang underwater, her skin wonderfully cool and vibrant. She stared upward; the water was a brilliant green, foam hovered on the surface. She broke through the surface where he waited. She splashed him. "You're a jerk! I just washed my hair!" The absurdity of her words made him laugh. His arms circled her waist and she twisted to push him away. His laughter was contagious. She started to laugh, her breasts grazing his chest, her hands relaxing on his shoulders. Danny leapt off the dock. She glanced briefly downward. She had napped without a bra on. Her shirt was transparent.

She and Rob were suddenly quiet. She looked at his angular lips, his broken nose, his bright blue eyes, the lips again. Like an undertow, a strong and invisible force pulled her mouth to his. She resisted. So did he. They bobbed silently for a moment, mildly aware of approaching dog paddles. Danny rested a hand on each of their shoulders, so they turned toward his small, delighted face. She returned the boy's smile and then backed off slowly as Rob released his hold on her waist. She swam in confusion toward the ladder. Climbing the algae-coated rungs, she was struck by the wet fabric pulling her downward, like the drowning weight of an anchor.

That evening there was a light tapping on her houseboat door. As she opened it, she leaned over.

"Grrrr..." she said, as if angry at being dunked.

Danny grinned, not terrified in the least. His sweatshirt had the large red S of Superman across the chest that she traced with her finger, tickling him.

"I have a message from Dad." He could barely contain his giggles. "He said to move your butt away from your laptop and watch fireworks with us." He was pleased with himself that he had remembered it so well. Plus he got to say the B word.

"Here's my message back."

"Okay!" he replied, thrilled with his new job as go-between.

"I'll go, but I'm not speaking to wicked trolls who throw women off docks."

"I got it!" He dashed off her boat.

She logged off, went to her cabin, and slipped on a hoodie to protect herself from mosquitos. She guzzled down some Glenlivet and gargled with mouthwash. The two were waiting on the dock. Rob carried an army blanket and small cooler, and Dan immediately offloaded the baseball equipment to her, wanting only to carry the flashlight. He grabbed her free hand and pulled her forward, chattering about the sea critters he had collected in his Seashore Life class at the science school in the village.

"I'm going to be either a marine biologist or a super hero," he explained. "But I can't decide which."

"Why don't you be both?" she proposed. "Maybe you could be Super Starfish Man who's a marine biologist, but has five arms with sticky tube feet for capturing bad guys."

The suggestion intrigued him for the rest of the evening. Rob wordlessly listened and straggled behind them as they walked over the spongy grass and mud of the marsh. They passed over the paved bike trail and waded through the soft sand of the dunes.

The beach faced directly east. Shark Rock was just offshore. Off to the right, Martha's Vineyard appeared like a large humpback. Like a necklace of yellow jewels, distant lights from boats and beach houses rimmed the coastline. On very clear days, directly ahead, one could see a low, dark stripe, Nantucket Island. To their left glowed the lights of Falmouth. In the waters off the town beach floated a firework barge.

She and Rob spread the blanket in the sand and weighed down the corners with stones in case the wind picked up.

Rob and Dan picked up their baseball gloves and tossed a glow-in-dark baseball down the beach from the blankets of families and couples in the sand. She searched the cooler but, sadly, found no beer. In fact, she had never seen Rob drink alcohol. How weird was that? The first firework of the night screeched skyward and burst into a rosette of gold and pink. Rob and Dan hurried back to the blanket. Dan noticed that her feet were buried in the sand so he placed himself in the V of her outstretched legs and peeled open the Velcro straps of his sandals. His squirming feet burrowed in the sand with hers, and they laughed at the tickling sensation.

"Dad, put your feet in the sand with ours," Danny suggested.

"That's alright," he replied evasively. His eyes looked skyward, anticipating the next spray of light.

Overhead fragments of burning light exploded again and again. Between her knees, Danny twisted and clapped, his crew cut skimming her chin. The barrage of questions continued... "What does Super Starfish Man's outfit look like? Does he wear a cape and have a mask? What villains does he battle? What do they wear?"... all while winding sandy licorice between her fingers. "Lin, what type of firework is your favorite?"

"Maybe the purple and orange ones that burst twice."

"I like the big round ones that are red, white, and blue. How about you, Dad?"

"They're all beautiful in different ways," Rob replied.

"No," Dan insisted, "you have to pick one."

"The green ones, since green is my favorite color," Rob answered.

That night Rob hardly made eye contact with her and was uncharacteristically reserved, and she wondered what offensive thing she might have said or done. The dunking still preoccupied her thoughts. She had been touched by quite a few men, in all sorts of ways. Why was this so distracting? This was ridiculous. She was a grown-up, she reminded myself. She forced her thoughts elsewhere. A couple was on a blanket not far from them. The woman lay on her back; the man was using her belly as a pillow.

She glanced back at Rob. His crew cut had grown out over the past few months. That's why he looked different to her; he had combed it for once. It was usually a flattened mat under his baseball cap. Now his hair was neatly parted and combed over with water.

Her view returned to the sea. The boundary between the black sky and black ocean was indistinguishable. Somewhere across the water was Iceland, then Ireland, then Scotland—where Duncan would not be watching spectacular flowers of fire in the night sky. For some time now, she had been certain that she no longer wanted to be married.

But Duncan would never divorce her. She was sure of it. She was too valuable a commodity for him to release. The Nolan-BioCorp Electrode had simply amassed too much money. Besides, she was so busy, had so many more important things to do at the lab right now than wrangle with lawyers to untangle the razor wire that tethered them together. The wind suddenly picked up. What would Rob would do it if she snuggled next to him on the blanket and slid her hands under his flannel shirt for warmth?

But those nagging jitters in her hands had begun again, so she hid them in the pocket of her hoodie. She stared skyward. And as fiery blossoms of color shattered overhead, the firework finale, there was only one thing she could think to do about it that night. Obliterate all thoughts of her marriage with a repeated infusion of highland malt whiskey in the quiet of her cabin.

Cambridge

The rumbling of Karen's stomach woke her. The last food she had eaten was funnel cake at Comic Con the day before. She couldn't believe her eyes when she saw the time on her cell phone. It was well after noon. And it was the 4th of July; in two hours she was to go to a barbecue, and watch fireworks over the Charles Rivers with friends from the Math Department. Distressed, she climbed into the shower; over 18 K had been charged to her American Express card the night before. What was done was done! At least she had saved face with the Guild.

After the shower, she wandered into the kitchen. A large aluminum tray of cat kibble that she had placed out for midnight snacks was empty. Puss-N-Boots trotted into the kitchen. She reached for two cans of Chicken Banquet in the cupboard and scraped the food into the pink and blue bowls. Puss-N-Boots quickly dug into his food. She poured herself a bowl of corn flakes, and started to eat. She, like Boots, was ravenous.

"Willow, chicken today," she called with a full mouth. "Willow?" She carried her cereal bowl into the living room. There was no Willow on the sofa. The door to the living room balcony was locked, and it was impossible that the cat could have escaped through the front door when she had talked to Mr. O'Leary, as she saw Willow after he left. She hurriedly searched the condo. There was no Willow in the coat closet, bedroom closet, or under the bed. The door to the office balcony was also locked, so the cat could not have gotten outside through that exit. She checked all the closets and under the bed for a second time.

In the living room she pushed her face into the small rooms of the carpeted cat gyms. She turned to her new entertainment center that held her CDs, DVDs, and high definition TV.

"Oh, thank god!"

Willow was curled into a ball on the lowest shelf. The black cat was camouflaged against the black wood of the entertainment center.

"Willow, breakfast!" She dropped to her knees and reached forward. There was no movement from the cat. She nudged Willow again, pressure building her in head. Instead the cat felt unnaturally hard. She tentatively lifted the animal from the shelf, and pressed her ear against the fur. Hot tears burst from her eyes like lava from a volcano. Willow had no heartbeat and rigor mortis had already set in.

Gazing into empty space, she sat on the sofa with Willow on her lap. What would she and Boots do without Willow? They were the Three Musketeers! She had raised Willow since she was a kitten. And what does one do with a dead cat? It was Sunday. No vet's office would be opened on Sunday, or on a holiday. She'd never dealt with the death of a pet before. Her first cat, Macavity, had wandered away never to be seen again, which had sent her to her first therapist. Larry, Curly, and Moe were given to her sister when she went away to Hopkins, but she faithfully visited them every vacation to check on their wellbeing.

Finally, she rose and walked to the bathroom where, with shaky hands, she wrapped the cat in a towel. How long before Willow would start to smell, the tissue start to decay... it was too depressingly horrid to contemplate! She wrapped the cat bundle in a large trash bag and placed it in the bathtub. She glanced at herself in the mirror. Her puffy eyes were nearly closed from the past hours of crying. Her nose was a scarlet red from persistent sniffling. No way she could go to a 4th of July barbecue looking like this! She found her cell phone to send a text to the host.

"Sadly, I'm unable to attend the barbecue," she typed. "There's been a death in the family."

Chapter 21

Rehab

Lindsey looked into the darkness beyond the hurricane fence. Nothing had changed since the fireworks on the beach with Rob and Danny, one year ago. She was a still a fly stuck in the marital web, and Duncan was still a spider, sucking life fluids from her. Other trapped animals, the patients lined the fence along side of her. Distant fireworks burst in the distance. In the addiction lottery, which of them would make it on the outside, and which of them would not live to see the next 4th of July? Some of the patients seemed silly and punchy. Their loud ohs and ahs were irritating, so she went inside to check on Ethan.

Over the last few days he'd become pale and withdrawn, frustrated that the pain in his foot was not subsiding. For the first time he'd asked to borrow her music and headphones. Her guess was that the fireworks sounded too much like the improvised explosive device that nearly blew off his foot. He was still suffering from shell shock, or, as they called it now, post-traumatic stress disorder. He complained hotly to the nurses that the prescribed painkillers were not strong enough.

She found him in the reading room, but he was not reading; his eyes stared blankly at the page. She placed her palm on his forehead. "You're burning up."

"I feel like hell," he uttered.

"Let me get you some cold water."

"That's not going to help. Nothing's going to help."

"We're all healing. Maybe slowly, but all of us are healing."

"This is my third fucking time in rehab," he growled, wanting none of her optimism. "My children think this is where I live! A minute doesn't go by that I don't think about a needle in my arm."

"Try to think of something else."

He lit a cigarette and grumbled, "To survive is the worst torture of all."

She shook a cigarette from her pack. His lighter flashed in front of her lips. She inhaled quickly. Her voice faltered, as she started toward the door. "I'm going to get some tea. I'll bring you back some ice water. Drink lots of water tonight."

Three quick circles around the ward did not calm her. Her heart, as if in a padded cell, slammed itself against her ribs and sternum. *To survive is the worst torture of all* replayed in her mind again and again. She'd heard that phase before, and recently, but where? She entered the Fishbowl where the Civil War re-enactor, Jonathan, and the Parrot Head, Glenn, played checkers at a card table. The Boston Pops played "America the Beautiful" on a TV that no one was watching. At the hot water dispenser, she dipped a teabag in and out a Styrofoam cup God knows how many times. She reached into the refrigerator for a water bottle for Ethan.

The Bottom Dwellers

Ethan could not sit still; he fidgeted and paced the halls more than she did. Like her, he was unable to share in meetings. But he had confided in her. Their problem was the same: they were trapped in loveless, incompatible marriages. Some years ago, while doing his surgical rotation in Boston, he had performed an emergency appendectomy on the son of a single mother. He cursed the day his scalpel sliced open that boy's lower right abdominal quadrant. The boy turned out to be the first grandson of Grayson Henry Harper of GHH Pharmaceuticals.

The old billionaire was used to getting what he wanted, and had decided that the pensive young surgeon might have a settling influence on his rambunctious daughter, Samantha. Ethan was courted by the curmudgeon, invited to The Club, charity galas, and polo tournaments. Ethan, who had moved to Boston knowing no one, was quickly surrounded by a large circle of alcohol- and drug-sodden sycophants trying to cuddle up to the old man's checkbook. The affair with Samantha burnt like a flare, brilliant and brief, but after, as they lay exhausted on silk sheets, they grappled for words to say to one another. None came. By that time they were engaged, and she was pregnant with the twins.

"Is that sucky music coming from the patio from one of your CDs?" Glenn asked her.

"I don't own anything remotely similar to Disco Inferno," she answered indignantly.

Curtis stuck his head into the Fishbowl. "Everyone's dancing outside. Join us, Lindsey. We need more ladies."

"In a bit," she replied.

She returned to the reading room with Ethan's water bottle, but he had vanished. She searched the hallway, and then stepped back into the reading room. A lamp illuminated the chair where he'd been sitting. On a nearby table were a full ashtray and a book. He was a prolific reader, finishing almost a book a day. She tilted her head to see what he was reading. *The Greek Myths.*

She moved to the windowsill with her tea. The lawn furniture had been dragged off to the perimeter of the patio, just like when she and Marcus had danced. Bodies pulsed and gyrated to seventies' dance music. Ethan was not outside. Footsteps approached from behind her. Lorena leaned next to her at the windowsill and watched the bodies bouncing in and out of the glare of the patio light. The big nurse hadn't been around earlier in the day and must have recently come on shift.

"How are you doing, honey?" the nurse asked.

"Good. And you?"

"Good. Happy 4th."

"You too." Bart and Ellen swirled on top of the picnic table and she worried that they might fall. "Lively crew tonight."

"Yes." The nurse's eyes crawled over her face, raising goosebumps.

"What?" Lindsey asked.

"What are you drinking?" Lorena inquired.

"Tea." She held out her cup for her inspection.

"Yum. What type?"

"Lemon Zinger," she answered, unnerved.

"Can I have a sip?"

"Of course," she agreed, offering her the cup.

Lorena took a sip and smiled broadly. Lindsey smiled back with misgivings, though she genuinely trusted this woman. A maternal warmth radiated from the nurse. She was the oldest employee on the ward, probably pushing seventy. She had a fun-loving manner, and was pulling for all of them to get clean. At the last weigh-in, Lorena had declared happily (in rehab, there was no such thing as political correctness), "Skinny white girl, you have gained five pounds!" Lindsey often called the nurse Good Cop when Kate Waters was in earshot. Lorena guffawed, understanding tacitly who was by default Bad Cop.

Lorena took a second sip. "Delicious," she said cheerfully, returning the cup that now had a bright red lipstick smudge on the rim. "I think I'll get myself a cup." She patted Lindsey's shoulder and left.

Tina Turner's version of "Proud Mary" caught Lindsey's attention. Hopefully dancing would dissipate her anxiousness. She placed the water bottle next to Ethan's book, then jogged downstairs and out the patio door. Vince immediately grabbed her around the waist and spun her around. He claimed to have a chronic lower back injury and hadn't worked in years, yet he played basketball and badminton whenever they unlocked the doors to the garden. He was a master of the disability scam. His lubricious charm had allowed him to insinuate himself into the life of a hard-working woman who changed bed linens all day at a tourist motel, while he lounged on her sofa watching daytime television, popped Nembutal, smoked weed, and banged the woman in the trailer next door.

The music was a string of oldies. "Proud Mary" was followed by "Psycho Killer," "Holiday," and then "Love Shack." She passed dizzily into the arms of Bart, Curtis, Connor, and then back to Vince. Bodies spun around her in a wild kaleidoscope of limbs and color, making her delirious and light-headed. Vince playfully pulled her out of the white patio lights and onto the shadowed lawn.

"What are we doing?" she asked, unsteadily.

"Something fun." Vince covered her eyes with his hands that smelled like cologne. His laugh was low and seductive. Bart held her hands and dragged her toward the darkness of the hedges. The men were arousing and frightening at once.

"What?" she repeated nervously.

"Just come with us. It's something you'll love," Vince coaxed.

"A treat for our pretty lady," Bart added slyly.

She peeled Vince's fingers from over her eyes. "Really, guys, what is it?"

Bart reached behind the air-conditioning unit, his hand searching amongst the weeds. Glass clinked across metal. Fear coursed through her like a wildfire. Vince's breath sifted through her hair and across the nape of her neck. His arms clasped her waist. "Party with us, baby."

"Don't," she protested, her hands tugging on his wrists.

Bart moved closer. The bottle hung inches in front of her face, briefly hypnotizing her. A quart of Jack Daniels. The lid was off. He slid the opening under her nose, the fumes colliding against her brain like a crashing wave.

"Let go," she ordered, but Vince's arms coiled around her like a python.

"One sip and you'll feel so good, honey," Bart whispered. His lips sucked on the bottle, and she heard the swish of fluid down the neck of the bottle, and then his deep swallows. He moved the opening toward her lips. "We'll never tell."

"Let me go. Please," she implored.

Bart's eyes glowed a demonic black. What the hell was he was high on? He'd had a lot of visitors that afternoon. A vial, pills, or slim piece of folded paper with coke or heroin would be easy enough to get through the security checkpoint, but how an entire bottle of JD? Vince's arms continued to tighten. With entrancing slowness, Bart glided the bottle's opening along her lower lip, down her chin, neck, circled each breast, and then drew spirals across her belly. Her panic skyrocketed. If she screamed, they'd all get thrown out.

Ethan stepped into the shadows. "Lin, dance with me." Vince's arms abruptly fell off of her. Bart whipped the bottle behind his back. Ethan pulled her quivering hand and led her back to a quiet corner of the patio. Everyone gyrated around them to some primal beat, but they slow danced through one thumping song after another.

"I didn't drink it!" she whispered. "I didn't drink it, I didn't drink it!"

"Shhh... I know." He stroked her hair while she shook into his body.

She curiously touched his cheek. He must have just shaved off his beard, giving him a cherubic, youthful appearance. She returned her arms to his waist and swayed slowly, careful not to jar his toes poking from his cast. They tightened their embrace.

Wampanoag Joe and Lorena had seen enough. One of them yanked the cord to the CD player and the chaotic motion on the patio came to a halt.

"This party's over!" Joe shouted. "Everyone's confined to the bedrooms for the rest of the night! The Fishbowl's closed!" He turned fiercely to Ethan and Lindsey who clung fearfully to one other. "You know the rules! Get your hands off each other!"

The patients fled to their rooms. Lindsey got cleaned up in the small bathroom and hid under the sheets. In her agitated state it would be impossible to get even a few hours of sleep. Worse, Ellen lay in her bed and blabbed uncontrollably about her boyfriends. On any other night her roommate's stories would have been titillating, but at the moment Ellen's exploits on a pool table with longliners off the swordfishing vessel *Salty One* held no interest. To tune out the chatter, Lindsey traced the eddies in the wood grain of the closet door and willed her mind to gentler places... swimming at Stony Beach with Sara and Zephyr... Danny blowing bubbles off her flybridge... coffee and pastries with Mort and Ella at the bakery... scraping icing off a cake that Rob and Danny made for her birthday.

Detox

"No more shots... no more needles!" Maggie cried, leaping off her bed as the nurse entered with a tray of syringes.

"So you can speak after all?" the nurse said, sounding surprised.

"Of course I can speak, you moron!" She crouched defensively behind the chair in the corner.

"You've been bitten by some animal. Was it a dog? It's infected. Can you tell us what it was?"

"Just stay the fuck away!"

"These are rabies shots and antibiotics. They're precautionary."

Rabies? Antibiotics? What the hell are those! Poisons? "Keep away from me!" Maggie yelled.

The nurse rounded the bed and approached the chair. "Please sit down. It'll just be a little stick. It won't hurt much."

Maggie presented her fists.

"Oh, for god's sake, don't be such a baby! They're just some shots."

Maggie's fists continued to shake. Never, ever had she struck a person, unlike Bess who'd had a fascination with violence. She glanced in a panic toward the doorway. If she could just escape this room… make it to the fire doors, she'd be home free! She suddenly leapt over the chair and shoved the nurse aside. The metal tray and syringes clattered to the floor. Out of her peripheral vision, she saw the nurse stumble at the foot of the bed. There was a faint thud. The red fire exit was a beacon. She dashed past the ghostly men in the blue cloud… over the coffee table… across the sofa… to the red light… her escape… almost there…

Boston

From her balcony, Karen watched a distant fireworks display off to the south. Maybe they were from Quincy or Weymouth or Braintree. They were too far away to have been launched from the Boston Harbor Islands. Much of the afternoon had been spent on the Internet looking for a vet that was opened on Sundays, and pet cremation services. Pussy Willow deserved the best, and Karen finally found a service that would cremate Willow and provide her with a small black cat statue, all for several hundred dollars. Her eyes were raw and no more tears would flow. She stared numbly into the night.

The fireworks were spectacular, but she could no longer sense or appreciate beauty. All was desolate and dark. It was unfair that she was assaulted and her backpack stolen. It was unfair that the armory was robbed on her watch. It was unfair that it would take her over a year to pay off an exorbitant credit card bill plus the extortionate interest. It was unfair that her beloved Willow had died! The cat had shown no signs of illness. Yesterday morning, she'd led a pleasant, orderly life. Twenty-four hours later all was havoc and horror!

How depressing was it to watch fireworks alone! She returned to her office before the fireworks show had ended, ensuring to lock the balcony door behind her, so that Puss-N-Boots did not escape. That's all she needed, for Boots for fall from the heights to his death! She dropped listlessly into the computer chair and turned on her computer. Control, Karen, control, she told to herself. Control must be restored, and at any cost. But how? She was in no mood to talk to the Guild members, especially after their snub the night before, and she was too emotionally spent to work on her manuscripts for work. It would perk her up a bit to talk to her mother about sewing her a new Diana gown. She checked the time on her smartphone. With the difference in time zones, her parents would still be at the yearly cookout in the backyard before heading off to watch fireworks at the high school with Grandma, Uncle Fred and Aunt Jill. And her mother would inevitably change the conversation to the wedding in Idaho. She shoved her phone out of reach.

She logged onto her work email, but there were only 4th of July greetings from her graduate students. "Hope you're having a wonderful 4th, Dr. Battersby!" Delete. She then opened up Facebook... again a terrible idea. Her American friends had already posted photos of parties and fireworks from their various locations across the country. Were there a Dislike option, she would have scrolled through the posts, systemically entering Dislike... Dislike... Dislike. Disgusted, she logged out of Facebook.

On her desktop was the folder labeled BND, her code for Baffling Nolan Device. She opened the folder and began to review the photos of the strange instrument again. Lindsey the Wonderful might be taking a respite from her "personal issues," as Sara described it, and was probably sitting in a hot tub, sipping champagne with her hunky husband at her seaside mansion. Or perhaps she had an expensive yacht and was having shrimp cocktail and dry martinis with Duncan while watching fireworks rain over Key West.

All while she was home alone on the 4th with puffy eyes, 18 K in the hole, a nose like Rudolph, and a dead cat in her bathtub.

Focus, Karen, focus! Focus on the device! She intently studied the various .jpgs. How clever to have snapped the device from all angles with her smartphone! A brief glimmer of control and confidence appeared. That was it! "Yes!" She pumped her fist into the air. The device was some type of printer! Yes, definitely. It was a printer! This was baffling in itself, as Lindsey was renowned for creating biomedical devices, not office equipment. But a look at the software interfacing with the device would tell her for sure. Somehow she'd need to get her hands on the software. And while she was at it, why not steal away that beautiful Polynesian engineer and the vast secrets held in her brilliant brain? She, Karen Battersby, was a Centurion, invincible and ruthlessly powerful! One more trip... no, a secret mission... to Woods Hole would be conducted as part of Operation Infiltrate!

Chapter 22

Rehab

"I want everyone up and out now! I don't care if you're not dressed. Get out here now!" Kate shouted, as a wake-up call to the ward.

There was no scent of breakfast. The patients shuffled uneasily into the hallway. The normal chatter of morning was absent.

"Everyone line up here!" Kate pointed to the rest room next to the dining room.

"I don't believe this. There's nothing in my system but nicotine and caffeine," Lindsey muttered irritably.

"Shut up and get in line! I don't want to hear a word from any of you!"

Kate and Ramon solemnly distributed plastic cups with patient name and ID number on it. For nearly an hour the only sound heard was Kate's imperious "Next," and the repeated flush of a toilet.

By noontime the urinalyses were completed. The violators were evicted while the rest of the patients sat tensely in a Twelve Step meeting, working on *Step Seven:*

The Bottom Dwellers

Humbly asked him to remove our shortcomings. After the meeting, the Fishbowl was abuzz with gossip. Urinalysis tests had revealed cocaine and alcohol metabolites in the urine of Ellen, Bart, Ted, and Vince. Alcohol was detected in Trisha and Sharon, who had shared a bottle of scotch and then heaved the empty over the hurricane fence into the tall grass beyond.

That afternoon the small counseling groups were to work on *Step Six: Were entirely ready to have God remove all these defects of character.* Lindsey had checked all of the boxes listed on the Defects of Character handout, and double-checked arrogance, self-centeredness, and unfaithfulness, but the events of the previous night were still distracting her. She simmered. Ellen's stupidity was staggering, the dismissal ensuring that she would never regain custody of her children. Also staggering was the stealth, cunningness, and tenacity of this disease that would cause a mother to forego a life with her children for a two-hour buzz. And what kind of sick mind would smuggle liquor and drugs into a rehab? The answer: another addict upset at losing a drugging or drinking buddy. Was this sicko aware that all of the patients had only four future options? If they used: insanity, incarceration, or death. Or, if they lived by one simple tenet, *just for this day I will not use*—a promise of life. The formula was that simple, but adhering to it was another story. A recovering addict had to respond to addiction with the urgency due a fire, not with the complacency of a fire drill.

Perhaps one of the IV drug users was responsible for the shoelace thefts and had been using over the past few weeks, as Myra and Ethan had both suggested. Before their expulsion, Ted, Bart, and Vince had remained a united and hostile front of denial about how the coke and booze had been smuggled onto the ward. All three of them were IV drug users; the shoelaces could have been stolen by anyone of them. No, it couldn't have been Bart, as he was admitted after the shoelaces thefts and Mitch's death. That left either Ted or Vince as the possible culprits; the two men were inseparable. Maybe they were using together? Perhaps one served as the lookout, while the other performed the theft? But why were so many laces required? And what was the significance of the laces in Mitch's sock? Had one of them helped him into the air duct? Lindsey's thoughts were interrupted when Ramon entered the meeting room and said that Kate wanted to see her.

She searched Ramon's face for an explanation, but he shrugged a concerned I-don't-know.

Lindsey left her counseling group and departed for Kate's office. "What?" she asked testily in the doorway.

Kate turned in her chair. "Sit down, please."

"I was with them, but I didn't drink any booze," she replied in self-defense. "They tricked me, lured me there!"

"You shouldn't have even gone off with them. It was a very bad decision. Please sit."

She moved toward the window, deliberating ignoring the request. "You found nothing in my urine. I can't believe you don't trust me. I've been completely honest with you since I got here."

"Honest? You've been bull-shitting me at every turn! So you did nothing with your husband in the bathroom? I'm guessing you were both in there washing your hands. And 'I went to Penn State where their mascot is the Hoya.' It's the Nittany Lion! I grew up in a Pennsylvania coal town. Everyone knows it's the Nittany Lion!" Kate shouted.

The Bottom Dwellers

Lindsey had forgotten about those incidents and shrunk against the windowsill. Her forehead flattened against the cool glass of the window. In the corner of the parking lot the Jeep sat under an undisturbed sheen of pollen.

Kate calmed herself. "But you're right. There were no traces of illegal substances in your urine." There was a delay in her words. "But there was something else."

Lindsey spun from the window, her mind scrambling for what a urinalysis test could indicate beside drug and alcohol metabolites... anemia, diabetes, kidney and liver diseases. But she was feeling so much better recently; it was doubtful that she had any of these disorders.

"Well... what?" she snapped.

Kate answered, her tone gentle compared to her usual bossy bark. Lindsey grasped the arm of the chair and decided to sit.

Woods Hole

It had been a surreal and nightmarish few days, Sara reflected. It all started on the evening of the 4th of July. She and Zephyr had been invited to Falmouth Beach to watch fireworks with Derick and his fiancée, Isabel. Big, big mistake. Her first impressions of Isabel had been spot on; the woman's smile was not a smile but a sneer of condescension. Derick was miserable and uncommonly silent that night. He tossed a foam football with Zephyr as a ploy to escape Isabel on the beach blanket, leaving her to make mindless small talk with Isabel. Thanks, Derick!

Isabel had mentioned repeatedly that she was a former Miss Georgia. Her family owned the Atlanta Organic Tea Company and an island near Hilton Head. Sara thought to mention that her car mirrors were held on with duct tape, her student loan debt might be paid off by her eightieth birthday, and her tiny apartment room took fifteen minutes to cross due to the congestion of bikes, plastic play equipment, computer table, and sleeping mat. But it was best to hold her tongue. She continued to assess Isabel as she did most fit women her age. Beauty queen or not, the Georgian was unattractive in every way.

"This wind," Isabel complained peevishly, "and this humidity are destroying my hair, and this annoying sand!"

"And this whining is destroying my ear drums," Sara wanted to reply. Again she held her tongue.

And Isabel had the IQ of a toad. All conversations revolved around shades of lipstick, skin exfoliants, and hair products. Were Lindsey here, they would have discussed cool stuff: electrodes, amplifiers, and historical aircraft, submarines, and boats. Sara looked desperately down the beach, overcome with a sudden urge to play football in the sand with the boys.

What did Derick, whose idea of fun was solitary motorcycle journeys across arid wastelands or backpacking excursions into the remote highlands of New Guinea, possibly have in common with a high-maintenance bimbo? Isabel ran a modeling agency; he was an infectious diseases expert with the Center for Disease Control, and an M.D.-Ph.D. In fact, his background was quite similar to Lindsey's. God, how she missed that mangy, infuriating, creative drunk!

Later that same night, as Sara was tucking a blanket around Zephyr, her cell phone vibrated. The text was from Karen Battersby.

"I have an urgent matter to attend to on the Cape. Aunt Edith's very ill. It's very short notice, but can we meet tomorrow?"

"Yes, of course," Sara texted back.

"Late afternoon? How about four?" Karen wrote.

"Four is fine."

On July 5th, Derick stopped by Sara's laboratory around noon. He was in his riding leathers with the armor plates for highway travel. There was a gloomy cast to his face.

"It appears that the upcoming wedding will be for Isabel and Jared," he said in a hard voice.

"What!" she said, stunned. "Where is she?"

"She left early this morning. There were too many fireworks last night. I'm going for a long ride."

"To where?"

"To anywhere. My phone's off. I'll be back in time to watch Zephyr when you go to Newport."

"Do you want to talk?" she asked hesitantly, though she already knew his response.

"No," he remarked fiercely. "I just need to ride." He kissed her cheek and rushed out the door.

"Be safe!" she called after him, but there was no answer.

Before Karen Battersby's arrival that afternoon, Sara had tinkered with the epileptic seizure simulator, as Lindsey would inevitably ask about it during her upcoming visit to the rehab. Theirs was a three-stage project. Her job was to build a device that simulated seizures in different brains areas, which she had done weeks ago!

Lindsey's job—which she had completely dropped the ball on!—was to build an electrode to detect the specific groups of abnormal nerve cells that generated the epileptic seizures. Of course, other types of electrodes had been designed to detect "hot spots," the site where the abnormal cells were located, but these electrodes were insensitive, and consequently large blocks of normal brain tissue were removed along with the abnormal cells during surgery. Current "en bloc" surgeries could eliminate the seizures, but sometimes resulted in impaired cognitive function, the result of removing surrounding normal tissue as well. Lindsey's electrode—if she ever built it!—would prevent this, as only the abnormal cells would be detected and removed.

Sara's epileptic seizure simulator, in conjunction with Lindsey's electrode, would be used to train neurosurgeons and preclude practicing on living tissue, such as from dogs or monkeys.

In the third and last phase of the project, Lindsey's electrode would first detect the "epileptic" cells in the brains of seizing patients AND also remove the aberrant cells with a tiny laser, instead of a surgeon's scalpel. The design of the micro-laser was months in the future.

Sara heard footsteps approaching in the hallway and glanced up at the clock. Karen had arrived promptly at four o'clock. Sara was taken aback by the change in the BTI engineer since their last meeting. First, Karen was dressed in a business suit and carried a briefcase. The only people dressed so formally at the marine lab were the occasional pushy sales representatives from a drug company, peddling some new antibody or receptor blocker. But the change ran deeper than her clothes. Her eyes had a bleary redness to them.

What if she's a boozer like Lindsey! Sara wondered. That's all I'd need, to move from one alcoholic boss to another.

For another thing, Karen's previous enthusiasm was gone. She was professional and friendly, but there was something else... something Sara couldn't quite put her finger on. Karen described in detail the thermodynamics project that she was interested in having her work on. "The defense department grant runs for a three-year period, so I can offer you a three-year contract. I'm fairly confident that the grant will be re-funded after three years, but of course there are no guarantees with the vagaries of the economy and cuts in military spending. But another war in the Middle East is imminent," she remarked with an upbeat tone. "That will increase the chances for the grant's re-funding.

Yeah, let's hope for war, Sara thought ironically.

The salary offered was 10 K more than what she was making at the marine lab, but that would be offset by a higher cost of living in Boston. The health benefits and retirement package were identical to those of her current job. There were so many variables to consider. She tried to focus on Karen's words, but the bloodshot eyes flitting nervously around the lab were disconcerting. This peculiar, paranoid mannerism had not been evident in their previous meeting.

"I really hope you'll consider my offer, Sara," Karen said, standing abruptly. She closed her briefcase. "You'll make a great addition to our research group. And don't hesitate to call me if you have any further questions. You have my office number and my cell."

Sara outstretched her hand. "Yes, thank you. I have a lot to consider. May I have a week to give you my answer?"

"Yes, of course. Now I'm off to Barnstable to see Aunt Edith."

"How's she doing?" she had inquired innocently.

"Not well," Karen replied sullenly. "She has pancreatic cancer."

This explained Karen's red eyes and tense demeanor. She reached out for Karen's hand. "I'm so sorry. You and your family will be in my thoughts and prayers."

"You are too kind, Sara," Karen responded as she departed.

Sara gazed at the vacated doorway, and shuddered inexplicably.

Five minutes later the fire alarm sounded, and the sound was deafening.

Plugging her ears, she had walked briskly down the hallway to the other lab where the summer students, graduate students, and post-docs worked.

"Drop what you're doing and walk quickly, do not run, from the building," she called.

The room clear, she circled the room, unplugging hot plates, balances, and other electrical equipment. Mort Somer's office was next. She spotted her boss hobbling with his cane toward the back stairwell.

"This is not a fire drill!" Mort informed her, his voice shaking. "I would have been told if we were to have a fire drill."

She rested her hand under his elbow and assisted him down the stairs. "I don't smell smoke or an electrical fire," she added curiously.

"Is every one out of the lab?" he inquired urgently.

"Yes, I checked."

"And Greta, the cleaning woman?"

"I didn't see her. The janitorial closet was closed. Maybe she's not at work yet."

"And Kumar?" Mort continued nervously.

"I'm coming, Mort!" Kumar cried fearfully from a flight above them.

Sara and Mort looked up at through the railings to see the old scientist and his walker maneuvering precariously down the stairs.

"This is horrible!" Kumar called in growing panic. "My sister died in a hospital fire in Calcutta!"

"Slow down, Kumar!" Mort shouted, his voice crackling. "You're going too fast. Sara, go help him. I can manage on my own."

"Okay. You be careful!" She dashed up the stairwell, skipping two steps at a time, but she was too late.

There was a terrible tumbling and clanking. Kumar lay sprawled across the landing, amidst a tangle of metal. Blood pooled around his ankle. She tentatively pulled up the leg of his pants. A shard of bone tore through the old scientist's shriveled skin. She whipped her cellphone from her pocket and called 911.

Chapter 23

Rehab

Dr. Lindsey Nolan had given countless talks during her career, in lecture halls and classrooms, dark auditoriums at conferences, the polished boardroom at BioCorp, even to elementary school children eager to touch the sea creatures in the buckets at the Science School. She could converse comfortably on a range of topics, from the design of an electrode to the electrical properties of nerve cells and muscle, or the action of neurotoxins. But in rehab, facing her circle of peers, she had found it impossible to speak.

At the AA meeting on the night of July 6, Lindsey finally raised her hand. Her words faltered. *"I'm Lindsey N. I'm an alcoholic."* This fact she had known at a subterranean level since junior high school. Normal people don't drink in the bedroom of their English teacher, or monitor their BACs before heading out to a bar. Normal people don't lose their cars, or total their sailboat on reefs... or forget entire boat shows and Boat Show Men in Trans Ams.

"About a month ago in a blackout I headed off to Newport. Somewhere I met up with two men." She slid a cigarette from the pack and flicked the lighter a few times before it caught. She silently castigated herself; the last thing she should be doing was smoking.

"And now I'm pregnant."

After the AA meeting, she stood in dumb confusion at the hurricane fence. Her urge to scale the fence and escape had disappeared some time ago. The black ribbon of the Sakonnet River unfurled into a black sea. Down the bluff, boats with their red and green running lights slowly wound their way up the river to rest at some mooring or marina. The sky was overcast and starless. The drag of Ethan's injured foot was heard in the grass. His hand blanketed hers on the fence.

"Congratulations. I think it's wonderful," he said genuinely. His scent was heavy with tobacco.

"This is a complete and utter disaster." She gazed forward through the mesh. "I live alone. I don't like people around me. I'm a solitary animal. I can't have this baby."

"You're a high functioning physician. You'll easily be able to raise this child. You'll be a great mother."

"I don't know...." She paused. "What if there's something genetically wrong with the father? I'll never know. I'm incapable of taking care of myself, much less a healthy child, much, much less a sick one."

"I'm sure the father is healthy. He could have sex with you, and drive you here, couldn't he?"

"What sleazebags," she remarked. "To do that to a drunk woman."

"Maybe they were drunk also?" he suggested.

She turned. "Is that supposed to make me feel better?"

"You're so pretty. Any red-blooded male would have done the same thing if he had the chance."

"I hate those men."

"They brought you here, didn't they? They weren't entirely bad. Horny yes, bad no. Have the child. My children keep me sane. And pregnancy's a great incentive to stay sober."

"I work all the time."

"Pathetic excuse. You know you don't have to."

"I never planned to have children."

"Your plans just changed. Children are the best thing in life."

"I'll never know who the father is," she lamented.

"What if the father was a Newport surgeon?"

His response startled her. "It wasn't you."

"We came in the same day."

"Ethan..." she said nervously.

"On June 13, Samantha threw me out when she found that I was shooting up again. I wasn't sure where to go. I was sitting in a bar on the waterfront when a hot woman in a short pink skirt and low-cut leopard blouse walked in. She slid onto the barstool next to me and ordered a Glenlivet on the rocks."

"I drink my scotch neat," she mentioned apprehensively.

"It was a blistering afternoon. We drank for a while and then headed over to Bowen's Wharf to look at the boats. You were drunk and I was high and we made a quite pair, stumbling, laughing, and holding one another up. It's a miracle we weren't arrested. We spent most of the time looking at Chris Crafts. There was one that you really loved. I said I'd buy it for you. You nearly fell climbing over a gunwale and scraped your leg."

Her fingers tightened on the mesh, remembering that mysterious injury that she noticed in detox.

"You tried to seduce me in the cabin of a display boat." He smiled. "I was more than willing, but unfortunately there were people wandering around checking out the staterooms so I called and got us a hotel room."

She shook her head, recalling none of this.

"We were great together." He paused. "Do you remember the strawberries and champagne?"

"No."

"I was eating strawberries and whipped cream off your..."

"My what?"

"Your everything!" he said with a laugh.

"I can't believe that I don't remember that. I love that."

He grinned again. "Where'd you learn that trick with the ropes?"

She paused. "Which one?"

He couldn't think up an answer fast enough. And things didn't add up.

"Que lenguas te hablas, medico?" she asked cunningly.

"What?"

"What languages do you speak, doctor?"

"French and Arabic."

"The men who brought me here spoke Spanish!" She whacked him playfully across the arm. "You're so not funny! That was *not* funny!"

He laughed. "There's no harm in fantasizing. I wish the child was mine," he said seriously. He hesitated and then admitted sadly, "But it's not."

She ventured aloud. "Maybe the father was a dashing Spaniard?"

"Probably."

"If I have it…"

"Which you will," he interrupted firmly.

"… I'll imagine that the father was a handsome playboy off one of the transoceanic racing yachts. And that we had a whirlwind love affair, made passionate love on the beach, and danced throughout the night in the clubs."

He smiled. "I'm sure that's what happened."

"Inevitably the child will ask about its father."

"And you can say that the father, a world-class sailor, had to sail back home to his diplomatic post in Barcelona."

"I'm in love with my Spaniard," she said an air of panache.

"Have the child, Lin," he insisted. "Your Higher Power made this happen for a reason."

His last words silenced her for a moment. "I will," she finally said. She threw her arms around his shoulders and pressed a sisterly kiss onto his cheek.

Rehab

"I'm so glad to be on this side of the security door!" the newcomer from detox announced with a gasp of relief. Lindsey turned from the coffee counter to listen to the fat English professor, Ernest. "There's a maniac in detox… a ferocious, insane Animal! The beast shoved a nurse and put twenty stitches in her head!" Ernest squeezed his immense body into a chair near Ethan and the Dead Head, Joshua. "Then the Animal tried to escape! It dashed across the detox, but a hefty nurse blockaded the fire exit with her body. So the nurses chased the Animal while it leapt over sofas and chairs and knocked over lamps. It was eventually cornered behind the nurses' station. Finally two giant orderlies arrived to catch it and restrain it. The only reason that it hasn't killed anyone is that it's been shot up with tranquilizers."

So this explained Kate's numerous departures to the detox over the past two days. As soon as The Animal was moved over to the rehab, it would be avoided at all costs, Lindsey decided; she would retreat into the reading room and immerse herself in smooth jazz and her doorknob project. The smartest strategy was to avoid it all together. Empty beds were in the rooms of the hacker, Connor, the Parrot Head, Glenn, and the mutual fund trader, Troy, since the expulsion of Bart, Vince, and Ted. One of those three guys could deal with it.

"The Animal has a two word vocabulary, Fuck and Off," Ernest snorted. "Social Services can't determine who it is. It has no name, no place of origin, no nothing."

"The *person* has to be from somewhere. Someone had to have brought the *person* here," Ethan said irascibly, stressing the word person. His dislike for the professor was obvious.

"Yes, the police. The beast was found unconscious in a crack house in Providence. And just to give you fair warning, it has every disease known to mankind, including HIV. Avoid it like the plague!"

And so she would, Lindsey concluded, especially being pregnant... a thought that was still unsettling.

"That Animal should go the psych ward, not the rehab, I told the nurses," Ernest carried on. "But no one listens to me. The lunatic's being moved over here sometime today!"

The guys on the men's side of the ward can definitely deal with him. This was not her problem. She headed back to her room for a short nap before the afternoon AA meeting. A faint, repellant odor near her room caused her steps to falter.

Please no... no more patients attempting to escape through the air ducts! She looked quickly upward, but no telltale green stains discolored the ceiling panels. She stepped tentatively toward the doorway, the odor intensifying. She stopped suddenly and fought back an upwelling nausea.

A teenage girl, who smelled like... it was unspeakable... was tearing wildly through the dresser drawers. She had crazy, deranged eyes. Next she lunged to Lindsey's bed, ripped the pillowcase off the pillow and flung it across the room. The sheets were ripped off next and the mattress flipped, the girl searching frantically for cash. She then rifled the blue Hopkins overnight bag. "Fuckin' finally!" She pulled a twenty dollar bill from the wallet and stole the cigarettes.

Lindsey watched for some time, unnoticed. Then it dawned on her... this was the Animal! It was a Jane, not a John Doe! And worst of all, since Ellen's dismissal, her room had a free bed. This was her new roommate! It was certain that Kate couldn't stand her, but this punishment, this roommate assignment, was cruel and inhumane!

The girl finally sensed Lindsey's presence and her body tensed. She stared defiantly, unfazed by her blatant thievery.

Lindsey grabbed her overnight bag and checked her wallet. The cash was gone but the credit cards and driver's license were present. "That was my last twenty." The girl reeked so badly she wasn't about to wrestle her for it. Besides, just a yard away in the metal base of the floor lamp was hidden the mystery cash from the Boat Show Men.

The girl had no intention of returning the money and stood rigidly holding her ground. The twenty and cigarettes were clenched in her fists.

"You smell like putrefying—shit, I don't know what, it's that bad," Lindsey said.

The girl was silent for some time. "What's... putrefying?"

Lindsey paused. The girl was an ignoramus. "A disgustingly atrocious smell. Like dead, rotting tissue. If you take a shower right now, I'll buy you a pack of cigarettes from the hospital store."

The girl viewed Lindsey through narrowed eyes. "Any type I want?" Her voice was slurred by some sedative.

"Yes. And if you never put on those rancid clothes again, I'll buy you a second pack."

"These are my only clothes!"

"Didn't you bring anything with you?"

"I travel light."

A raggedy tarp tied up with blackened rope sat on the foot of her bed. "What about that? Don't you have clothes in there?" Lindsey asked, pointing.

"No."

"What is it?"

"A tarp, you moron! Don't you know what a fuckin' tarp is?"

"What's it for?"

"Sleeping. What else! As long as I stay dry, I don't get cold."

Lindsey shook her head, mortified. "It's filthy. Put it under the bed." Though bedrooms were not designated smoking areas, she pulled a pack of cigarettes from her pocket and lit a cigarette to cover up the smell of foul air. She offered one to her roommate, which the girl readily accepted. The girl was slightly taller but skinnier than she was. It was hard to tell, but Lindsey guessed that she was about Kelly's age.

"We're about the same size. You can wear some of my clothes until you get some new ones," Lindsey said.

The teenager wavered slightly and grabbed onto the back of the chair to catch her balance. The doctors in detox had tremendously over-sedated her; there was a long stretch of time before she answered.

"Two packs," Lindsey repeated, temptingly. "That's forty cigarettes."

The girl smoked silently by the window, ignoring her.

Lindsey tucked in her sheets and recovered her pillow. "Forty cigarettes."

"For what again?"

"Showering and putting on clean clothes," she repeated slowly.

Finishing her cigarette, the girl stubbed it into an ashtray. "Deal, Fuckhead."

She immodestly stripped off the stained, torn clothes—clothes that should not be touched with bare hands, but lifted with tongs and tossed directly into an incinerator. Ribs and the bony rims of her small, boyish hips protruded through lackluster, malnourished skin. The skin of her arms appeared like the lunar surface, cigarette burn craters, razor cut gullies, and scarring from needle use. A large gauze bandage wrapped her ankle. The girl grabbed Lindsey's towel off a door hook, wrapped it around herself, and headed toward the women's shower room.

Lindsey called after her, "There's something in there called shampoo and soap."

The girl called back, "Fuck you. I know what those things are."

"Good, then use them. What brand do you want?"

"Anything non-filters."

"I'm buying you anything filters," she yelled.

She bolted toward Kate Waters' office and shoved through the door without knocking. "Dana has an empty bed in her room! They're closer in age! The Animal would be better with Dana."

"Do I not recall someone's offer to help the teenage girls with their studies? The Animal," Kate chuckled, "would eat Dana alive. Besides, you're going to be her Peer Mentor. I think you'll get along famously."

"Who is she? She's just a child."

"We're clueless. She's says nothing to the social workers. We guess that she's a runaway. She has gonorrhea and is HIV positive."

"I'm pregnant. This is a huge liability issue."

"Not unless you're planning on having sex with her, or sharing needles."

"Yeah, right," Lindsey replied sarcastically.

"Since you're a physician, you can help counsel the girl with her health issues."

"Christ, she better not be using my toothbrush!" Lindsey cried, dashing back to her room.

Day Fuckin' One

That seat far in the corner would be the best place to eat without interruption and distraction, Maggie decided, hurrying her tray across the dining room. It was so hard to concentrate and stay awake! If she sat by herself, she wouldn't have to talk to any-fuckin-one. Lindsey N., her weirdo roommate, pointed to a chair next to hers and that blond man named Ethan, but she obstinately shook her head. She'd had enough of that dweeb for one day. Only good thing about Lindsey was that she used big words like putrefying, rancid, and atrocious. It was possible that she knew more big words than Bess. That was impressive. And amazingly, Lindsey hadn't struck her when she tore up the room and stole her twenty. If she had ransacked Bess' stuff... shit, she didn't want think about what would have happened!

Lindsey's boyfriend, Ethan was adorable and looked vaguely like an old version of Jed, but she wasn't thinking about asshole surfers ever again. It was Ethan's wife, Samantha, who brought her several days' worth of sick, new clothes, and all designer brands. Sadly, they'd have to be left behind when she got out of this nuthouse. The best of Samantha's purchases were the new sneakers. Her feet were sore and torn up from the mad run through alleyways in Stamford, and walking the highway in flip flops stolen from the bathhouse in southern Rhode Island on the same evening those assholes abandoned her! Stealing all of the coke that she stole from Sneek! Samantha had brought her nail-clippers, a completely worthless device—it was easier to just bite off her nails—and a perfume called Chanel No. 5, which Lindsey asked to borrow.

"Only for another pack of cigarettes, gum, and chocolate bars," Maggie had bargained. The fat, nice nurse, Lorena, made a run to the hospital store every day for the patients. That was very useful information.

"You're a con woman and extortionist! All that for a squirt of Chanel?" Lindsey had exclaimed.

"I know what those words mean," she had replied proudly.

"Of course you do," Lindsey had said good-humoredly. "I'm sure you know all the words associated with criminal activities."

"So, do you agree to my terms?"

"Yes," Lindsey had answered.

Maggie's attention returned to her food tray. Warm, wonderful food! There was no time to bother opening up the plastic bag with the plastic utensils; she was that hungry. Besides, spaghetti and meatballs could easily be eaten with one's hands. So could rolls, jello, and salad.

"Jane Doe," Lindsey called, holding up the plastic utensils. "Use these."

Jane Doe... she hated that name that Lindsey called her, but no way was anyone finding anything about her personal business. She scowled at Lindsey and flipped her the bird. Lindsey just shrugged and returned to her conversation with Ethan and a man in ugly plaid pants named Curtis. OMG... if she had ever flipped the bird to Bess, her entire body would be black and blue within minutes! Lindsey didn't care anything about anything except that contraption in the reading room, and Chanel No. 5. That, too, was very useful information. Maggie finished her dinner within minutes, lifted her plate to her face and licked it clean. Then something wonderful happened!

"Here, baby girl," Lorena said, placing a second food tray in front of her. "One of my boyfriends works in the kitchen. I can sweet-talk him into anything."

"The food here is delicious! And it's warm!" she said to Lorena.

That nosey roommate must have overheard. "Actually, Jane, it's just some unknown, synthetic substance resembling food whose covalent bonds are digestible by the hydrolytic enzymes in our gastrointestinal tracts," Lindsey N. explained in her know-it-all voice. The N stood for NERD!

Maggie looked quizzically at her roommate, burst into laughter, and then dug joyously into her second plate of food.

Newport

Sara Kauni's bag was carefully searched before she was admitted to the rehab wing of the Narragansett Eastbay Clinic. Given the okay, a large nurse pointed her down the hallway to the third room on the left, the reading room. Lindsey's back was to the door; she was working at a table covered with notepads and tools. In a chair next to her colleague sat a teenage girl blowing smoke rings at the ceiling. She gazed at Sara with hostile, suspicious eyes.

"Someone's here to see you," the girl warned in a low, gravelly voice.

Lindsey turned cautiously. She then popped out of her chair and threw her arms around Sara. "What a surprise! I'm so glad to see you. Let's go outside." Before Sara could respond, Lindsey dragged her by the hand down the hallway and outside to a garden. They walked to the far side of the lawn, toward a bench under a maple. The teenager followed and sat next to them.

"Now tell me everything!" Lindsey said excitedly.

Sara was unsettled by the warm welcome, but did her best to respond in kind. "Mort and Ella sent you some pastries. They're from the village bakery." She pulled a box out of a brown grocery bag.

Lindsey opened the pastry box. "Scones. Thank you. Jane Doe, try one of these."

"Don't fuckin' call me that," the girl mumbled as she grabbed pastries from the box.

Sara glanced uneasily at the teenager. "Who's this?"

"My roommate," Lindsey explained. "She doesn't have a name or any place of origin, so I'm guessing that she was dropped on this planet by an alien spaceship."

The girl grimaced and continued to munch.

"Mort says to get better soon. He told me to tell you that your best work's still to come," Sara said thoughtfully.

The encouraging words moved and silenced Lindsey for a moment. "Send him my thank-you. And tell Ella, thanks for the scones. I know she bought these."

"Mort meant it. He has every confidence in you," Sara added.

"I wish I did," Lindsey admitted sadly. "How are you and Zephyr?"

"We're good. Zephyr's snorkeling on Stony Beach this afternoon with Derick Briggs."

"I'd love to be on Stony Beach right now," Lindsey sighed wishfully. "Who's Derick Briggs?"

"He's a friend from grad school."

"What else is happening at the lab?"

"Nothing really. We're all just working away on our various projects. A strange thing happened this week. The fire alarm went off, and while leaving the building, Kumar tripped down the stairs and broke his leg. It was a greenstick fracture. He's still in the hospital because they can't control the infection."

"That's terrible," Lindsey said, frowning. "Whose lab was the fire in?"

"No one's. Some prankster pulled the fire alarm."

"That's odd." Lindsey hesitated. "Why didn't you visit me before now?"

Sara paused. Best to be honest and put it all on the table. "Because I've been so pissed at you!" she blurted. "We've done nothing significant in the lab for months. Our work and publications have slowed to… nothing."

"I hardly remember the past few months," Lindsey confessed. "I need to make amends to you."

"Amends?" Sara protested.

"*Step 9: Made direct amends to such people wherever possible, except when to do so would injure them or others.* They're like war reparations, I guess. I'm being brainwashed here. There are these Twelve Steps…"

"I know what the Twelve Steps are!" Sara interrupted hotly. "Fuck the amends. Amends aren't going to bring back months of lost productivity!"

"I'll try to make it up to you. Really," Lindsey said weakly.

"How, Lin?" Sara demanded, unconvinced.

"I don't know." Lindsey felt pathetic. "Maybe I can't. I'm terrified of leaving here," she confessed again.

"Shit," Sara said quietly.

"I wish I could, but I can't promise you anything."

Troy, the mutual fund broker, combed his hair over with his hand and strutted across the lawn. "Lindsey, would you like to introduce me to your friend?"

"Get lost!" Lindsey and Sara shouted in unison. He scuttled back to the patio.

"I found another job," Sara finally disclosed.

Lindsey exhaled as if she'd been punched. "Was I really that bad?"

"The worst. I'm furious that you were having sex in the lab, in your work closet!"

The teenager burst out in laughter.

"Shut up, Jane Doe!" Lindsey turned defensively toward Sara. "I would never have sex in the lab! I don't even bring boyfriends to my boat. Those are sacred places, my sanctuaries."

"Don't lie to me! There were condoms and sex lube in the work closet!" Sara accused.

The girl's giggling continued, and she reached for another scone.

Then Lindsey laughed softly to herself.

Sara glowered. "You two are so disturbed. It's not funny!"

"The rubber in condoms is the perfect material to make rubber membranes to separate saline compartments in the ion diffuser," Lindsey explained. "And lube has the perfect viscosity to hold the membranes together. Don't ask me why, but they just work better than anything I can get from a scientific equipment supplier."

"Only you would know this," Sara muttered contritely.

"Where's the job at?" Lindsey asked sadly.

"BTI. In Karen Battersby's lab."

Lindsey was quiet again. "That should be a good place for you. Karen does good work and has a reputation for being a good mentor to her grad students and post-docs. There will be more opportunities for you at BTI. The marine lab can be pretty isolating, especially in the winter." They sat awkwardly. "I'm sad for me, but I'm really glad for you."

Sara's heart pounded. "I haven't accepted the position yet."

"When do you have to let her know?" Lindsey asked apprehensively.

"In less than a week," Sara said moodily.

"Where are you with the epileptic seizure simulator?"

"It's done. Here. I took some photos for you." Sara pulled her smartphone from her pocket and handed it to her partner, who studied the photos scrolling by.

The teenager lit a cigarette and blew smoke into the canopy of leaves above.

"Jane, can I have one of those?" Lindsey asked. "I left my pack in the reading room. I'm sure they've walked by now. Sara, I've given up one vice that was going to give me cirrhosis, and replaced it with another that will give me lung cancer."

"What will you give me for it?" the girl asked slyly.

"Five pieces of bubble gum?" Lindsey proposed.

"Ten," the girl countered.

"Okay, ten. Sara, this kid is robbing me blind."

The girl handed over a cigarette and a lighter.

Lindsey smoked and said nothing for a while. "How long would you be willing to stay on after you accept Karen's offer?" She was already resigned to the fact that Sara was leaving.

"Two weeks."

"Good, because the simulator's not quite finished yet."

"It's not?" Sara replied, baffled.

"Right now it's a metal oval structure, but it needs to be the exact anatomical shape of a human brain. Remember that it's a training instrument for neurosurgeons. You'll need to embed your simulator into a precise model of the brain. The material, some plastic or rubber, will need to have the exact same resistivity as real brain tissue to accurately simulate the movement of an electrical current, the seizure, from the source, the hot spot or epileptic focus, to the surface of the brain. You'll need to figure out what substance will work best to construct it. And you'll need to create foci in different brain areas where seizures are most prevalent."

Ramon, wearing the aqua and white jersey of Dan Marino, called from the door of the garden, "Visitation's over."

Sara couldn't believe her ears. "You want me to build a seizure-generating, three-dimensional brain in only two weeks?"

Lindsey smiled. "No. Four of them, a brain of an adult, teenager, child, and infant."

Chapter 24

Rehab

Jane Doe's unshakable presence and demands chafed; all she wanted to know was the meaning of words.

"Don't you want to hang out with Kelly, Dana, and Melissa and talk about sex, drugs, and rock n' roll, or watch mindless reality TV with them?" Lindsey asked.

Jane stared back. "No!"

Not once had Lindsey noticed Jane speaking to the other teenage girls; the girl was a confirmed loner. Well, she empathized with that. She shrugged and turned back to the sensor portion of the Drunkard's Doorknob, which was almost complete. Kate hated the name of the new device. Ramon, a man of delicacy and diplomacy, had suggested that the doorknob might be used by arthritics that could no longer manage keys and locks, and proposed the name, the Arthritic Access Aid. The triple A... not.

While Lindsey tinkered, the girl seemed content to study the wall map of the U.S. Fluorescent stickers marked the cities and towns where the patients had come from. Lindsey had placed a small sticker over her hometown the first week there. She glanced over her shoulder to see where Jane might place a sticker, but instead the girl dropped down into a chair and did nothing.

The girl did infuriatingly nothing all the time! That behavior was inconceivable; Lindsey had to keep compulsively busy all the time. The doctors were still over-medicating the girl to prevent another staff injury, but Lindsey saw no indication of violence from her, except a clenched fist if approached too closely by an unwelcome man.

Jane's parentage was evident. She was the product of an interracial marriage, love affair, one-night-stand, who knows what. Her skin was mocha brown. Her ash blonde hair was in cornrows, their ends accented with small white beads. As her health improved, Jane's looks emerged and were noticed by the men on the ward. Her blue eyes were large and exotic, her cheek bones high, her lips pink and sensual. The men's come-ons and compliments came fast, but she was having none of it. She was a prostitute and had no illusions about what they wanted. As soon as a word was spoken from any man, she stopped them with, "This is gonna to cost ya," which caused a predictable, hasty retreat.

Ethan was the only man allowed entry into the girl's vigilantly guarded world. They often smoked together at the fence where he taught her the different types of boats winding down the river toward the Rhode Island Sound; she was quick to identify ketches, yawls, sloops, and catboats. If Lindsey approached, she was told to "get lost, nerd."

Jane had a calming influence on Ethan, and for a time he was not so preoccupied by his foot. He had Samantha bring in an assortment of children's books that sat in an undisturbed stack in the reading room. The girl had bragged to him that she could read, but Lindsey seriously doubted it, as the girl never once touched a book. The boast, she guessed, was said to impress him.

Irked by the girl's ceaseless inactivity, Lindsey asked, "Can you really read?"

The girl turned from the map. "Of course. I finished half of fourth grade." Deliberately changing the topic, she stated in a supercilious tone, "I've been to every state."

"Even Alaska and Hawaii?" Lindsey asked.

The girl paused. "No," she admitted, a bit miffed.

"Then you haven't been to every state. You were probably born right here in Rhode Island, and haven't even stepped foot into Connecticut."

Jane Doe gnawed on her thumbnail. Lindsey expected her to lash out with the usual expletives, but instead she lit another cigarette and considered.

"I'm from Arizona," the girl revealed a few minutes later.

Lindsey searched the toolbox for the right resistor. "Since you've been everywhere, what's the Pacific Ocean like?"

"I only saw it from far away."

"You went all the way to the Pacific Ocean and never swam in it?"

"No!"

"Why?"

"I hate the water. I can't swim."

"You're so full of shit. You're a Rhode Island girl. This is the Ocean State. You can swim."

"I'm from Tucson."

After a few minutes of silence, Lindsey said, "I have to call you something. Since you won't tell me your real name, I'm going to make one for you. Since you're a probably a Rhode Islander, I'll call you Quahog."

The girl's hands shot to her hips. "What the hell is that? I hate that name!"

"It's a clam."

"Sit on it, a-hole, you're not calling me that!"

"Since you're from the Wild West, how about Cowpie?"

"No!" The girl stormed away.

Best to back off on the circuitous questions and strategies of reverse psychology, Lindsey decided. For the rest of the day the girl grumbled, "Fuckhead" every time they passed in the hallway or Fishbowl, and Lindsey wondered briefly if that might be the name by which the other patients had stereotyped her.

Boston

Karen Battersby's home office was dark except for the glow of the computer monitor. She leaned on the windowsill and gazed down to the street below. The few people on the sidewalk beside the bay appeared to her as ants. Sara Kauni had not gotten back to her with further questions about the job, or a decision. But it was of no consequence anymore if Sara joined the team or not. Besides, Sara was a sucker for falling for that ridiculous story about Aunt Edith's pancreatic cancer. She'd nearly burst out in laughter when Sara had grabbed her hand and said, "You and your family will be in my thoughts and prayers."

In Sara's printer she'd noticed a piece of paper with MapQuest instructions on how to get to a place called the Narragansett Eastbay Clinic. When she Googled the clinic, she found that it was drug and alcohol rehabilitation hospital. Lindsey Nolan had been quite the party girl at Hopkins. Karen had often seen her huddled over the keg at various frat parties. At every lacrosse game, Lindsey had cheered on the Blue Jays with a beer bottle in her hand. And there were rumors of a terrible car accident during her freshman year. Could a drinking problem be the "personal issue" that Lindsey was dealing with, and the reason for the slowed productivity that Sara eluded to? While Googling Duncan McLeod, Karen found that he was an assistant professor of history at a puny, third-rate college in northern Virginia. He and Lindsey didn't even live together anymore! They were not taking a romantic holiday together in Paris or the Mayan Rivera. Lindsey was probably drying out in a rehab, and the couple was separated or divorced. Karen felt better by the minute.

Nor was there a reason to ever go back to the marine lab. What Karen needed to 'acquire' from the Nolan lab was now safely stored on her hard drive.

"I'm a genius!" she proclaimed gleefully. Hearing her voice, two black domestic shorthaired kittens that she had adopted from the SPCA ran into the room. She dropped to her knees to play.

The whole mission had been brilliantly planned and executed. After meeting with Sara, she'd ducked into a janitor's closet down the corridor from her lab. When the hallway was clear, she ran out, pulled the fire alarm, and ducked back into the closet again. Through a tiny crack in the doorway, she watched the commotion unfold. Sara had quickly ushered the younger scientists from a lab down the hallway, and then left the floor with an old man with a shock of white hair. Karen then darted into the Nolan lab, went into the small workroom, closed the door, and downloaded everything onto an external hard drive from her briefcase. It took only minutes. Lindsey Nolan's laptops were stupidly—

yes, she was certainly a lush—not password protected! She had then rushed to a stairwell at the opposite end of the building from where Sara and her research group had exited. A fireman passed her on the stairs and told her to hurry out of the building. In her business suit, she melted into a group of employees and administrators from the marine lab's library, and then slipped away to her car.

Escaping across the Bourne Bridge, she was still in a state of nervous exhilaration; she felt like a super spy who'd successfully stolen secrets from a rogue government. The whole episode was almost as exciting as an adventure with the Centurions. All of the information needed to scoop her drunken nemesis was in her briefcase on the front seat of her Honda Civic.

Chapter 25

Rehab

The next day Jane Doe had forgiven her, and again pulled her chair next to the worktable. The girl smelled wonderful, like Chanel No. 5, and Lindsey wondered what it would cost her next time to get another spritz.

Lindsey was despondent for a number of reasons. The thought of working without Sara was devastating. She had always imagined that she and Sara would be partners... forever. Sara wouldn't even allow her to make amends. Whether Sara was at the marine lab or BTI, something meaningful would have to be done beyond just saying "I'm sorry" if their relationship was to be salvaged.

Then, somewhere, maybe outside by the picnic table, where she often took them off, she'd misplaced her sneakers. She'd scoured the ward, Jane Doe taunting her with "numbskull," "peabrain", and "dumbass." But despite the diligent search, the shoes had vanished, and so she returned to wearing sandals. Worse, the lost shoes resurrected her paranoia about a strangler or another IV drug user on the ward. Perhaps it was one of the new patients, like one of the creepy meth cooks that had just come over from detox.

And Melissa was getting ready to be discharged and nagged her; everyone's impatience to discover Boat Show Man's identity was growing. Lindsey tried to convince Kate Waters to bring in a hypnotist to dislodge his identity from her mental mush, but Kate answered with the usual canned response, "Focus on getting sober!"

Lastly, Lindsey was a total failure as a Peer Mentor. The girl refused to reveal anything about herself or her drug addiction. All of her strategies fell flat. She'd described her years as a drunken teenager, college student, med student, and scientist, all while Jane Doe had twisted gum around her fingers in total boredom. The girl didn't even notice when she'd finished talking, as she'd fallen asleep. At that point, without telling Kate, Lindsey fired herself from the job of Peer Mentor.

The girl seemed dumbly content to watch her solder capacitors and resistors into a circuit board. "What are you making?" she asked one day.

"It's called the Drunkard's Doorknob. It reads handprints so drunks don't need to worry about keys."

"It's a stupid invention. All of the drunks I know sleep outside."

The last comment was the tipping point. It was not a stupid invention! It was an ingenious invention! Lindsey grabbed a yellow legal pad and wrote across it in large, simple print, "Why don't you ever do anything? You're a coward." She held the pad up to the girl's face. "Can you read that?"

The note struck a nerve as the girl's eyes widened and she fell silent. One thing was certain... she could clearly read.

Lindsey felt a surge of guilt, as the girl was both steamed and wounded. Jane yanked the pad from her hands and picked up the pencil. For minutes she scrawled frantically on the pad. The girl was a lefty like herself.

She shoved the pad into Lindsey's face. "Can you read that?" she shouted.

The paper read: "You are an arrogant, self-important asshole! I have Self-esteem because I can read and draw."

It was elementary school handwriting, but the spelling and punctuation were correct. So that was it... the girl had self-esteem issues. Maybe she'd been shuttled between relatives during a nasty divorce, or had an abusive father, or an icy, unloving tiger mother, like her own, whose expectations were unrealistic and unreasonable. Any number of conditions could prompt a girl to flee home and take to a life on the streets. But another thing on the page caught Lindsey's eye.

It was a quick sketch of seagulls perched on the hurricane fence.

The drawing was remarkably good. No, it was better than that.

"Cowgirl, do want a job?" Lindsey asked.

"No!" She paused. "What is it?"

"Watch how I'm soldering the wires into the back of the board."

"Okay," she grumbled.

"See how I'm using very small dabs of solder?" Lindsey held up a completed circuit board and handed her a blank one. "Can you make a circuit board just like this one? With all of the colorful pieces in the exact same places on the board? My hands have bad shakes. Yours are steady."

"What will you give me if I do?" Jane asked shrewdly.

"What do you want?"

"Peanut brittle from the hospital store. Two packs."

"Can you do it in one hour?"

Jane nodded.

"Deal." She rose from her chair. "I'll be back in an hour. Don't burn yourself. That thing's very hot."

"I know that! You think I'm an idiot?"

"Not anymore."

After her group counseling session, Lindsey returned to the reading room. Jane Doe was in front of the map again.

"Which dot is you?" the girl asked.

"The one by Annapolis, Maryland."

"That's the state capital, you know."

"You're right."

"I've been there. I've been to every state capital. Name any state and I'll tell you the capital."

"North Dakota?"

"Bismarck.

"Maine?"

"Augusta."

"Minnesota?"

"St. Paul. You won't stump me. I've pulled tricks in every state capital," the girl bragged.

"Now I'm really impressed. That might get you into the Guinness Book of World Records." Lindsey wandered over to the table. "Let's see how you did."

Jane held up the circuit board. All of the resistors and capacitors were in the right place. The solder job was crude, but all wires were firmly attached.

"Not bad." She handed the girl three packs of peanut brittle. "The Twelve Step meeting's in five minutes. Don't sleep through this one."

Day Four

My roommate has issues! Maggie realized. Her memory is shot and she got knocked up by two Latinos that she can't even remember! That can't happen to me, because I haven't had my period yet. Bess had taught her about Reproduction.

And Lindsey had evil and tormenting creatures stuck inside her hands called tremors, or DTs. "When are the tremors going to stop, Lin?" she asked testily. "Stop them. Get better!"

"I don't have voluntary control over them. They just happen."

"I hate them. I want them to stop." She grabbed Lindsey's hands and pinned them to the working table as if to scare the shakes out of them. "Stop it!" she shouted at the hands.

The mean old bitch, Kate Waters, stuck her head in the door. "What the hell are you two doing?"

Maggie quickly retracted her hands and hid them in her pockets.

"Nothing," she and Lindsey answered in unison.

Kate gave them a doubtful, pissed off look and departed.

"What am I soldering today?" Soldering was good for Self-esteem and acquiring peanut brittle.

"Nothing. I've run out of some components. Kate will bring us supplies tomorrow when she stops at the hardware store after work. Until then we're going to read."

"No fuckin' way," she said firmly.

"I'm going to read and you can listen, if you want to. It's an exciting tale about Viking princesses."

She grimaced and lit a cigarette.

The Bottom Dwellers

Lindsey pulled a book from Samantha's stack. She dropped into a chair. "A series of dangerous adventures beset our heroine, Freya and younger sister, Helga....'"

"Heroin?" she asked curiously from a nearby chair.

"Not that kind. This is heroine with an e. It means a female hero. Look." Lindsey pointed at the word. "'A series of dangerous adventures beset our heroine, Freya and younger sister, Helga as they travel across the North Atlantic.' Hmmm,"—she flipped pages and skimmed ahead. "Their longboat is trapped in a maelstrom—which is a giant whirlpool of spinning water—off the Lofoton Islands. Captain Larvik and half the crew are pulled into the cruel jaws of a great krakken."

"What's a krakken?" she interrupted.

"A huge octopus-like creature with grabbing tentacles and a shredding beak," Lindsey exclaimed in a dramatic voice like actresses on TV.

"That's why I'll never swim in an ocean!"

Lindsey continued with verve. "Without the captain, Freya learned to steer the Star Board. Icy swells sweep across the bow as they approach Newfoundland. Helga is nearly swept overboard, but Freya quickly grabs her and pulls her aboard by her long blonde braids! As the longboat approaches the Vinland settlement, the girls are attacked by Skraelings. Spears and arrows shower the"—She stopped and looked at her watch. "Whoa, I'm in trouble," she said, standing. "I was supposed to meet with Ramon five minutes ago. Maybe we can finish this up tomorrow."

She grasped Lindsey's shirttail. Her voice quavered and shifted an octave. "Wait! What's a Skraeling? What happens to the girls?"

Lindsey handed her the book. "Here, Cowgirl. Find out for yourself. Later."

Later that afternoon, the old bitch, Kate, returned to the reading room. "I've been looking all over for you. You missed your small group session!"

Maggie pulled her eyes grudgingly off the page. The scolding didn't faze her one fuckin' bit because she was brimming with Self-esteem. She hadn't moved off the chair all afternoon and had read all the way to page fifty-four... on her own!

Chapter 26

Rehab

At 3:43 am Lindsey pulled herself from under the sheets and passed silently to the window. As she leaned on the windowsill, her elbow pushed into the curtain. A crumpling sound was heard so she peered behind the curtain. A hidden stash of bags of potato chips and tortilla chips was tucked into the corner. She glanced back at the sleeping girl, still rattled and saddened by their earlier conversation.

While the two of them were cleaning up for bed that night, Jane Doe finally began to talk. Her drug use varied according to U. S. geography, it seemed. Crack and heroin in the cities, and meth or whatever she could get her hands on in more rural areas. She'd been using for just about two years. The girl never drank alcohol, as she didn't like its taste. How was that even possible? Alcohol was delicious, the elixir of life! When she was Jane's age, she was sniffing out booze daily from her various watering holes... her father's liquor cabinet, Megan's basement, and Mark Willis' refrigerator.

Jane usually traveled alone, but sometimes hooked up with another migratory teenager en route to whatever direction on the compass rose they might find a buzz, food, shelter, or the friend-of-a friend. For a couple of years she'd roamed the country with a sixteen-year old prostitute named Bess.

"Where's Bess now?" she'd asked.

"We're parted ways in Tennessee," the girl had said shortly, without further elaboration.

Jane avoided men, pimps, whenever possible, as they invariably tried to enslave her for their profit. "Once," she'd mentioned with a shudder, "I was stuck bad, in Minnesota, but I don't want to talk about it."

It was best not to prod, Lindsey had decided. Jane traveled the country in trucks and cars, exchanging for rides and food the one service she could offer the driver. In the fall she hitched south to avoid bad weather and boasted that she knew the coastlines of Alabama, Louisiana, and Florida like the back of her hand. Her sleeping accommodations were junked cars, woods, abandoned warehouses, drainage pipes, or under boardwalks. "Beds are awesome. I love to sleep in beds!" she'd declared happily.

"My name's Maggie," the girl had revealed.

"Where are your folks?"

"I don't know. I never knew them. I fuckin' hate the girls' homes and orphanages. Traveling's not so bad once you get used to it. And I really have seen all of the states, except Alaska and Hawaii!"

"I believe you. How old are you?"

"Fifteen."

"Which is your favorite state?"

"Massachusetts."

"Really? That's where I live. On a pirate ship with pirates."

"You're bull-shittin' me."

"Yeah, I am. Actually it's just an old houseboat full of pirates made of coconuts."

"The whole body's made of coconuts?"

"No, just their heads. So why do you like Massachusetts?"

"Because of the seagulls."

"If you lived in Massachusetts, you'd have to learn how to swim."

"Forget it, then! I'm not going back there."

"What's your next stop after rehab?"

The question stuck a nerve. "That's my fuckin' business," Maggie had said in a surly tone. She had climbed into bed and turned toward the wall.

The next morning Kate and Lindsey smoked at the psychologist's windowsill. Lindsey felt traitorous and guilty.

"She says her name is Maggie May. She's from Arizona. She's fifteen," she disclosed, hating herself more with every revelation.

"Maggie May? Like the Rod Stewart song? What a ridiculous alias," Kate remarked cynically.

Lindsey kept to herself the fact that Maggie was hoarding food behind the curtain and obsessively checked, sometimes many times a day, to see that her tarp remained under the bed. Maggie had no intention of staying the thirty days. Something the social worker had said had put her on edge; she'd returned from their interview sullen and silent.

"What happens to the kid after rehab?" Lindsey asked.

"She's going to a juvenile detention center," answered Kate. "The place has security. She can't be running around the streets with HIV. She's a Typhoid Mary."

"You can't lock her up! She's committed no crime. The crimes have been committed against her." She stared hotly at Kate. "The place sounds like a goddamn prison!"

"It's in the hands of the courts," Kate said dismally.

Woods Hole

"What are you thinking about?" Derick wondered. His bare foot rocked the old rope hammock as Sara lay gazing up at the stars.

"My father, for some odd reason. I rarely think about him anymore. It was the visit to Lindsey that made me think of him."

He sipped wine from one of Zephyr's plastic Super Hero cups. The wine and the crickets in the woods next to Sara's tiny apartment had a relaxing effect. "Why's that?"

"Every birthday my father would give me a plane model for a gift. I was crazy with anticipation, wondering which model I'd get next. Since our island was so remote, he'd have to send away for it through the Internet. For weeks I'd be wondering if the new plane would be a Curtis Jenny, a Junkers, the Red Baron plane, or something else. Once I received it, I'd study its history so that I knew every obscure fact about it. While assembling it I'd install a small battery-operated motor so that it would fly. Sometimes it worked, and sometimes it didn't. I'd conduct the test flights on the beach so that if the plane crashed—which it usually did—it wouldn't sustain too much damage."

"That's pretty amazing. How old were you?"

"A teenager."

"When I was a teenager, my only interest was racing dirt bikes through the fields and getting my hand into the shirt of the cute teenager on the neighboring farm."

Sara smiled. "Did you?"

"Yes," he replied, his thoughts in a faraway place. "Sex was fun and sweet then." His mood darkened. "Now I feel sick about it. I'm going to kill Jared."

Sara sipped her wine. "You'll feel better when you get back to Indonesia to do your research, and put some distance and time between you and Isabel."

"Anyway, my grandmother, who runs the family business with him, will probably kill him for me. Back to your father—what does he have to do with Lindsey?"

"Do you know what task she gave me before I go to Karen Battersby's lab?"

"Are you definitely going?" he interrupted.

"I don't know!" she exclaimed, raking her fingers through her hair.

"When do you have to let her know?"

"Tomorrow," she answered woefully.

"What task did Lindsey give you?"

"To build her four models."

"Plane models?" he asked perplexed.

"No, brain models. Four epileptic brains of differing ages. I've never ever had so much fun! I'm embedding metal plates in the different brain areas that are hooked up to a current source to simulate different types of seizures. I think about the project day and night, and nothing else. I'm on an adrenaline high all day in the lab constructing these brains. Tomorrow I'll embed wires crisscrossing the entire cortex to produce grand mal seizures. So, why did she give me such a great project? She had to know I'd love building brain models. As a going-away present? Or to reignite my interest in the lab and keep me here?"

"I think you're reading too much into this. She probably just needed the work done, and you were the best person to build the models." He paused. "Was she clear enough to have had those other motives? How did she seem?"

"Really different. I was talking to a complete stranger. She was almost unrecognizable. First of all, she was wearing someone else's clothes. They were neat and elegant. She's usually disheveled, like she's just emerged from an orgy."

"She sounds fun. Introduce us," he said facetiously.

"I thought that you weren't thinking about women," she reminded him in an admonishing tone.

"You're right. I'm not," he quickly replied.

"And she was clear-eyed and clean. In the past, if one lit a match near her, she'd combust from the alcohol fumes wafting off her." She was silent for a moment. "So I can stay here and work for a total stranger, or go to BTI, and work for a total stranger. In either case, my future's a complete unknown."

"Which research impresses and inspires you more?"

"If I stay here, I do electrophysiology and biomedical research. If I go to BTI, I do heat conduction in military weaponry. I like the biomedical research better, but what if Lindsey can't stay sober, and I've missed a great opportunity at BTI? And another thing… right as I was leaving, she told me that she was pregnant. In February, she said, she'd be taking some maternity leave."

"Who's the father?"

"She doesn't even know!"

Derick's eyebrows rose.

Sara struggled out of the hammock with her empty cup, and leaned toward the wine bottle. "Do you want some more?"

"No thanks, I'm good."

"Look." A firefly sat on the cork and she held it out for Derick to see. "Bioluminescent animals are the coolest." For a moment, she studied the black and red bug, and then blew it gently into the air. It emitted a glow as it flew up into the trees.

"What's your gut telling you?" he asked.

"It's telling me to listen to Mort Somers," she stated decisively. "He has unwavering confidence in her. I can't stop thinking about the message he had me deliver to her."

"What was that?"

"That her best work is yet to come."

Day Five

My roommate's criminal mind is admirable, Maggie thought to herself, noticing the dictionary and the thesaurus on the foot of her bed. Lindsey had clearly stolen them from the reading room on her behalf. And the radio from the janitor's closet had mysteriously appeared in their bedroom.

"It's much more fun to bounce on the beds to Beyoncé and Missy Elliot than to your old fart jazz," Maggie had casually mentioned.

"I don't know what you're talking about. I see and hear nothing," Lindsey had said.

Bess called that admirable quality Discretion.

Maggie discovered another important fact about her roommate. Lin—that's what Sara called her—had a fetish, but not a weird one like the old, disgusting Slugs. It was a pirate fetish. Maggie caught her roommate reading *Treasure Island* and the *Pirate Queens* about Anne Bonny and Mary Read. Lin showed no interest in the other books that Maggie had moved into their bedroom, like the *Jewel Princess* stories, *A Tree Grows in Brooklyn, Harry Potter,* or *The Outsiders.* Only pirate stories. Her houseboat on Cape Cod had pirate flags on the rigging, in addition to the pirate coconuts that lined her bookshelves.

"Are you up to playing a pirate game with me? It's called the Black Spot," Lindsey said, upon entering their bedroom.

Maggie looked up from her sketchpad. "Maybe," she said nonchalantly, though listening with rapt attention.

"Here's how you play. Each day," Lindsey continued, "you and I, the two pirate queens and captains of this Ship of Fools, will assign some doomed pirate the Black Spot. For the rest of the day we'll find words in the dictionary or thesaurus that best describe our victim. Permissible words in this game have to be over four letters in length, hence eliminating most obscenities and your entire vocabulary."

"I'll play if I can be Mary Read," Maggie cut in. "You should be Anne Bonny since she's a slut."

"Thank you," Lindsey said ironically.

"I will soooo beat you in this game because my brain works again since they stopped the sedatives. And I'm smarter."

"Don't be so sure about that, small-fry."

"Who gets the Black Spot first?" she said excitedly.

"Let's doom several pirates at once," Lindsey suggested mischievously. "How about Curtis, Dana, and the fat pontificator, Ernest?"

"And Ethan," Maggie added.

Lindsey nodded. "Mary, we'll meet here at the ship's wheel at the end of the day. Have your list ready for inspection. We'll hold a pirate council and vote on who has the better list."

"Okay!" she said, springing off the bed.

"Yo ho," Anne Bonny said.

"Yo ho!" Mary Read replied.

The best place to observe the pirates cursed with the Black Spot was the Fishbowl, so Maggie positioned herself in the wicker chair next to the coffee table with the ashtrays.

"What are you doing, baby girl?" Lorena asked, poking her head in the doorway.

"Nothing. Just drawing." She flipped through the pages and held up a sketch of Kate.

"That's excellent! It looks just like her. Though I've never noticed the horns and devil tail," Lorena remarked, laughing.

Maggie smiled back. The rehab wasn't that bad a place. Her three favorite things were here: beds with sheets, warm food, and kind people. Lorena called her baby girl; Ethan called her honey or sweetheart; and Lindsey called her funny names that weren't so bad like Magpie, Cowgirl, or small fry. And now Mary Read... how cool was that!

What timing! The fat pontificator walked over to the coffee counter and dumped packets of hot chocolate into a Styrofoam cup. Maggie thumbed quickly through the thesaurus. A number of words corresponded with the word *fat*. *Corpulent* sounded like a cork springing from a bottle. She double-checked its meaning in the dictionary. There was no way Anne Bonny could possibly win the Black Spot game!

The task accomplished, she reviewed her word list for Ernest: *corpulent, slovenly, dullard,* and *vitriolic.* Then Curtis wandered through the Fishbowl, searching for the sports page. The best words that described him were *jocular, amenable, affable,* and *polyester.* Then she slyly watched Dana through the glass windows of the Fishbowl as she chatted in the hallway with Ramon. The words *coquettish, featherbrained, fractious,* and *petulant* suited her. Mary Read was sooo going to win this game! Then the *debonair* and *elusive* Ethan entered the room with the old Dead Head, Joshua.

"Do you mind if we watch the news before dinner?" he asked her.

"Go ahead." She intentionally reached for her cigarettes, as she knew the *gallant* and *charming* Ethan would swish the lighter from his pocket and *suavely* light her cigarette. Her next comment would really impress him. "Dinner tonight is *scrumptious* pizza!"

Ethan grinned. "Scrumptious pizza is my favorite."

If pizza was Ethan's favorite, it was hers also. "Mine too."

He aimed the remote at the TV and found the local news. Joshua stretched out on the sofa next to him. Through the weather and sports, she created a picture for Lindsey of the pirate queens digging up a treasure chest on a tropical shoreline. During the news story on a whale that washed up on Narragansett Beach, she sketched Lorena dispensing vitamins from the medicine cart. If she could pick her grandmother, her first choice would be Lorena. Suddenly the anchorman said in a grave tone, "Breaking news... stay tuned for a press conference by the senator from Maine, Richard Hamilton, regarding the execution-style murder of his son, Jed Hamilton and his roommate, Antonio Baker."

Maggie looked up from her sketchpad and gnawed on her thumbnail.

"The remains of the two Yale sophomores were found in their van outside of Boston yesterday, where their van had been set on fire. The two college students were avid surfers and had spent the summer traveling up the east coast from Georgia..."

"It sounds like a drug deal gone bad," Joshua said.

"Most definitely," Ethan agreed.

"The police are following a number of leads..." the anchorman continued.

Cambridge

In a small pizzeria Agnes Holcomb scrolled through the data on Karen Battersby's new laptop. "Your friend writes code very strangely. Maybe that's how they do it in Germany. I don't know. At some places, it's very logical, and at other places, it doesn't make sense. It's gibberish."

Karen pulled another slice of pepperoni pizza from the pan. "She's not a computer scientist. She's an engineer trying to write code. And she's been very sick, which might explain the gibberish. She was in amazing shape, a marathon runner, when we were grad students together. Then she returned to a job in Bonn, and was soon diagnosed with pancreatic cancer. She's been on chemo for months. Now she's getting morbid and fatalistic on me. She sent me this software. I'm quite concerned. Her email read, 'in case something happens to me, see if you can do something with this device.' There are .jpgs also."

"I'll look at those in a sec," Agnes replied, still staring curiously into the monitor. "You should have come dancing with us after Comic Con. I danced all night with Lieutenant

Worf. His friend, Data, was pretty cute and he didn't have a date."

Karen shook more grated cheese onto her slice and took another bite. "I'm trying not to think about that night. It was one series of disasters after another. Next time we stay together."

But having Agnes unwittingly decipher the code from Lindsey Nolan's laptop, she thought to herself, was consolation for a run of horrible luck.

Agnes continued to study the code. "Your German friend is trying to get the processors to do something extremely rapidly. Something is being reproduced very fast, but I can't figure out what. Besides, current processors don't work as fast as she's wanting them to. If I didn't know better, I say that she's trying to write code for a program to reproduce molecules or cells at an extraordinary rate. There's a mention of RNA polymerase. Is she trying to make proteins, or something like that? Is her research biological in nature? She's factoring in enzyme kinetics. Is she studying enzyme reaction rates?"

"I have no clue what the device does. I emailed her, but she hasn't gotten back to me. I'm hoping that she's not too sick. Or worse, dead! We were so close in grad school."

A waitress appeared at their table. "Do you want more drinks?"

"Yes. I'll have another Cherry Coke," Karen responded.

"Another Sprite for me, please," Agnes added.

The waitress left with the drink orders.

Karen leaned toward the laptop. "Let me show you pictures of the device. Whatever it is, it's in its very early stages of development. Here." She turned the images toward

Agnes. "Do you think it's a very fast printer? Can she be reproducing words very quickly?"

Agnes shrugged with uncertainty. "You're the engineer." She gazed at the monitor as she streamed through the .jpgs. "But where's slot for the paper? And where does the ink or toner go? And what's the function of the RNA polymerase?"

"Who knows! She hasn't been well. What if it doesn't use ink or toner?"

"What printer doesn't use ink or toner?"

"And what's the purpose of the tiny coolers? Heat must be generated in some way to need coolers."

"What if she's designing some futuristic device for German spaceships?" Agnes suggested playfully. "Maybe the Germans have a super advanced, secret space program that the rest of the world doesn't know about. Maybe your friend is a double agent, and is leaking the information to you in the U.S.? Maybe the information is encrypted somehow in this top secret code?" She grinned. "At this very moment, German secret agents are sneaking into the country to steal this code back from you."

"Yikes! Then I'm in trouble!" Karen grinned also. "What if it's a time machine?"

"It's way too small. Maybe it's a prototype photon torpedo!" Agnes added, giggling.

"Or a worm-hole generator!"

"What about a cloaking device?"

"It's way too small for humans! What about for cloaking German cats..."

The two women laughed hysterically at the preposterous notions.

Chapter 27

Rehab

A nudge against her shoulder woke Lindsey in the middle of the night. She squinted into the darkness. "What?" she said sleepily.

Maggie stood trembling in the darkness.

"What is it?" Lindsey asked, sitting up.

"I hate the homes, Lin," she whispered fiercely. "I can't go to this one. I'll never get out. This one's a lock-down."

Lindsey's eyes adapted to the darkness and suddenly it registered. Maggie was fully dressed. The blue Hopkins gym bag hung from her shoulder. "Think this through, Maggie. You're not safe on the streets. Especially alone!"

"I've always wanted to see Alaska. I'll go through Canada."

Lindsey climbed out of bed. "Don't do this. Canada's cold, even at this time of year."

"Don't tell anyone where I'm going. Promise me that," Maggie insisted.

"Why do you have to go now? Wait a few more weeks. You're doing so well with the Steps. Stay for the whole thirty days. Maybe you don't have to go to a detention center! Maybe something can be worked out. I can talk to a lawyer —"

"They're gonna fuckin' lock me up!" Maggie cut in. "Cops might arrive tomorrow and lock me up for fuckin' ever!"

Lindsey shook her head in confusion. "The detention center won't be like that. You'll be able to go to school again."

"Promise!" Maggie whispered emphatically. "You won't tell!"

"Okay," she agreed hesitantly.

"It's important that I leave tonight... NOW!"

Lindsey's alert system switched on. "Something's happened. What is it?"

"Nothing! But I need to leave now!"

"Did one of those creepy meth cooks say or doing some to you?" she asked warily.

"No! I gotta go!" Maggie stepped toward the door.

"Wait a sec." She tiptoed to her drawer. From inside a sock, she pulled a roll of bills, the remaining money from the Boat Show Men that she had removed from the lamp to pay for cigarettes and candy. "Take this to buy food and warm stuff." She handed Maggie the money. "And this sweater and extra socks. I want to give you my address and phone number. You call or write me to let me know you're all right, or if you need anything. Okay? Anything! A place to stay... money... food... anything."

Maggie shook her head stubbornly. "No. You're going to have to get on without me. I hope your tremors go away." She quietly unzipped the overnight bag and stuffed the bills and clothes inside. She nimbly attached the rolled tarp onto the shoulder strap of the bag. The two roommates paused and then collapsed into an embrace. Finally, Maggie pushed away and backed quickly toward the doorway, a yellow rectangle of light in the darkness. She hesitated.

"Stay sober, Lindsey N."

"Long clean life, Maggie M." Lindsey murmured weakly to the silhouette in the doorway,

"Maybe we'll eat crab cakes together in Annapolis one day," Maggie said with some bravado.

"Let's do that," she replied, shaken.

Maggie waited a second longer. "Yo ho, Anne." She peered surreptitiously into the hallway.

"Maggie, wait!"

But the teenager disappeared out the door.

She heard nothing as Maggie darted down the hallway. It then occurred to her to wonder how Maggie was escaping. She walked silently down the hall to the reading room. Her screwdriver was gone from the worktable. Next to the locked patio door downstairs was a ladies' room where a small window, perhaps only the dimension of a cinderblock, was high in the wall over the sink. There was no way an adult could squeeze through such an opening, but a skinny teenager, maybe.

Maggie must have dropped through the opening head first, for Lindsey heard a small thud and quiet curse. Her forehead pressed against the glass, she watched the teenager pick herself up and run swiftly along the shadow of the hedge toward the corner of the fence. The bag-tarp bundle was flung in a black arc and landed silently in the grass on the other side. Maggie climbed effortlessly up the wire mesh of the hurricane fence. At the top she gingerly slung her long legs over the sharp wires, and then sprang outward, falling into the grass. For a moment she searched the tall grass for the bag. Slinging the bundle over her shoulder, Maggie disappeared down the bluff on a trek to perceived freedom.

"I live in a place called Woods Hole... Dave's Marina," Lindsey whispered to no one.

Chapter 28

Rehab

Drs. Kate Waters and Ethan Eldridge sat at the picnic table, chain-smoking in the morning heat. They looked in skeptical anger at Lindsey when she approached.

"Are you sure you had nothing to do with this?" Kate demanded accusingly. "Did you piss her off in some way?"

"No! I told you. I was asleep. I woke up. She was gone."

"Her name actually is Maggie May," Kate said. "We finally found out who she is. She's a ward of the Arizona State Program of Child Services in Tucson. She was abandoned in a trailer in the Sonoran Desert. The parole officer who found her named her after her favorite song. Based on the child's dentition and bone development, the physician who examined her at that time estimated that she was two years old and so arbitrarily set her birthday for two years before the date she was found. She disappeared from a girls' home four years ago after complaining to a staff member that a cook had been bothering her. Where she went from there is unclear, but she was arrested for shoplifting in Texas and

Florida, and for prostitution in Oregon and Wisconsin. Maggie's not fifteen, but thirteen."

"Samantha and I could have adopted her," Ethan said, bereft. "We have a big house and three children already." He stood and walked agitated circles around the patio. "We could have dealt with her emotional and medical needs."

"I can't envision her sitting still anywhere," Kate pointed out, "much less in Newport high society. In each city of her arrest, she'd been taken to homes, all of which she fled within weeks. At each facility her pattern of behavior was identical: she'd stay just long enough to get meds, eat, and gain weight and strength for her next journey." Kate turned to Lindsey. "The social workers are going to want to talk to you later this morning."

"I told you. I didn't do anything to her," she said defensively. "We got along okay." She pulled a cigarette from her pack but Ethan made no movement to light it for her.

"I should have assigned her to Dana," Kate said bitterly.

With that not so subtle insult, Lindsey walked to the fence, replaying over and over her every interaction with the girl. Though she could find nothing inappropriate in her words or actions, she was still overcome with an unshakeable guilt. They did get along okay! That was the truth. Yes, there was tension at times, but a bond had developed between the two of them. She was not the cause of Maggie's flight! Something else happened yesterday afternoon, possibly while Maggie was in the Fishbowl playing the Black Spot. At dinner Maggie had said little and eaten only one slice of pizza rather than three or four. Nor did she dance on the beds after showers to music from the stolen radio.

Something happened yesterday afternoon, and now Maggie was gone. It wasn't her fault... was it?

From the top of the fence, a seagull peered down at her, perhaps looking for a scrap of bread. There was only one thing to do at that moment. The Serenity Prayer was posted all over the ward. Her Higher Power had restored her ability to memorize the entire thing. She repeated it again and again while her fingers hung off the fence.

God grant me the serenity to accept the things I cannot change, change the things I can, and the wisdom to know the difference.

But she could find no serenity or wisdom in this world.

A forest north of Newport

If she stayed off the main interstates and traveled only at night, she might make it to the Canadian border without being killed by Sneek, Maggie figured. Could fingerprints be detected on a burnt-up van? Would the police be able to identify her that way? Her fingerprints were on file in four states! What if the cops thought that she killed Jed and Tony? Fuck! In additional to Sneek, state troopers and the FBI were combing the highways! Her face was probably on the Ten Most Wanted List and flashing on all of the crime billboards between New York and Boston by now!

If Sneek could track down Jed and Tony so quickly, he would certainly be able to find her! His scouts must be searching for her at that very minute. She was a sitting duck stuck in one place like a rehab! Those creepy meth cooks were probably Sneek's spies! Despite the clean bed, warm food, and a fun roommate who knew long words, there was no choice but to flee. That was the hardest... worst fuckin' decision ever. It was best to travel in the darkness of night.

The Bottom Dwellers

That was the plan. That's how she and Bess escaped Minnesota, after Bess whacked Janine.

Angry storm clouds were about to burst open. She climbed over a guardrail and slid down an embankment into a forest. There was a cranberry bog beyond the trees, and the soil was wet and spongy. Just up the highway was the interchange. 195 East headed toward New Bedford and Cape Cod, and 195 West was the road toward Providence and destinations north. When darkness fell, she'd climb up the embankment and stick out her thumb. With any luck some driver or trucker might take her as far as Vermont or Maine. In a day or two she'd be a permanent resident of Canada. Canadians spoke English, didn't they?

She searched the forest until she found high ground, and trees and bushes the right distance apart. She unrolled the tarp and strung it between the branches, adjusting the tarp angle so that the rainwater would run away from her. Cold was bad enough, but cold and wet was the fuckin' worst. She crawled underneath and pulled on Lindsey's sweater. No way could she build a fire to dry her damp sneakers or warm her feet. Sneek and the state troopers would certainly spot the smoke. Now what? Travel and wait, travel and wait... the story of her miserable life. That's all she and Bess ever fuckin' did. Travel and wait, and get stoned and pull tricks, she remembered gloomily. In rehab, at least there were books to read, boards to solder, chocolate bars and peanut brittle to extort, and interesting, smart people to listen to. Now what? She frantically chewed on her thumbnail until it started to bleed.

That nervous... itchy... lonely feeling set in. Getting fucked up used to pass the time. She could probably get to Providence within an hour. NO! Shooting up was out of the question. No more dope to escape In World. She lit a cigarette and smoked urgently. *Give me strength... give me wisdom.* No more crack or smack or meth in Providence, no more crack houses visited. Providence would be bypassed all together. If Lindsey N. could stay sober for nearly four weeks, then so could she! Long clean life, Maggie M., Lindsey had said. She was now Maggie M. Slippery, shadowy creeps would be avoided at all costs. Besides, they might know Sneek and tip him off to her whereabouts. Rhode Island was not that far from Connecticut. With one phone call, Sneek could speed up 95N and be there in an hour. He'd probably kill her slowly, torturing her for weeks on end until she finally died. She could only hope for a fast execution style murder...

That lonely, frantic itch persisted, but she was now a clean and sober girl, she desperately reminded herself. *Give me strength... give me wisdom.* Think of other things... enjoyable things... like pirates.

She whipped a pencil and pad from the Hopkins gym bag and quickly sketched Anne and Mary on a treasure galleon. Pirate coconut heads lined the deck as the pirate queens had a smoke together. Pirate flags fluttered overhead, next to soaring seagulls. Sunlight burst from a happy sun. If she had colored pencils, the sun would be spirals of orange, red and yellow.

God, did she destroy her roommate in the Black Spot game! It wasn't even close! Anne Bonny and she, Mary Read, voted at Pirate Council that her word list was much better.

"I hope I don't have to walk the plank for losing," Anne had said with dread. "How about we doom the scallywags, Lorena, Connor, Joshua, and Nancy tomorrow?"

Maggie had nodded sadly, knowing by then she'd be long gone.

Lindsey N. was a kind person, a child in a woman's body, just like Kate said. God, she would miss her! And that angel-faced Ethan. When they were talking back at the fence, he had told her about the explosion that fucked him up. No wondered he was mopey and sad at times. His heart was broken. She could barely refrain from crying while listening to him. She flipped the pages on her pad and started to sketch him. It would be a happy, smiling Ethan; an Ethan who was thinking about scrumptious pizza. She drew pizza slices in thought bubbles over his head.

He had worked in a place called Sudan. Sudan was in Africa because she had checked an atlas in the reading room later that night. His friends were two other pediatric surgeons, Colin Price from England, and Mario Carpellio from Italy. When their contracts ended with an international health organization, the three doctors joined a mobile medical hospital of the UN and were sent to Afghanistan. Afghanistan is where they grow poppies to make heroin, she recalled. The doctors worked closely with Army medics. One medic was the reservist, Nicole Johnston, called to active duty from her job as a junior high health teacher in Springfield, Illinois. Weird coincidence... the state capital. She'd been to Nicole's town. Maybe they'd even passed each other on the street?

The medical team was eating breakfast in the mess when they got the call, Ethan had said. Strapping on flak jackets and helmets, they ran across the hard sand of the compound to the Humvees. Colin, Nicole, and Mario climbed into the first vehicle. Ethan and a young medic from Georgia jumped into an ambulance truck carrying the medical supplies. In total, two armored military Humvees and two medical vehicles sped up the dusty road to a village where a car bomb had injured civilians.

The heat of the truck bay was stifling. He had made love with Nicole just hours before. He prayed that Samantha and the old man would grant him a divorce. Nicole was single and free to marry him. He sat on a cargo box directly behind the cab, looking through the grimy cab window over the shoulders of the two drivers at the two Humvees in front of them. The Georgian mentioned that he had just finished making car payments on his new four-by-four when they heard explosions. The Georgian leapt to his feet, pressed his face next to Ethan's at the cab window, and yelled an obscenity. Billowing black and orange flames engulfed the frames of what had been the two Humvees in front of their truck. In a second of time, Colin, Mario and Nicole were gone. "Trap!" Ethan shrieked. Another explosion ripped the scorched air. A wave of fire crashed down upon the truck, tossing Ethan, the Georgian, and burning shards of metal through the canvas and into a dry ravine across the road.

Rain began to drop onto the tarp. Maggie slid the pad and pencil back into the bag, and tucked herself into a ball to stay warm. She would pray to her Higher Power to heal Ethan's sad heart and Lindsey's tremors, and deliver her safely to Canada. Shit!... she hated the cold. She was a child of the desert. Canada was going to be insufferably cold. And worst of all, she hated whoring to make money. "Stop the fuckin' whining, Maggie," Bess used to growl at her. "Get fuckin' used to it."

Chapter 29

Rehab

The images in the dream moved swiftly, like a train clacking through a mountain of dark tunnels... a sand dollar, a black Trans Am, sandy sheets, a flask suspended in a cloudless blue sky. Then a faceless man kissed her. She struggled to identify him, but the image suddenly vanished. She blinked awake in the gray dawn.

A ghost in white stood at the foot of her bed.

She blinked again. The apparition remained, watching over her as if it were a sentry. Her eyes came into focus and she was struck by a horrid odor. It was the smell of dying tissue, remembered viscerally from the hospital in Baltimore, and more recently, the ceiling in the laundry room.

She bolted up. "Ethan?"

"Nicole," he murmured dreamily.

His eyes were wide and black like marbles, staring aimlessly outward. His hair was damp and matted, and he wavered slightly. She glanced for a moment to the open door, to the yellow fluorescent lights in the hallway. Then she noticed it. A dark, glistening trail had followed him into the room, blood dragged across waxy floor tiles. His foot was wrapped haphazardly in disintegrating pieces of bloody toilet paper. His bleeding hand was clenched onto the bed sheet toga that wrapped his body. A small puddle of blood spread under his foot.

She lifted his free arm around her shoulders and they hobbled to the Fishbowl, following the red trail back to his terrible surgical theater. She helped him onto a sofa and placed his foot on an armrest so that it was elevated above his heart. She rushed for a trashcan by the coffee counter and placed it under his foot. Blood dripped onto spent Styrofoam coffee cups, measuring off the minutes like a ticking clock.

She sprinted down the hallway, but the nurses' station was abandoned. Where the hell were the night nurses? If she opened the security doors at the end of the hallway, an alarm would sound and the whole ward would awake in a panic. And none of them had cell phones. She would have to wait for the nurses to return. She unwound the soaked toilet paper from his foot.

Ethan's ramblings made no sense. He was speaking the names of foreigners, perhaps people he'd worked with abroad. *Mario... Pasithea... Colin... Hypnos... Icelus... Morpheus...*

He stared upward at the ceiling and chattered on. His phalanges 1-3 had been severed from the metatarsals. The procedure had not been done by a surgeon's deft hand. Instead the skin was hacked and torn as if by a madman. Sawn tendons and ligaments had retracted into the small red caves that were his toe sockets. Slow drips of blood continued to fall from the sockets, rebounding off Styrofoam in the silence.

The Bottom Dwellers

On a coffee table was his surgical instrument, a doubled-edge razor taken from a man's shaver. She decided against a tourniquet upstream as blood flow to his foot was already impaired. She would pack the wounds and apply pressure locally. She placed another pillow under his foot and repositioned the trashcan. The razor cuts on his fingers were small and had clotted on their own. She glanced down the hallway, but a nurse was still nowhere in sight.

His mumbles changed from English to French, again interspersed with names of colleagues or friends... *Phobetor... Phantasos...* then shifted to an Arabian dialect, and then stopped entirely as he drifted to sleep.

Also on the coffee table, three severed toes lay in small red pools on the glossy cover of a beauty magazine. The toes should have been removed days ago, but the cast had been on, and that meant everything was fine, right? Lindsey had known doctors and nurses who pencil-whipped their rounds. Their smell was gagging. She grabbed a roll of paper towels from the coffee counter and, averting her face, picked up the toes and wrapped them in a trashcan liner. Ethan snoozed soundly. With damp paper towels, she got down on her hands and knees and mopped up the maroon trail connecting the Fishbowl to her room.

A low electric hum sounded at the end of the hallway, followed by quiet voices: a night nurse and a security guard at the threshold of the door. Lindsey stormed down the hallway. The security guard stepped protectively in front of the young nurse, and then realized that something was terribly wrong. Lindsey told the nurse to call Kate Waters and the ER to have a surgical team in place to sew up Ethan's foot. The security guard rushed out the door, and the nurse grabbed her cell phone.

Lindsey returned to check on Ethan and collapsed into a wicker chair, her head falling back onto the cushion. His previous words wound vaporously through her thoughts. The names had a distant familiarity, but she couldn't remember why. All day he had paced the Fishbowl, lighting one cigarette off another, complaining histrionically about droughts and Ebola in Africa, Maggie's poor health, and on and on...

Kate arrived shortly, not having changed from what she was sleeping in, sweat pants and a T-shirt. Striding quickly down the hall, she whispered a series of commands into her cell phone. She stood over Lindsey. "Thank you, Lin," she said earnestly. The red paper towels in the trashcan caught her eye. "When did this happen?"

Lindsey stood. "I don't know for sure. After he did it, he showed up in my room."

Another electric hum sounded, and then the rubbery squeak of gurney wheels. Two orderlies moved into the Fishbowl and lifted Ethan's slender body onto the white sheets. Lindsey placed a sofa pillow under his foot. The hushed voices and jouncing roused him.

Sleepily, he raised himself on his elbows and turned to Lindsey. "Kiss me, love."

The orderlies tightened. Kate watched uneasily. Lindsey stepped hesitantly forward. His was not a brotherly kiss. She backed away.

Kate put her hand on Lindsey's shoulder. "Go sleep."

Lindsey nodded numbly. As the orderlies maneuvered the gurney through the Fishbowl doors, Ethan turned to her once again. "Peaceful dreams, Nicole."

Too shaken to sleep, she walked down to the reading room and scanned the bookshelf. She finally found it. *The*

The Bottom Dwellers

Greek Myths. She had read a lot of literature while spread across Mr. Willis' sheets, though she hardly remembered the Lesser Gods. She thumbed through the pages. The Grace, Pasithea, and the God of Sleep, Hypnos, had four sons: Icelus, Phobetor, Phantasos, and Morpheus. Icelus controlled dreams reflecting reality, Phobetor, nightmares or phobias, and Phantasos, fantastical dreams. Morpheus, who could appear in human form, controlled the dreams of kings and heroes. Ethan certainly knew that Morpheus was the word origin for his obsession, a dream-inducing drug called morphine.

Kate's door was ajar the next morning. At the windowsill, she faced outward, still wearing her sweats from the night before. Strands of hair had slipped from a large clip at the nape of her neck. The usual background music, soft rock from her computer, was absent.

Lindsey approached apprehensively. Wordlessly, Kate offered her a cigarette from a shaking pack. Lindsey pulled a lighter from her pocket and lit their two cigarettes. She followed Kate's eyes out the window to the same black asphalt and yellow lines of paint that had been her view for the past twenty-nine mornings. The next morning she would drive away in her Jeep, a thought that evoked both excitement and terror. She turned her head and searched Kate's face. Her eyelashes glistened with tears.

"What's happened?" Lindsey asked, her voice tight.

"It's Ethan," Kate replied quietly.

The two of them smoked in silence for a while. Lindsey's lungs, as if encased in lead, could barely move the smoke.

"How?" she finally rallied the courage to ask.

"With shoelaces and clothes line. He had stashed them in his cast. We never thought to check there."

Chapter 30

Rehab

Later that day a bouquet of wildflowers was delivered to the room of Lindsey N. "Your Birds are four and a half games behind the Immortal Sox," was written a small card tucked amidst the blossoms.

"These are beautiful. Are they from Duncan?" Kate asked, stepping into the room.

"No, they're from my neighbor." Lindsey looked down at the card, curious to know how he knew where she was. "Rob Jenkins. He lives on the boat next to mine. Strange. I never knew that Jenkins was his last name. His boy, Danny, told me once that his full name was Daniello Roberto Ruiz."

Kate pulled her nose out of the flowers. "What name did you just say?"

"Daniello Roberto Ruiz."

"No, the father's name."

"Rob Jenkins."

"Robert Jenkins, the baseball player?"

"No, he's a sports blogger."

"Handsome guy, black hair, blue eyes, a Sox tattoo?"

Lindsey nodded curiously. "How do you know him?"

"Every local knows him. He used to play for the Paw Sox, and then for the Red Sox very briefly, but his career was over before it started. They brought him up from the Minors way too young. He couldn't handle the distractions. He was a real problem child. I think he drifted around the Caribbean leagues for a while, and then disappeared off the radar screen."

Lindsey read the entirety of the note. "He brought me here!"

Kate's eyes looked as though they would pop from their orbits. She burst out laughing.

"This is so not funny, Kate!"

"This is so incredibly funny," Kate laughed.

"Duncan's flying back from Scotland to pick me up!"

"Bad, bad Robert," Kate chuckled, while departing, "messing with you, a toxic girl."

She stared in confusion at the flowers. She had no recollection of the car ride to the rehab! Rob didn't drive a Trans Am; nor was he Hispanic. Had she slept with him? Impossible. If they had fought, then why the kind note? Nothing made sense!

On the day of their last conversation, she remembered waking with a paralyzing hangover... like every morning....

With a groan, she lifted her head from the pillow. She was a wreck, her hair crossing her face like bars of a prison cell. On the nightstand were a glass and an empty bottle of scotch. How much scotch was in the bottle at the beginning of the night? And this brand was swill, not Glenlivet. She vaguely recalled drinking beers at the Kidd, but not the scotch. She just couldn't remember. No matter. What she needed was in the refrigerator.

Twenty goddamn feet... if she could make it twenty goddamn feet to the fridge she could start the day. She slung her legs over the side of the bed, checked the shakes in her hands. Like every other morning, they were there. She lumbered to the kitchen, empty bottle and glass in hand, and dropped the bottle into a green recycling bin. Unsteadily placing the glass in the sink, she noticed that the sink was clean and dry, devoid of dishes from the night before. Dinner had been skipped again. A few nights before it had taken her nearly five minutes to figure out which buttons to press on the microwave to cook a frozen dinner, which she had barfed up anyway.

She bent into the refrigerator for a long neck beer and guzzled down the amber liquid. A wonderful combination of the ice cold fluid and the hot burn from carbonation bubbles caused a brief frisson within her.

She struggled to focus on the wall clock. It was almost noon. After a protracted search, her cell phone was finally located under a heap of dirty clothes. She rasped into the phone, "Sara, I'm having my period and..."

"Who are you fucking kidding? Sleep it off," Sara interrupted bitterly. She hung up without further comment.

Her inventory of the refrigerator revealed that there were only two beers left. Two beers! It would be impossible to make it through the day with just two beers and no Glenlivet! Besides, the beers were breakfast.

She stumbled to the head to wash up. Next, searching the living room for her car keys, she heard a murmur of male voices and looked out the window to see that same curious assortment of men congregated in lawn chairs on Rob's stern. They drove in on Ninja sport bikes, rusty pickups, station wagons, SUVs, and Jaguars. They were a mix of ethnicities and ages, and she wondered if she was witness to some secret society of leftist revolutionaries conspiring to dethrone the greedy one percent at the top of the global food chain. These men smoked and sipped from extra-large cups of Dunkin Donuts coffee. What freakin weirdos! When a bunch of men get together, they're supposed to drink beer.

As she stepped onto her deck, all heads turned to stare at her, their words suddenly silenced. She felt a sudden panic; had she remembered to put on clothes? She glanced down, hugely relieved; the clothes were the same ones that she had passed out in the night before. Her hair was a nest of tangles, as she had forgotten to comb it. She raked her fingers through it and gave her head a quick dog-shake as if the wild, chaotic look was the look she was going for that day.

She looked at Rob; his eyes were brooding and shadowed under his ball cap visor. Fear shot briefly through her. She was sure that she had returned home quietly last night and tiptoed down the dock and onto her boat so as not to wake his sleeping son. Hadn't she?

A branch was wedged between the fender and grill of her Jeep. How the hell had that gotten there? She wrestled with it for a few minutes, trying to dislodge it. Fuck it, it was no use. It wouldn't budge. Anyway, the car would drive just fine whether the branch was there or not.

"Great time four wheeling yesterday!" she called toward the men on the dock. But there was no response. "Dullards," she muttered to herself, climbing into the car.

The glove compartment had a calendar of her visits to the local package stores, as it was clever not to visit the same one too frequently. They might think she was a lush or something. It had been three weeks since she had bought booze at Beer King. She could casually mention to the clerk that she was stocking up for... what holiday was coming up? How about the Cinco de Mayo? Wait, was it still May, or was it June?

In the liquor store she strolled the aisles and loaded a shopping cart with a case of Glenlivet and two cases of Molsons, with the happy realization that within minutes she'd be back in the parking lot quaffing down lunch—glorious Canadian ales. If she stopped and bought produce at a farm stand, a six-pack and a bottle of Glen could be stashed under the vegetables. The booze could be carried inconspicuously past the men. "I'm turning vegan," she might mention.

By the time she returned to the marina, beer marinated her brain and the parking lot was mercifully clear of the men's vehicles. She didn't want to think about men, or have them anywhere near her. Duncan was visiting that coming weekend, which meant that she'd have to be moderate. Until then, she'd let loose all week.

She managed a fairly straight walk down the dock. Rob sat outside with his laptop across knees. "How are you feeling today?"

She grinned stupidly. "Fabulous."

"No work today?"

"I've given myself a personal day."

"You took a personal day yesterday and the day before."

"And I might take another one tomorrow."

"It must be wonderful to be the Empress of the Universe," he said.

"It is," she replied, heading inside with her bag of vegetables.

Woods Hole

Four seizing brain models, as requested, sat on Dr. Lindsey Nolan's desk, and an unsent email to Dr. Karen Battersby sat on Sara's laptop. Any day now Lindsey would be returning to the lab, a fact that unsettled Sara. To calm herself, she sent another model aloft. The Jenny Curtis now circled the air space with the *Wright Flyer*, the *Hindenburg* and a Klingon Bird-of-Prey. With her cup of coffee in hand, she gazed out to Eel Pond.

The last morning Lindsey had been in the lab had been a complete disaster. First were the nagging calls from the Grants Office requesting the grant extension forms, which Sara doubted Lindsey had ever submitted. That delayed their paychecks! "Dr. Nolan's really busy today... but she'll call you soon." Why was she lying for this incompetent asshole?

Seconds later came the crash from the small workroom. Sara had flung open the door. A bottle of vodka had smashed next to the oscilloscope and amplifier. That was it. She exploded.

"Idiot! Fluids and electricity should *never* be in the same space! You're going to cause a fire! You might not care for your safety, but I value my life and have a five-year old depending on me. You're so unbelievably self-centered. And you look and smell like a piece of shit. You're a drunk. Get help!"

Most of the time Lindsey would shuffle wordlessly by, but that morning, she slung her backpack over her shoulder.

"Fuck off, Sara," she had mumbled. "I'll be working from home."

Then the unforgivable had happened. On her way out the door, Lindsey swatted at a plane... one of Sara's favorites! *The Spirit of St. Louis* careened across the lab, struck the chemical cabinet, and shattered into countless pieces!

Sara's lungs heaved, over a month later, just thinking about that plane crash. She returned to her laptop and stood for indecisive minutes, her hands on her hips. Her response to Karen's job offer stared her down, taunting and daring her. With a sinking feeling in her stomach, she reached forward and pressed SEND.

The Muck of Bottom

Deja vu. A passed-out woman in a car. When Rob had played ball, these were the staples of his life: groupies and party girls. And at the time he'd felt obliged to sample every one of them. He glanced at the passenger's seat of the Jeep. Her hair fluttered out the window as they wound along the coastal road. How had he gotten himself into this mess? He knew better than to have anything to do with her! But there was no choice. Dave had threatened to tow her houseboat into the Vineyard Sound, hoping that she'd drift away in the night. For days there had been no activity on her houseboat. Nothing at all. Her mistreated Jeep sat unmoved, and days of mail overflowed from her mailbox. Finally he and Dave had decided to check her boat; they'd stepped warily onto her deck.

"Her door's locked," Rob had said, twisting the knob.

Dave had pressed his face against her window. "I can see her. She's at the galley table. Passed out. Or dead. I could be so lucky."

"Maybe I can get through the window." He'd punched in her screen, slid the coconut pirates off her shelf, and climbed in, then opened the door for Dave.

"Is she dead?" Dave had asked, stepping inside.

Rob had checked. "No, she's breathing."

"Too bad," Dave had said, half kiddingly.

Her body was draped across the galley table, limp like a puppet. Her outfit was outlandish and slutty, not her usual rumbled t-shirts and jeans.

"I like her outfit," Dave admitted.

"Yeah, me too. She's going somewhere," he'd said, noticing a blue gym bag on the futon.

Dave moved toward her the full recycling bin. It was overflowing with amber bottles and beer cans. "She's really been knocking them back."

Rob had scanned the papers on the table. The drunken scrawl on a yellow Post-It note took him some time to decipher. "I guess this says June 14, Gull Inn. That's on the coastal road southeast of Newport. I know all of the back roads of Rhode Island from my time at Pawtucket. She has an e-ticket for a boat show for today."

Dave stared at her outfit once again. "The Gull Inn... some guy's in for a wild time tonight."

Rob had studied another paper that showed directions to a rehab in Rhode Island. "I'm not sure, but it looks like she's checked herself into a rehab in Newport. Tomorrow, June 15 a bed will be available, I think it says."

"My prayers have been answered!" Dave declaimed to the heavens. "We might have some peace and quiet around here for a few weeks. You drive her. Sheila and I will watch Danny."

"Shit, why do I have to take her?"

"Because she's a menace on the road. She'll kill someone. And there's no way Sheila'd ever let me get into a car with her, especially in that miniskirt!" Dave said, laughing. "Besides, if I took her, she'd never get to Newport. I'd murder her first and dump her body in some cranberry bog."

"Yeah, you probably would," Rob had said, only half facetiously.

"So, you're taking her, right?"

"Do I have any choice? She's dying," he'd said seriously. "I'll tell Danny I'm taking her to catch a plane. She's going on vacation."

From Woods Hole to the motel, she had not stirred once; a crease from the bucket seat formed an imprint across her cheek. He studied the limp body. His neighbor was repugnant to him in so many ways. She had an impossible combination of personality traits, none of which he could stand: drunkenness, unfaithfulness, and arrogance.

Through the dusty windshield he spotted the Gull Inn and turned into the parking lot. In her present state, it was best to park away from the motel office. No wonder she was able to book a room there despite it being peak season. The place was a dive, a no-tell-motel. As long as the bedding and bathroom were clean, it would be okay for an overnight.

Having received the room key, he moved the Jeep down to a parking space in front of Room 11, two doors down from a pack of Harleys. How to extract her from the car? Wake her? She looked so peaceful. He unlocked the door to the room and returned to open the passenger side door. The pink miniskirt had ridden up. His neighbor had forgotten to put on panties. He scanned the parking lot and, seeing it empty, scooped up the dangling body and carried it inside.

The air-conditioning had cooled the air to near frigid temperatures, so he placed her on the bed and wrapped her in a blanket. He inspected the room and bathroom. It was spartan and adequately clean. A TV, dresser, small circular table, queen-sized bed. A schlocky oil painting of sailboats hung over the headboard. After carrying in the bags, he pulled off his shirt and kicked off his sneakers, as he hated the constricting feeling of clothes on his skin. Clumping the pillow against the headboard, he grabbed the remote and scanned the cable channels. Nascar, no. Bowling, no. Spanish soap operas, no. Cooking channel, no. The Movie Channel. *Bridge Over the River Kwai...* yes. Alec Guinness movies were the best.

She still had not moved. He placed his hand lightly on her forehead. She was burning a fever, a clammy sweat broke across her face. She was unlike the party girls he had known in his life (if you could call it that) before his bottom. Her mind, he had realized immediately when he moved to the marina, was rare. Strolling around her boat deck, her cell phone to her ear, she spoke to colleagues in a foreign tongue, a language of gigohms and capacitors. Work was her love, and he was sure, whatever she actually did at the marine lab, she was probably very good at it, even if she wasn't good at marriage. The moment her husband's car pulled out of the marina after one of his visits, she seemed to come alive, and, backpack slung over her shoulder, she'd pedal off to the lab.

Her intelligence glaringly eclipsed her husband's. The man, clearly adoring her in his grabbing, oafish way, was awkward in her presence, his mind an ooze of insecurities and manipulations. Duncan spoke compulsively in his wimpy southern accent about himself over their dinners outside on the deck, as if to validate himself, prove his worth.

The Bottom Dwellers

Never did he ask about her work, her wellbeing, never a basic and courteous inquiry of concern, "How are you doing?" He had to know she was sick! Instead, he blathered on about his teaching load and excessive committee meetings, paper rejections, rebuttals to editors, and being scooped by competitors. She would listen politely, but her eyes might be fixated on ripples undulating across the pond, or a sudden burst of sparrows out of the marsh. Occasionally her view wandered over to his boat.

On warmer nights during the husband's visits, he'd hear her quietly pad to the bow of her houseboat. For some inexplicable reason he always slept badly when her husband was around; he might be up reading a book by his dim cabin light. The pssst of an opening beer would alert him to her presence outside. The glow of his digital clock might read three or four o'clock. Was this a nightcap or breakfast? A shimmering robe, a silk kimono, indicated her movements in the darkness. Unaware that anyone was awake on the pond, the robe was knotted loosely, sometimes not at all. She stood in the same stance each time, her hands leaning on the railing, her long curtain of hair obscuring her face as she searched the black water. Was she making a light-hearted wish, or offering a solemn prayer to the gods of the pond to release her from some unspeakable servitude?

She turned on the motel bed, her breath heating a patch of his thigh. He lifted a wisp of her hair and let it drop onto the pillow. He was suddenly ravenous, as he had not eaten since breakfast with Dan. He glanced at the TV, at Colonel Nicholson's release from the claustrophobic prison-box, the oven. Dan had never seen the *Star Wars* series, he realized. That's what he'd get his son for his birthday next month. Lindsey was a scientist of some sort and must like science fiction; she might want to watch the DVDs with the two of them when she finished treatment.

He stepped outside onto the warm cement and called Sheila. Danny was too busy to talk, as they were just about to ride bikes to play at Taft Park and get ice cream. A good sign; he was not being missed in the least. His second call was to his former teammate, Manuel, who offered to follow him to the hospital tomorrow morning and drive him back to Woods Hole. His thoughts again turned to his neighbor on the bed, and he tried to decide what type of food she'd be able to keep down, if she wanted to eat at all. He wandered back inside to find the restaurant guide.

After a pizza was delivered and the bridge over the river was detonated, he stepped outside again. A frumpish middle-aged couple struggled up the rocks across the street and headed toward Room 5. There was a way down the cliff and, though it was steep and treacherous, the couple told him, the beach below was secluded and worth the climb. He walked across the parking lot, slung his leg over the guardrail, and leaned over the edge of the cliff. A narrow trail with a rickety wood railing wound through the rocks to a narrow strip of sand below. During a storm, such a narrow beach would be completely submerged by the pounding surf, but that afternoon it was golden and beckoning.

He returned to the room. The blanket that he had folded her in was empty. A yellow stripe glowed from under the bathroom door. By the sink was a new bottle of scotch. He flipped open the pizza box and grabbed a slice, noticing that one piece had some small bites taken out of it. She emerged from the bathroom, mussed and disoriented. She grasped tightly onto the bathroom doorknob for support. "Where am I?"

"A hotel. Do you want me to take you to see the boats?"

"Later. My head's spinning. Is there a pool here?"

"No, a beach."

"Maybe a swim would wake me up."

"Your suit and towel are there." He pointed toward her gym bag.

She stepped over to the dresser and pulled off her clothes as casually as if she was in a locker room with the girls. He decided to appreciate the view and did not avert his eyes. Holding on to the dresser for balance, she stepped precariously into the bikini bottoms first, and then slid the top up her arms and shoulders. She struggled with the clasp between her shoulder blades for some time. After watching her inept fingers, he stepped forward to help.

He held her hand across the parking lot to the cliff's edge. Scree tumbled and bounced downward as he navigated them along the trail. Where the path narrowed and curved, her calf grazed a plank from a wooden railing, leaving a large red scrape. She laughed recklessly.

"It's not funny," he said. "It'll sting in the salt water."

"I feel nothing," she replied bitterly. "In fact, I never want to feel anything ever again."

Next to a rock outcrop on the beach they dropped their towels and stepped out of their sandals. He still held securely onto her hand. The tide was low so they walked out to a large black boulder in the emerald shallows.

He circled the boulder, and climbed gingerly upward, avoiding the barnacles and mussels. On the highest ledge, he stood with his hands on his hips and scanned the sea below him. She stared shoreward, toward the cliff.

"Lin?" he called to distract her.

"What?" she answered, her view still fixated on the steep rock face.

"Stop looking at that."

"At one time, I would have been able to calculate the force of the impact, should I jump off that cliff, factoring in my weight, the height of the cliff, and gravitational pull. But now I'm brain dead." She added despairingly, "And I don't know that if I jumped, I could even kill myself effectively!"

"You're not jumping, so forget about it."

"Rehab's going to be a waste of time. I'll never be able to stop drinking," she said despondently.

"Have you ever tried?"

"Yes, a thousand times. I can't even make it to noontime. It's hopeless." She turned back toward the cliff. "If I landed on the rocks, instead of the sand, it might work."

"Stop it. You're not jumping."

"But I deserve to be dead."

"And why's that?"

"Because I ended someone's life."

"Who? When?"

"My best friend. In a car crash during college. I was loaded."

"She died?"

"All but. It should have been me. The worst thing of all is to survive." She fell silent and walked through the water, her fingertips grazing the surface of the water.

The inlet was so clear and tranquil that he could see her painted toenails like pink cockles moving across the white sand. "Lin!" he called to distract her from the cliff.

She looked upward, her hand a visor across her eyebrows. He leapt outward, curling himself into a cannonball. He hit the water deliberately close, showering her with saltwater.

He popped into the air to see her sad smile. Then she spotted something of interest in the sand. A sand dollar. She flipped it over with her toe.

She waded over to where he floated on his back. Her face now held that expression that he observed from time to time; a look that caused his blood to ignite. Her closeness surprised him and he stood abruptly, unsure of her next move. Her hands on his shoulders, she jumped slightly and hugged her legs around his waist, her ankles locked at the small of his back. Her boldness was startling. He composed himself and then began to sway her back and forth in the water. The rhythm brushed her hair across the green surface, reminding him of a gold paintbrush moving through green watercolors.

Her face was inscrutable. When she spoke at last, her words were still slurred. "The program's thirty days, I think. You'll water my plants?"

"Yes."

"And collect my mail?"

"Yes."

"You can find my check book, right? You'll send off my bills on time?"

"Yes. You need to pay Dave for the sign also."

"What sign?"

"You drove over the front sign the other night, the large wood one by the highway that reads Dave's Marina. Before hitting it, you drove through his flowerbed, plowing it all up. He's furious. He wants you to leave the marina. He thinks you're a liability and driving away customers."

"Where would I go?"

"You need to buy him lumber, paint, and new flowers."

"Of course. Convince him to let me stay!" she pleaded. "I have nowhere else to go!"

"He knows that you're going to rehab. That cooled him down a bit."

"There's one other thing I need you to do for me?"

"What's that?"

"Have sex with me." She grinned invitingly.

"No," he replied swiftly.

"Why not?"

"You're loaded. I'd be taking advantage of you."

"So? What if I don't remember?"

He stared at her, perplexed. "Then why do it?"

"Because you're my FILF," she confided, laughing.

"Sorry, but I'm not going to be a just another name in your contact list. And you're married. You're the worst wife I've ever seen."

"That's why you should take this opportunity to take advantage of me. Just this once."

He pondered the distorted logic. "And why's that?"

"Because once I'm sober, I'll never stray again."

He didn't respond for a moment, profoundly bothered by these words. She pressed her lips into his. His were as unflinching as stone. She pulled back and searched his face.

He stated firmly, "I won't have sex with a drunk woman."

"No one turns me down! Ever!" she exclaimed astonished. She unwound herself from him. "Are you gay?"

"No. I was married to a woman. You know that."

She shrugged. "Some people change their sexual orientation."

"But I'm not one of them," he answered matter-of-factly.

"Then who are all of the guys on your boat?"

"They're my brothers in crime," he replied. "It's a men's Twelve Step group. We rotate houses. How did you not know this? Have you ever seen me drink?"

"Since you're not gay, then just fuck me," she said vexed. "We have lots of time to kill."

"No."

"Your loss, buddy," she replied hotly. She waded back to shore.

He remained in the water, settling his thoughts, and letting other things settle. On the beach her towel unfurled into the wind and then luffed downward into the sand. She drained most of a water bottle. She tugged off her bikini top and laid herself belly down across a Corona beer towel, a carefree gesture as if she was on the Riviera where topless sunbathing was the norm. He watched dumbfounded, none of her actions making the least bit of sense. She was loaded... why would they? He glanced protectively up the bluff, wondering if someone had observed her actions. Where were the guys with the Harleys? Was the act intentional, meant to tease or taunt him? He wandered out of the surf and spread his towel next to hers. There was no comment from her, for she was already passed out.

She was so fair; she'd fry in this haze. He wound her hair into a thick rope and slid it off her back. He placed the Panama hat on the side of her face to shield her from the sun. Slowly circling sunscreen across her back, his eyes moved over the waves and troughs of her body. Tan hair and tan skin. Was she not on a white towel she'd be camouflaged perfectly amidst the grains of sand. And he shouldn't even be looking. He forced his eyes seaward where a catamaran slid over white caps in the Rhode Island Sound. A regatta of

Sunfish from a local sailing school dotted the horizon to the west.

Since Paola's death he had not been with a woman, or been remotely interested. He and his wife had been compatible in every way. When she died, it was as though a steel cable wound around his heart. The offers by friends to introduce him to "a hot babe from the office" he had politely declined, and he nearly choked when someone suggested that he set up a profile on Capesingles.com. He had settled comfortably into a widower's life. In fact he relished his ordinary days on the houseboat with his son; he had become accustomed to the rhythms and seasons on the pond, and possibly the woman next door. It was a load off his mind to have sold the house in Bourne to the young family who had been renting it. Possibly when Dan was a teenager and needed more privacy they'd have to move, but that wouldn't be for years.

He glanced down at her once again. No, no, and again no! Her behavior was generally abyssal. Was Dave ever ballistic about the sign! He lovingly tended to his flowerbeds like his children. Then there was the time she had driven MacPherson's Jet Ski straight into the marsh grass, clogged up the jets with mud, so that it had to be towed back to the marina and the engine rebuilt. God only knows what had happened to her sailboat! Who names their boat the *Naughty Nymph*! She had headed out to sea one sunny day with a cooler of beer, only to show up days later in the arms of a Coast Guard officer. When he'd asked her where the boat was, she remarked obtusely that she was "simplifying her life." Never once did she invite her boyfriends, like the Coastie or the Jamaican, onto her boat for dinner or conversation. Instead she'd lean through their car window and dismiss them with a long kiss. Then, retrieving her laptop, she'd settle down to work on the flybridge, having already forgotten them.

Yet, he was thankful to his neighbor in small ways, as their lively conversations engaged him. Like Paola, who knew every statistic about players in the Dominican League, Lindsey knew her American League baseball. Nothing was a more of a turn-on than a woman who could talk intelligently about the nuances of baseball. On the first day he met her—that sassy jibe about the Red Sox and Yankees being over-rated, as she stood in that neon pink bikini with her hip cocked to the side, hit his brain like the clash of cymbals.

Two Jet Skis whined across the opening of the small inlet and still she did not move. What was her loveliest feature? The unruly flow of hair? Miles of skinny legs? Her head rested across her folded arms. Inches away from his hand on the towel, round and white, was the outer side of her breast. He had seen it before, many times when she was snoozing or reading on her boat, but always hidden at least partially by the fabric of her bikini top. Something stirred in him. A twinge. It was a hunger pain, nothing more. The steel cable was secure and intractable, he was certain. He picked up the tube of sunscreen and squirted a gob of lotion into his palm, realizing that he had forgotten to do her legs.

Sometime during her slumber she turned onto her back. He repositioned the straw hat over her face. There was no way he could doze now; the scenery was too beautiful. He sat upright, lit a cigar, and dug holes in the sand with his heels. She periodically shuddered.

A tern swooped overhead, shrieking at another seabird picking at a fish in the sand. She stirred, and then awoke, pushing the hat aside. She looked suspiciously down at herself speckled with sand and glistening with perspiration. Her glare was fierce and accusatory. He looked back guiltlessly and with complete disinterest, and dropped the straw hat on his head.

The sun had shifted toward the west and was hanging low over Narragansett Bay. The clock in her head bonged that it was witching hour, a chanting, stomping, pounding for a renewed bacchanal. She had no patience to fumble around with her top on the beach. In a fury of withdrawal, she snatched up the towel and wrapped it around her body.

She shook the water bottle and found it empty. As she did so, he caught the scent of whiskey from it. That hadn't been water she had been drinking, then.

"I need to go to the room now," she snapped. "Do you have the key?"

He rose also. "I'll help you up the trail. It's dangerous."

"I don't need your help! I need the goddamn key!"

He dangled it in front of her. She grabbed it and clambered up the trail, slipping twice in the scree. He followed quickly, jumping over a tiny avalanche of stones cascading upon him. She made a beeline for Room 8.

"Not that room," he called. "We're Room 11."

Finding the right door, she jammed the key into the lock, but her hand quaked and the door would not give.

"Here." He jiggled the key into the slit and pushed open the door.

She shoved passed him and furiously kicked off her sandals; one flipped into the mirror and landed on the dresser, the other on the bed. Stepping to retrieve the sandal, he inadvertently moved too close to the bottle on the dresser. She pushed him aside and possessively grabbed the bottle.

"Don't touch that!" she yelled. "I'm drinking the whole thing. You touch it and I don't go to the hospital."

"That much will kill you."

"I can only hope." She put the bottle to her lips and swallowed one large glug after another.

He started off toward the bathroom. "Then kill yourself."

After his shower, he exited the bathroom with a towel around his waist. She slouched against the headboard, taking slow sips from the bottle. Her mood was proportionally related to her blood alcohol concentration. "Who's with us now? Dr. Jekyll-Nolan or Ms. Hyde?" he asked cautiously.

"Definitely Ms. Hyde," she replied pleasantly.

"You got sand all over the bed." He wandered back to the sink and ran a towel over his head.

She rose, still wrapped in the Corona towel. "The sand's only on your side." She grinned at his reflection in the mirror.

"Thanks," he replied. "I ran you tub water. Don't slip."

She flashed him another brash smile as her pointer finger drew a horizontal stripe across his rear end as she passed through the bathroom door. Her bikini bottom dropped onto the bath mat. He heard her urinate and a toilet flush. He then heard her feet step into the tub, a splash of water, then wild laughter.

"I can't hold onto the soap." More raucous laughter echoed off the tiles.

"God help me," he said, pushing open the bathroom door. She had feebly managed to work shampoo through her long hair. "You are a sorry thing." He knelt next to the tub and soaped up a washcloth.

"I know," she agreed amicably.

He scanned the slippery tan skin. "And you are stunning."

"Irresistible?" she queried, smiling salaciously.

"Resistible," he answered, firmly.

He stroked the soapy cloth in slow circles around her feet and between her toes. She retracted her foot, laughing.

"Ticklish?" he said.

"Everywhere. Don't you want to find out?"

"No."

He moved a washcloth up her calf, then thigh while her sleepy, green eyes watched his. Her finger outlined the tattoo on his arm, and then traced the scar on the bridge of his nose. "How did you break your nose?"

"A Frisbee?"

"Really?"

"You guess. Choice A: A beer bottle. Choice B: A flying hubcap. Choice C: Fist of a stripper."

"What was Choice A again?"

"A beer bottle."

"Hmm. Choice C?"

"No, it was a hubcap."

"Ouch," she remarked, cringing.

"I didn't feel a thing until the next day." Having soaped her up, he placed the dripping washcloth over a faucet.

"You missed some areas," she said suggestively. "My offer of mind-blowing sex still stands."

"My answer's still the same."

Anger flashed quickly in her eyes, then dissipated.

He left the bathroom before he did something regrettable. He parted the heavy plastic curtains, cranked open the window, and lit a cigar. Her cell phone, shell necklace, and dive watch were lying on the table next to him. The necklace was one that could be bought in any tourist shop on Cape

Cod for five bucks. No rings, no bracelets. Lindsey never wore bracelets.

Paola always wore bracelets, their jingle alerting him to her presence. On the night of his bottom, her brown, jangling wrist stretched across the table, unloading another round of sweating bottles of Cerveza to the grimy ball players. He was determined not look up at her, or attempt to talk to her, ever again. That conceited waitress, Manuel's cousin. Paola Ruiz with the crucifix swaying into the V of her blouse and a white apron tied around her full hips.

"Forget about it, amigo. No one has a prayer with her," Manuel had told him.

Despite her attempt to eat an uninterrupted dinner at the end of the bar, he approached nightly, hoping that his rough Spanish would not distort his meaning. And nightly she'd dismiss him. "Drunken yankee... beat it."

But that night he shielded his face from her. The night before, the Cuban shortstop had broken his nose with a hubcap. One eye was swollen shut. He'd have put up a better fight had he not been doing shots of tequila. What was the fight about anyway? Manuel and Nigel had dragged his flailing body out of the cantina, Paola yelling after him, "Yankee bum! Don't come back here!"

But he had returned the next night, just like every other, to drink at the corner table under the swaying wire of lights. In the jungle behind the fence, insects sang their nightly song and a jukebox played American tunes from decades before. No, he decided, that night he would not speak to her. She was not worth his time. Clearly she didn't know who he was. And he had been one of the Boston Red Sox, for almost an entire season. His batting average, albeit only for a few months, was 0.399.

He pulled some crumpled bills from his pockets and placed them on the table while Bobby Darin crooned "Mack the Knife." He mumbled his mañanas to his teammates and wandered into the darkness. That night he decided to sleep in the steamy shithole of a room that he was renting by the week, instead of on the beach. The bugs were biting and, even as drunk as he was, he'd feel it. The rum and beer had done nothing to numb his throbbing nose and eye. He stepped off the dirt road to piss in the bushes rather than use the disgusting toilet at the end of the hall in his rooming house. Finally, he approached the stucco building. He put his key in the lock and the rusty hinges creaked open. For a change, the couple upstairs were not beating on each other. A decaying old man, who probably had leprosy, snored like a metronome in the room next to his.

He pulled off his shirt and shoes, and flopped onto a lumpy mattress. Moonlight sifted through the palm fronds into his room. As shadows shifted across the cracked plaster wall, he inventoried everything that had gone wrong in the past year. He'd been too impaired to visit his father while he was dying; then he missed the funeral in South Boston. He had never met his niece, his sister's firstborn; it would kill his mother and sisters to see him this condition. A million dollar contract had been drunken away. No team would touch him now. And there was a beautiful woman on this godforsaken island who would never be his. Overwhelmed by sorrow, he pressed his face into the matted pillow and wept like boy.

The next afternoon after practice he walked by Nigel's dive shop, determined never to return to the cantina. The Brit gave him a used mask and snorkel and a floral bathing suit that was so garish it could not be sold. He swam out to the reef, and again the next afternoon, and the next, for many weeks, the queasiness slowly sweating from his body. The padre told him of a group of men with his same problem that met nightly on a barge by the fishing processing plant. After a while the temptations at the cantina rarely crossed his mind.

A few weeks later he walked from the surf, inspecting a cowrie shell he had found on a sandbar. He stopped short in the sand. Paola Ruiz sat on his towel. "Tuesday is my night off," she said. "You can pick me up at seven."

Such vivid memories of the Dominican Republic had not occupied his thoughts for quite a while. Lindsey's long swallow from a bottle drew him back to the present. Though she was standing only in a small towel, he would not watch her ingest her poison. He turned his attention across the road, out to sea. On the horizon was a blue island that he guessed might be Block Island. He glanced behind him once again. In front of the sink, she struggled to pull his small black comb through her hair.

He checked his watch. "The boat show closes in a few hours. We should get going."

"I'm in no shape to go."

"But I promised I'd take you."

"I'd rather stay here and sleep."

He nodded and turned outside again. A burnt orange sun hung low over the black mainland across the water. He stubbed out the cigar and took a long sip of Coke. He approached the sink and put his hand on her forehead.

"How am I?" she asked.

"Still warm."

Her finger scratched nervously at the label on the whiskey bottle. Without looking up from it, she whispered almost shyly, "Let me make love to you."

He leaned on the counter staring at the gold flecks in the Formica. His need was no longer a dull ache. Why a drunk woman of all possible women in the world to have resuscitated him and started his heart to beat again? Could one man have such catastrophically bad luck?

"Just this once." She paused. "When I get sober, I'm going to have to go back to him."

"What do *you* want?" he asked a bit too forcefully.

"I don't know. I don't know anything right now."

She studied his image next to hers in the mirror, and then reluctantly tilted the bottle of whiskey over the sink. The amber fluid circled the white porcelain and vanished. He watched in disbelief. That gesture for an alcoholic was monumental. The withdrawal would be very uncomfortable; it would be a long night. He slowly pulled the towel from around his waist, and then gently dropped hers to her feet also. He slid his arm around her waist, pulling her hip into his. The symbolism was not lost on her. For a moment, they stood imprinting the image of the other. Their fingers entwined and they walked toward the sandy bed.

The next morning, Lindsey slipped from under the lead weight of his arm. She paced the hotel room searching for her clothes. Pink skirt, see-though bra, awful shirt. Hideous clothes! Whose are these? Fine... whatever she could throw on.

"Where are you going?" Rob mumbled from the bed, still half asleep.

"To get my cosmetic bag from the car. It has my birth control pills."

"How are you feeling?"

"Fine," she lied.

Her thoughts were squirrelly and mean. There was no time to talk to him or any other fucker, for that matter! She quickly pulled on the clothes and, cracking open the door, squinted into the harsh glare off the cement. The pavement was already warm and she stepped cautiously around the pebbles and glass fragments in the parking lot. She fumbled under the passenger's side seat of the Jeep and finally felt the cool reassuring metal. Oh thank god! She twisted her Emergency Flask from between the springs and yanked off the stopper. The burning fluid coursed down her throat. Relief!

She climbed over the guardrail and walked to the edge of the cliff. On the beach in the distance a man tossed a stick to a golden retriever, and an elderly couple, shoes in hand, strolled through the surf. Never would she have a beloved dog, or walk a beach with a soul mate, or live to be an old woman. She stepped closer to the edge. Desperate, giant swallows emptied the flask. She inched closer. It was she who should have died in that wreck. God had shown her no mercy. The worst thing was to survive. No way could she ever stop drinking... alcohol was her blood. Her toes hung over the edge. She peered over. If she jumped in that direction, she'd certainly crash onto that jagged boulder. No one could survive such a leap.

She heard a sound behind her and turned with a sudden gasp.

"I, I couldn't find it," she stammered.

"What?"

"The cosmetic bag."

He grabbed her hand, pulling her from the ledge. "But you found something else." He yanked the flask from her hand. "You promised last night that you were done. That was the deal. No more drinking, then I'd have sex with you. You broke your promise!" With full force, the flask was flung high into a cloudless blue sky; it was suspended momentarily, and then dropped into the surf. He grabbed her hand again and dragged her toward the car. She dug her heels into the sand and thrust her weight back, resisting.

"Get away from me, I'm not going!" she wailed, pushing him away.

"Yes, you are." He lifted her onto his shoulder—she kicked and punched—and carried her toward the car.

"Get these fucking things off me!" Lindsey strained against the cables on her wrists. Her right hand was tied to an armrest on the door, the left one to the base of the parking brake. That bastard had the audacity to tie her up with her own electrical cables from her box of electronics!

Rob swerved the car on to the shoulder of the road. "Shut-up... please! I had enough trouble with the cops when I played ball. I don't need your rants causing them to pull us over. And I'm guessing that you've had enough of the police with your DWIs."

She fumed. "Take them off!"

"Don't pull and they won't hurt. Come hell or high water I'm getting you to rehab today! I'm not taking the chance that you'll jump out of the car on the highway, or at an intersection, or pull some other crazy bullshit. You're not causing an accident with me in the car. Danny has one parent and I need to get home to him in one piece!" He paused. "You need to calm down so we don't have any accidents."

Her eyes narrowed and she looked in the rearview mirror at a black Trans Am. "Who's the asshole who helped tie me up? Why's he following us?"

"It's Manuel. He's going to drive me home. I'm leaving your car at the hospital."

"Who is he?"

"A friend. We played ball together in the Dominican league. Unfortunately he burned out his rotator cuff before he ever got to the majors. He had an amazing slider. You should have seen it."

He veered the Jeep back onto the coastal road. The threat of police had silenced her for the moment.

"We're going to the boat show, right?" she asked absently.

He stared incredulously at her. "The boat show was yesterday."

"Did we have fun? I don't remember it."

"We didn't go," he answered calmly.

They drove in silence for many miles. "I've lost my shoes," she eventually noticed.

"All of your stuff's in your gym bag."

She squirmed in the seat. "And I don't have on panties! Did you take them?"

"Why would I take your panties?" he asked wryly.

"Who knows? As a trophy?"

"You're no trophy."

"Take me home! I'm not going! The deal was that you take me to the boat show, then I go to rehab."

"I offered to take you," he reminded her. "Instead you wanted to make love all night." He paused. "Believe me, I'm not complaining." In fact, the entire experience was confounding. The single word to describe her was expert. And exhausting. His lower back screamed for aspirin, but it was so worth it.

"I wasn't making love. I was just fucking you. Nothing more."

"*I* wasn't. I don't *just* fuck." At a red light he fumbled with radio, and then turned resolutely to her. "You'll never know how hard I've tried not to fall for you. And I have no clue why. You're an absolute lunatic."

She fiddled unsuccessfully with the cables, as she struggled to unwind his words. "If you cared for me, you wouldn't make me go," she said, her voice becoming frantic. "Duncan would never make me go..."

"I'm nothing like Duncan!" he broke in.

He put on the turn signal and swerved into a strip mall. The car lurched to a stop in front of an ATM, the Trans Am idling loudly behind them. He pulled the keys from the ignition and rose from the car, pulling his wallet from a pocket. Waiting for cash to be dispensed from the ATM, he watched her struggle furiously with the cables. Cash stuffed in his pocket, he returned to the car, leaned through the passenger's side window and laid a kiss on her hair. She continued to ignore him.

Manuel stuck his head out his car window and said with a rich laugh, "Patético, amigo."

He uttered gloomily, "No me lo recuerdes." He started the car, pulled the visor of his baseball cap down over his sunglasses, and turned back onto the road toward the Sakonnet River. A periodic blue and white H sign along the roadside confirmed that they were heading in the right direction.

The Bottom Dwellers

The hospital finally appeared. A low brick wall accented with a bed of flowers read The Narragansett Eastbay Clinic. He stopped the Jeep. At the passenger's side door, he released her seat belt and untied her wrists. She leapt from the car and flung a furious fist at his face, but he quickly jumped back. Her knuckles smashed into the car door.

"Ow!" she shouted, shaking out her hand.

"If you hadn't had a flask of whiskey for breakfast, you might have been a little quicker."

"Bastard." She slumped against the car and watched blood ooze from her knuckles.

"Have a nurse get you some ice for your hand."

"I need to sleep," she said listlessly.

"All you have to do is rest, listen, and heal." He stretched into the backseat, which had been used as a trash bin, and pulled out her gym bag. He returned the cables to her box of electronics. He checked his watch again. No time to clean the car out now. He'd told Sheila that he'd be back to get Dan by noon.

He unzipped her bag on the hood of the Jeep, stuffed her car keys into the bottom of it and slid the crisp bills into her wallet. His hand under her elbow, he directed her toward the emergency room entrance. The Trans Am waited in a loading area. With a cell phone at his ear, Manuel leaned against the hood and spoke in Spanish to his wife.

She slogged barefooted across the pavement. "I can't do this."

"You'll die otherwise."

The automatic glass doors of the ER were dangerously close, ominously snapping open and closed like the mouth of a monster. A wave of terror broke over her. She halted. "I've learned my lesson. I'm sure if I really, really try, I can—"

He interrupted quickly, "You're going." His arms stretched toward her. "Let me hold you for a moment, baby."

"I'm not going!" she shouted.

"Yes, you are. If I have to carry you in there..." He stepped toward her.

"Don't touch me!" She shoved him away.

A nurse and X-ray technician next to an ashbin stared at them. She spun toward them and roared, "Can you get a fucking life?" The employees stubbed out their cigarettes and retreated hastily inside.

She snatched her bag from his hand.

He continued calmly, "When you get out, you're going to be a different person. I will not interfere with your recovery in any way. You'll call the shots. And I know about the rule."

She turned confusedly. "What rule?"

"The no-sexual-relations-of-any-kind-for-six-months rule."

"What!"

"You've got to follow the rules, or you'll never get better. You've got to get on your feet on your own, and not be distracted by anything. Just go to lots of meetings. You'll feel better about yourself."

"No sex? You're kidding me. When I get out of here, I'm screwing every man in Massachusetts. Except you!"

He laughed. "Then you're going to be a very tired woman." He reached for the bag. "Let me help you register."

She stepped away and held the bag protectively across her chest. "Read my lips! Get lost!"

He approached, his arms outstretched. "A kiss for the road?" She stepped back again, her foot triggering the automatic door. He advanced toward her again with a mock menacing grin.

"Fuck off, loser!" She fled across the threshold.

"Work hard, sweetheart! When you want to talk, you know where I live," he called. He agilely stepped back as the sliding door closed between them.

Chapter 31

Release

Six patients had played Texas Hold'em in the detox on the night of June 15. Five men and one woman. One month later, two of them left the rehab. Addicts' lives were a game of numbers, probabilities, attrition, and sometimes survival. The wife and teenage son of Curtis H. had come up to the ward for him earlier that morning. It was Lindsey N.'s turn to be discharged. She waited by the security doors with a plastic bag of clothes. Duncan, who was still banned from the ward, was forced to wait in the lobby on the first floor. Kate had been downstairs to speak with him and had given him a packet of Al-Anon literature, then returned to her office to sign off on her paperwork.

It was an odd sensation, Lindsey thought, to feel car keys and a cell phone back in her pockets after carrying only cigarettes, a lighter, and gum for a month.

She had said her goodbyes to her girlfriends, Julia, Kesha, Sierra, Cheng, and Juanita, and clicked a selfie with them. None of the guys she particularly wanted to keep in touch with. While waiting for Kate, she reviewed the photos in her cell phone and lamented that fact that she didn't have photos of Marcus, Anton, Kelly, Melissa, Lorena, and especially Ethan, and her roommate Maggie. There was one image in her photo gallery that she couldn't keep her eyes from. The date of the photo was June 14 at 10:53 pm. Rob must have been holding the camera with an outstretched arm. They were sitting upright against a headboard. The motel room was brightly lit. A white sheet wrapped them together. His eyes were glistening and alert, hers glassy and far away. His arm encircled her shoulder, her hair dangled across his chest. What stuck her was the relaxed way that their heads leaned together.

Kate scuffled down the hallway toward her. She showed the image to the counselor. "If you'd let me have my cell phone, I wouldn't have been agonizing over this for a month."

Kate studied the photo for a moment. "I saw Jenks play once, many years ago. He hit a home run over the wall, out to Causeway Street."

"What did you call him?" she asked in surprise.

"Jenks. That's what everyone called him. You just went white. Are you alright?" Kate asked.

"I'm not ready for this! You should really let me stay a little longer," she insisted, shoving her phone into her pocket.

Kate couldn't wait to be rid of her. "You're ready, believe me. One meeting, more if necessary, a day."

"I'm petrified."

"Be petrified. I still am. Even after sixteen years. Never be complacent, or cocky, or let your guard down, even for a second. This disease is too smart." She handed Lindsey a folder.

"What's this?"

"A list of meetings in your area. Go to women's meetings if possible."

Lindsey slid the folder into the plastic bag holding her clothes. "Thank you for everything," she said sincerely. The two women shook hands.

"You're welcome." Kate moved toward the keypad lock on the doors.

"Allow me." Lindsey's fingertips tapped lightly across the numbers. The doors emitted an electrical hum and swung open.

"You're a pain in the ass! How the hell did you get that key code?" Kate asked, distressed.

"I had many sleepless nights."

"Get out of here," Kate ordered, shaking her head.

Stepping backwards through the security doors, Lindsey said, feigning optimism, "I'm going to email you when I have one year, then two, then three..."

"Don't get cocky!" Kate then added, "Those are my favorite emails. I'll look forward them." Her face darkened. "One of these days you're going to have to confront your demons, and talk about that first DWI when you were in college. It's the only way you'll heal."

The security doors closed between them and Lindsey stood, unraveled by Kate's words. Finally she descended the stairwell to the lobby.

Duncan was perusing—with dread—the Al-Anon pamphlets when she approached. "Let's get out of here," he insisted, pulling her through the sliding glass doors. "I hate this place."

In the loading area, where orderlies assisted patients from wheelchairs into cars, he spotted a trashcan and deposited the Al-Anon literature. They crossed the parking lot and stopped next to her Jeep. Each of them paused to take in the other.

He was almost unrecognizable. He was dressed in gray dress pants and a white short-sleeved dress shirt. In all the years she'd known him, his hair had never been that short. His blonde-red beard and ponytail were gone. His appearance was disturbingly suburban; some time ago her wild Scot had vanished. Perhaps he was dressed for an elegant restaurant, had booked them into a quiet seaside inn for a few days to relax and reacquaint.

She forced the key into the lock and opened the door. The scent of flowers overwhelmed her. The night before, she and Ramon had carried the bouquet and box of electronics down to her car. They had also cleaned out the empty booze bottles and tried to brush out some of the beach that was her backseat. She flung the plastic bag into the seat next to the bouquet and turned back to him.

"Who are the flowers from?" he asked.

"A friend."

"That's nice," he replied vapidly.

She couldn't wait until the restaurant. "I have something to tell you..."

"I have something to tell you too," he cut in.

He was laboring to say something, was laboring to meet her eyes. "What, Duncan?" she prodded.

"I got the grant to work in Edinburgh for a year."

"Congratulations!" she said genuinely. "When do you leave?"

"I'm... flying from Logan later today."

"Today?" she replied, stunned.

He avoided her eyes and stared at the keys to his rental car. Then it occurred to her. Some authority, indifferent to—or maybe delighted by—her precarious state, had ordered him to make the cut swift and clean. Slumping against the car door, she fumbled for a cigarette.

"I didn't know you smoked," he remarked.

"There are a lot of things you don't know about me," she replied ironically. He looked at her as if she were mad. They stood in rigid silence.

"Your weird neighbor cleaned the booze off your boat before I got there," he said to break the silence. "I put *Bluejay* in at your marina. I could never drive that thing like you could anyway."

"The hull. It's black and grey," she remarked. "The boat needs a new name."

"Sure. Whatever." He watched her closely. "You look... great."

Maybe he expected her to say "thank you." She didn't. She took a few more drags from her cigarette.

He stepped urgently toward her and pressed his lips against hers, wanting more, she sensed, but something held him back. It was the most pathetically guilty kiss she'd ever felt.

"Go," she urged gently.

"Okay," he answered, sheepishly backing away.

Just as he was bending into his rental car, she called to him. He looked up, lost and befuddled.

"Duncan, it's all right," she said, releasing them both.

She sensed everything in him crumble. She had her agenda (meetings, find a sponsor, work the steps, meetings, meetings, meetings, stay clean, stay clean) with or without him. Without him.

As he passed her, he lowered the driver's side window. "I'll be back soon. Really, I will," he lied. "What was it you wanted to tell me?"

"I forgot."

She turned the key in the ignition. After a few coughs and protests, the engine finally turned over. She consulted the Internet map that she had, in a silent scream of desperation, printed out more than a month ago. Five miles to the north was the exit to Fall River and a straight shot down 195 East to the Cape. But if she headed southeast, she could pick up a small coastal road that would be slower and more scenic. She headed for the coast. Her first impulse was to pop in a music CD, blare some lively New Orleans jazz, to announce her discharge and freedom. But she stopped herself, needing to hear the banal sounds of the outside world, even if it was just a trash truck crashing a dumpster of debris into its backend at a gas station.

A montage of fast-food restaurants, gas stations, nail salons, and tourist shops passed by the open window. The colors of the morning had a hallucinogenic intensity. At a red light, her hand scrambled through the glove compartment, searching for her sunglasses, with no success. Out of her peripheral vision was a seductive flash of neon. Bud Lite in blinking red and blue, Narragansett Beer in yellow and green, Heineken in gold. Cases of discount beer were stacked on either side of the front door—what an amazing price for a case of Guinness!

All the car had to do was cruise fifty feet across the parking lot, and she could obliterate the image of the Scottish girlfriend from her thoughts. It had to be the administrator that Duncan had been working with over the years, an older woman of position and clout, with definite demands and expectations, who would dress him in office clothes, make him cut his beautiful hair, and mold him into her model of academic respectability. Duncan's future flashed in front of her eyes. Those who could not publish would teach. Those who could not publish or teach would administrate. He would become academic driftwood floating through the flotsam and jetsam of forms and papers for the next thirty years.

Accustomed to the chill of the ward, the air in her car seemed humid and stifling. An ice cold Heineken would slide down nicely right about now. The light turned green without her notice. A rude blast from a horn in the car behind her (or her Higher Power?) startled her and her foot jumped onto the gas pedal. She quickly drove past the package store and through the intersection.

A few miles up the road was a tourist shop where she bought sunglasses, a six pack of ginger ales, and sourdough pretzels. She also picked up saltwater taffies for Sara's incorrigible sweet tooth—if she hadn't moved to Boston yet—and for Danny and Zephyr, a plastic shark head on a stick that when you pulled the trigger its mouth chomped open and close. Very cool. She spotted a pirate flag for the *Bluejay*. Danny would love this. She searched for some Red Sox souvenir, but saw no gaudy bauble that Rob didn't already have. Anyway, she had special gift for him. A sudden and irrational craving for a Creamsicle drew her to the refrigerators in the back.

She licked the fast dripping ice cream and drove on. Amazingly her car ignored and passed other liquor stores and no longer felt compelled to pull in. She remembered Kate's words. Cars don't ignore; cars don't feel compelled. She was driving the car; she was making the decisions. And she remembered that she had not lived with Duncan for nearly three years; he was a human being and was not a possession to hold or give away, a thought that lightened her spirits.

She passed a sign for a state beach up ahead. It would be too late to go to work that day. Her only plan was to get groceries, nap in her cabin, and find a meeting for tonight. Tomorrow she'd return to work. Would Sara even be there?

She was now certain how to change the sensitivity of the electrode to reach seizures generated in deeper neuronal layers. The problem was not with the diameter of the axial wire or its electroplating, as she had originally suspected, but with the conductivity of the electrode housing. That problem could be easily fixed. Moreover, the size of electrode would be reduced to a nanofilament to minimize tissue damage. If she were to affix a microscopic laser to the electrode, then there would only have to be one point of entry into the brain to neutralize the activity of the epileptic cells.

An idea for her next project was to develop a device to localize sites of potential ischemic events in individuals predisposed to strokes. Then with proper drug treatment the strokes could be precluded. Still another idea was to aerosolize vaccine molecules so rooms of people (perhaps an entire school auditorium of children) could be inoculated at once. Maybe, if Sara decided to stay at the marine lab, she'd want to start on one of these projects while she wrapped up the first one?

At the beach she paid ten dollars to the parking attendant and slowly navigated the car between parents and children juggling coolers, chairs, and beach toys. Even at this early hour, the parking lot was nearly full. No wonder; it was July 15, the peak of the summer season. She leaned into the backseat and grabbed her bathing suit and towel. The towel was unfamiliar; it was brand new. Solid white terrycloth with no logo. The Corona Beer towel had disappeared. She would email Kate Waters a "thanks" sometime soon. Rob's bathing suit, Panama hat, and flip-flops lay in the back seat as well. She grabbed the hat and plunked it on her head.

There was a wait for an available changing stall in the bathhouse, so she watched three chattering teenagers primp in front of the mirrors. Suddenly saddened, she thought of another teenager who might never enjoy a summer day with girlfriends, who might never kick through the surf because she could not swim. Maggie would be over the Canadian border by now, hopefully traveling with some kind-hearted trucker.

A leathery grandmother leaned over to help her tiny grandson pee into a toilet. A mother changed the diaper of a squirming baby on a plastic table that unfolded from the wall. The air was a blend of sand, salt, sunscreen, and dirty diapers. When a stall was vacant and she began to change, she could barely stuff her breasts into the black bikini top. She looked at herself in astonishment; she had breasts and hips. Her belly was still flat, though for how much longer? She was a healthy woman for the first time... ever.

The sand was wonderfully warm under her feet as she walked the beach. In her other life she would have walked as far down the beach as possible to drink in inconspicuous isolation. Instead she picked a parcel of sand between the lifeguard chair and the concession stand, dropped her wad of clothes and spread out her new towel. Frisbees soared overhead and teenage boys kicked up sprays of sand in their lunges for it. Children scurried with buckets and shovels around emerging sand castles. A mixture of good and bad music played from various radios. A news broadcast reported on a roadside bombing in Iraq, and she wondered how Samantha and her children were coping.

A memory surfaced. Over breakfast in detox, Hayseed had chatted about stereo speakers, basements, and rat nests. With a small plastic knife from his food tray he sawed a shoelace into two pieces. She had curiously watched him relace his high tops with the halves.

"What are you doing?" she had asked.

"I lost a shoelace somewhere," he had replied.

Sorrow coursed through her; followed by anger. During his nocturnal wanderings, Ethan had stuffed shoelaces into the sock of a dead man and replaced the grate—all to deflect attention from himself. She struggled to slow her breathing. From day one, he'd never intended to leave that hospital. Had all their conversations about getting together with their respective children after rehab been a ruse, a smokescreen, or had he ever felt glimmers of hope? She slathered sunscreen across her skin and let the sun soak into her, heal her, restore her. Help her to forgive him, as she prayed for his grieving family.

Overhead a yellow biplane droned along the coastline, unfurled behind it was a banner with a roguish pirate, "Captain Morgan's Rum." She could not sit still and walked the wrack line, searching for shells to distract herself from the colliding emotions. She picked up a purple fragment of the *Venus* clam, some blue sea glass, and a whorl from the whelk *Busycon*. Kicking through the surf were two twenty-something-men who smiled at her and said, "Hello." The one with the wild dark hair was quite handsome. No, she said swiftly to herself. She responded with a "Hello" that was polite, but not forthcoming. She continued on her way.

Jets arced skyward from the south, transatlantic flights from JFK in New York to various European destinations. Planes would be leaving with the same periodicity from Logan to the northeast. She had a sudden urge to swim.

A small girl with a bucket had followed her along the foamy sand. Lindsey turned. "Do you want my shells?"

"Yes!" the girl replied enthusiastically.

"Look at this one," she remarked, holding up one in particular, "a surf clam. This one is perfect."

The girl pushed her bucket forward, and she carefully placed the shells inside. The child had light blue eyes and freckles.

Lindsey dashed for the water. It was unseasonably warm. Like a porpoise, she dove again and again under each bowing wave, resurfacing on the backside, and sucking in deep breaths of salt air. Out beyond the breakers the water was smooth and calm. Her mantra of sobriety would be different than the normal AA slogans frequently seen on bumper stickers. Hers would be *My child will have a clear-headed mother*. At that moment, everything in her life seemed surreal, euphoric, hilarious and staggeringly painful at once. She was a mad sane woman bobbing in the sea. With her plaintive laughter, a bottle was uncorked, a bottle that had been jostling in the swells for years. From it streamed salty tears of release, her tears raising the sea level of the Rhode Island Sound that July morning.

Chapter 32

Prologue

The thermometer at the lifeguard station read ninety-six degrees, so Lindsey decided to drive home in her bathing suit. She returned to her car and wrapped the towel around her waist like a long skirt. She twisted her hair into a briny clump and tucked it inside the Panama hat. In the front seat she cracked open a lukewarm ginger ale and pulled on her sunglasses. If she stayed on the ocean road, it would drop her somewhere near the Bourne Bridge, then it was just a straight shot into Falmouth and Woods Hole.

Twice she got lost. First she turned off too soon by a seafood restaurant built into the shape of a lighthouse, and the second time by a mini-golf complex. In her other life, she would have fumed and honked at incompetent drivers, and run every yellow light and possibly some reds to make up time. She moved through time differently now. Not frenetically chasing her next drink with the tenacity of bloodhound. Time was something to accumulate and bank. She had a thirty-day chip in her wallet. Her sights were set on a sixty-day chip. She craved a cigarette but instead made herself eat another pretzel. She cautiously drove the speed limit, treating her body respectfully, for it was harboring a mysterious treasure.

Why was she certain that this child was a girl? How did mothers know such things? In the past month, the neurons of the child's central nervous system had been forming their clever connections. Small limb buds, precursors of arms and legs would have sprouted. Pulsing myocytes would align themselves and a primordial heart would begin to beat.

She had loved hanging out with the girls during freshman year. Girls like her, who were crazed Orioles fans. She and Megan had scrounged money from their summer jobs and bought season tickets, the cheap seats high over right field at Camden Yards. Megan was infatuated with that rookie from Boston who was getting so much hype.

They drank a lot of beer that singular disastrous afternoon. Megan had repeatedly flashed that young player's photo from the program in front of her roommates' faces. His eyes were a transparent light blue, contrasting with the long black hair. A devil-may-care smile. "Not my type," Lindsey had said, fixated on the Birds' pitcher on the rubber who was on the verge of a meltdown. The Sox had the bases loaded. A home run would put them ahead by two in the ninth inning, with the lame end of the Orioles batting order next! That lanky rookie stepped up to the plate. He taunted the pitcher, having detected cracks in his composure.

Megan had hammered Lindsey's knee. "I want him!"

"I want him to strike out!" she'd cried back.

The young Red Sox had thirty-five thousand sets of eyes boring into him. Like the rookie, she too was eighteen, but her only concern was whether or not she was going to get an A or A+ in general chemistry. The first pitch was a strike.

The Bottom Dwellers

Like a bull, the batter toed the dirt. He was astute and cunning, features she only admired in Orioles players. The second pitch was low and off the outside corner. He swung and missed. Again he toed the dirt and flashed the pitcher a challenging grin. The next pitch floated so slow that even she could have hit it.

Thirty-five thousand voices fell silent. The crack of bat to ball was piercing, even in their nosebleed seats. The ball arced their way. In the next section sat a group of rowdy guys on a road trip from the University of New Hampshire. They'd been flirting with the Hopkins girls all afternoon. The Hampshire guys rose in unison, fists in the air. "Jenks!" they shouted as the ball spun over their heads.

She pulled into the marina in the middle of the afternoon. The new sign and flowerbed at the entrance to the marina were lovely. Meticulous Dave was always keen on making improvements around the marina. She spotted the black and grey cruiser from Baltimore, walked down the dock, and climbed onboard. The name *Bluejay* wasn't fitting. The old dive boat needed a new name... new identify... a resurrection. *Blackbeard*... yes... perfect! It badly needed sweeping and scrubbing. She yanked the cord on the outboard engine. Nothing. She tugged again. Not even a sputter. Duncan was unable to differentiate a wrench from pliers. The engine would need its gas lines and plugs replaced, the fluid compartments drained and cleaned. It would be oily, grimy work, but she looked forward to tending to the boat after years of neglect. The first cruise would be out around the Elizabeth Islands. She wondered if Rob would let her take Danny for rides on *Blackbeard*, or let her anywhere near the boy.

Returning to the car, she slung the plastic garbage bag over her shoulder and juggled the bag from the tourist store in her other arm. Men were seated on plastic lawn chairs around his deck. She felt exposed in her bathing suit and towel, and walked briskly along the dock. She glanced askance at him from behind her sunglasses. Elbows on his knees, he was leaning forward, watching his cigar glow and listening to the words of a man who struggled with English.

"Lindsey!" a small voice squealed. A flash of red and blue, Danny in Spiderman swimming trunks darted between the maze of chairs. She lowered her bags as he flung his tiny arms around her waist and squeezed a breath from her. His cheek was sticky against her belly and his shoulders slippery from sunscreen.

She squeezed back and rubbed her hands over his fuzzy crew cut. "How's my little velvet head?"

Danny's grin was wide and orange from a recent Popsicle. "Great! How was your vacation?"

"Terrible," she declared, "because I missed you every minute."

"Dan," the father called firmly, "let her get settled."

She stooped to pick up her bags and stepped onto her deck. Her neighbors had taken the liberty of decorating her boat while she was gone. An ostentatious electric palm tree stood next to the transom. Plastic seagulls swayed from its fronds. A string of red chili pepper party lights rimmed the flybridge. She pushed through the door with relief. Rob had opened all of the windows. The interior was warm but breezy, and smelled wonderfully of sea salt and marsh grass. A vase of wild flowers from the marsh was on the galley table next to a child's drawing. 'Welcome Home' was penned in magic markers. A white envelope was also on the table.

"Beautiful picture, Dan."

"I know," he agreed, springing in pleased steps across her futon. His hand grazed her wind chimes.

"I almost forgot. I got you a little gift." She reached into the paper bag and pulled out the plastic shark toy. His eyes widened, and he wrapped his arms around her again. A fast, wet kiss was planted on her belly before he tore outside to the men. One man sounded the theme music for *Jaws* while the shark nipped the brims of caps, sunglasses, and fingers.

She dropped fearfully onto the futon, the white envelope in hand. The single word on it, Lindsey, was Sara's handwriting. She tore it open with a shaky hand. It read:

I know you're going to be sifting through hundreds of emails and voicemails so I wanted to be sure that you got this message first. I've decided to stay at the marine lab. And you can make amends to me. Here's how.

1. Arrive every morning at 8:00 am sharp.
2. Convince Mort to give me a raise of 10K to match Battersby's offer.
3. Don't ever tell me "fuck off, Sara" again!
4. No fluids—of any kind!—in the workroom.
5. Never lay a finger on one of my planes again!
6. Stay sober.

Can't wait to see you. Sara XO

Lindsey scrambled for her smart phone and sent an email.

I'll try to negotiate a raise of 15 K because we have many challenging projects to get started on ASAP. Did I really tell you to fuck off? SORRY! Did I really drink near live electronics? SORRY! Did I break one of your planes? I'm SO, SO SORRY! I love your planes! Will go to a meeting a day, more if necessary, and work the steps to stay sober. Thank you for staying. I'd be lost without you. Mañana at 8.

She headed to the shower. Stepping into the head, she halted. Her pink cosmetic bag had been sitting on the back of the toilet for the past month.

Opening up her computer after her shower, she found over five hundred emails in her Inbox. Sara was right... this would take forever to sort through. Anne and Julius Davids had sent many over the past month, nervous as to her health and whereabouts. For ten years she had been Anne's pride and plague. She zipped off a quick note, telling Anne that she was good, that she'd call tomorrow to tell her everything. E-greetings from Kelly and Melissa, and Marcus would be visiting next weekend. No word from Myra.

The latest entry had been sent from an e-café in Logan Airport that afternoon. It was apologetic and groveling. She had a very bad feeling about the new girlfriend, her claws in Duncan's heart snagged deeply. He and a Scottish friend had made a bad investment on a castle restoration project, the email explained. He had borrowed from the Nolan BioCorp Electrode account... he'd pay her back... he promised...

"Shithead!" She stared at the computer screen in shock. Pressure welled behind her temples. His salary over many lifetimes could not pay back that money! She frantically logged onto her bank accounts. Columns of zeros filled the screen! Pilfered bank accounts were too overwhelming a task to deal with at that moment. It would be a massive amount of work with an accountant and lawyer—but later. She checked the wall clock. A women's meeting would start at a Methodist church in Falmouth in a few hours. There was something that she badly needed to share, to vent, to finally purge.

Stepping outside into the late afternoon, she swiped her hand across the plastic gulls, causing them to swing like pendulums. She climbed up to her flybridge to inspect the general state of affairs around the marina. The men on Rob's deck must have left while she showered. Through the window next door Danny and Max lay on the sofa, giggling while the plastic shark snapped at action figures of Thor and Ironman.

A lazy path of olive water threaded through the marsh toward the sea. Two herons stood on toothpick legs at the fringe of spartina grass. A bass boat floated by a muddy sandbar. She climbed down the ladder and headed toward the bow. As she sidestepped along the gunwale, she was startled. Rob was on his gunwale, waiting for her to round the corner, a yard or so across the water. Warm pond water lapped quietly between their two hulls as they stood wordlessly.

She finally asked, "Do you remember what you were doing on May third ten years ago?"

"I have no clue," he answered. His gaze became curious.

"I do. You hit two home runs to almost the same location. The right field stands at Camden Yards."

It had been a double header. They had been swilling warm beers all afternoon under a relentless sun, carousing and carrying on. She had her mother's car for the weekend. Stumbling across the parking lot at Camden Yards, one of the girls shouted, "Road trip!"

"Ocean City!"

"Lifeguards!"

On their way out of Baltimore, the Lexus flipped on the interstate. Joanne sustained a bad concussion. Kelsey broke her pelvis and femur. Megan's spinal cord was crushed at the lumbar 2 level; she would never walk or ride her horse again. She, the driver, walked away with nothing more than bruises and a broken wrist. She never hung out with the girls much after that. Instead, she drowned herself in a bottle and in a toxic relationship with a boy named Duncan McLeod.

Rob watched squalls move through her thoughts. "That's ancient history," he said. He had been cut by the Sox months later, and never played in the Majors again. "How are you doing?"

"I feel like a child. Everything is new." The response sounded trite and ridiculous in her own ears; she had not figured out how to tell him The News.

They were wordless again.

"Thank you," she said, breaking the silence. "For the ride to rehab, for everything."

"It was your idea. I just drove you."

"No, you did more than that."

"You would have done the same for me."

"You're right." She hesitated. "I barely remember anything."

"I'm not surprised."

She hesitated. "Did I behave badly?"

Rob turned to make sure that Dan was out of earshot. "You were very sick and very loaded," he whispered, "but you had your moments."

What was meant by that? she wondered.

He paused. "I didn't want to, not while you were in that state. It was wrong of me. It's just that you were so..."

"So what?"

"Persuasive."

She sighed in embarrassment. "Sometime you'll fill in the blanks?"

He nodded. His expression was peculiar and difficult to interpret. His head tilted back against the bulkhead of his boat. He was sizing her up from foot to head. Perhaps he noticed something different about her? Impossible. There was no way he could tell after only one month. Could he? No, it was impossible.

"Some people came by looking for you."

"Marcus?"

"No. No one by that name. Your friend, Sara, with a giant biker on a motorcycle. She brought a letter."

"I saw it. Thank you."

"And then a teenage girl."

"Kelly? Melissa?"

"No, a kid called Maggie."

"You're kidding me!" Lindsey surged forward. "How did she know where I lived? She didn't take my address!"

He shook his head.

"Do you know where she went?" she asked excitedly. She wanted to dash to her car, but where would she begin to look?

"She was hitching north. She hung around the parking lot for about a day. She had your travel bag, so I assumed you gave it to her."

"She's a little thief," she remarked with affection.

"It took me a while to convince her that it was safe to walk on the dock and the houseboats. She came by to see your coconut-headed pirates. She was starving. She ate four peanut butter and jelly sandwiches and drank an entire carton of orange juice. Then she played some ball with us. She didn't know how to hold a bat, but once I showed her, she could crack the tennis ball over the highway." He grinned. "Dan thought that she and her colorful language were wonderful. It poured later that night. I hope you don't mind, but I let her sleep on your futon. I hope she didn't steal anything."

"It's okay if she did."

He said wryly, "The next morning she offered to perform a certain service if I made her more sandwiches."

She grimaced.

He shook his head sadly and sighed. "Jesus, Lin, she's just a child!"

"Lots of men find that attractive," Lin said bitterly, remembering all the attention Maggie and the other girls had drawn at the clinic.

"My sexual deviance seems to be impregnating drunk women," he said ironically.

Her breath caught in her throat. She leaned off the gunwale and looked toward the stern. There were four seagulls hanging on the electric palm tree.

"The baby's mine, isn't it?"

She nodded.

"Good." He stretched his hand over the green water. She leaned outward. Her fingertips were just able to graze his.

"Permission to board your boat?" he asked.

"Permission granted."

It was dark when Lindsey N. returned home from a women's AA meeting where a ten-year secret had been released from the prison of her conscience. A free-spirited old hippie who had thirty-three years of sobriety told her to come early next time and set up the coffee pots with her. She lugged a bag of groceries from her front seat. The party lights trimming the two houseboats cast spatters of color across the black pond. Danny and Max were on the dock with their fishing rods and Styrofoam cups of earthworms. She spotted Rob in the repair shed with Dave. Six months might as well be six millennia. On the other hand, Kate Waters had never defined what acts were and were not permissible under The No Sex Rule...

Rob approached and lifted Dan's bike from where it had been abandoned in the gravel and wheeled it toward the boats. "You have a visitor," he said in a serious tone.

Her head snapped toward her boat, her mood plunging. There was no sign of Duncan on her deck chair, hunched over in a mean brood.

"She wouldn't talk to me. She only wants to talk to you," he elaborated.

She walked cautiously toward her boat, but saw no one. She peered over the gunwale. Maggie was curled into a fetal position under the yellow and green lights of the electric palm; she sobbed into a torn-up sweater.

Lindsey reached for Maggie's hand and pulled her to her feet. She was filthy and disheveled. Her face was bloodied from a cut under her eye.

"I hate fuckin' men... I just hate them!" Maggie cried.

"What happened?" she asked, distraught. "Have you been using?"

"No."

Lindsey held the door open and flipped the light switch. "Come into the light so I can see your face."

Maggie burrowed into Lindsey's shoulder and cried for a while.

"When did this happen?" Lindsey finally asked.

Maggie slumped into a chair. "Tonight. I was hitching back from Hyannis. They were two mean drunks. I hate fuckin' drunks. They're the worst assholes of all! They didn't pay me!"

Lindsey put some ice cubes into a dishtowel. "Here, hold that against your eye. It's swollen. How'd you know where I live?"

"I memorized the address on your driver's license."

"The cut should be cleaned. Luckily, you won't need stitches." She returned to the sink and soaped up a washcloth.

"It's gonna hurt!" Maggie yelped.

"Don't be a baby. I've got to do it," Lindsey urged, cleaning her face with the cloth.

"I'm so fuckin' exhausted..."

"Do you want to stay here for a while?"

"Badly!" As if suddenly remembering some vital thing, Maggie grabbed Lindsey's hands and assessed her tremors. "You knew I'd be back to take care of you."

The girl's resilience and swagger was impressive. "I am so, so glad to see you," Lindsey said.

The comment stunned the girl. "No one's ever been glad to see me."

"I am." Lindsey unpacked the bag of groceries. "I'll get dinner on. Go get a shower, and clean yourself, everywhere. Those rancid clothes are going into the dumpster tonight."

There was no argument from Maggie. She returned from her shower in Lindsey's shorts and well-worn Hopkins Medicine t-shirt. After dinner, they climbed up to the flybridge and took in the nocturnal sounds and sights of the pond.

"Where am I sleeping?" Maggie asked, lighting a cigarette.

"On the futon bed in the salon."

"What's a salon?"

"A living room on a boat."

"I love that bed!"

"The vile tarp is getting tossed in the dumpster also. Look. There's the Big Dipper," Lindsey said, pointing upward.

"Where?"

"There," Lindsey replied. "This is a drink, drug, and sex-free boat. No more men, no more tricks."

"I fuckin' hate it... more than anything! But it's the only way I can make money," Maggie said grimly.

"You're a smart girl. If you're interested in a job, I'll pay you out of my grant as a summer student, which, by the way, doesn't pay one hundred dollars an hour. But you'll earn student wages and put the money you earn into a bank account." Maggie feigned disinterest and continued to scan the sky. Lindsey continued, "After work, we'll go to AA meetings every evening."

"What kinds of things would I do at work?"

"You'll pick up animals for Sara and me from the tanks in the aquarium building. I'll show you how to do the nerve dissection. You'll make us chemicals and salines. And solder circuit boards. You'll learn how to use a computer, enter data for us, and make graphs. You'll make deliveries for us around the lab buildings and pick up our books from the library."

Lindsey gazed down the dock. Maggie craned her head, wondering what Lindsey was looking at. "On the weekends we're going to tear apart *Blackbeard*'s engine," she said, pointing toward the boat, "and get him up and running. I need a dive buddy. You're going to learn to swim. If you decide to stay as long as the fall, then you're going back to school. I'll tutor you to get you caught up. Look, Cowgirl, that's the North Star." She pointed northwest toward the bright star off the Big Dipper. "If you don't like my plan, Alaska is that way," she jested, "where the state capital is Anchorage."

"Juneau," Maggie corrected quickly.

"Anchorage," Lindsey countered, goading her.

"Juneau, you moron!"

Lindsey grinned triumphantly.

"Moron," Maggie mumbled.

"That's my plan. What do you think of it?"

The overwhelming proposition silenced Maggie. Lindsey half expected some obscenity, and for Maggie to bolt toward the highway. Instead, she pulled another cigarette from her pack, dropped into the captain's seat, and rested her bare feet on the control panel. She tilted her head back and blew languorous smoke rings at the stars.

"Well...?" Lindsey inquired.

"I hate the fuckin' water and am now living on a fuckin' houseboat and working at a fuckin' marine lab," Maggie said.

Children were about, and Lindsey looked down at Rob's boat where he was tucking Danny into the living room sofa bed. They appeared to be saying prayers. "There are lots of kids around here, so you're not using the f bomb anymore."

Maggie scowled at the reprimand and gazed across the pond. After a moment she responded; her voice had frightening clarity and traces of maturity. "I'll work hard. And then more. I won't disappoint you. Or me."

Bemused, Lindsey stood. "Okay then. Let's get your bed set up."

"Lin," Maggie said reluctantly, "sometime we need to talk." She paused. "About something that happened in Connecticut this summer, and last winter in Minnesota. Just in case."

"Just in case?" Lindsey said ominously. "Is it long?"

"Really long."

"Can it wait until tomorrow?"

"Yeah. But it's top secret and must always stay between Anne and Mary, and no one else. Can you promise me that?"

"Anne Bonny will take it to her watery grave at Davy Jones Locker. Let's get some zzzzs. We're at work tomorrow at 7:30."

Tomorrow there were a zillion phone calls to make and emails to send. It was a priority to sell the Drunkard's Doorknob design ASAP to restore her depleted fortunes. Besides, the girls needed a bigger boat.

Chapter 33

Boston, two years later

Karen Battersby had a recurring nightmare. *That she was found out.* In the dream, she was spotted on a security camera on the third floor of Lindsey Nolan's laboratory building as she snuck from the janitor's closet and pulled the fire alarm. Then, at a most public event, where she stood giddily at a podium, readying herself to receive the award for the Best Invention of the Year and with it a significant check, Lindsey Nolan appeared out of nowhere, claiming the printer as her own. Next in the dream, ferocious policemen surrounded Karen, smacked her into handcuffs and leg irons, and dragged her away to spend eternity in a dank, bug-infested dungeon. Two years had passed, she reminded herself, and there was no fallout from her actions at the Nolan-Kauni laboratory in Woods Hole.

She anxiously scanned the floor of the convention center for colleagues from other Engineering Departments. Her printer would be the talk of the Boston Engineering Expo! She adjusted the diamond cat pin on the lapel of her new business suit and looked around the hall again. She gasped aloud! Was her nightmare becoming a reality? That woman wandering the exhibitions closely resembled of all people... Lindsey Nolan! Though it had been over ten years since she had seen Lindsey in person (probably in a fraternity house), she often Googled her nemesis; Dr. Samuels would never know. Lindsey still worked in Woods Hole with Sara Kauni, and they'd had a number of interesting publications in the past months. No... impossible... it couldn't be Lindsey Nolan. This woman was far too attractive. It was not her. Karen turned her back to the crowd.

But what if it *was* Lindsey? What if she was stealthily waiting for this public event to expose Karen and the Battersby-Holcomb printer? Karen glanced slyly over her shoulder. Perhaps Lindsey might yell aloud to all of the engineers in the large hall that this was *her* invention, stolen from *her* lab! She had the software and prototype to prove it! Karen's thoughts flopped and floundered haphazardly for a plausible defense. "Many research teams come upon the same findings or inventions simultaneously," she could contend. "Take, for example, Charles Darwin and Alfred Russel Wallace, independently formulating the concept of speciation by natural selection! The printer was a co-discovery," she would concede. It would be almost impossible to disprove that claim in court.

The Lindsey Nolan look-alike was getting closer! Karen's heart pounded. Maybe she could make a quick retreat to the ladies' room and hide in a stall until Lindsey left the convention center? But she'd promised Agnes that she'd man their exhibition table with the glossy brochures and the demo printer until Agnes returned from lunch. What if, in the legal settlement, Lindsey also wanted the new Audi—and the cats? Breathe, Karen, breathe deeply. Twenty times, just breathe. Besides, it might not be Lindsey Nolan at all. Lindsey always dressed in jeans and a Hopkins hoodie. This elegant woman wore a silk blouse, pearls, and tight black pants.

The Lindsey Nolan clone was less than twenty feet away! Karen nervously rearranged the brochures on the table. *Breathe, Karen, breathe!*

"Dr. Battersby?" It was a female voice.

Karen's knees jittered; she turned with dread. "Yes?"

"We've never met before, but I'm a fellow alumna from the Hopkins Engineering Department. I'm familiar with your work." The woman extended her hand.

Karen cautiously shook her hand. *'Careful, careful, don't be fooled by the woman's deceptively pleasant tone.'*

"I'm sure you don't remember me, as I graduated a few classes ahead of you. I'm Lindsey Nolan."

Best to remain silent so as not to incriminate oneself in court. Best just to nod.

"I read about your printer in Business Technology and Invention magazine," Lindsey continued. "I was really excited when I saw that one would be on display here. Do you mind if I have a look?"

"No. Please do," she managed, gesturing rigidly toward the table.

Lindsey studied the printer from different angles. "Can I open it?"

"Of course."

Lindsey leaned over, nearly putting her head in the instrument, and studied the interior components.

At any minute Lindsey Nolan will scream aloud that this is her design! Karen imagined in growing panic.

"I love this printer," Lindsey stated. "The idea of a tonerless, inkless printer is pure genius."

It's a trap... the conniver's lulling you into a trap!

"The single most annoying thing is to run out of toner," Lindsey complained. "It always happens right before I need to print out something important. Then, when I go to order the toner, it's always on back order."

"Here's what the script looks like." She extended a page of text, trying to steady her shaky hand.

Lindsey studied the letters. "Nice. The font's much crisper than a laser printer. I read the specs in the article. The other thing I like about it is the smart phone app. So I could be in a lab meeting, press the print commands into my phone, and have a five hundred page document waiting in my printer in less than two minutes? Is that really correct?"

"Yes."

"Impressive."

"Agnes Holcomb, my partner, wrote the software. I can't take credit for that."

"Well, kudos to you both. I hope to buy two of them when they go on the market. One for my office, and one for the post-docs."

"Thank you for your kind words," she replied, warily.

Lindsey stared back at the printer, her head slightly tilted. She laughed to herself. "Do you want to hear a crazy thing?"

"Okay," Karen answered uneasily.

"A few years ago, I built a device that looked just like this."

Karen grasped the edge of the table for support. Her knees knocked together.

"But only from the outside. But it wasn't a printer," Lindsey added.

"What was it?" Karen blurted, overcome by curiosity.

"You're going to think I'm insane." Lindsey grinned. "It was a replicator."

"What were you trying to replicate?"

Lindsey answered with a burst of laughter. "Humans! I thought that in the future, when transporting a human across interplanetary space, one should make a copy of them first so that if something went wrong, there would still be an original version of that person."

"In transporting across space, you mean like 'Beam me up, Scotty'?" Karen asked incredulously.

"Yes!" Lindsey laughed again. "Just like that! But of course, the science, especially our understanding of physics, centuries away from doing this, so I thought I'd start very simply by breaking and make the molecular bonds in a single-celled organism, a bacterium. Still, a bacterium is composed of billions of organic molecules, and trying to figure out the exothermic and endothermic reactions that make and break the chemical bonds made my head explode. So I focused only on the cell membrane, but even that was too daunting a task." She grinned again. "And my head was muddled at the time, so I gave up on that silly, far-fetched idea to work on more feasible projects, better suited for this century. Besides, the more I think about it, it would just be easier to send the instructions to some other planet and assemble the organism there, rather than attempt to send atoms and molecules through space." She checked her watch. "I have to get back to my daughters."

"They're here?" Karen asked.

"Yes," Lindsey said, pointing. "At the food concession."

The Bottom Dwellers

Karen squinted through the crowd to see Sara Kauni talking to a toddler in a stroller. An African-American teenager staring into a smartphone sat next to Sara.

"Sara and Maggie have been feeding Ava funnel cake all day. She'll probably never touch mashed peas again," Lindsey said humorously. "Thanks for taking the time to show me your printer. And again, congratulations!"

Lindsey Nolan gave her a friendly wave and disappeared into the crowd.

Karen stood wide-eyed and confounded. A wave of joyous victory washed over her. *She had gotten away with it... intellectual theft.* Enormous profits were to flow into her bank account from the sale of the printer. No more nightmares would jolt her awake at night! Any expensive healing potion or magic staff from the *World of Warcraft* cyberstore was hers. She could hit BUY, BUY, BUY without a thought of cost! Maybe different Diana gowns might be designed for the various seasons when the Comic Cons were held... a daisy gown for the summer, a heart gown for February... an orange and black gown at Halloween. What a freaking stooge Lindsey Nolan was! She was staring straight at her own instrument! The software running the lightning-fast printing was Lindsey's own computer code that Agnes only had to tweak!

Agnes Holcomb hurried through the crowd and handed Karen a Cherry Coke and a hot dog. "When you get a chance," Agnes said excitedly, "go to the biomedical exhibition area. These two scientists from Cape Cod built the most astonishing device. Everyone in the crowd is talking about a Nobel Prize for its creators. There's two parts to it, an artificial epileptic brain for training neurosurgeons, and a microscopic electrode-laser probe that can both find the abnormal cells, and then surgically remove them. It's amazingly cool!"

Karen struggled to calm rising horror in her mind and the quaver in her voice. "Cape Cod? Who... who are the scientists?"

"Two women named Nolan and Kauni." Agnes paused. "Are you all right? You look green!"

Tons of cement and metal girders of the convention center roof seemed to crash down upon Karen Battersby.

As long as Lindsey Nolan and she co-existed in the same time-space continuum, her presence would always be cosmically inconsequential.

The End

Prologue for
Ægir's Curse
Book Two of the Wood's Hole Series

Vinland 1149

Thorsen mustered the last of his strength to heave Einar over the prow of the longboat. The dead man hit the dark water on his back, the heavy leather boots and air pocket in his tunic tilting him upright as if he were treading water and cajoling Thorsen to join him for a swim. As a boy Einar loved to swim, Thorsen remembered, even when other children were too timid to venture into the chill of the fjord. Now his cousin's corpse stared dull-eyed toward a muted orange sky —what past sin deserved such a punishment, a death of abdomen stabs, coughs of blood, and a fire in the head? Thorsen prayed that the tide would be swift and drag the body of his cousin from the inlet and out to rest in the sea realm of the god Ægir.

Einar had been the most skilled of navigators, measuring with his notched stick positions of the North Star and the sun, observing changes in bird flights, seaweeds, and water color to determine the location of the timber ships. Never with Einar on the steerboard did the Greenlanders sail by the inlet of their summer encampment. And it was he who first found this camp with arrow-straight trees and forests of wild grapes. Now Einar, like the rest of the mariners, was gone, his body ravished by a cruel plague.

When the first two mariners collapsed in sickness, the men cast torches into their dwellings to rid themselves of the contagion, as the red men, Skraelings, in the shadows of the leaves watched the Greenlanders in bafflement. The Mainlanders' grain that had been traded for furs of the white bear must have been infected with plague, the men agreed. The Greenlanders then scrambled onto the longboats anchored in the inlet, leaving the grain stores and huts aflame. But the retreat came too late and another dead mariner, then another, broke the still waters.

Thorsen struggled to prop himself against the single mast, his body wracked by involuntary convulsions. All was silent except for a hushed scurry of rats below in the ballast stones and the chirp of insects in the marsh grass. Thorsen lamented—the timbers lashed to the deck would never be masts or wagons or beams of long houses in Greenland or Iceland. Casks of berries below deck would never be wine. His journey would be for naught. The blisters on his hands yesterday had begun to ooze blood. His hands, so horrible now, would never touch his beautiful Jorun again.

The pain in his head surged like storm waves, the same agony that caused Didrik, who could not swim, to thrust himself overboard, and Kjell to slice open his own throat. The new land must be cleansed of this sickness forever! Thorsen dragged himself toward the shards of jasper to light the longboat on fire.

*****

Six days sail from Vinland in eastern Greenland Jorun had a premonition. The timber ships would not be returning over the western horizon. The unease was strong in her belly; this time Thorsen was not returning. The plague that ravaged the coastal villages was not carried by birds, waves, or wind, but had been transported on the trading ships from the continent to Greenland. She was sure of it. That meant that the timber ships of the Greenlanders could have spread the sickness westward to Helluland, Markland, and possibly as far south as Vinland. Mercifully a few outlying farms like hers and the monastery had been spared the agonizing death by their remoteness from the ports.

Jorun remembered the map and shuddered.

The summer before, after much convincing, Brother Vegar had shown Thorsen and Einar how to create maps, as the two mariners were intrigued by the priest's drawings of the Greenland and Iceland coastlines. One night Thorsen and Einar leaned over her table and conjured memories from their Vinland voyages. Thorsen drew a large peninsula with bays, rivers, and inlets. The mead that Einar had brought from the village was strong and she drank too much of it. The children were finally asleep. She wished that Einar would find a woman in the village, but he only wanted the woman who was won from him by a gambler. Now he slept on a fur mat by the fire pit and worked on the farm beside Thorsen when not navigating some ship across the northern seas. Jorun looked restlessly at Thorsen, hoping he would notice the subtle wandering of her eyes. But his hand continued to draw black lines across a reindeer skin, with Einar nodding or grabbing Thorsen's wrist before he drew some bay too shallow or too deep.

"It's done!" Thorsen finally announced.

Jorun rose from where she had been lying by the fire and peered over the men's shoulders. The place looked to her like a bent arm. The sailors' camp, marked by a black circle of dye, was situated in the armpit. Tiny islands trailed off to the southwest, while two larger ones lay southeast in deeper waters. Thorsen turned on a stool and pulled her onto his lap, remarking that he often dreamt of swimming with her off the sunny beaches of Vinland.

What would warm air and water feel like surrounding her body? It was unimaginable, she concluded; her world had always been wet, windy, and cold. She dropped her face into Thorsen's neck, slid her hands inside his tunic, and drew in the scent of him, mead, fire smoke, and man. Winter winds howled fiercer now. Her hands slid further beneath the leather. Glaciers from the north were encroaching on once fertile pastures. The soil scarcely produced enough winter hay to feed the livestock. Even the richest plots that the Church had appropriated would not sprout wheat or barley. Trading vessels rarely came to their shores anymore since walrus ivory and white bear furs were no longer valuable commodities to the Mainlanders.

Now the timber ships were not returning. Jorun told her oldest daughter to watch the young ones while she wrapped a cape around her frail shoulders. She grabbed the hide map and pushed through the winds to the monastery across a barren promontory. At a door in the rampart, she inquired of Brother Vegar. After some time shivering against the stone wall, a wizened priest appeared.

She anxiously extended the map to him.

The old priest unrolled the hide and studied the fine workmanship. A singular black dot on the parchment was puzzling and he asked of its meaning.

"It is a place of forests, beaches, wineberries, and butternuts," Jorun answered. "And a cache of coins is there to trade with the Skraelings, but they do not want coins; they only want swords. Take it, Brother. Hide it among your other maps, but no sailors should see it or return to Vinland. The place is cursed."

About The Author
Leah Devlin

Leah Devlin is a marine biologist who grew up in the Washington, DC area. She has undergraduate degrees in English Literature, Biology, and Environmental Science, a MS in Zoology and a PhD in Neurophysiology.

In addition to being a writer of novels, Leah Devlin is a biology professor with research specializations in neuromuscular control in marine invertebrates and biological exploration in the Arctic in the early nineteenth century.

The Bottom Dwellers, Ægir's Curse and *The Bends* comprise a trilogy of mysteries and thrillers centered on the scientific village of Woods Hole, Massachusetts, where Leah was a scientist at the Marine Biological Laboratory for over ten summers. The novels focus on the adventures of the brilliant yet troubled Nobel Laureate, Lindsey Nolan, her colleagues and family.

Leah's second series of thrillers, the Chesapeake Tugboat Murders, are set in the fictional village of River Glen in the upper Chesapeake Bay. The first novel in this series, *The Vital Spark*, a modern pirate yarn, has just been completed. The second novel in this series, *Spider*, is underway.

Leah enjoys outdoor adventures of all kinds: motorcycle journeys along winding back roads, boating, diving, rock-climbing, skiing, and long-distance trekking. When not traveling, she divides her time between Philadelphia and her boat on the Chesapeake.

Force 12 in German Bight

by
James Boschert

Considering that oil and gas have been flowing from under the North Sea for the best part of half a century, it is perhaps surprising that more writers have not taken the uncompromising conditions that are experienced in this area – which extends from the north of Scotland to the coasts of Norway and Germany – for the setting of a novel. James Boschert's latest redresses the balance.

The book takes its title from the name of an area regularly referred to in the legendary BBC Shipping Forecast, one which experiences some of the worst weather conditions around the British Isles. It is a fast-paced story which smacks of authenticity in every line. A world of hard men, hard liquor, hard drugs and cold-blooded murder. The reality of the setting and the characters, ex-military men from both sides of the Atlantic, crooked wheeler-dealers, and Danish detectives, male and female, are all in on the action.

This is not story telling akin to a latter day Bulldog Drummond, nor a James Bond, but simply a snortingly good yarn which will jangle the nerve ends, fill your nose with the smell of salt and diesel oil, your ears with the deafening sound of machinery aboard a monster pipe-dredging ship and, above all, make you remember never to underestimate the power of the sea.

–Roger Paine, former Commander, Royal Navy .

PENMORE PRESS
www.penmorepress.com

WILDFIRE IN THE DESERT

BY

BRUNO JAMBOR

Action Adventure, Crime, Mystery,
Southwest History

Highly entertaining, well researched and original:

A Navy veteran returns home to his ancestral land to escape the pace of modern life. His nephew begs him to hide the drugs he is transporting to escape his pursuers.

An astronomer trying to find a replacement for his estranged wife finds solace in his work with the stars.

Police and the drug cartel try to recover the missing shipment, regardless of consequences, ready to sacrifice any opponent.

The antagonists crisscross the desert of Southern Arizona in a chess game where the loser will be eliminated.

Unexpected help comes from a famous missionary who blazed new paths through the same desert three centuries ago.

The climactic resolution will captivate readers of this thriller with deep spiritual undertones.

PENMORE PRESS
www.penmorepress.com

The Chosen Man

by

J. G Harlond

From the bulb of a rare flower bloom ambition and scandal

Rome, 1635: As Flanders braces for another long year of war, a Spanish count presents the Vatican with a means of disrupting the Dutch rebels' booming economy. His plan is brilliant. They just need the right man to implement it.

They choose Ludovico da Portovenere, a charismatic spice and silk merchant. Intrigued by the Vatican's proposal—and hungry for profit—Ludo sets off for Amsterdam to sow greed and venture capitalism for a disastrous harvest, hampered by a timid English priest sent from Rome, accompanied by a quick-witted young admirer he will use as a spy, and bothered by the memory of the beautiful young lady he refused to take with him.

Set in a world of international politics and domestic intrigue, *The Chosen Man* spins an engrossing tale about the Dutch financial scandal known as tulip mania—and how decisions made in high places can have terrible repercussions on innocent lives.

PENMORE PRESS
www.penmorepress.com

www.ingramcontent.com/pod-product-compliance
Lightning Source LLC
Chambersburg PA
CBHW070419170726

48291CB00002B/277